Praise for *USA TODAY* bestselling author Jennifer Snow's Wild River series

"This first title in the Wild River series is passionate, sensual, and very sexy. The freezing, winter-cold portrayal of the Alaskan ski slopes is not the only thing sending chills through one's body."

—*New York Journal of Books*

"Set in the wilds of Alaska, the beauty of winter and the cold shine through."

—*Fresh Fiction*

"Heartwarming, romantic, and utterly enjoyable."
—*New York Times* bestselling author Melissa Foster

"Jennifer Snow's Alaska setting and search-and-rescue element are interesting twists, and the romance is smart and sexy… An exciting contemporary series debut with a wildly unique Alaskan setting."

—*Kirkus Reviews*

"Readers will enjoy the mix of sexy love scenes, tense missions, and amiable banter. This entertaining introduction to Wild River will encourage fans of small-town contemporaries to follow the series."

—*Publishers Weekly*

"*An Alaskan Christmas* drew me in from the first page to the last. I tried to read slower so that I could savor the story and feel every emotion. I reveled in every nuance, felt the cold, the wind and snow, and loved the small town and the mountains… I can't wait to return to Wild River."

—*Romance Junkies*

JENNIFER SNOW

Stars Over Alaska

Recycling programs for this product may not exist in your area.

ISBN-13: 978-1-335-92844-3

Stars Over Alaska
Copyright © 2021 by Jennifer Snow

A Wild River Match
First published in February 2021.
This edition published in April 2021.
Copyright © 2021 by Jennifer Snow

ISBN-13: 978-1-335-92844-3

Stars Over Alaska
Copyright © 2021 by Jennifer Snow

A Wild River Match
First published in February 2021.
This edition published in April 2021.
Copyright © 2021 by Jennifer Snow

This edition published by arrangement with Harlequin Books S.A.

For questions and comments about the quality of this book, please contact us at CustomerService@Harlequin.com.

HQN
22 Adelaide St. West, 40th Floor
Toronto, Ontario M5H 4E3, Canada
www.Harlequin.com

Printed in U.S.A.

CONTENTS

For my mom, the strongest person I know.
Thank you for everything. XO

Stars Over Alaska

CHAPTER ONE

Somewhere outside Wild River...

FIFTY-SEVEN HOURS TRAPPED in a vehicle with Selena Hudson had Leslie Sanders contemplating just how important it really was to keep the woman alive.

Selena continued to twitch in the passenger seat. She stretched her long legs out in front of her and scanned the surrounding scenery, which consisted of snow-covered evergreen trees as far as she could see. "How much longer?"

If Leslie had to answer that question one more time, her head might actually explode. "Just a few minutes." More like twenty, but each second cooped up in the vehicle felt like an eternity.

"But there's nothing around here. I haven't seen a house or business or crappy gas station convenience store for over an hour. This area looks deserted."

That was the point.

Leslie slowed down and scanned for the opening in the trees where the trail, just wide enough for a car, led into the forest. It had been a while since she'd driven out here by herself and this stretch of Alaska Highway was unremarkable.

Seeing the opening at the last second, she took the sharp turn as carefully as possible on the snow-covered roads.

Her all-season tires on her secondhand car weren't a great match for the early spring conditions.

Tall, thick trees on either side blocked the view of the setting sun and cast an ominous shadow ahead.

"I thought you were trying to save my life. This place looks like something out of a horror flick."

Selena Hudson's active imagination was an occupational hazard from growing up on movie sets. The Disney child star turned rom-com queen couldn't recognize the real world when it wasn't illuminated by fake lighting. "Believe me, this will be the safest place for you." Hopefully Leslie sounded more convincing than she felt. The farther they'd driven away from LA, the less confident she was.

"Is this even a road?"

"Yes." Not a great one. Her small car struggled to push through the three feet of snow. Her foot was pressed to the floor and the tires spun, lacking significant traction.

"You sure this car can make it?" Selena asked.

"Yes." With a small miracle on their side. Getting out and walking the rest of the way didn't appeal to her. "Just sit tight. We're almost there."

Selena sighed but sat back against the seat.

A few minutes and a lot of praying later, Leslie stopped the car and put it in Park in front of a small, secluded log cabin.

"Tell me this is not where we're staying." Selena's unimpressed expression was one Leslie had been prepared for. Only five-star, luxury accommodations were to the star's liking. "The car ran out of steam, right? That's why we're stopping?"

"Nope. This is it. My family's cabin. It's safe."

"Does it even have running water?"

"Yes." Hopefully. If the pipes weren't shut off to avoid

freezing during the winter months. Truth was, she hadn't been here in years. Leslie's decision to bring the movie star to the Alaskan wilderness outside of her hometown of Wild River had been an impulsive one. One she hadn't gotten official clearance for and one that could very well cost her her job with the Executive Protection Agency in LA. One she hadn't had time to fully prepare for. But she'd had to make the split-second decision and this was it.

Of course she'd also had to bend the truth a little to get the movie star to go along with her insane idea to drive from California to Alaska, and now the look of terror on Selena's face suggested she'd never be assigned another client again.

But she'd taken the job to protect people and this had felt like the best and only response to Selena's stalker moving in.

"You said we were going to a ski resort."

Leslie nodded. "You can cross-country ski out here." Her family kept skis and snowshoes in the small shed behind the cabin. Of course they'd need to shovel a path to the shed first.

Selena stared at her. "You know that's not what I assumed."

"Well, you know what they say about assumptions."

"Leslie! You lied to me. In fact, you lied about a lot of things. You took me away from Unicorn—who is an emotional support animal, by the way—and you said this road trip would be fun. It wasn't. You said we could stop and see things along the way. We didn't. You said this time together would bring us closer. Spoiler alert—I don't feel closer to you at all."

Leslie cut the engine of the vehicle. "Look, I knew you wouldn't come along if I told you the complete truth and there wasn't time to get Unicorn before leaving town." The star's five-pound Chihuahua had been at the Posh Puppy Spa when they'd made their hasty exit out of LA.

Selena's pinched expression revealed her annoyance had reached a breaking point, but she wiggled in the seat. "We're not staying here, but I really have to pee, so here's the plan. We go inside. I pee. Then we get the hell out of here before Jason shows up in a hockey mask and murders us."

Leslie's teeth clenched. She could accommodate the first two parts of that plan, but Selena was going to have to accept that they wouldn't be leaving. Not until Leslie figured out what to do next. "Let's go in," she said. "I'm sure you'll feel better once you see the inside."

"Don't count on it," Selena muttered. She stared out the window. "How are we even supposed to get to the door?"

"Um…" Leslie glanced at their feet. Selena's running shoes and her work shoes weren't a match for the trek through three feet of snow.

No one had been to the cabin since the summer before; her sister, Katherine, habitually came here for several weeks a year to regroup. She claimed that the pleasant acoustics and being surrounded by the natural exposed wood helped her relax, get away from the stress of her job as a homicide detective with the Alaska state troopers' office. Outside of that annual visit, no one in their family really used the cabin anymore. Not since their father died and the family dynamics became tense. And definitely not during the winter months when access to the cabin and outdoor activities was limited, hence the lack of maintenance.

Leslie knew the heat wouldn't be turned on inside either and neither of them was dressed for Alaska weather, wearing only fall jackets and thin stretchy dollar gloves from the last gas station before they hit Alaska.

Admittedly, she hadn't thought the logistics of this rushed decision through carefully…or at all. It was a heartbeat reaction to a dangerous situation. Her fight-or-flight instinct kicked into high gear and she'd chosen flight, unsure of what they were fighting against. Her training taught her that going in unprepared was always a disadvantage and she hadn't wanted to put Selena in more danger, waiting it out in LA.

Selena's gaze burned into hers. "Well?"

She wouldn't panic or look unprepared to her client. *Stay cool.*

Leslie reached down to untie her boot. They had extra winter clothing and boots inside the cabin. They just needed to get there. "We'll switch."

"Gross. Absolutely not."

"You think you can make it through the snow in those?" She nodded toward the bright pink-and-teal running shoes.

"Nope. So, I guess you'll have to carry me to the door."

This woman was officially out of her goddamn mind. "You want me to carry you?"

"Look, becoming a bodyguard was your life choice. Therefore, you signed up to protect my body—all of it, any way you need to. And if you want to do a traditionally man's job…"

Jesus, they were back to this again. Selena's disbelief and disappointment that she'd been assigned a female guard. For the first month on assignment, all she'd heard was Selena's skepticism that Leslie could actually protect her in a life-and-death situation. Leslie's credentials—five years as an Alaska state trooper, graduating third in her class at the academy, and her intensive twenty-eight-day protective detail training along with her black belts in jujitsu and karate hadn't worked to ease the star's mind. Leslie had learned to tune out the comments muttered under her breath and those said not so quietly when Selena was in a mood. If the star wanted reassurance that Leslie could do her job, this was her opportunity to prove it.

"How much do you weigh?"

"That's rude."

Leslie scanned her. Five foot six, but supermodel thin, she couldn't be more than a hundred pounds. Unfortunately, Leslie wasn't a heavyweight herself, but she was strong and determined and that beat size any day. Or at least that's what she'd told herself repeatedly over the last seven years through the rigorous and demanding training whenever she'd been tempted to quit.

Leslie opened the door, pushing hard against the deep snow, then climbed out and trudged toward the passenger side. Wet snow fell into her boots and clung to the fabric of her jeans and the damp air chilled her. Snow started to fall and the big, thick flakes covered her thin jacket within seconds. She opened the passenger door and turned around, bending at the knees. "Hop on." She'd piggyback Selena inside.

"This is not how I meant."

"Do you want to get inside or not?"

"Not really," Selena said but she sighed and wrapped her arms around Leslie's neck and her legs around her waist.

Leslie gripped her tight and stood, then kicked the door closed with her foot.

The temptation to "accidentally" drop Selena into the snowbank was so incredibly enticing, but if there was a sliver of hope that she could keep her job after this fiasco, Leslie was grasping for it. She wasn't expecting a five-star review of her performance after this was over, but if she kept the woman safe, that had to count for something.

She hoped.

A former Alaska state trooper, working highway patrol for five years, Leslie had only ever known careers in protective services. It was in her blood—her mother had been the second official female state trooper in the northern state and her older sister and younger brother were in the force as well. Leslie didn't want to be a cop anymore, and this new path suited her...and normally she enjoyed her job. Enjoyed the different challenges and obstacles, the element of high pressure and danger. It kept her adrenaline high and therefore reminded her she was alive.

She was one of the best—an especially impressive feat given that she was a woman and smaller than the other agents at the agency. So far she'd excelled at all of the assignments she'd been given.

But this assignment had quickly become her toughest one.

With the others, she'd been hired as a security measure... extra precaution during high-stress and high-visibility times for the client. But this time, there was an imminent threat to the person's safety.

Failing this first real test of her skills wasn't an option.

The snow was even deeper than it looked from the car and Leslie sank up to her knees with each step. Her feet were going numb and she struggled to take a deep breath in the cold mountain air that was thinner at this altitude than any of the hikes she'd done in the California mountain ranges.

Not much could prepare someone for the Alaskan wilderness in the colder months.

At the deck, she reached along the top of the door, through the coating of snow and ice and found the extra key.

"That's safe," Selena said.

"We're in the middle of nowhere and there really isn't anything of value inside the cabin, anyway."

"Wow. Way to sell it," Selena mumbled.

Leslie unlocked the door and stepped inside. She immediately dropped Selena back to her feet and rotated her shoulders. Between the mounting stress and carrying the other woman, her back and neck were a mess of tense knots. She'd deserve a week off once all of this was over.

She flicked on the lights and the place illuminated. Immediately Leslie's stomach fell—memories of family time in that cabin rushing back at the worst possible time.

This place had been the last place she remembered feeling happy—truly happy, like only a kid with no worries could be. It wasn't big and luxurious like those belonging to wealthy families closer to the water's edge, but it was cozy with its loft-style bedrooms with their slanted ceilings, a real wood-burning stove and exposed log interior. She and her older sister shared one room and her brother had the other. Their parents had the bedroom downstairs. A small living space with exposed wood on the walls and ceiling, skylights allowing the stars and northern lights to shine down on them, a wood burning fireplace and some comfy furniture that they'd moved from the house in Wild River once it started showing its age. On the walls hung scenery photos of the surrounding trails and rivers. And several family photos from when she and her siblings were young—a lifetime ago.

The place even smelled the same, despite no one being up there in months. The lingering scent of firewood and slightly musty surroundings. Her mouth watered and she could almost taste the s'mores they'd roast over the open fire every night.

She shook it off. She wasn't here on vacation or with her

family. There was no time for nostalgia, she had to get her head straight and figure out what the hell she was going to do now that they were here...in the middle of nowhere, with no one to know where they were.

"Stay here. I'll get the things from the car." Not that she needed to tell Selena not to help. For the last three months since she'd been assigned the star's protective detail, she hadn't had any success making Selena realize that Leslie was there as her bodyguard, not her personal assistant, not her personal valet when she shopped, not a shoulder to cry on when the latest co-star broke things off and not her friend.

She trudged back through the deep snow to the car. After opening the back door, she reached inside for the several shopping bags of food from the last convenience store they'd passed before turning off the highway and escaping any sign of civilization.

It wasn't fresh mahi-mahi or whatever Selena's macro diet demanded she consume, but at least Leslie was giving her the option to not starve to death while they were stuck here.

Anxiety made her chest tighten. Just how long would that be? Being "home" or in close proximity was already stressing her out and the circumstances around it were enough to cause a severe panic attack. She hadn't had one in over a year, but now seemed like the perfect time for old psychological ailments to return. She forced a chilly breath as she kicked the door closed with her foot and headed back inside the cabin.

Selena still stood exactly where she'd left her. "It's freezing," Selena said, dancing from one foot to the other, rubbing her arms in her thin jacket. "Where's the thermostat?"

Right. 'Cause cabins in remote Alaskan wilderness had electric heat.

Leslie brought the groceries to the kitchen, placing the bags on the counter, then went straight to the hall closet. She carried a stack of blankets back to the living room. "Sit and wrap up in these. I'll start a fire right away."

Selena remained standing, looking around the cabin. "Take me back to LA."

"So your stalker can kill you?"

She huffed. "You think I've never had a stalker before?"

As if it was something to be proud of. Though based on the number of social media followers these VIP people had, fandom was almost low-grade stalking anyway. They craved the attention and validation they received from society. "Not like this one," she said.

"What makes this one so dang…dangerous?" Selena's teeth chattered and she reluctantly grabbed a blanket and wrapped it around her shoulders, though she stayed standing near the door.

"He was in your bedroom, that's what." That was all she'd reveal to her. Selena didn't need the sordid details… not yet anyway. If she continued to not take this seriously, then that might be the time to be brutally honest with her. Scared straight kinda thing, if all else failed.

Leslie's hands trembled from the cold as she stacked several logs into the fireplace and lit a match. Grabbing some old newspapers, she lit the end and tossed it in, then closed the protective metal gate.

"All I'm saying is that if I were in that much danger, wouldn't they have assigned some big, burly—preferably hot—bodyguard to keep me safe instead of you?"

Leslie ignored the question she'd already answered a dozen times. She was assigned because she was just as capable, if not better trained than any of the men at the agency and she…blended in better. Selena's management had been clear that the star's brand depended on her being seen as approachable by her fans. A thick-headed guard didn't go well with the image they were trying to portray.

"But we are only here for a few days, right?"

Leslie's grunt was noncommittal.

"Leslie…" Selena's tone was a warning bell. "How long are we staying here?"

A three-year-old would be easier to deal with. "Until it's safe to go back."

Selena's eyes widened. "What about my commitments? I'm starting on a new movie in three weeks. I have a promotional tour for my upcoming movie starting next week."

Yeah, she most likely wouldn't be making that tour. The thought depressed Leslie just as much. She wasn't exactly thrilled to be putting her own life on hold indefinitely either. Not that she had much of a life outside of work, but still… "Look, I'll get you back to LA as soon as I can. I need to call the office for updates. Hopefully, the stalker will be caught and arrested quickly."

Selena's eyes narrowed. "You flinched just now when you mentioned the office. Do they know you took me out of LA?"

Damn. Lie or tell the truth? If she expected Selena to trust her, better to be honest. "No."

"But you cleared this with my management, right?"

"It might have been an inside job. Someone was in your house—they had to have gained access somehow." Leslie couldn't trust even the people closest to Selena right now. That house was well secured, so the possibility that someone on her team might be in on it was very real.

"Does *anyone* even know where we are?"

Shit. Leslie bit her lip.

Selena's eyes widened. "What the fuck? No one knows where I am and you've taken away my cell phone?"

The cell phone was left behind on purpose. Selena was glued to the thing and it was easy enough to track, unlike Leslie's, which had a ghost app. "It was the only way to make sure your stalker doesn't find out where you are."

"So, essentially, you've kidnapped me."

"Don't be so dramatic."

"How do I know I can trust you?"

"Are you serious?"

"A hundred percent. You could be working with my stalker. This could all be a setup." Frantic eyes darted around the room.

"Calm down."

Selena threw off the blanket and struck a kung fu pose. "I'm a black belt."

"And I have a gun."

"Help! Someone help!" Selena whipped open the front door and started yelling into the void. Her voice echoed on the nothingness around them.

"Hey, shhh… Calm down!" Leslie said, closing the door. "I'm not kidnapping you or going to kill you." As tempting as it was. "If I was going to do that, I would have done it already and dumped your body along the deserted stretch of highway, not wait until we were in my family's cabin."

Selena still didn't let her guard down. "How do I know this is your family's cabin?"

Leslie pointed to the picture of her and her siblings above the fireplace. "The one in the middle? That's me."

Selena peered at it, her arms lowering slowly to her sides. "The one with the boy's haircut and braces?"

Leslie's teeth clenched as she nodded. "Yes."

Selena's face gave way to a look of amusement. "Oh my God…talk about an awkward stage! Do you have any more photos like that?"

Leslie sighed. "In the ottoman, there's a family photo album." To further confirm that she wasn't lying or to make fun of her some more, Leslie didn't care.

As long as the pain-in-the-ass movie star stopped screaming for help

CHAPTER TWO

Fairbanks, Alaska

LEVI STARED ACROSS his desk at the interviewee, Tyler Forrester. Ironic choice of name for someone wanting to become a smoke jumper in the Alaskan wilderness. The guy was well trained—volunteer firefighter for eight years. Lead rescue on the search and rescue team in Wild River. Avalanche training. Drone training. Definitely met the higher-level requirements. He looked physically fit and had passed all of the written applications. But Levi wasn't convinced.

"I see you've recently relocated to Fairbanks from Wild River," Levi said. This, he'd need to explore a little. Not many people left a ski resort town to move into a more remote area of Alaska unless they were running from something…or toward it.

"Yes, sir." The guy's face broke into a smile.

Toward it. Levi's guess would be a woman was the motivating target. "Your girlfriend lives here." Not a question. He'd seen it before.

"Yes, sir…fiancée, actually. Well, hopefully. I plan on proposing tomorrow night." The smile faded slightly. "But, I'm fairly confident she's going to say yes." Tyler shifted in the seat. "We were high school sweethearts… Things got complicated…"

Levi sat back and listened to the guy ramble on about his relationship drama. As head of the Alaska smoke jumping team, he'd mastered the art of active listening to relationship ups and downs with his open-door policy—which the men on his team took to mean resident therapist. Hearing everyone else's issues made him grateful that he was solidly single.

Funny enough, everyone in his life kept pushing him to date. Misery loved company, right? Life balance, everyone said. He knew relationships just complicated the hell out of things, but no one was listening to his protests.

The ping of his cell phone indicating a new Tinder match on the account his co-worker, Chad, had set up for him was evidence of that.

When Tyler stopped talking, Levi sat forward and shook his head. "I'm sorry, Tyler, I just don't see this being a good fit."

The guy's face fell. "What? Why? I meet the requirements, right?"

All but a very important one: no serious attachments.

It wasn't technically a job requirement, but it *was* a Levi Grayson prerequisite of sorts. The guys on his team liked to date; casual relationships that lasted several weeks at most, but they were essentially like him—single, no family, unattached. They all happily shared a canine at the station cabin, Smokester, a retired rescue German shepherd who was currently snoring loudly in his dog bed in the corner of the office. Other than that, there was no one in the back of their minds when they threw themselves out of a plane and dropped into the middle of a raging wildfire. The job may not be a year-round gig, but during the on season, hours were long and unpredictable. Usually men moved on to more stable, regular firefighting positions once they settled down and started families. The demands of the job were a little too much for most at that stage in their lives.

Tyler's expression when he talked about his fiancée told Levi that there would definitely be someone to distract Tyler, and his crew's safety depended on no distractions. "I'm sorry, Tyler, but I just don't think this is the right fit... for either of us."

Tyler looked determined as he reached forward and pointed to the impressive skill list on his résumé. "Come on, man. I even have additional certifications the job doesn't call for."

Levi spotted an exposed tattoo on his forearm—a watercolor of the aurora borealis. He took a chance. "What's your girlfriend's name?"

Tyler frowned as he said, "Aurora."

Bingo.

Levi hated to turn down an amazingly qualified candidate, but he'd try to explain things to Tyler as best he could. "Okay, let me give you a 'what if.'"

Tyler nodded slowly. "Okay."

"What if we get a call about raging fires in Swan Lake and at the same time, you get a call that your wife is in labor. What do you do?"

Tyler's eyes widened. "Dude, I haven't even proposed yet."

"Right, but you plan to and engagements lead to marriage and I suspect kids at some point?"

Tyler cleared his throat and tugged at his tie. "I guess so... I mean...yeah, I think. We haven't really planned that far ahead."

"To you, that timeline might seem far away, but when I'm recruiting, I have to look at least five years into a candidate's future. A lot of training and time and effort goes into new recruits and I need my crew to be focused at all times. We run a skeleton crew because not many recruits have what it takes to succeed in this career."

"I do," Tyler said.

"Yeah, you do...which makes it tough for me to say this, but I can't offer you a place on the team."

Tyler looked annoyed. "So, you're telling me none of the other guys on the crew have relationships?"

"Not serious ones, no."

Tyler seemed to struggle with his next point of argument. "But...they have other family members. Aren't those distractions?"

"Okay let me rephrase my question: What if we get a call to a fire and at the same time your *sister* went into labor. What do you do?"

"Obviously take care of the fire."

Levi smiled. He rested his case.

Tyler sighed. "I'm pretty sure you can't turn down my application because I'm in love."

"You're in your right to file a complaint, but I'm sticking to my decision."

Tyler looked ready to argue but common sense obviously prevailed. Getting a hot head wasn't the way to go and he had to give the guy even more credit for having the sense to know it.

Damn, this guy would have been a good one.

Tyler extended a hand to Levi and he accepted it.

"This isn't the last you'll see of me," he said before leaving the office.

Part of Levi hoped the guy was right, the other part hoped his girlfriend said yes to his proposal.

Chad entered the office as the station door slammed shut. "You know you have to stop turning candidates away because they have a personal life. We're going to get sued for discrimination." Chad was the longest-standing member on the team and his ten years of experience made him the perfect spotter. It was only the two of them who worked the station year-round, the only full-time employees, and Chad was happy to defer to Levi for most decisions, but recruiting was one issue they argued about.

"There were other reasons," Levi said.

"Sure. Like what?" Chad folded his arms, the new addition to his sleeve tattoo still wrapped in a bandage.

"He's from Wild River."

"So are you."

"I'm not really from anywhere. I lived in Wild River as a kid, but I've lived all over Alaska." And all over the world on different military bases. "Tyler's never been anywhere but the ski resort town, which is about as far from real Alaska as you can get."

Chad leaned against the door frame. "*Real* Alaska?"

"You know what I mean. Rugged, outback wilderness Alaska. Besides, he's in Fairbanks because he's chasing a woman. I give him six months before he's convincing her to move back to Wild River with him."

Chad glanced at Levi's cell phone on the desk as it pinged with another Tinder match. "Look, just because you strike out with the ladies doesn't mean we all do."

Levi ignored the comment. He couldn't argue with facts. He never claimed to be good at relationships. How could he be?

His parents had divorced when he was a kid. His mom readily let his father take over raising him and Levi hadn't heard from her since. He'd moved from one military base to another, until his father decided *he* wasn't the best option to raise him either and shipped him back to Wild River to live with his grandmother. She was in her sixties by then and she did her best, but she'd already raised her children and had little interest in or energy to do it again.

The only family he ever felt he had was in his two best friends, Dawson and Leslie, both of whom left him three years ago…in different ways.

His alarm sounded on his phone and he stood. "Shit, I gotta go."

"Well, I know it's not a hot date," Chad said, rolling his eyes as Levi grabbed his jacket and keys and left the station.

Chad was wrong about one part of that sentence. Mrs. Powell was certainly coming in hot…or coming toward him hot. Did that phrase still work?

"Levi! So nice to see you," she said as he entered the restaurant in downtown Fairbanks a half hour later. "Thank you for meeting me here."

He accepted her hug and forced a smile when he pulled away. He wasn't looking forward to that day's meeting. But she'd left several voicemails for him in the last few weeks and he couldn't avoid her forever.

Plans to start a Dawson Powell memorial foundation for supporting mental health had him experiencing every mixed emotion his body was capable of.

He thought it was very honorable of the Powell family to do this—set up a charity in their son's name after he'd died in a high-speed chase with a man on a suicide mission. Showing forgiveness in the form of trying to help support programs that assisted in mental health was an amazingly charitable way to preserve Dawson's memory and do something good in the process. Levi just wasn't sure how he felt taking a leadership role in it.

He wanted to honor his friend's memory, and the Powells had hardly given him much choice in being involved. They said he'd been Dawson's best friend, so he was the natural choice to be the face of the foundation. He'd practically been raised by the family—they'd treated him like a son, having given him clothes, food, sporting equipment—the list went on. But more than that, they'd given him structure, discipline and advice.

He could hardly say no to this now.

It was just that he was more of a behind-the-scenes kinda guy. Unlike Dawson, he didn't like the spotlight. He'd be happier doing the heavy lifting with fundraising campaigns and such, rather than being front and center.

But how did he communicate that without it coming out wrong?

"Levi, I'd like you to meet Angelica. She's going to be helping us with the legal side of things—the paperwork and getting established as a charity, that kind of thing," Mrs. Powell said, stepping back to reveal a pretty redheaded woman who definitely lived up to her name. Pale skin, emerald green eyes, dressed in a pale pink dress—she did look angelic.

Unfortunately, the look on Mrs. Powell's face was rather devilish. She obviously had more than a working relationship in mind for the two of them. "Nice to meet you," he mumbled.

"Likewise. Karlene speaks very highly of you. A smoke jumper—wow, that must be incredibly exciting," Angelica said, eyeing him with open attraction.

Attracting a woman wasn't the issue, it was lack of "game" that had him struggling with lasting relationships. "Yeah... I mean, no, it's actually quite intense during the fire season and almost boring during the off-season. The gear is hot and uncomfortable and a bunch of smelly, dirty guys sleeping in tents at base camps isn't exactly bachelor living…"

Angelica nodded politely as he rambled, but Mrs. Powell shot him a look that said "less is more," so he zipped it.

"Let's get started," she said. "There's so much to do before we can announce the first charity event later this spring."

Wow, she was really moving full steam ahead on this. She'd first approached him with the idea only months after Dawson's death, and had thrown herself into researching these kinds of charities and applying for the appropriate licenses and aligning herself with the mental health institute of Alaska. She'd jumped in headfirst and it had become her new mission. Levi understood why. This was her way of coping, of not breaking down and disappearing behind a wall of despair. Everyone grieved in their own way. Karlene Powell planned and organized and felt better giving back to the world in some way in memory of her son.

Levi followed them to the table near the window. He pulled out both of their chairs and sat between the two women, doing his best to look and sound engaged, all in, but he was secretly hoping for an emergency call to get him out of there and back to keeping his best friend's memory in his own way.

By remembering…

That kid was going to break his neck, but he'd be immortalized as the king of the playground.

His first day at Wild River Elementary, Levi stood at the border of the playground, watching all the other kids play. He knew this "new kid" routine well, having moved from one military base to another with his father for ten years. He never bothered to make a lot of friends or deep connections with the other kids, knowing he wouldn't be there long.

This time was different. Or so his dad had said. This time, he'd be staying in the small ski resort town, living with his grandmother, who owned a bookstore on Main Street. Traveling around the country wasn't right for a kid, his father had said.

Levi knew how hard it was on his father to leave him there, so he'd squared his shoulders, put on a brave face and shook his father's hand as his dad left for another tour overseas.

Then he was desperate to keep up the brave act, facing yet another new school, another set of kids. Right now, he couldn't take his eyes off the one balancing on top of the monkey bars—ten feet high, slick with ice so thick it glistened in the Alaskan winter sunshine. The boy looked about his age, but he was smaller than Levi. He'd removed his winter coat and gloves and was making his way across the bars, arms outstretched for balance. Not an amazing stunt during warmer months, but just then the entire metal surface was like a sheet of ice.

He was almost to the other side when his foot caught the edge of a rung and he lost his footing.

Instinctively, Levi dove and he didn't exactly catch the other kid, but his body served as a crash mat beneath him.

"Hey, man, thanks," the kid said.

"Yeah…no problem." His ribs felt broken and the wind had been knocked from his lungs, but it was an easier way to make friends than having to actually walk up to a group and try to fit in.

"You're the new kid, right?" the boy asked, getting to his feet and extending a hand to help Levi up from the ground.

"Levi," he said.

"Nice to meet you, Levi. I'm Dawson," he said just as a girl, tall and thin with short blond hair sticking out from under a purple hat, came toward them. She was the prettiest thing Levi had ever seen and he felt like his tongue had swollen.

"I got it," she said, turning a small portable hand recording device toward Dawson. She eyed Levi and her piercing territorial look had him sweating. "Who are you?"

"This is Levi… He just saved my life," Dawson said, glancing at the footage replay.

The girl scoffed. "You could have made the landing." She shrugged. "No biggie. I'll edit him out."

Sounded about right. Wasn't he always being edited out?

"See ya," he said to Dawson as he started to retreat to the playground border again. He could take a hint. It was the same everywhere. By grade four, friendships had been formed, groups were established and no one liked to open their circle to the new kid.

"Wait… Come back," Dawson called after him.

"What are you doing?" he heard the girl hiss.

"We could use him in the movie."

They were making a movie?

"Hey, we're making a movie about a stunt kid who learns he actually has superpowers and…"

"Shhh," the girl had said.

"Come on, Leslie. He'd be great," Dawson said to her.

Her cheeks flushed under Dawson's gaze and she sighed as she turned to Levi. "Look, the only other part in the movie is the villain. We were going to ask my brother, Eddie…"

Dawson touched her shoulder. "Don't take this the wrong way, but Eddie's not the right person to play the villain… He's too much of a tattletale. He will run to your mom and rat us out every time we try something even a little bit dangerous. And besides, Levi here is huge."

Leslie thought for a moment, eyeing him.

Levi, who had been a chubby, tall kid for his age and normally slouched to fit in, stood even taller. For once his size might be a good thing. Or at least not something he needed to be embarrassed about.

"Fine," Leslie said reluctantly. "You can be in the movie, but Dawson is the star of the show."

His buddy always was and Levi had never had a problem letting him have the spotlight.

Mrs. Powell touched his arm on the table. "Levi, you still with us?"

He blinked and nodded. "Yeah, sorry... I drifted off there for a second, but I'm back. Full attention. Focused," he said.

Angelica smiled at him and damn if he didn't wish that made him feel any type of way.

CHAPTER THREE

SIX HOURS AT the cabin and Leslie was losing her mind. Strategy was eluding her and she needed advice on what to do next. She'd never exactly been in a situation like this one. She pulled on her boots and a heavy coat from the closet.

"Where are you going?" Selena asked, coming out of the bathroom, where she'd taken the longest shower in history, despite Leslie's warning that the water tank heated only so much at a time.

"Just outside for some air. I'll be back in a few minutes," she said, slipping out and closing the door behind her. She walked to the other end of the wraparound deck and took her cell phone out of her pocket. She hesitated, staring off at the heavy snow clouds in the darkening sky. Normally, she found the quiet stillness helped to bring clarity, but that evening it only made her that much more aware that she was completely alone in this.

Her next moves still unclear, she dialed the number before she could overthink it. She needed to tell someone that they were okay at least.

Her co-worker and…casual hookup answered on the first ring. "Oh my God—I've been going out of my mind. Where are you?"

Eoghan's worry made her even more uncertain. She'd missed sixteen calls from him already and a dozen from the agency. Everyone was trying to reach her, but she wasn't sure who to trust. "Can't say."

"Selena's with you? You're both safe?" he asked. His thick Australian accent usually made her smile but right now she only heard the seriousness of the predicament she was in.

"Yes. We're out of LA." That's all she'd say for now. "I didn't know what else to do. Her bedroom…" Leslie had seen some pretty messed-up shit working first as an officer of the law and now working high-end security, but the vulgar, disgusting message left for Selena a few days before had unsettled her like nothing else. Thank God Selena hadn't seen it. Although maybe if she had, she'd realize the danger she was in.

"I know," Eoghan said, his tone softening. "That was some heavy shit. You okay?"

"Yeah…of course." If anyone could sense she was lying, it would be Eoghan. Working together for the last year and sleeping together almost as long, they were friends, co-workers, casual daters… But she refused to let him too close. After the tragic death of her fellow state trooper fiancé in a high-speed crash, Leslie was far from ready for another relationship.

She'd grieved. She'd moved on, but she wasn't prepared to open herself up again.

Luckily, Eoghan knew her well enough not to coddle her. "Have you checked in with the agency?"

She caught the note of warning in his tone. "No. I wasn't sure if I should just yet." She wouldn't admit her suspicions that there might be someone there she couldn't trust. He'd think she was being paranoid.

Or not. "Good," he said. "I'll let them know you're safe and will keep updating through me," he said.

"Thank you." It was a small relief to at least have someone with her on this.

"Of course. So what's your plan?" he asked.

"I'll let you know as soon as I have one." Looking at the time on her phone, she disconnected the call. A minute or less would be the limit on her contact with the outside world until Selena's stalker was caught.

Leaning against the rail, she stared at the dark mountains in the distance. This place had always grounded her. The silence had helped block out the noise and she was desperate for some of its healing powers now. A cold evening breeze blew her hair across her face as her phone buzzed with a text from Eoghan.

Stay safe. We will figure this out.

After heading back inside, she closed and locked the door. At least they were safe here for now. That's what mattered.

"What astrology sign are you?" Selena asked, flipping through the pages of a magazine left behind by Katherine. Trashy celebrity magazines were Katherine's guilty pleasure. Obviously these were left behind by mistake. Or her sister thought no one else would be there to find them.

"I don't know." It wasn't the complete truth. She knew she was a Cancer sign, but she'd never put any stock into horoscopes and she didn't think astrology predictions were going to help her figure out this mess.

"Well, when's your birthday?" Selena asked.

Yeah, she wasn't revealing that. Her clients were on a need-to-know basis, and Selena really didn't need that info, but the star was relentless in her annoyingness. She sighed. "I'm a Cancer."

"I could have guessed that."

Leslie didn't care what that meant so she didn't ask.

"It says… 'This month brings changes for you. You will have to decide whether to follow your heart or your head. Let your passion guide your decision.'"

Wow. So insightful.

"Of course this was from a million years ago." Selena tossed the rag aside and reached for another one. "Hey, let's take this quiz. Which *Friends* character are you?"

Leslie rubbed her temples. "I'm not interested. Can you just let me think?"

Selena shrugged, grabbing a pen to take the quiz.

Leslie paced. She knew she'd done the right thing removing Selena from immediate danger, but she may have played right into the stalker's game. Unlike serial killers who hunted and killed, stalkers liked the chase—they liked to toy with their victims as long as possible. Make them feel afraid. It was part of the high for them to watch their target get more and more paranoid, protective… Taking Selena away might not deter the stalker, it might just give him more of a challenge.

"You got Chandler," Selena said.

"What?"

"You're Chandler from *Friends*. See?" Selena held up the magazine.

Leslie swiped it away. "I didn't even answer any questions." She refused to take the silly quizzes in the magazines. She had slightly more pressing issues at the moment.

But Chandler? Really? Not even one of the fun, flirty female characters? Selena obviously didn't answer the questions properly on her behalf.

"I answered them for you and you got Chandler. It says, 'You are outspoken and sarcastic. You focus on the future and avoid your past and family life. You make decisions based on logic and have low emotional stability and are often immature when it comes to developing new relationships. You turn to humor to avoid dealing with real emotions.'"

Couldn't argue with almost all of that. "I'm going to go take a shower."

Selena shrugged, but Leslie caught her quick glance toward Leslie's cell phone. Leslie grabbed it from the table. Just in case.

Man, it really did feel like she had abducted the woman, but she couldn't trust her not to put her life in even more danger. When Selena had discovered that Leslie had purposely left her own cell phone and purse back at her house, she'd thrown one of the worst tantrums Leslie had ever seen. Being unable to post selfies every hour on the hour was going to be like a prison sentence for the movie star, but Leslie couldn't take the chance that the phone or credit cards could be tracked or that Selena might not follow her rules.

Inside the bathroom, she locked the door and sighed, resting against the sink.

Outside the bathroom window, she could see the dark lake in the distance through the trees. Memories of summers spent here with her family had her seriously rethinking this. Making the decisions of what to do next would be hard enough without her past haunting her. Why hadn't she taken Selena to Tijuana or something?

Looking at the lake, she saw all the best days of her life flash like a bad eighties movie montage in her mind. Jumping off the dock into the freezing water in late June, throwing the football around and taking the Sea-Doo out. Fires on the shore late at night, roasting marshmallows, long passionate make-out sessions with Dawson, listening to the water lap onto the rocks, under the stars when everyone else was in bed. Dawson waking her up before everyone else and dragging her out onto the lake in the canoe to watch the sunrise, her cuddled between his knees, a blanket draped over them as they watched the sun crest over the mountains in the distance. He'd told her he loved her for the first time out there on the lake...

She undressed quickly and got into the shower. Exhaustion hit her like the hot water cascading down her back. It took all of her energy to lather her body with a bar of soap that had been sitting there for who knew how long.

For two and a half days, she'd been on high alert and hadn't slept more than a few hours at a time. This was what her body was trained for, but she was unavoidably crashing now that they were safe. Safer, at least.

But what the hell had she done? Coming here could have been a huge mistake.

No. She had to stay confident in her decision. She'd gone through the proper procedures for weeks. She'd provided the company with a detailed stalker behavioral report and surveillance monitoring that proved Selena was in danger. No one had listened.

The smaller incidents made everyone more cautious, but not enough.

That creep getting into Selena's house...into her bedroom.

Leslie shivered, chilled despite the heat from the water.

Whoever was stalking Selena was clearly disturbed. They were motivated by obsession and wanting to "own" the star. Leslie knew their intent wasn't to kill, but to capture and torment, forcing Selena to be a possession. Worse than death.

Moving to LA for the position, she'd assumed she'd get some hard-to-handle clients, having chosen to specialize in Celebrity Protection, but this assignment had pushed her to the limit of her abilities.

Adapt or Quit was the motto she'd repeated to herself ad nauseam over the past three months.

Now the choice might not be hers to make. She might get fired.

But she had to stay the course. She'd made her decision—for right or wrong. Right now, Selena was alive and safe and that was all that mattered…

The wailing of the smoke detector made her jump.

Except now the cabin was on fire?

Leslie blinked, suddenly wide awake again as she jumped out of the shower, grabbed a towel and rushed into the living room.

She had to have fallen asleep in the shower. This had to be a nightmare. The flames engulfing the living room couldn't be real.

Selena's scream destroyed any notion that she was dreaming.

Flames bordered the entire room, having caught the curtains at the window and the nearby armchair. The smell of thick black smoke circling the room had her instantly coughing and squinting to see through the haze.

Selena stood frozen in the center of it all. "The fire was going out. I tried to add more paper," she said.

Leslie saw the torn pages from the magazine, several with perfume samples attached. "Those pages contain highly flammable substances," she said, looking around for a way to extinguish the flames.

"How the hell was I supposed to know that?" Selena said, backing up toward the door.

Grabbing the fire extinguisher, Leslie attempted to spray the wild flames but the thing wouldn't work. Damn it! Who knew the last time it had been checked?

They had to get out. She tossed it aside, grabbed her car keys and wallet from the table and hurried toward Selena. Flames caught the edge of her towel and she quickly patted them, the heat burning into her flesh. "Ow! Jesus!"

She shoved her feet into a pair of oversized rubber boots near the door and opened it, ushering Selena outside and through the deep snow to the car, away from the cabin, as quickly as possible. The windows could blow or the place could collapse any second.

She jumped into the driver's side and threw the car in Reverse, as the windows shattered and the wooden support beams began to fall. She stared into the mirror as the entire cabin was engulfed in flames. Her heart raced and her chest tightened. Thank God they'd made it out in time.

"What now?" Selena asked, her voice quivering. In the passenger seat, she shook with cold or fright, Leslie wasn't sure which.

Leslie wanted to reassure her or say something clearheaded, but the truth was, she had no idea.

Her one and only plan went up in flames along with her family's cabin.

EVERYONE THOUGHT THAT jumping out of a plane into the middle of a burning forest was the toughest part of being a smoke jumper, but for Levi, inspecting the parachutes—having his crew's safety in his hands—was where the real pressure came from.

Standing in the parachute loft, he took his time inspecting the gear. The chutes needing repairs would be brought into the station before being repacked for use. Luckily, most appeared to be in good shape. A few tears in the canopies and netting, but nothing major.

His cell phone rang, creating a loud echo throughout the loft. He glanced at the caller ID and, seeing the station number, shook his head as he answered. "What's the matter? Couldn't walk the ten feet to come get me?"

"There's a fire reported in Mason County area…a log cabin," Chad said

Levi's smirk disappeared and he was instantly on high alert. "That's the Sanders family cabin," he said, as he sprinted out of the loft. It was the only cabin in that area. The Sanders family had owned that land for generations. With a lake on one side and forest on the other, the family had cleared enough of a trail to get their vehicles in and out during the milder months of the year, but had preserved as much of the area wildlife as possible.

Great for the environment. Not great in this case, when a cabin fire could and would quickly spread to nearby trees. And getting to the cabin would require smoke jumper assistance.

"I've put the call out to the on-call team and I'm getting the plane ready," Chad said.

They were operating on a skeleton crew with it being off-season. Only two supervisors were eligible for year-round employment. Luckily, their on-call crew were all nearby in Fairbanks. "I'm on the way." He disconnected the call and then hit speed dial for the Wild River state trooper office and asked for Eddie Sanders.

A moment later, Eddie picked up. "Hey, Levi, what's up?"

His cabin. Up in flames. "Hey, are any of your family members at the cabin this week?" That was the most important thing— establishing if anyone could be in danger.

"Not that I know of. Katherine only goes out there during the summer."

"Your mom or grandma?"

"Nah. They wouldn't try driving out there this time of year. Something wrong?"

"I hate to tell you this, buddy, but the cabin is on fire."

"Shit. Let me call around to make sure no one's there and I'll call you back. Thanks for the heads-up," Eddie said.

After going inside the cabin, Levi grabbed his gear from the wall in his room. He undressed in record time.

Eddie's quick return call revealed none of the Sanders family were there that week, which was a relief, but it wasn't unusual for homeless people to break into abandoned cabins and squat for the winter. Levi suspected the fire was an accident and not an act of arson and hoped no one was still inside.

Hurrying back out, he climbed into the C-212 with the others. No emergency was ideal, but this one was particularly unsettling.

He knew the Sanders family well. One member in particular—too well. His childhood...and adulthood (until a few years ago) best friend, Leslie. Luckily he knew there was no way she would have been at the cabin. She'd been living in LA for three years now and it took small miracles to get her back to Alaska.

Levi certainly didn't qualify as important enough.

They flew through the snow toward the location of the cabin and his heart pounded a little, seeing the flames illuminating the darkness in the distance. He'd spent a lot of summers at that cabin with Leslie, her family and their close friends. As kids, they would all go hiking and swimming and play capture the flag in the woods. They'd have campfires by the lake, and then as older teens, they'd head to the cabin to host parties without parental supervision.

So many good memories were wrapped up in that cabin. Now it was gone.

As they drew near, they prepared to jump. Chad located the best jump site and signaled them when it was time.

Levi exited the plane and parachuted to the ground, just yards from the burning cabin. The fire had spread to the surrounding trees and after stockpiling their equipment, the team spread out to create a fire line to prevent further spreading. Using crosscut saws, the team cut back the brush and Levi immediately started digging a trench below the deep snow to stop the flames in their tracks.

The aircraft circled above, dropping water onto the blaze and minutes later, the area was secured. Unfortunately, the cabin had completely burned to the ground, now just a large pile of smoldering debris. Luckily, no one had been inside.

Chad radioed as the team toured the area to make sure the flames were out. "I see a car…looks stuck on the in-road about a mile from the cabin. Vehicle is running. Can't confirm passengers inside."

Levi led the team to where the car sat idling and approached with caution.

The passenger door opened and a young woman dressed in jeans and winter boots with a blanket wrapped around her shoulders came hurrying toward them. "Oh thank God…" She nearly collapsed into his arms and Levi struggled to steady her.

"Hey…it's okay. What are you doing out here? Were you in the cabin?" The singed edges of the blanket and the smell of smoke on her hair suggested she was, but who the hell was she?

"Yes…it was so terrifying," she said, her lips trembling.

The driver's side door opened and another woman got out…wearing only a towel and rubber boots that looked miles too big. She turned and his heart stopped beating.

"Leslie?" She was back? She'd somehow burned down her family's cabin?

She was in a towel.

His mouth was a desert and he swallowed several times. Hard.

"Hi, Levi," she said tightly, shifting uncomfortably in big oversized boots and the towel.

Hi, Levi. That was it?

He continued to stare at her, until Miller, one of his crewmates, nudged his arm. "Your friend's probably cold," he muttered, guiding the other young woman out of Levi's arms.

Shit. Right. Levi quickly removed his jacket and wrapped it around Leslie's shoulders.

"Thanks," she said, sliding her arms into the coat sleeves and pulling it around her body. It was far too big for her, but gave her some warmth and coverage at least.

"What happened?" he asked.

"My…uh…friend isn't familiar with flammable substances."

Was it his imagination or did she look murderous when she glanced toward her "friend," who was getting checked on—and checked out—by the other rescue members. She was a stunning woman with long dark hair and big blue eyes. If he were to guess, she must be someone famous. "What were you doing out here? I thought you were in LA?"

"I was." She looked hesitant, her dark blue eyes sliding toward the others as she lowered her voice and moved closer to him. His pulse soared to an unhealthy rate. Having her this close, after so long… "Okay, look Levi, you have to take in what I'm about to say with strict confidence and zero judgment."

As if she'd ever need to ask him for either. He'd only been in love with her since the fifth grade but he admired and respected the hell out of her enough never to tell her. Whatever she was about to say couldn't possibly compare to that. "You got it," he said.

"She's not exactly a friend. She's a client. And I brought her here for protection." Her expression said she clearly saw the irony in their current situation, so he didn't make a comment. "The problem is, no one authorized my actions or knows where she is...where we are."

His eyes widened. "So, you essentially kidnapped her?"

She shook her wet hair, the blond strands nearly hitting him in the face. "No. I had to get her out of LA."

"Surely, there were other—safer—following-protocol ways to have done that."

"Hey, maybe I didn't specify, but I wasn't looking for advice either. I just...trust you and someone should know... in case the stalker does happen to find us."

She trusted him. Sure, she'd stumbled over the word, which annoyed him because she should know that she could trust him with anything and everything, but at least she was choosing to tell him, out of anyone she could have confided in, including her law enforcement family...or a confidant (maybe boyfriend?) back in LA. "What do you need?"

Leslie glanced down at the towel under his jacket. "Right now? Clothes and a ride into Wild River." She looked ruefully at the car stuck deep into the snowbank. "And we'll have to get the car towed somehow."

"Keep my jacket as long as you need and I'll call this in once we reach town. We'll get you two a ride from the station."

She nodded and started toward the trail, to hike out through the deep snow to where the plane was waiting. Then she turned back abruptly, nearly colliding with him. "Oh, and one more thing."

He waited.

"Tell no one about this."

He grinned. No doubt this was embarrassing for her. She would hate for anyone to know she'd been in this situation... especially as compromised as she was. "I won't say a word."

CHAPTER FOUR

"I REALLY DON'T think it's necessary to go to the hospital," Leslie argued in the back of Levi's truck as they passed the Welcome to Wild River sign a few hours later. Already, six smoke jumpers and rescuers knew Selena was there… She wanted to trust that none of them would go spreading the gossip, after she'd explained the situation, but the more people who knew, the riskier it was.

"Better to be safe than sorry," Levi said. He glanced at her bandaged hand. "And a real doctor should check that out."

She barely even noticed the painful tingling under the bandages. She swallowed hard but no matter how many times she did, she couldn't get rid of the lump in her throat. Emotions she was usually so in control of were now close to the surface.

Her family cabin was gone. Despite not having used it much in the last ten years, she'd always liked knowing it was still there. A standing memory of good times when her father was alive. Before everything changed, started to fall apart. Now it was gone. And she was to blame.

Would she always be the one responsible for tearing her family apart?

This entire situation was made a million times worse because Levi was a part of it. She could hold things together when she was surrounded by strangers but her estranged best friend, a person she could trust if she needed to give in to her exhaustion and stress—was weakening her when she needed her strength the most.

He had seemed surprised, but happy to see her, which made her cool exterior that much harder. It was obvious which of the two of them had essentially walked away from the friendship.

As they pulled up in front of the hospital, he opened the doors to help them out. Selena was more than willing to accept any and all attention after her "ordeal," but Leslie refused his hand when he extended it to her.

If he noticed, he didn't show it as he closed the truck door behind her. "Do you want me to come in?" he asked.

"No...no need." She cleared her throat. "Thank you for your assistance."

He nodded. "Of course, Leslie. Anytime."

The words weren't casual. They were full of feeling—compassionate, kind and slightly questioning. She knew he had to be wondering why she'd basically disappeared from his life, but right now wasn't the time.

She caught Selena staring at them. Better wrap this up. "So, remember, tell my family..."

His disappointment about her asking him to lie was clear as he said, "We aren't sure yet how the fire started." He nodded. "I got it, but we can only keep that up for about twenty-four hours."

He'd have to file his report with the details...the truth. Her family would know she was in town soon enough. But she appreciated the twenty-four hour reprieve. The head start. Time to process being in Wild River without having to face them. She would have to eventually. She owed them an apology for the fire. Her gut tightened at the thought. "That's great. Thanks again," she said.

Levi turned to Selena. "Pleasure meeting you, Ms. Hudson. Enjoy your time in Wild River," he said before climbing into the truck.

Leslie turned to head into the hospital.

Shit, she was still wearing his jacket.

She turned back and tapped on the window.

Levi's hopeful expression was too much as he rolled it down. "Yeah?"

"Your jacket…"

"Keep it until you can get some clothes."

She wanted it off as fast as possible. Seeing him was like seeing a ghost from her past. Having his familiar smell wrapped around her just confirmed he was definitely real…and so were the memories threatening to destroy her. "Okay, I'll get it back to you somehow."

He hesitated. "Are you sure you don't want me to call Katherine or Eddie…or your mom or grandma? They could bring you some clothes." He reached for his phone.

"No!"

Selena turned to look at her.

"No," she repeated more quietly. "No. It's okay. I'll figure something out." Her grandma would be the person she'd call if she needed to…but everyone else was going to be devastated when they heard about the cabin and more than likely pissed off at her. Especially her sister, who now wouldn't be able to use the cabin for her yearly solitary retreats.

"You sure?" Levi asked.

"Yes." Guilt wrapped around her, but she fought it. She'd face them all soon enough. Just not yet.

"Okay." Levi put the phone away.

"Thank you…again. I'll be sure to send your jacket back."

He nodded. "Take care." The intensity in his ocean blue eyes made her shiver and she averted her gaze. Of all the people to come to their rescue—of all people to run into immediately upon being in Alaska—it had to be Levi. The one person who could break her, if she let him.

Turning away from the truck, she hurried inside the hospital with Selena, and moments later the admitting nurse directed them to a small examination room.

Selena eyed her as she climbed onto the examination table, leaving Leslie—the injured one—with the uncomfortable plastic chair. "You two have a history."

Understatement, but she'd play dumb. "Who?"

"You and that unbelievably good-looking fire-hero guy."

"Nope." This was not a conversation she was eager to have anytime, least of all with her client. Sharing personal details of her life with Selena was unnecessary and unprofessional.

"You totally do."

"No. We don't." She pretended to examine the bandages on her burned hand.

"Then why did he look at you like Ryan Reynolds's character looked at Amy Smart's character in *Just Friends* when they saw one another for the first time after she'd broken his heart by friend zoning him in high school…"

Leslie held up her uninjured hand to stop the rom-com recap. The way Selena likened everything to movies was almost more painful than the burn. "We don't have a history. We're both from Wild River. We went to school together."

Selena was unconvinced, but she shrugged. "Fine… If you say so."

"I do." Of course she was lying.

Truth was, seeing Levi had made her temperature rise higher than the flames burning her family's cabin to the ground. And she'd longed for metaphorical flames to engulf her as well.

Three years since she'd last seen him. Three years of trying to put the tragedy from her past aside and focus on her future. Three years of ignoring any contact he'd tried to make.

She had no real reason for it other than a desperation to leave everything and everyone that reminded her of Dawson behind, and there were few memories of her former fiancé that weren't closely linked to Levi.

Just looking at him hurt.

The accident, everything that happened, was not his fault and she didn't blame him. It was just difficult to be around someone who represented both the best times in her life and the hardest. He knew her better than most people and that made her vulnerable to him and vulnerable was the last thing she wanted to be.

Especially right now.

Twenty minutes later, her hand feeling pleasantly numb in fresh bandages, Leslie left the hospital in scrubs, with no idea what to do next.

CHAPTER FIVE

Three years earlier...

SHE WASN'T A DRESS person by nature, but it had to be true what they said—wedding dresses were designed to make every bride look her very best. Leslie almost didn't recognize herself in the mirror as she slipped her feet into her ballet flats. The floor-length, off-white gown with its intricate beading along the bodice and A-line skirt was flattering to her figure, while still modest and her style. No frills or lace, but something uniquely special for the day.

She hadn't even planned on wearing a real wedding dress, since it was going to be a small ceremony at the courthouse—just the two of them, plus her grandmother and Levi to act as witnesses. But at the last minute, she'd decided to splurge on the dress. At least part of the whole thing would be following tradition. Without their parents' full support, it didn't make sense to hold an elaborate event with a large guest list and a massive, unnecessary budget.

She moved closer to the mirror in the B and B honeymoon suite where they planned on spending their first night together as a married couple and applied her pale pink lipstick with a shaky hand. Her stomach twisted and she forced a breath.

This was the right thing. This was what she wanted.

It was just nerves getting to her.

She loved Dawson. He loved her. That was all that mattered.

"Ready to—" Levi's voice broke off and he cleared his throat "—go," he said, entering the room behind her.

She turned with a smile, seeing him in a gray suit and white dress shirt, a smart-ass comment about his lack of jeans and T-shirt on the tip of her tongue, but then her smile faded, seeing his expression.

Completely unreadable as he stared at her like she was a stranger. Stared at her made-up face, her blond curls hanging loose around her shoulders, and then he stared for a really long time at the dress.

"It's just a dress, Levi," she said with a laugh, hoping to break some of the tension filling the air around them. His reaction was only increasing her nerves.

He shook his head and immediately her friend was back. "It's beautiful. You're beautiful," he said, looking away and reaching for her purse on the table. "We should go or we're going to miss your timeslot."

She nodded, forcing her best confident look. She was ready for this. They'd been together for years. Life without Dawson didn't make sense, so why not get married?

"Thank you," she said, accepting the purse from him.

She followed him out of the room. And neither of them heard her forgotten cell phone ringing.

HE COULD DO THIS.

He had to do this.

His best friends were getting married—the two people in the world who meant the most to him were going to commit to a lifetime of love and happiness and Levi would not get in the way of that.

He'd kept his feelings for Leslie to himself this long. What was another lifetime?

His mouth watered and he rushed to the shared bathroom in the hallway of the B and B, where Leslie and Dawson would be spending their wedding night. Vomiting, he splashed water onto his face and stared at his reflection in the mirror.

He wasn't letting her go. He never had her in the first place. She loved Dawson, had always loved Dawson, and always would. He wouldn't even be in the running, even if his best friend wasn't in the picture. She'd never seen him that way. They were friends. Full stop.

Unrequited love happened all the time.

Unfortunately, unlike other rejected, jilted, heartbroken people, Levi couldn't just walk away from the source of pain and torment. He'd had a front row seat to it for years and now he would be standing next to his best friend, offering all the support he wanted desperately to feel as he vowed to love and cherish the woman Levi was in love with.

If only he could break whatever spell Leslie had on him, whatever power she held over his heart. Over the years, he'd tried to get over these insane feelings he had for her. But no other woman made his body, mind and heart react the way she did.

He'd even tried stepping away for a while, pulling back...but not having them both in his life was just that much more painful. They were more than friends, they were family, and he'd support them the way he always did.

He left the room and walked down the hall to Leslie's room. He knocked once and entered.

And his entire world spun out of control.

She was breathtaking in the floor-length, simple but elegant off-white satin gown, and he forgot how to function as he took in the sight of her.

"It's just a dress, Levi," she said with a shy laugh.

It was so much more than a dress. It was a symbol of his inability to ever be honest with her. To ever tell her how he really felt. It was an even bigger symbol of the fact that he would never have the love of his life. He'd have to be content never fully loving anyone else to his full capacity. He'd never share a life with her. It was so much more than a dress.

But *she'd* be happy.

And that was what mattered to him most.

He cleared his throat. "It's beautiful. You're beautiful." He hoped it sounded natural, normal. It's what you said to a bride on her wedding day.

He handed over her purse and checked his watch as they left the room. He had an hour before he gave the woman he loved away to his best friend.

LEAVE IT TO Dawson to be late.

Leslie checked the clock on the wall at the courthouse and reached into her purse. She'd text him to remind her often-absentminded fiancé that their wedding was supposed to have started five minutes ago. His inability to be on time for anything was one of those quirks of his that she'd been forced to come to love, otherwise she would have murdered him by now.

Three other couples were scheduled to get married that day and their window of opportunity was closing.

Unfortunately, her cell phone wasn't in her purse.

Damn it, she'd left it in the honeymoon suite at the B and B.

She scanned the courthouse hallway for Levi and saw him guzzling a bottle of water near the vending machine. He looked pale and slightly ill. He was probably freaking out about having to stand up there in front of half a dozen people. Little crowd, big crowd, didn't matter—he got stage fright something fierce. She walked toward him and heard him mutter something undecipherable under his breath.

"Hey, you okay?" she asked.

He wiped the back of his hand across his lips. "Yeah... great. We ready?"

"No. Dawson's not here yet. Can you call him? I left my cell at the B and B."

"Sure... I'm sure he's just stuck in traffic or something," he said.

She raised an eyebrow. "Or maybe he's getting cold feet." She was joking, but her chest tightened, thinking about that very real possibility.

LEVI STEPPED OUTSIDE the courthouse and dialed Dawson's cell. The fresh air helped his nauseated state, but now his annoyance was growing.

"Hey, Levi. Can I call you back?" Dawson answered.

"No. You're supposed to be at the courthouse right now. For your wedding," Levi said. Unbelievable. Classic Dawson.

"Yeah, I know. I'm just running a little late."

He was in his vehicle. Levi could tell he was on speakerphone. "Where are you?" Please let the man be on his way.

"Answering a call."

Damn it. "You're off duty."

"We're never off duty. You know that. Look, it's just a break-and-enter call. I'm the closest unit. I can't ignore it. I'll be there soon."

Normally, he'd agree with the greater-good-comes-first code that his best friend lived by, but not in this case, not when it meant disappointing Leslie. "Dude, it's your wedding day. The ceremony was supposed to start five minutes ago. Let someone else take this one."

"I already responded," Dawson said.

"Dawson." He couldn't remember ever being so pissed at his friend. This was selfish and unnecessary. Hurting Leslie like this wasn't cool. "Don't be a dick and get your ass to the courthouse."

"Gotta go, Levi. Take care of my girl until I see her again."

The line went dead and Levi swore under his breath. How was he supposed to go in there and tell Leslie that Dawson was going to be late for his own wedding? Or that he may not be making it at all? And did he tell her the truth and worry her or say he was running late?

Damn his friend for putting him in this position. As soon as he showed up and said his vows, Levi was going to kick his ass.

Still no word from Dawson as the clock ran out on their assigned timeslot. Leslie was trying to appear unfazed, but she wasn't fooling Levi. She hugged her grandmother on the courthouse steps and forced a laugh as she said, "A rescheduled wedding date to be announced…thanks for coming out and sorry about this. I'm sure the call must have been important."

Her grandmother nodded, kissing her head. "You're beautiful. Give him hell for me when you see him."

Because Leslie wouldn't give him hell on her own. She'd let Dawson off the hook like she always did.

His cell phone rang in his pocket and he prepared his own earful as he reached for it. But his blood ran cold seeing the state troopers' office number lighting up the call display instead. "Hello?" Had he said the word out loud? He barely heard it.

"Is Leslie with you?" Captain Clarkson said. No pleasantries...

"Yeah, she's here." His hand shook violently as he handed his cell phone to her. Her expression immediately turned to fear as she listened and his heart pounded in his chest.

"What? What...? I mean...where is he?" Her voice was strained. "He's...no...that's not possible. He was coming here...we were supposed to get married."

Were. Past tense. It didn't escape anyone's notice.

Her grandmother immediately moved in closer, supporting Leslie's weight as she looked pale and about to faint.

Levi's chest was about to explode as he watched all the color drain from her cheeks. Her eyes teared up and her lips trembled violently.

He caught the phone as she dropped it, then moved fast to catch her as her knees gave way. He didn't have to ask. He knew.

Dawson was gone.

Shock passed quickly and anger was the first emotion he felt. Damn his best friend for answering that call on his wedding day. Damn him for always putting the job first. And damn him for breaking all of their hearts.

Leslie felt limp in his arms as they both lowered to the courthouse steps. He held her while tears soaked his dress shirt and her body trembled.

He didn't even know what was happening around them. Levi knew he had only one job in that moment. Sit there, hold her tight, and make sure she had something to grab ahold of while her world came crashing down.

BEAMS OF SUNLIGHT shone through the stained glass windows of the church the day of the funeral. Levi stood tall, straight, unwavering as the priest talked about Dawson in the past tense.

He refused to give in to the desire to run out of the church and away from the pain and sadness threatening to engulf him. He had to be strong for Leslie. She needed a rock, something she could use to get her own bearings... He'd be that for her.

And his best friend deserved his respect, honoring the life he'd led, the sacrifices he'd made and the man he hadn't gotten a chance to be, the future he hadn't lived.

"The community and the department honor Dawson as the hero he was. He selflessly put his life on the line to protect others...and on that day paid the ultimate sacrifice for a lifetime of serving others. We salute him and we ask God to take him into his..."

The words echoing all around him in the silent church seemed far away and Levi shook off a wave of dizziness as he prepared to carry his best friend's casket to its final resting place.

Leslie gripped the pew in front of her. Her pale knuckles losing any remaining color as she held tight. Levi's hand covered hers and he shivered at how icy it was.

She hadn't eaten or spoken much in days. Mostly sat in a trance as Dawson's family made all the preparations around her. Not that she was in the mindset to deal with these decisions, but it angered Levi that no one asked her for her opinion on anything. No one acknowledged that she'd been about to be Dawson's wife.

But maybe in the end, this would be easier on her.

The cold way his family had always treated her had simply continued...

It was one of the things that had always bothered him—their lack of respect and love for Leslie. He never understood it. The family had opened their hearts and home to him so willingly and he owed them so much...but he hated the way they'd never accepted Leslie. Had always treated her like she wasn't good enough for their son.

THE CEREMONY ENDED with a final prayer and moment of silence and Levi knew there was not enough time to compose himself and prepare for what came next.

Along with Dawson's cousins and two members of the police force, he carried the coffin out of the church and down the path toward the burial site. Tears burned his throat and he couldn't feel his legs, just the heavy weight of the coffin pressing against his left shoulder and all the regret of a life that ended far too soon.

As the coffin lowered into the ground, his buddy's last words to him played on his mind.

Take care of my girl until I see her again.

SHE WAS NUMB. Which was the best way to be... Leslie knew the reprieve from the ache in her chest and pain in her stomach was temporary. She knew the stages of grief, having gone through them too many times already. They would all appear eventually, but right now all she knew was that she had to get away. Escape the constant reminder of the future that had been stolen and distance herself from all the kind, caring sympathy that made her want to throw up.

She wasn't sure how she felt—angry, sad, disappointed, heartbroken... Nothing seemed powerful enough to capture the emotions running through her.

As she walked through the station, head down, avoiding gazes, blocking out the sound of sympathetic wishes as she passed her fellow state troopers, desperate to look anywhere but at the open cubicle desk where Dawson's unfilled paperwork was still piled high in his in tray, she focused only on what she was there to do.

If she thought about it too long, she might change her mind.

Entering her boss's office, she placed her gun and badge on his desk and walked out before she could fall apart.

CHAPTER SIX

Present day

LEVI WAS HALFWAY back to the station when he pulled his truck to the side of the road. He'd nearly turned around a dozen times already, but for what?

Leslie hadn't exactly seemed thrilled to see him. She'd barely spoken to him beyond what was necessary and she'd struggled to look him in the eye. Granted, the circumstances could hardly get worse, so he was desperate not to read too much into her standoffish coldness.

Seeing her had made him anything but cold.

The image of her getting out of her car in just a towel was likely to plague him for a long time. He'd add it to his inventory of memories. The ones he didn't want to try to forget. Yes, some of them were painful and full of heartache, but there had been a lot of good times too.

Even if he'd been the third wheel.

And unfortunately, he couldn't help but question if maybe he wouldn't have been the third wheel if he hadn't frozen on the day that had changed everything...

Since that day on the playground, the three of them had been inseparable. Leslie and Dawson's passion for movie making had never really rubbed off on Levi, but he accepted the roles they gave him without complaint. Then as they got older, even as their interests changed and new friends were made, they were all still close.

And with Dawson involved in every sport imaginable, it had been he and Leslie who had spent more time together going to movies, hanging out at Dawson's sports games, studying... He remembered the day he felt the shift. At thirteen, they were starting to get interested in dating and kissing and she'd been the one to initiate the conversation as they'd collected their books from their lockers after school.

"Have you kissed anyone yet?" she asked.

He wanted to be cool so badly, but he knew there was no point in lying to her. His palms had sweat and his mouth was chalky as he'd shaken his head. "You?"

"No..." She twirled a piece of her blond hair around her finger as she stared at her high-top sneakers. "I was thinking that maybe it might be a good idea to learn...practice with a friend before either of us tries to kiss someone we really like and mess it up."

His heart was beating so loudly in his ears that she had to have heard it. She wanted to kiss him. But not because she really liked him—because she wanted to practice on someone safe. Unfortunately, he really did like her and if he was going to kiss her, he wanted it to be special. He didn't want to be the trial run guy, the safe friends-only guy...

While he struggled with the words to form a confession, to finally tell her how he felt and put himself out there, she'd misread his silence as being not interested.

Her cheeks had flushed and she'd laughed. "I was totally kidding, Levi. Man, you should have seen your face."

"Oh...um..."

She'd turned and hurried away as the bell rang. And he'd stood there so long in shock, regret and confusion that he'd gotten a hall slip from the monitor.

All day, he'd replayed it, kicking himself for not agreeing to it and for not making his own feelings clear.

He had to stop being such a wimp. Leslie had wanted to kiss him and he'd made a huge mess of it. Now he had to make things right. He'd ask her to the winter formal dance, then if it seemed like she was into him too, he'd go in for a real kiss. One he was prepared for. One that conveyed his true feelings for her. Move away from friends-only and have the relationship he'd been wanting with her since that first day on the playground.

After school, he caught up to her as she was unpacking her locker.

Play it cool. Apologize for freezing earlier that day and ask her to the dance.

But as he approached, he saw Dawson heading down the hall toward them from the other direction. He slowed his pace a little. Damn, he didn't want to ask in front of Dawson. That part of things was going to be potentially awkward as it was if he and Leslie started dating.

How would their dynamic change if two of them were more than just friends? Would Dawson want to double-date with them? If he ever got serious about anything other than sports? Or would they spend more time apart?

Dawson reached Leslie first and Levi's stomach knotted as his buddy produced two winter formal dance tickets from behind his back.

Two. Not three.

Shit. No. This wasn't supposed to happen. Since when was Dawson into Leslie that way? He'd never shown any interest… Was he asking her to go as friends? But then, he would have bought a third ticket and they would all have gone together.

Levi's heart raced as he neared them and heard Dawson say the word *date*.

Leslie hesitated before answering. She caught sight of Levi and her expression was slightly conflicted.

Maybe there had been more to the practice kiss she'd been wanting...

Say something! Do something! Don't let your buddy steal your girl!

Unfortunately, as usual, he waited too long, and then it was too late.

Leslie looked away from him and smiled at Dawson. She nodded her head and Dawson grinned like a moron.

And that was the first time seeing his two best friends together had broken his heart.

But no matter how hard it had been over the years, having the two of them in his life had meant everything to him. They were his family.

And family supported one another. Leslie might be the last person on earth who would ask for help or admit she may be in over her head this time, but he'd be there for her if she needed him. Decision was made, he was staying in the ski resort town for a few nights.

He dialed the station and Chad answered on the third ring. The unmistakable sound of Mario Kart in the background confirmed that Levi taking a few days off shouldn't be a problem. "Hey man, I've decided to stay in Wild River for a few days... You cool holding down the fort on your own?"

"No problem...damn it, Yoshi took me out," Chad said.

"Okay, call me if there's an emergency," Levi said, disconnecting the call. Then, checking the traffic, he took a deep breath and did a U-turn on the highway, heading back toward Wild River.

For one last attempt to get back at least one of the friends he'd lost.

CHAPTER SEVEN

"Ahhhh...now this is more like it."

Shocking. The Wild River Resort was to Selena's liking. Stretched across four hundred acres, the posh, luxurious accommodations boasted three hundred guest rooms, a five-star spa, two high-end, expensive dining options, and provided tourists the most spectacular views of the mountains.

Unfortunately, the price tag was astronomical. Wild River was a small town, boasting only four other modest hotels and a local B and B, but everything else was booked solid. Some bestselling fantasy writer was hosting a knitting retreat and book signing that week.

"This place is amazing. I had no idea there were resorts like this in Alaska. You've definitely redeemed yourself," Selena said.

"Wonderful. I was worried," Leslie said as they approached the check-in desk.

"How can I help you?" the man dressed in a resort uniform behind the desk asked.

"We need a room, please."

"For how many nights?"

She hesitated. "I'm not entirely sure. Can we book three for now and then extend our stay if necessary?" Hopefully it wouldn't come to that.

The clerk nodded. "I'll need your ID and credit card, please."

That wouldn't be happening. She couldn't risk leaving a trail. She opened her wallet and took out a wad of cash that she'd taken from an ATM before leaving LA. "I'd prefer to pay cash if possible."

The clerk hesitated. "You'd need to leave a sizeable deposit for any incidentals…"

Leslie nodded. "That's fine," she said, handing over the money and saying a silent goodbye to her savings. It wasn't like she'd be able to submit an expense report for this one. She signed the paperwork for their room with her left, unbandaged hand, the signature barely legible.

"Great," the check-in clerk said. "Here are your room keys…"

"We only need one," Leslie said.

Selena rolled her eyes. "You don't even trust me with a room key?"

"You won't be going anywhere alone."

The clerk sent them an odd look, but having the forty-year-old guy think she was in some weird as shit relationship was the least of her worries right now. "One key is fine," she said.

"Okay… Elevators are down the hall, across from the restaurant. Your room is on the third floor. Room service is twenty-four hours and the spa is open from eight a.m. until nine p.m. Enjoy your stay and please let us know if you need anything."

The last part of his sentence was directed at Selena and Leslie sighed as she moved away from the desk. She didn't care how strange this must look—her in a pair of hospital scrubs and oversized rubber boots, checking into an expensive resort with no luggage and a woman that looked half her age. She couldn't wait to get to their room and take a hot shower. A nap would be amazing as well if she was successful in shutting her overactive brain off for five minutes.

She ignored the odd looks from other guests as they headed toward the elevators. Then she immediately spotted someone that had her looking for an escape route. "Oh shit."

"What? What's wrong?" Selena followed her gaze. "Is it the stalker?" She moved to stand behind Leslie, ducking low behind her shoulders.

"Nope." Worse. For Leslie at least.

She scanned the lobby, but its open concept layout provided nowhere to hide and Eddie spotted her. His expression was a mix of shock and amusement as he came toward them and eyed her clothing.

"Do we know him?" Selena whispered.

Unfortunately. "Selena, this is my brother, Eddie," she said as he stopped his wheelchair in front of them. "Um… what are you doing here?" He lived three blocks away. Why was he at the resort? She'd thought they were safe from running into any locals, especially her family.

"Montana's parents are in town," he said. "We were just having dinner at the restaurant. Better question is, what are *you* doing here?" He glanced at her hand and she knew that he knew she was responsible for the cabin fire.

"Protecting me from my stalker," Selena said, stepping out from behind her.

Jesus. Hadn't she told her not to reveal herself or the reason they were there to anyone? She shot her a look. "Eddie, this is Selena Hudson and this conversation is highly confidential," Leslie said quietly, scanning the hallway. Locals might have a hard time recognizing the star, but tourists might not.

Eddie grinned as he extended a hand to Selena. "My

lips are sealed. Nice to meet you. I can only assume that you're famous?"

"'Cause I have a stalker?" Selena asked.

"'Cause my sister doesn't have any friends, so you have to be a client of hers."

Selena laughed as though Eddie were the funniest comedian on earth.

Oh come on...

"Does Mom know you're here?" Eddie asked.

"No one was supposed to know I'm here." Her irritation skyrocketed at the mention of her mother. She was walking a fine stress line that day that felt ready to snap at any moment.

"She had us hiding out in the woods until the cabin went up in flames," Selena said, obviously having immediately bonded with Eddie.

Leslie was going to murder the star herself.

Eddie's face was insincere shock. "*You* burned down the family cabin?"

Yes, and she was the woman in a towel rescued by the local smoke jumpers that everyone must be talking about as well.

"It was my fault," Selena said quickly. "I'll pay to have the cabin rebuilt."

She would?

Eddie's girlfriend, Montana Banks, approached and Eddie turned in his wheelchair to make the introductions. "Hey, Danger, meet Leslie's new client, Selena... I'm sorry, what did you say your last name was?"

Selena laughed, tossing her dark hair over one shoulder as though glamming it up might make her more recognizable. "Hudson. Have I really arrived in a town that hasn't heard of me?"

No ego, just genuine surprise. "I told you," Leslie said.

Montana smiled warmly, her striking features even more beautiful. "Nice to meet you and great to see you again, Leslie."

"You too." It wasn't fake politeness either. Leslie really liked her brother's girlfriend. A single mom who'd suffered a tragic brain injury years before and was back in Wild River to have a relationship with her daughter, Montana had helped Eddie overcome his own tragedy, getting shot months ago. The two of them were great together and Leslie was happy to see her brother happy. If circumstances were different, she'd love to spend time with Montana, but that would require spending more time in Wild River with her family.

"How long will you be staying in town? We should have dinner," she said.

"Um… I'm not sure. Hopefully not too long."

"Dinner sounds cool though," Selena said.

No one was asking her.

Leslie checked an imaginary watch. "We should get going… We have to run into town for a few things." A shower and a nap would have to wait. They needed better clothing and she really needed a new cell phone right away. There could be updates from Eoghan and being out of touch for too long wasn't a great idea. Her sanity would also depend on the short, infrequent calls.

Selena frowned as she looked at her. "How are we getting there? Your car is still stuck in a snowbank, remember?"

"There's a shuttle from the resort into town." Getting on the public shuttle dressed in scrubs was the least of her concerns right now.

But Eddie shook his head. "We're headed home. We'll drop you off on Main Street."

"Perfect!" Selena said.

Leslie wanted to argue, but at this point, she was choosing her battles and conserving her energy. "Great," she mumbled.

In the back seat of Eddie's van a minute later, Leslie tried to put as much distance between her and Selena as possible, but the star kept moving closer to peer out the window as they drove toward Main Street. "You have your own window," she muttered.

"There's just trees on my side," Selena said, practically leaning on Leslie's lap.

"So, is the cabin completely gone?" Eddie asked, glancing at her in the mirror.

"I'm not sure…but I think so." The lump was back in her throat and she swallowed hard. What was wrong with her? It was just an old cabin that she hadn't bothered to visit in a very long time. She'd left it in her past years ago, along with everything else. This overwhelming regret needed to subside quickly so she could go back to focusing on the mess she was currently in.

"I'm so relieved you two are okay," Montana said.

Was she? Physically maybe.

Selena's audible gasp next to her made her jump. "What? What is it?"

"O-M-G this street actually looks just like the studio lot set for the *Back to the Future* series."

Leslie shot her a look. "You have been outside a movie set before, right?"

"Yes, but not outside of LA and let's face it, Hollywood is really just one big studio lot."

No arguments there. "So, wait—you've never been outside of LA?"

Selena nodded. "Of course I have, but mostly when we are on tour for movie promo, so I've never actually seen Small Town, USA. I've been in movies since I was a toddler and between my filming schedule and Dad's…we're too busy to travel for fun."

So money couldn't buy everything. Leslie's family relationships weren't perfect, but some of her best memories growing up were of traveling together—mostly with their father before he died. He was a brilliant artist with a passion for photography, something Leslie had inherited, and he'd captured the most breathtaking scenic shots wherever they went. Photos that were now lost in that fire. She'd lost him years ago when she'd needed him most and now she'd lost those precious, irreplaceable images as well.

"You can put the sympathetic eyes away," Selena said, mistaking Leslie's own memory lane trip as sympathy for her. "I love my life and LA. There's nowhere I would have wanted to go anyway," she said, then her attention was elsewhere. She pointed to North Mountain Sports Company on the right side of the street. "That looks like a place to find decent winter clothes."

Right. At killer prices. The big chain store had only recently opened in Wild River and despite the locals' attempts to keep it away, it seemed everyone had quickly embraced the store and its high-end offering. Leslie wasn't sure it went with Wild River's aesthetic, but they were trying to appeal to the luxury traveler and outdoor enthusiasts. Or in cases like Selena, brand snobs.

"This where you'd like to get dropped off?" Eddie asked, pulling his van in front of the store.

"Yes, please," Selena said.

"I'll pretend I don't see you shopping at my competitor," Montana said with a wink. She'd recently partnered with her ex's new girlfriend at her company SnowTrek Tours. North Mountain Sports Company had once threatened to put them out of business, but Montana's background in extreme sports and BASE jumping gave SnowTrek Tours something different to offer and according to Eddie, the company was no longer worried about the big chain store's effect on their bottom line.

"Sorry Montana. I promise we won't book any excursions," Leslie said, opening the van door and climbing out. "Thanks, Eddie."

Her brother nodded. "Anytime. And I'll call you about dinner."

Fantastic. She didn't commit as she closed the door.

"How long has your brother been in a wheelchair?" Selena asked as the van drove away.

"About eight months." Felt like a lifetime ago already when her brother's heroic act had given them all quite a scare and had him questioning his future on the police force.

"What happened?"

"He was shot. Took a bullet for…Montana actually. She wasn't his girlfriend at the time."

"Who could resist a man that heroic though, huh?"

Leslie shrugged. "They had a connection before that, but I would think Eddie's bravery didn't hurt to make Montana fall even harder." Her brother had sacrificed everything in that split second—his life, his career… Things could have been a lot worse. But it was in their genetics to be selfless and he'd acted the way anyone in their family would have. The way Leslie was prepared to in her line of work.

She opened the door to the new sporting goods store

and followed Selena inside. Chart-topping music played throughout the store and sales clerks restocked shelves and manned the dressing rooms, but she was relieved that the store was quiet, it being the off-season and almost closing time.

Selena nodded. "Is it...was it tough on him? Adjusting to life in the chair?"

Why the sudden interest in her family? "I'm sure it was. But he's doing well."

"He mentioned he's a cop."

She nodded. "He's still working on the force, developing a drug awareness program."

"That's great." She paused. "My father is in a wheelchair."

Leslie frowned. "Mel Hudson?" The heartthrob actor from the eighties wasn't injured as far as she knew, but she'd only met him and Selena's mother the one time when she'd first taken over as Selena's personal security detail.

"That's my stepdad. My real father was in the US Army. A war vet, injured overseas. My management team didn't think he fit my brand, so we don't talk about him much and he doesn't make any appearances with me or anything. The media thinks Mel is my father and he's been the one raising me for so long..."

"I had no idea," Leslie said, unsure how to feel about the star confiding something as personal as that, but there was definitely a hint of sympathy developing for Selena.

"Yeah. Anyway... Oh my God, that ski suit is amazing," Selena said, hurrying toward the rack of overpriced, name-brand winter gear.

And just like that, any resemblance to a normal, caring human being was gone.

"You should get one too," Selena said, combing through the rack for her size.

Leslie glanced at the price tag and winced. Three hundred dollars. No way. That ski suit could stay right where it was on the hanger. As it was, she'd be paying for whatever Selena bought.

An hour and six hundred dollars later, they exited the store with new clothing to get them through their time there—bras and underwear, workout clothes, jeans. Selena was in a ski suit that was too warm for that day's weather and Leslie was in a pair of yoga pants and oversized sweatshirt from the sales rack.

"Where to next?" Selena asked, looking like she was ready to take on Main Street as if it were Rodeo Drive.

"I have to get a new cell phone," Leslie said, heading toward the tech shop a block away.

"Me too," Selena said.

"No. Not yet. Once it's safe." She glanced both ways before crossing on the walk.

"Why do you get one?"

"Because I need to check in at the office for updates and keep an eye on all the LA news sources."

Selena stopped outside the Chocolate Shoppe and looked through the large storefront window, where the chocolatier was making chocolate-covered candy apples. "I haven't had one of those in years."

"No surprise there." And at twelve dollars each, the star wasn't breaking her sugar-free streak on Leslie's dime either. She checked her watch. "The stores are closing in ten minutes. We have to hurry."

Selena reluctantly continued along the sidewalk next to her and Leslie pushed through the doors of Techies R Us. Thank God she'd never gotten a new phone when she moved to LA. Though she refused to read much into the decision. Right now, having access to the provider where she'd set up her phone number was a blessing. She turned to the guy behind the counter. "Hi. I know you'll be closing soon, but I need to get a new phone with this number as soon as possible." She wrote her cell number on a piece of paper and handed it to him.

The young man smiled. "No problem. Do you want the same phone—the Android 8?"

"Yes, please. And can you add a ghost app?"

"Sure thing," the guy said. "I'll just need your ID to call up your account."

"Everything on file attached to the number should be the same," she said, reluctantly flashing her ID. Right now wasn't a great time to update her account.

The guy shrugged. "Okay, just give me a few minutes."

As she waited, Leslie scanned the row of cameras along the wall. She picked up the Nikon Z 7 and peered through the lens. She'd been saving for one, thinking the almost five-thousand-dollar price tag was a nice goal to shoot for by her thirtieth-fifth birthday in June, but this trip would definitely set that aspiration on hold.

"You like photography?" Selena asked.

"Just a hobby I used to have." Still did, but she wasn't eager to share any personal life details with the star. Her father's passion for photography had transferred to Leslie at a young age. He'd take photos wherever they went and she'd always been intrigued by the apparatus he always wore around his neck.

He'd bought her a Canon of her own at age six and they'd taken several photography courses together. He hadn't needed them, but it had been an amazing bonding experience with her dad. Her first real shot, one of the sun setting over Suncrest Peak, one she'd set up and waited hours for, to get it just at the right moment when the disappearing light cast a final illumination over the valley below, her father had framed and hung on the living room wall.

"Are you any good?" Selena asked.

"I don't know. Not really," she said. She used her cell phone's camera mostly to capture shots in and around LA, but now thanks to the fire, those were gone. She doubted there was any way to retrieve the memory from her phone, if it was to be found.

"Well, if you want some practice, I could use some new shots for my portfolio. Some of the backdrops around here would definitely give me something different."

Backdrops. Selena saw all of this beauty and wilderness surrounding her as just backdrops to her own experience. "I'm more into scenery than people." And if she were to start taking photos of people, Selena wouldn't be her first choice. She'd seen the star on set and that was one headache she wouldn't bring upon herself.

Selena shrugged as though that was boring and moved on to play with a laptop. No doubt hoping it was connected to the internet.

"Your phone's ready," the guy said, taking it from the box.

Leslie reluctantly moved away from the cameras and approached the desk as he unlocked the screen and displayed the home screen apps. "It's good to use?"

"Yep. All set."

"My contacts weren't miraculously saved and transferred over to this device, were they?"

The guy laughed. "Unfortunately, I'd need your old phone for that."

Right. The phone that held her lifelines, her photos…

gone in the fiery blaze. Thanks to Selena. "Okay," she said, signing the paperwork for the new phone.

He handed her the box with the charging cables. "Anything else?"

She hesitated, glancing over her shoulder at the Nikon Z 7. There was no way she could buy it now. "No, that's it. Thank you."

"I'm starving," Selena said as they left the shop and made their way toward the bus stop where the resort shuttle was scheduled in five minutes.

Leslie was hungry too, but she wasn't willing to spend thirty-six dollars on a room service hamburger, so she sighed as she passed the bus stop and kept walking. "I know a place we can eat. Great food and you won't be recognized," she said, leading the way to The Drunk Tank, the locals' preferred bar and eatery.

"I think I prefer the restaurant at the resort," Selena said, eyeing the wooden double doors and the neon sign.

"No doubt you would, but we are eating here. Welcome to the local Small Town, USA, hot spot," Leslie said, opening the doors and going inside. At this point, she almost didn't care if Selena followed.

But a second later, Selena stood beside her, her eyes widening as she noticed the man behind the bar. "Holy shit, that dude is big."

"That would be Tank."

Selena nodded. "Obviously."

Leslie held her back as she flicked her long dark brown hair and straightened her shoulders, causing her chest to stick out farther in the body-hugging ski suit. "Don't even think about it. He has a girlfriend."

"What?" Selena's innocent look was a testament to her acting abilities. "I didn't say anything."

"You didn't have to." Every woman in Wild River had, at some point, wanted to take the single dad off the market before his longtime best friend succeeded in doing it last year. At six-foot-five and about a thousand pounds of solid muscle, Tank would make even the Rock jealous. And despite his ominous size, he was one of the nicest guys in town. An irresistible combination for many a local.

Selena scanned the nearly empty bar. "I thought you said this was a hot spot?"

"It is," Leslie said, heading toward the bar. The Drunk Tank was the best place in Wild River to hang out any night of the week. It was busy during tourist seasons, but that night it was filled with the usual locals—and by filled, Leslie meant with about forty people. Not exactly LA hot spot standards, but that's why she was comfortable bringing Selena there. She'd bet her job—if she still had one—on the fact that no one would even recognize Selena.

And this experience should be entertaining at least. If anyone in Wild River could put Little Miss Movie Star in her place, it was the local watering hole owner. She smiled at him behind Selena's head when they reached two empty bar stools and Selena was still scanning the bar like she was stuck in an old Western movie and didn't know how to get out. "Hey, Tank."

He nodded toward her. "Heard you were in town," he said with a smirk he failed to hide.

Leslie's own grin faded. Damn. She should have known that the search and rescue crew would have heard about what happened with the cabin…and the rescue…and her unfortunate wardrobe. And Tank was a member of the team. "Yeah, well… I like to make an entrance."

He laughed because it was furthest from the truth.

Her "friend" on the other hand…

"Hi. What do you serve that's skinny?" Selena asked, climbing onto a bar stool and looking for a drink menu.

Tank reached for new coasters and set them on the bar in front of her. "Besides you?" He rested his palms against the bar and even Leslie had trouble averting her gaze from the rippling muscles in his forearms. Tank was off limits, but guys like Tank definitely were her type. Big, muscular, strong… Someone who didn't make her feel like the manlier one in the relationship.

Selena smiled at the perceived compliment. "I meant calorie-wise, like a skinny margarita or martini?"

Tank shook his head. "Just regular margaritas and martinis but I can pour it into a skinny glass if it makes you feel better."

Selena's smile faded. "That will be fine."

Tank looked at Leslie. "For you?"

"Diet soda, please." She would kill for one of Tank's famous martinis but she was technically on the clock.

Tank moved away to get their drinks and Selena twirled on the bar stool to face her. "You tricked me again."

"No, I didn't. Believe it or not, this is as wild as it gets here on an off-season Tuesday night."

"I'd slit my wrists if I lived here," she mumbled. Something caught her eye and she grabbed Leslie's arm to hide partially behind her. "That guy's staring at me. Do you think he recognizes me?"

Leslie sighed. Doubtful. The guy she was pointing to was Rob from the hardware store. "He's staring at you because you still have the price tag hanging from your jacket." She yanked it off.

"I don't feel safe. I think you were right. We should just hide out at the resort," Selena said.

Leslie wasn't falling for that. The star had been desperate to explore the town—until she realized that there was little to explore. Wild River was a quiet ski resort town with a few shops along Main Street, a steak house boasting fancy dining and the pub. People came here to ski and hike and fish...not "be seen" red carpet–style.

So, naturally, Selena was eager to return to the only high-end place in town, where she felt more at home.

"You're actually safer here. No one in this bar has any idea who you are," Leslie said.

A loud shriek made her jump.

Tank's twelve-year-old daughter, Kaia, was coming from the kitchen, carrying buckets of ice. Her mouth was wide open in shock as she stared at Selena.

"I guess you were wrong. *Someone* in this town recognizes me," Selena said, obviously happy to have a fan.

Kaia walked slowly toward them and Leslie's mind reeled. How did she convince the preteen that she had to keep this encounter to herself and off all social media when it was probably the coolest thing to happen to the kid in months?

"Hi, Kaia," she said carefully. "Um... I guess you recognize my friend..."

Kaia was nodding, eyes still locked on Selena. "I've seen *High School Romance* at least a hundred times," she said.

"That she has," Tank muttered.

Selena's smile was warm. "Well, thank you. That was a fun movie to make... Kaia, is it?"

Kaia nodded. "Yes, Kaia... I'm Kaia."

Starstruck was what the poor kid was. That had worn off quickly for Leslie. LA had a way of going from charming and exciting to fake and flashy fast. In her few years living there, she'd gone from enamored to disillusioned quickly.

But she wouldn't burst Kaia's bubble. "Maybe Selena could give you an autograph?"

"Could we take a selfie?" the young girl asked.

"Of course!"

"No!" Leslie offered a sympathetic look at Kaia. "I'm sorry Kaia, but…" She lowered her voice to a conspirator's level. If Kaia was part of the plan to keep Selena safe, she'd cherish that more than a photo anyway. The kid was already a self-appointed unofficial, junior member of the search and rescue crew and taught outback safety courses to kids in the town. "Selena is here in Wild River hiding out. So, we need to keep her presence here low-key to keep her safe. That means, unfortunately, no photos."

As predicted, Kaia immediately looked serious and determined. "Absolutely." To Selena she said, "You're safe here."

Leslie winked at her.

But then Kaia frowned, glancing at Selena's drink. "Hey, is that alcohol?"

"Yes."

"Are you even old enough to drink?"

Tank reached for the glass but Selena pulled it away. "Yes, I'm twenty-four. I was twenty-one acting like a seventeen-year-old in *High School Romance*," she told Kaia.

"Wow. Really?" Kaia put down the ice buckets and climbed up onto the bar stool next to Selena.

Tank sighed, coming around the bar to retrieve the buckets. "Don't worry. I'll take care of the ice," he said loudly, but Kaia wasn't listening. She was enamored by the star.

"Hey, you're super cute," Selena said, pushing Kaia's dark, messy hair away from her face. "Have you ever thought about acting? I could hook you up with my agent's email…"

"She's all set," Tank said quickly. "School, sports... She's busy."

Kaia laughed. "Chill, Dad. I have no interest in Hollywood." She paused. "Though I did just get the lead in the spring play at school. Maybe you could help me with my lines sometime?" she asked Selena. "If you're not busy," she added quickly.

Selena shot Leslie a look. "Believe me, that would be the highlight of my time here." Turning back to Kaia, she smiled. "I'd love to help if I'm in town long enough."

Kaia beamed. "Awesome."

Huh, so maybe the star wasn't all bad. Leslie knew Selena did actually care about her fans. She had several charities focused on children's needs in LA and she was an active participant, volunteering her time as well as donating money.

"Great, but right now, you have homework," Tank told Kaia.

The girl looked disappointed, but she climbed off the bar stool. "I gotta go, but it was really awesome to meet you and if you need anything..."

Selena reached for her coaster and a pen on the bar and signed it. "Here you go, and we'll find a way to sneak a selfie before I leave town, I promise," she said.

Kaia hugged the coaster to her chest as she headed into the back room. "I can't believe I can't tell my friends about this," they heard her mumble.

Leslie knew she wouldn't. They took care of one another in Wild River. Subconsciously, maybe that was why she'd come.

And at least Selena looked happier. Being away from her life couldn't be easy on her either. "What a cutie," she said as her gaze drifted toward the door. "And speaking of cuties…"

Leslie followed her gaze and almost choked on her drink, seeing Levi enter the bar. What the hell was he still doing in town? Didn't he have a forest to protect?

"So there is a history," Selena said, eyeing her.

"Nope. There isn't."

"Well, why does your face look simultaneously pale and flushed?"

"Just surprised to see him here," she mumbled.

"So, you'd be cool with me buying him a drink then? For saving my life?" Selena baited her.

Technically, *Leslie* had saved Selena's life. Levi had saved *hers*. "He's probably meeting people…"

Or not. Levi spotted them and headed their way. "Hey."

"What are you still doing here?" Leslie asked before she could stop herself.

Levi looked uncomfortable and Leslie immediately turned her attention back to the melting ice in her glass. This awkwardness would only get worse the more time they were together. Didn't he realize that as well? No real contact in years had already made their previous, necessary encounter tense.

"Be more rude," Selena said to her, before turning a warm smile in Levi's direction. "I think what she meant to say was, have a seat—I'll buy you a drink. With Leslie's money." The smile might have made up for Leslie's coolness if Levi had seen it, but his gaze was still locked on Leslie. She could see his reflection in the mirror behind the bar, but she didn't need to. She could feel his gaze burning into her.

"Come on, join us," Selena said when Levi hesitated.

"I'll sit, but ladies don't buy the drinks," Levi said, climbing onto the bar stool next to her.

"They do when they're rich," Selena said, reaching for Leslie's wallet. Levi went to protest, but Leslie still wanted an answer to her question, though she did reword it to sound less offensive. "So, are you heading back to the station tonight?"

Selena's side-eye was murderous. Obviously still not subtle enough. Leslie knew how it sounded, like she wanted Levi out of town ASAP, and she did. Being in Wild River was tough enough without spending time with him. Something Selena wouldn't understand and something Leslie wasn't planning to explain.

But if Levi caught her vibe, he was choosing to fight against it. "I took a few days off, decided to stay in town… since you were here. Thought we could catch up."

Catching up was the last thing she wanted.

"So, you two went to school together?" Selena said, positioning herself to block Leslie's view of Levi, obviously annoyed that the man's attention had been solely focused on Leslie so far.

Levi cleared his throat. "Yeah…we've been friends for years."

Best friends. The three amigos. Leslie was closer to Levi than almost anyone else and she knew what he was doing right now. The same thing he always did. Pushing his way in. Refusing to acknowledge her pushing him away. As kids, whenever she was upset and didn't want to talk, to open up, he'd always barreled his way into being there for her and eventually she'd give in and tell him what was wrong and he'd be the shoulder to cry on. That was his role in their little group. He was the rock for her and Dawson. The sounding board. The fixer. The advice giver.

Damn, she could use some of him right now…

But no. They weren't kids anymore and this was a problem she needed to find a way out of herself.

And not let nostalgia and "catching up" get in the way.

Luckily, Selena launched into a recap of Levi's heroics that day and the two quickly seemed to forget that Leslie existed. Which was fine. She'd sit there in peace and enjoy her flat, watered-down diet soda. She wasn't interested in hearing all the details of how the smoke jumpers executed the rescue. She wouldn't intercept with her own questions, even if Levi's job was super exciting and intriguing…

Selena laughed at something he said and her hand landed on Levi's arm causing Leslie's stomach to twist.

This was fine. Someone else to entertain Selena for a while was good. She could use a break and at least when the star had a captive audience, the whining and complaining was reduced to a minimum.

Levi's cell rang on the bar in front of him and he glanced at the caller ID. "Sorry, I have to take this," he told Selena.

"No problem," Selena said. "I have to check my phone too…oh wait, I'm not allowed to have one." Her pointed glare was directed at Leslie.

Leslie ignored it. Being without a cell phone wouldn't kill her. Actually, a social media hiatus would be good for Selena. Social media for validation wasn't great for one's mental health.

She glanced at the caller ID, vaguely recognizing the phone number, then listened as Levi answered the call. "Hi, Mrs. Powell… Yeah, that's no problem. Never too busy for you. What's up?"

Mrs. Powell? Dawson's mother was calling Levi? Why? The two of them were still close obviously…but calling him at nine at night on a weekday seemed slightly unusual.

Leslie studied him but he avoided her questioning gaze as he listened.

Leslie could hear the woman's voice on the other end of the line and strained to hear what she was saying.

"He's so nice," Selena said, checking her reflection in the mirror across the bar.

"Yep."

"And really good-looking."

"Sure." Leslie could hear Mrs. Powell laugh and Levi was nodding. What were they talking about? Seemed important based on Levi's expression as he listened intently. He was doing the one-eye-closed thing he always did when he was trying to commit details to memory. She'd always teased him about the habit but secretly thought it was cute. Seeing it now was completely messing with her ability to remain distant and neutral.

Selena was looking around the bar. "Hey, you want to play darts?"

"No."

"Pool?"

Oh, so now the star appreciated the bar. "No. Shhh…" she muttered. Levi was talking now. Something about an event?

"Can I go to the washroom at least?" Selena asked.

"Yes. Go," Leslie said through gritted teeth.

Selena left the bar and headed toward the restrooms and Leslie pretended to be keeping an eye on her and not listening to Levi's call. But she was desperate to know what they were talking about. She leaned closer and caught herself as she slid off the bar stool.

Levi glanced her way and she quickly retrieved her new cell phone and busied herself with it.

"Yeah, just send over the documents and I'll sign them and scan them back to you in the morning," he was saying.

Documents? What was going on? She hadn't spoken to Dawson's mother since the funeral. She'd left town shortly after and there was never a good time to reach out from LA. She'd had so much to deal with, so many life transitions that she'd easily found an excuse not to. They'd never gotten along anyway and now that they weren't going to be forced family anymore, staying in contact had seemed pointless and unnecessary.

Mrs. Powell had obviously felt the same.

Leslie hadn't been bothered by the shutting out until now. She couldn't help but feel jealous of the relationship that Levi had with the people who were supposed to have become Leslie's family. The Powells had always loved and accepted Levi, treating him like a second son and he'd always tried his best to connect them all, to no avail.

"Great. Thank you... Take care," Levi said, disconnecting the call. He tucked the phone into his pocket and picked up his beer glass. Empty beer glass. He brought it to his lips anyway and drained the remaining drops. Then he scanned the bar. Looking everywhere but at her.

"Are you really going to make me ask what that was about?"

He shrugged. "You don't have to."

Was he serious? "Levi..."

He sighed, leaning forward on the bar. His forearm muscles flexed and momentarily caught her attention, until he spoke... "She's setting up a charity in Dawson's name, that's all."

"What kind of charity?" Sure, she was no longer going to be Mrs. Dawson Powell, but it hurt that Levi knew about the family's plans and she didn't. No one had reached out to her about it. What would she have done if they had? Would she have wanted to be involved? Would she have answered a call if she'd seen Mrs. Powell's number lighting up her cell? And what would her involvement have required? For her to stay locked in the past, reliving the hurt, constantly remembering a better time in her life and having to recount the tragedy over and over to strangers… Probably for the best that she hadn't been contacted.

"She wants to start a foundation in support of mental health. I guess it's their way of showing forgiveness and honoring Dawson's memory at the same time," he said.

The edge in his voice rang loud and clear. They all thought *she* wasn't honoring him. Leaving town right after the funeral, never returning to Wild River unless absolutely necessary and leaving them all behind. Just running from the memories. Well, they were damn right about that. Who wanted to remember when remembering made it difficult to breathe?

"That's nice of them," she said tightly. She hesitated. It was none of her business. But she was curious against her better judgment. "And you're involved?"

He nodded, not looking overly pleased about it. Or maybe he just didn't want to discuss it with her. "She wants me to help with the fundraising events…be sort of the spokesperson, the face of the foundation, I guess."

Her eyes widened. Levi? A spokesperson? "You hate public speaking."

"That's correct."

"And you get awkward in big crowds and formal events."

"Yep."

"And yet you agreed to do it?"

He turned on the bar stool and stared straight into her eyes. "What choice do I have, Les?"

The sound of her nickname made her heart race. He was the only person who called her that. She'd beat the crap out of anyone else who tried. But she'd always let him get away with it.

And now, the sound of it had her heart racing in an unfamiliar way. Or maybe it was the way he said it—the tone in his voice that held traces of longing and regret.

She simply stared back, not sure how to answer. He was right. He really couldn't refuse to help after everything the Powells had done for him over the years and how close he and Dawson had been. The fact that he was stepping out of his comfort zone for the family said a lot about his character. Same old Levi.

Selena rejoined them. "The restroom was surprisingly clean," she said.

Neither Leslie nor Levi answered her.

"What are we talking about?" She looked back and forth between them. "Did I hear you say something about fundraising?" she asked Levi.

"Yeah," he said reluctantly, breaking his gaze with Leslie. "I'm just helping a friend's family with a charity organization in his name."

Selena looked like she was in love.

Oh come on…

"I can help," she said. "I run several charities back in LA."

"I'm sure Levi has it covered," Leslie said quickly.

Levi shook his head. "Actually, I have no idea what I'm doing."

Selena looked ready to pull out a day planner and start organizing. She really must be bored out of her mind. Leslie had witnessed the woman's schedule and it had been intense. She knew what the star was giving up, the risk to her career this impromptu hiatus from her life might cost her, but Leslie couldn't focus on all of that. None of that would matter if the star was dead, and her stalker had made his intentions very clear.

But if helping Levi could give her something to do, something to take her mind off things and keep her from harassing the shit out of Leslie, Leslie would keep her own feelings about it to herself.

"Well, I have experience with all aspects of fundraising, from the permits to executing events that people want to attend and will open their wallets for," Selena was telling Levi.

Levi hesitated, but then when he glanced at Leslie and she didn't oppose, he nodded. "Thanks. If you're in town for a while, I may take you up on that."

"Well, for the first time since arriving, I hope we stick around for a while." The two clinked their empty glasses, then signaled Tank for another round.

Fantastic. Her former best friend and the women she was hiding from the world were joining forces to plan charitable events in her ex-fiancé's memory and no one wanted her involved.

On the clock or not, Leslie deserved a drink.

LEVI WASN'T AN expert on women. Not by a long shot. But he knew two things. Selena was flirting with him and Leslie didn't like it.

Unfortunately, he was smart enough not to allow himself the thought that it could be jealousy. She'd been annoyed with him and by him since he'd rescued her ass in the forest.

He wasn't looking for a thank-you…or maybe he was. Maybe a "thanks, Levi, for not leaving me to freeze to death in the wilderness in only a towel, and by the way, great to see you…" might be exactly what he was looking for from her. Or hoping for, at least.

He'd stayed in Wild River to see her. He'd thought the shock of the fire and the circumstances surrounding her "visit" had made her more prickly earlier that day, understandably. But her mood hadn't changed, even after the scotch on the rocks she'd drunk in record time. She'd changed into a pair of leggings and an oversized sweatshirt with a picture of a moose on it and it was so typically Leslie that it made him smile on the inside, knowing that somewhere deep inside, she was the same woman who lived for comfort clothes and looked hot as hell in them. Admittedly, that part was mildly inconvenient—the attraction he'd always had for her hadn't faded in the least.

Selena was a chatterbox, thank God, otherwise the silence would have been too much to endure and he'd have left moments after arriving. Unfortunately, he'd barely been paying attention to anything the young Hollywood star had been saying.

"So, what kind of fundraiser were you planning?" she asked him now.

Damn, he'd hoped to avoid the conversation about this again that evening. Leslie's expression when he'd told her had hardly been the veiled one she'd been going for. She'd been hurt and he could understand that, but what had she expected? She'd disappeared just weeks after the funeral and he knew if she hadn't wanted to keep in touch with him, she certainly wasn't keeping in touch with Mrs. Powell.

She'd wanted to get away from everything and everyone.

"Um… I think it's a dinner," he said. "At the Wild River Resort here in town."

Selena looked unimpressed. "Dinners are okay, but

you'll need more than food to draw a crowd at a hundred dollars a plate."

"A hundred dollars a plate?" The resort restaurant was expensive, but Selena was right. Even the richest people in Wild River would want more than just a well-cooked steak for that ticket price.

"Have you thought of a silent auction? Or fashion show? Or bachelor auction?" She smiled up at him under long dark lashes. She was absolutely stunning, like most models and actresses, and he wished just once some other woman could catch his eye, make his body react the way it did when he saw Leslie. "I'm sure you could bring in a decent penny," she said.

"Oh my God..." he heard Leslie mutter.

His neck grew red and he cleared his throat. Yes, he knew she'd disagree on that point. She wouldn't open up her wallet for a date with him. That had always been painfully obvious. As much as he'd only ever had eyes for her, she'd only had eyes for Dawson.

And Selena's flirting was making him uncomfortable now. He had at least ten years on the woman and she wasn't really his type, even if his heart was available. It was true that he could use help with the fundraiser to offer some sort of knowledge and support to Mrs. Powell, but he didn't want to encourage anything else. He checked his watch. Might be time to call it a night.

Leslie's cell phone rang and she answered on the first ring. That was surprising. He'd figured she'd be keeping a low profile.

"Hi, Eoghan..." he heard her say.

Eoghan? Boyfriend? Had she moved on with her life in LA? Maybe that was the reason she hadn't wanted to keep in touch.

"Not great. Please tell me they caught the guy," she said, resting her elbow on the bar and her forehead in her hand.

Wow, she really wanted to get out of here.

Selena turned her attention to the call as well.

"Not yet." Leslie glanced at Selena. "She's fine."

"That's debatable," Selena said. "Though I am much better now." She placed a hand on his arm again and Leslie caught the gesture and stood abruptly, letting the bar stool topple on its legs as she walked toward the pool tables in the back.

Shit. He was only making things worse for her. She was stressed enough and now he was allowing this flirting with Selena to irritate her further.

"Don't worry. It's just Eoghan," Selena said, wrinkling her nose as though getting a whiff of something gross.

He couldn't help it. He needed to know. "Who's Eoghan?" He took a chug of beer.

"Another agent at the agency. Leslie's boning him, I think."

Levi coughed on his beer. "She's—" he refused to say *boning* "—dating someone in LA?"

"I wouldn't say dating. That would require clothing and an ability to connect with other human beings…"

Well, she had Leslie pegged on the emotional distancing part anyway. Or at least the persona that Leslie was trying to give off. Levi knew she had an impressive ability to hide what she was actually feeling. But it was often an unsuccessful attempt with him. He knew her every tell from the confrontational stance she took as a self-defense mechanism to the restlessness she'd been exhibiting at the bar tapping her fingers, looking around, sighing as quietly as possible. She was struggling to keep it in check.

"I think they are mostly just sleeping together," Selena said and shuddered.

"You don't like him?"

"Not particularly. He's Australian, so naturally I found the accent hot at first, but every time I'm around him, I get a douchey vibe."

Weird that Leslie wouldn't get a similar vibe if the guy was a jerk. Her radar for assholes was usually strong. "What's he like?"

"Tall, muscular... I mean, not Tank muscular."

"No one is Tank muscular." The bar owner was an anomaly.

"He has dark blond hair that's slightly longer, wears a man bun..."

"Okay, I see where the douchey vibe comes from," he said. Man bun? Really, Leslie? Seems she'd strayed as far from the Dawson type—clean-cut, tall, dark and handsome—as she could. "But is he a good agent? Can she trust him?" That's what mattered most right now.

Selena frowned. "I'm not sure. But I trust her and if she says he's good, I guess he's good."

Unfortunately, Leslie didn't look good when she returned to the bar moments later. If possible, she looked even more stressed.

It killed him to see her this way. Levi wanted to hug her, hold her, force her to confide in him, let him help...or at least be a sounding board.

He didn't like that she was confiding in this Eoghan guy.

"We should call it a night," she told Selena, reaching for her jacket.

"Already?" Selena said.

But Levi was ready to go too. Obviously, his former best

friend had no interest in reconnecting and the longer he was around her, the more he'd get caught up in her drama that she didn't want him a part of and which would just eat away at his sanity. "I should go too."

"You're staying at the resort too, right?" Selena said, suddenly good to go.

"Yes…"

"You are?" Leslie looked confused.

"Everything else was booked," he said.

"Right. The famous author in town."

Selena beamed up at him as he stood. "So, we're all headed the same way."

Wow, Selena was as subtle as a wrecking ball. "We are. I'll give you both a ride?"

"We'd love one," Selena said.

"Sure," Leslie said, as though she'd rather be accepting a ride from Selena's stalker, then hurriedly led the way out of the bar.

Selena linked her arm through his as they followed and Levi got an odd nostalgia-like feeling of another love triangle. But once again, he was not on the right side of it.

CHAPTER EIGHT

THE BED WAS turned down when they got back to the room and Selena collapsed backward onto it as soon as she'd kicked off her boots and removed her ski suit. "I call dibs on the bed."

Leslie sighed. "It's a king. Neither of us are huge. I think we can share." She rubbed her forehead, the stress of the last twenty-four hours accumulating in a vein in the front of her head. Eoghan's update hadn't been promising. Still no leads and the police hadn't been able to get any prints or DNA from Selena's bedroom. The stalker was smart... which made him even more dangerous.

"Why didn't you get a room with two beds?" Selena asked.

"This was all they had available."

She opened their shopping bags and hung the items in the closet.

Damn... Levi's jacket. She hadn't been sure how or when she'd have an opportunity to return it, but now he was just on the floor above them... Room 406. After turning down Selena's suggestion to grab another drink in the lobby bar, they'd parted ways, but not before he'd let them know which room he was in, in case they needed anything.

They wouldn't.

But she should return the jacket now and get it over with.

She didn't want to have to see him again. That evening had been enough time.

Enough time for her to feel the pain of the past creeping in again. Enough time to recognize that a lot of life had happened in the last few years and enough time to realize she missed him. Which was the last thing she needed right now. Listening to him chat with Selena—it had been torture not to just let her guard down and try to enjoy the evening with him, take a much-needed break from the stress and laugh with him, talk to him, reconnect with him.

But if she had, walking away again once all of this was over would be hard. She'd be opening herself up to having to start over with the distancing she'd achieved. Distancing that was necessary to keep moving forward.

"I'll be back in forty seconds. I just need to return..." She stopped, noticing Selena out cold on the bed. Mouth agape, a soft, low snoring came from her. Hopefully, she was out for the night. Unfortunately, she was sprawled across the center of the bed, so Leslie would be sleeping in the armchair.

She quietly grabbed the room key and the jacket and slipped out of the room. A too-short elevator ride later, she knocked on Levi's door.

His expression was a mix of concern and happiness to see her. Better make this quick. Without Selena there as a buffer, this could go off the rails fast. She held up the jacket. "Thanks again." He took it and she turned to leave. "Night."

"Leslie!"

Could she pretend not to have heard him? How rude would it be to just ignore him? Too many years of friendship prevented her from being an asshole, especially when he had helped them that day. Reluctantly, she turned around. "Yeah?"

"I'm sorry if I did or said something wrong," he said, leaning against the open hotel room door frame.

She shrugged. "You didn't. In fact, I think you've got yourself your own stalker." Joke. Be sarcastic. Anything but show real emotion. Wow, maybe she really was a Chandler.

"Leslie, you can stop," he said.

She should have ignored him. This was too dangerous. Being alone with him. The two of them sharing the tragic bond of losing someone they cared about. Having so much history between them. "Stop what?"

"The smoke and mirrors act. I can see through it."

"Wow, the smoke I knew about, but mirrors too, huh?" Keep it light. Don't let him bait you into this.

"You don't have to keep acting tough around me," he said, letting the door to the room close as he walked toward her.

"You better catch the…" It came up short against the bolt lock and stayed open.

"No one else is here now," he said, almost pleading with her to let her guard down, to be vulnerable, to show him some sign of the friend he'd known. His dark, penetrating eyes burrowed into hers, looking for any sign of the friendship they'd once had. "You can talk to me."

"I'm fine, Levi. I don't need to talk. I've moved on." Denial, refusal to acknowledge the pain was a way of moving on… Wallowing in the past wasn't her way of dealing with things.

"Well, then, you're going to have to tell me how," he said, his tone slightly desperate. "Because I'm still not okay. I was supposed to be the best man at my best friend's wedding and instead, a week later, I'm wearing the same damn suit carrying his coffin."

Leslie winced. This was exactly why she'd avoided talking to him. There was no way he'd just leave the past in the past, where she needed it to stay. Levi was the kind of person who needed to fix things, solve things by addressing issues head on…but he couldn't fix this, damn it, and talking about how they were both living with holes in their hearts where their best friend used to be wouldn't help. Nothing—no amount of talking— could bring Dawson back. "Look, Levi, if you're struggling, maybe you need to talk to someone…"

"I'm *trying* to talk to someone right now. My best friend." He searched her face, obviously looking for that person but she knew he wouldn't find her. "I'm not okay and I know you aren't either." He took a step closer and touched her shoulder.

The contact weakened her resolve far too much and she stepped back and folded her arms, desperate to hold the emotions in. If she broke even a little, she'd crack wide open. "We used to be best friends, but I haven't been here in years. We haven't even spoken in years." Surely, he couldn't still believe they were as close as before…or that she wanted to be. Why was he pressing the issue?

"That's exactly how I know you're still processing and mourning," he said. "You avoid any reminder of him— including me. On the surface anyway." His sympathetic expression only angered her. Why couldn't he just accept that she was fine burying things and moving forward? Why was he looking at her like it was okay to break, like he wanted her to break, maybe even needed her to as some sort of self-validation?

She should not respond and walk away, but he'd hit a nerve assuming he knew what she was feeling. "What's that supposed to mean?" she asked.

"Just that I bet you still have that message."

Her stomach turned as though she'd been kicked. This was too much. He had no right to do this. She didn't ask for his help or for him to hang around town. She wanted nothing from him, so how dare he try to make her feel bad for surviving the only way she knew how.

And he wasn't letting up. "The phone message from him—the last one before he died. You can't bring yourself to erase it, can you? Because that would mean he's really gone," he said softly but with determination.

Angry tears were too close and there was no way in hell she'd allow him to see her cry or know how close to the truth his words were. "You don't know what you're talking about, Levi, so please just stay out of my business."

She stalked away and punched the button for the elevator.

Levi stood there in the hallway, hands shoved deep into the pockets of his jeans.

That damn elevator could hurry the hell up. The lump in her throat threatened to choke her and her exterior felt ready to crumble.

It chimed and the doors opened and she disappeared inside before her best friend could see the scar he'd torn wide open.

STAYING IN WILD RIVER had been a bad decision. Leslie wanted nothing to do with him. It broke his heart that he couldn't get through her defenses. She was still hurting despite the brave face. People who'd moved on could face their past. Leslie was still running from it.

He'd thought maybe her coming back home when she'd needed somewhere safe to go had been a sign that this was still that safe place for her. But maybe she'd just been trying to get Selena as far away from California as possible.

If the cabin hadn't caught fire, no one would have even known she was back.

Inside his hotel room, Levi sighed as he lifted his T-shirt over his head and tossed it onto the chair next to the window.

First thing in the morning, he was headed back to the station. He'd paid for the room, might as well enjoy a comfortable bed and expensive coffee before going back. He was exhausted, his brain was a fog and his muscles ached from tension and stress.

A knock on the door had his heart racing.

Opening it to Leslie, his mouth was dry. "Hey..."

She held her cell phone with a shaking hand as she dialed her voicemail.

Dawson's voice on the recorded message made his throat constrict. He hadn't heard it in over three years. He'd started to forget what it sounded like...now, all the hurt of having lost his best friend way too soon came flooding back.

I won't be long... Don't start forever without me, Dawson was saying.

Levi's chest tightened. Dawson had no idea when he answered that call that his forever would be cut short. No one ever knew when it was their last day. When they'd run out of chances to do the things they wanted to do, say the things they needed to say. It was a harsh reminder to live life like any moment could be the last.

Still, he was unable to voice his truth. Some things couldn't be said.

Leslie looked wrecked as the message ended. "So, maybe I'm not okay."

He opened his arms and she stepped into them. The earth shifted around him. She'd always been his best friend—and the woman he secretly loved. He'd held her a million times. But not like this.

All the pain and the memories of the past—the good and bad and tragic—all wrapped around them. They'd each experienced the grief of loss and they'd each tried to move on, but separately. They'd not only lost Dawson, they'd lost each other.

Holding her now, Levi's emotions raged. He'd wanted her to open up to him. He'd wanted his best friend back... but these emotions running through him were more than that. The feel of her in his arms was one he never wanted to forget. It was fulfilling a part of him that longed to be the one she needed. "Shhh...it's okay." He murmured into her ear. He breathed in the scent of her skin at her neck and his mouth watered. His palms sweat and his heart pounded even louder in his chest. He tangled one hand into her hair and pulled back slightly to look at her.

Her pain-filled expression met his and the longing and hurt changed to a flicker of confusion then something else. Desire and realization.

Her gaze lowered to his bare chest and the intimacy of the moment seemed to hit her. Her arms lowered from around his neck and slid down his chest slowly, cautiously... as if on their own.

Levi's heart pounded beneath them. Her touch was foreign but not unwelcome. The feel of her fingers on his skin had him swallowing hard and fighting to resist the urge to pull her closer and press his lips to hers. He stared at the top of her head, unmoving, arms still wrapped around her waist as she caressed his bare body, almost as though in a trance...unaware of her actions and the effect they were having on him.

She traced the shape of his pectoral muscles as her tears slowly stopped, her sobbing eased, then her fingers tickled along his waist.

He couldn't stand it. "Leslie…" It came out as a low, strangled sound and it snapped her attention back to his face. How he felt about her, had felt for so long, had to be written all over his expression and he expected her to run from it.

She should run from it.

Instead, she reached up to cup his face between her hands. She stood on tiptoes and her mouth connected with his.

Surprise had him momentarily paralyzed, but then he was backing up into the hotel room and closing the door behind her. She kept moving them forward, toward the bed and he stumbled over his discarded boots, gripping her tighter to steady himself.

The back of his legs hit the edge of the bed and they fell onto it. Leslie's body straddled him and her mouth never broke contact with his. Hungry, desperate kisses, as though she were searching for air to breathe, as though she'd find healing from the pain.

His fingers dug into her waist as he felt himself grow thick. What the hell was he supposed to do? He never wanted to stop kissing her. This was a moment he'd only fantasized about, but right now he couldn't enjoy it when he had no idea what was fueling it. She was upset and stressed and obviously needing someone. But just anyone?

He couldn't be that guy. He was the last one who could ever be that guy for her. He loved her too much to be just an impulsive act—one she'd regret, one that would just push them even further apart.

Leslie's hands reached for the button on his jeans and it took all his willpower to stop her.

"Leslie..." He grabbed her hands and held tight.

She shook her head. "I don't want to talk."

Damn. Obviously not, but could he actually do this? Be with her? Give in to what he'd always wanted? Turn his brain off and go with the way his body was craving her? Even if it was only one time. Right here and now?

No. He knew her actions were coming from her over-whelming sadness and grief and he didn't want to take advantage of that. They needed to talk. He had no idea how much he was willing to tell her right now, but they couldn't jump from no contact in years, both still strug-gling to move past the hurt, to getting physical in a mo-ment of emotional stress.

"Leslie, I want you." There was no denying that. She'd already seen it on his face, felt it in his touch, saw the ev-idence in the bulge in his pants. "But not like this." He squeezed her hands and released a deep breath.

She blinked and yanked her hands away. Climbing off him quickly, she looked around the room as though un-sure where she was or how she'd gotten there. Her hand flew to her lips, glossy and pink from their kisses. "Shit," she muttered.

He stood quickly and walked toward her. "Hey... Let's sit and talk."

She shook her head. "No... That was...um." Her gaze took in his shirtless state and her cheeks flamed red. "No. I don't even know. Oh my God." She turned in a circle as though looking for an exit, somehow not seeing the hotel room door right in front of her. She took a strangled-sounding breath and pressed a hand to her chest.

She was freaking out. Great. Remorse, regret, he'd expected that, but she was completely unraveling. "Look, you weren't wrong to... You read the situation correctly," he said, unsure how to make her feel better about her actions. She didn't need to feel embarrassed. He needed her to know that he'd wanted to kiss her just as badly. He wanted her.

She scoffed. "This is insane. I have no idea what came over me." She ran a hand over her hair and when her gaze landed on his bare body once again, she made a beeline toward the door.

"Wait...please. Don't run away. Let's talk," he said.

She kept going. "There's nothing to talk about." She reached for the door handle, then swung back, anger the only emotion on her face now. "You're something else, you know that? You poke and poke until you find the crack you're looking for, then you act all valiant when I finally break. Well, screw you, Levi. I was fine before I got back here and I'll be fine again. I don't need you to try to help me in whatever twisted way you think you can." She opened the door.

Damn, she had this whole situation all wrong. He hurried after her, refusing to let her go believing that he'd had some secret agenda or a goal of hurting her. "Listen, I'm sorry. I just wanted you to open up to me. Let me in..."

"So you could reject me?"

What the hell? "That's not what's happening." Not even close. He just knew her advances weren't real. Not about him. It was all frustration and a need to take the edge off the intense emotions she'd been roller-coastering through the last few days. Anyone would seek any sort of release after the shit she'd been through so far that week.

"It doesn't matter. Nothing's happening between us."

Not even a rekindled friendship. He heard her loud and clear.

"Bye, Levi." She left the room, letting the door close behind her.

Once again, leaving him to stare after her, more conflicted than ever.

CHAPTER NINE

WHAT A NIGHTMARE. Only Leslie wasn't sleeping. Hadn't slept a wink since her embarrassing encounter with Levi the night before. How had her life turned into such a mess so quickly? She needed to pull it together and figure out a game plan stat. This adventure had already gone on too long. She ripped the tags from the new workout clothes she'd bought the day before and changed quickly. Then she paced in front of the bed, checking her watch.

Selena's snore was loud and steady. It was tempting to record it to use as ammunition the next time the star drove her up the wall. Threaten to post it online. How long could she stay asleep, anyway? Leslie coughed several times—nothing. She opened the bathroom door and slammed it. The star didn't even budge.

She couldn't stand it any longer. She touched Selena's shoulder. "Time to get up," she said.

Selena lifted one side of the silk eye mask provided by the resort that Leslie's cash deposit would no doubt get dinged for and squinted up at her. "What time is it?"

"Seven a.m."

Selena lowered the mask and rolled away from her, sprawling across the bed and hugging a pillow.

Leslie released an annoyed breath. "Hey, I'm serious. Get up."

"*I'm* serious. Fuck off," came Selena's muffled reply.

"I need to work out," she said, shifting from one foot to the other. She was edgy and jittery and the lack of her morning five-mile run had her severely grumpy. Working out was her way to relieve stress and, well, there weren't enough miles in the world to eliminate what she was feeling currently, but she had to start somewhere. A good workout would help her focus and hopefully exertion would help erase the memory of her hands all over Levi's naked upper body.

"I need to sleep," Selena said. "I'm still jet-lagged from traveling."

"It's an hour difference and technically it's *eight a.m.* for your internal clock, so get out of bed." Back in LA, the movie star would have already been on set for hours.

"Why are you bugging me? Just go work out and when you're done, come get me for breakfast." Selena reached back with a lazy arm and bopped Leslie on the head. "Like a human snooze button."

That's it. She'd officially snapped.

Leslie grabbed the blankets and pulled them off the end of the bed.

"Hey, what is your deal?" Selena sat up and raised the mask over her forehead.

"I told you. I need to go to the gym and you need to come with me because I can't leave you alone."

"You think my stalker knows where I am?"

Leslie hesitated. Lying and saying yes would make this conversation a whole lot smoother, but she didn't want Selena freaked out. "No. I don't trust you." If she made a phone call from the resort, everyone would know where they were within minutes and all of this would have been for nothing. And all of this could not have been for nothing. She changed her tone, knowing she was getting nowhere with the drill sergeant routine. "Please, Selena. There's a hot tub and sauna. You said your skin was feeling dry from the cold weather."

Selena looked annoyed at being patronized, but she swung her legs over the side of the bed. "Fine. But only because I'm turning into a lizard."

Whatever it took.

Ten minutes later, Leslie cranked the speed on the treadmill in the otherwise empty workout room and forced her exhausted body to move. What speed and distance would erase a terrible decision from her memory?

Unfortunately, there was no way she could outrun her poor judgment and stupid impulsivity the night before. Kissing Levi? What the actual fuck? It was almost as though the memory of it had happened to someone else. An out-of-body experience...that had felt really good. His shirtless body pressed against her and the passion in his kiss had made her body spring to life as she'd grabbed ahold of any emotion that didn't make her feel anxious or numb.

She groaned inwardly and cranked the speed higher.

It had to be temporary insanity from the high-stress situation she was in, adrenaline-filled, emotionally-fueled actions, spurred on by Levi poking old wounds. She wasn't attracted to Levi. She'd never let herself see him in that light...except for one time. As teens. When she'd put herself out there with the idea of a practice kiss. But he'd rejected her then too... At that moment, she'd drawn a line between them, placing him firmly into the friend category and never allowing herself to think of him in any other way.

Until the night before, apparently.

Jesus. She kept making a bigger mess of things.

She inclined the machine, feeling the burn in her shins. A punishment for her actions.

On the stationary bike next to her, Selena's legs barely rotated as she flipped through a recent celebrity news magazine. "Do you think Brad and Jen are ever going to wake up and realize they are meant to be together?"

Leslie didn't care, even if she knew who Brad and Jen were. She had her own issues at the moment.

"I mean the whole Angie thing was just sexual chemistry."

More flipping. Less pedaling.

How the woman stayed in shape was a mystery. Her workout routines with her trainer were more gossip session than sweat. Had to be her young metabolism...and diet. Leslie could easily keep the weight off by eating healthy alone, but she liked to feel strong, powerful... She loved how having muscles made her feel overall.

That's it. Think about the workout. Focus on breathing and sweating...

"Speaking of sexual chemistry..." Selena said, "there was a shit ton last night at the bar."

Leslie tripped and grabbed the handles of the treadmill before she could fall on her face. "What are you talking about? I told you Levi and I are just old friends." With a history, with a past, with shared trauma and now a passionate...regrettable kiss between them.

Selena looked at her like she was dense. "I was talking about me and him."

"Oh."

"Think he'd have dinner with me?"

"We're not here on a vacation." She wasn't jealous of the idea. It was just dumb. They weren't there to have fun, they were there to keep her alive. And if Leslie wasn't enjoying herself, why should Selena?

"But we are stuck here, right? Might as well make the

most of it." She climbed off the bike and headed toward the sauna.

Leslie didn't answer. It didn't matter. Selena could ask Levi out, but he'd never say yes. Selena was too young for him and not his type.

Levi preferred strong, sturdy, practical women.

A flash of the expression on his face when he was holding her, right before she kissed him, replayed in her mind. It was that look that had ultimately gotten to her. Pure, raw attraction mixed with hurt and yearning. It had terrified her, then intrigued her, then made her jump off the deep end by throwing herself at him.

Stopping the treadmill, she got off and checked on Selena before heading to the showers. The star was asleep in the sauna.

But when Leslie reemerged ten minutes later, she heard her talking to someone. Her heart raced as she listened. Was there someone else in the workout room? She peeked around the shower room door to see Selena casually curling a two-pound dumbbell with Leslie's cell phone to her ear.

What the…?

Damn it! She'd left her phone unattended on the treadmill. How the hell had Selena even unlocked it and who had she called? Grabbing a towel quickly, she nearly fell on the wet, slippery floor as she hurried toward her. "Who are you talking to?" she said, reaching for the phone.

Selena swiped her hand away and shot her a look. "It's your brother," she said.

Eddie? He must have called and Selena answered. Leslie's shoulders sagged in relief. That was better. At least it wasn't anyone from LA.

"Yeah, we can totally be there for then… Leslie's just

finishing a workout so hopefully runner's high is a thing," she said, laughing into the phone.

Seriously?

"I know, right?" she said.

"What did he just say about me?" she asked, annoyed at Selena for chumming it up with everyone and annoyed at herself for giving a shit. She reached for the phone again. "Give it to me."

Selena pulled it away. "Okay…see you then," she said, disconnecting the call before handing the phone to Leslie.

"What was that about?"

"We were invited to lunch," she said, setting the two-pound weight back down in the wrong spot.

Leslie sighed. "Fine." There were far worse ways to spend the day than hanging out with Eddie.

"It's at your mom's house," Selena said.

Right there. That was the worst way.

LEVI PUNCHED THE button for the elevator and fought the feeling of drowsiness washing over him. Zero sleep the night before, his overthinking was on autopilot.

That kiss had him all kinds of messed up. He'd wanted Leslie to open up. He'd wanted his friend back. If he was being completely truthful, he wanted her. Especially after that kiss. He knew what was driving it, but what if there was more? He'd felt all her emotions spiraling out of control, but there definitely had been passion and attraction in her eyes when she'd looked at him. He'd been right not to take advantage of the situation, but he couldn't help but wonder if maybe they could somehow find themselves there again, someday, with less hurt and more attraction between them.

And then he felt guilty as shit. He'd never made a play for Leslie because she was his best friend's girl and now she was his best friend's widow, essentially. That made her just as off-limits as before. Even more so.

His phone lit up and a glance at the caller display only amplified his conflicted state.

He sent Mrs. Powell's call to voicemail, knowing there was no way he could sound normal that morning, let alone happy to hear from her or able to discuss Dawson in any way without his guilt destroying him.

The elevator doors opened on his floor and he stepped in. He wanted to see Leslie before he headed back to the station. Apologize for the night before and make sure she knew he was there for her anytime she needed someone, but he knew he'd have to quit trying so hard to force it. She'd come to him on her own time if she still wanted a friendship.

The elevator doors opened on the second floor and there she stood.

Again, wet and wearing a towel.

Was fate having fun messing with him?

"Levi!" Selena said, excitedly getting into the elevator. "So happy to run into you."

He reluctantly pulled his gaze from Leslie's flushed expression as she hesitantly stepped inside the elevator, her workout clothes and runners clutched close to her body. They didn't help to cover the long, gorgeous legs or sexy shoulders and collarbone. He could still feel her hands on his chest and stomach and remember the way she'd tasted.

Damn, he hadn't heard a single word Selena had said and now she was staring at him expectantly.

And so was Leslie.

Both expressions so completely different. Selena's hopeful. Leslie's murderous.

Shit. What had he missed? "Um..."

"I'm sure he has other plans," Leslie said quickly.

So Selena had invited him somewhere.

"Um…"

"I'm sure he'd rather hang out with me…us," the star said, shooting him a flirty grin that no doubt worked on most men. Unfortunately, she was not his type at all and the woman he was crazy about was standing right there for comparison, so the flirting had zero effect. Though the idea of spending time with Leslie appealed to his lack of common sense.

And if he had to pretend to agree to hang out with Selena to make it happen…well, maybe he would. "Actually, I'm not in a rush to head back to the station." Damn, he was truly a sucker for punishment.

Leslie's eyes widened and Selena smiled. "Great! And you can drive."

He nodded. Drive where? Guess he'd find out.

The elevator doors opened on their floor and they stepped out. "Meet you in the lobby around eleven?" Selena said.

"Sure."

Leslie hung back as the star disappeared down the hall. "What are you doing?" she hissed.

"Spending time with an interesting woman," he said, staring straight at her.

Her mouth gaped as the doors started to close.

He stopped them, unable to help himself from saying, "And by the way, I'm digging this new towel fashion trend you've got going."

CHAPTER TEN

"THIS IS WHERE you grew up?" Selena asked from the passenger seat of Levi's truck as he pulled into the driveway of Leslie's family home.

"Sort of." Just the sight of the two-story, modest townhome had so many conflicted thoughts swirling through her. This was her home until she was fifteen. Until the arguments with her mother had turned unbearable and she'd gone to live with her grandmother. Until one of the toughest days in her life taught her that family wasn't always supportive when you needed them to be.

Finding out she was pregnant had been terrifying. She was on the Pill and, sure, she'd forgotten a couple that month, but she and Dawson had had sex only that one time, before they both agreed they weren't ready and decided to wait until graduation to do it again.

Telling her mother hadn't been her choice. She'd walked out of her doctor's appointment in a hazy fog, disbelieving, scared and unsure, and her mother had read the truth in her expression.

Their arguments went from bad to worse. Her mother had never approved of Dawson. After he'd been charged with vandalism with a group of boys in the few months that he'd fallen in with the wrong crowd, she said he was reckless and impulsive and his rich, privileged upbringing hadn't given him a sense of responsibility or discipline.

This unplanned pregnancy had seemed to only justify her position. She'd used it as a way to somehow prove to Leslie that the relationship wasn't healthy and the pressure to end it increased.

Leslie had been alone and scared. They told no one about it and her mother talked incessantly about her "options."

Leslie hadn't wanted any option that didn't include raising the child...with Dawson. She'd been young and in love and stubborn to a fault, but things had also changed for her, knowing she now had someone else to think of and consider and it hadn't taken long for her to turn her fears into strength.

Then she'd lost the baby. Before she'd gotten the nerve to tell Dawson. Away with his hockey team that weekend, she'd been all alone. He'd never known. She'd kept it to herself, feeling the weight and pain of it, despite the poor timing and situation.

Her mother had been relieved. Said it was a blessing in disguise.

Leslie had moved in with her grandmother that same day...

It had been raining as she'd packed her things. Tears had streamed down her face, as uncontrollable as the rain hitting the windshield of Levi's old pickup truck. He was the one she'd called for help and he'd been there, no questions asked.

He'd helped her unload her things and carried her bed and mattress into her grandmother's spare bedroom without needing her to explain her impulsive decision. He'd been a quiet, unjudging source of support and strength. Everything she'd needed that day with Dawson still away with the hockey team.

Once she was settled, he'd sat next to her on the porch

swing and she'd rested her head on his shoulder as she struggled with the emotions whirling through her. She told him about the baby and she hadn't needed to ask him not to tell anyone. She knew her secret was safe with him.

He'd held her on the swing all day and without knowing it, he'd helped her damaged heart start to heal.

Staring at the family home now, her chest tightened. She hadn't seen her mother since her grandmother's wedding—her *third* wedding—months ago. Whenever they were around one another, the air was tense and awkward and everyone felt it. It was easier to keep contact to a minimum. And now, by the look of the cars in the driveway, they had a full house for lunch that day.

"Are we going in?" Selena asked when neither Levi nor Leslie made any move to get out of the truck.

Levi was waiting on her to adjust, to mentally prepare. She appreciated that he knew her so well but it also just made everything worse. His caring, intuitive nature was something she'd always loved about him. Dawson had been slightly clueless about feelings and he'd always seen her strength and assumed she was never vulnerable. Levi had seen that side of her and therefore had always been the compassionate ear.

But right now she wished no one knew how hard this was going to be for her. It was easier to keep up the facade when there was no one who could see through it.

She still couldn't believe he'd agreed to join them for lunch. She knew it wasn't about Selena. He wanted to spend time with her, but she was still processing what had happened the night before and it was harder to do when she was around him. She'd expected the embarrassment and the feelings of annoyance but she hadn't been prepared for the lingering simmer of physical attraction he was evoking.

"What's happening?" Selena asked.

"Yeah, we're going in," Leslie said quickly, removing her seat belt and opening the door.

Outside the truck, Selena stopped her. "Hey, look, I get it. Families can be complicated. If you want to leave, just use the safe word 'hashtag' and I'll fake an illness."

Rare moments of Selena's true character caught her off guard. Her intuition was spot on in this situation and it made Leslie even more uncomfortable that she was so easily readable. "Thanks. I'll keep it in mind."

They made their way up the steps and she composed herself as she opened the door. Inside, she was relieved to hear her grandmother's voice in the kitchen.

Thank God. Her grandmother served as an amazing buffer for her. Her neutrality in the conflict seemed to help deflect any arguments from starting and her silent support for both Leslie and her mother made them both feel like they had a safe spot.

"Hi, darling. So wonderful to see you," her grandma said, as they entered the kitchen. She hugged her tight.

Leslie didn't want to let go because that meant turning to her mother next. But, she couldn't stay in her grandmother's arms forever. "Hi, Mom," she said, desperate to sound casual with Selena and Levi watching.

"Hi." Her mother's single word and unreadable expression revealed she was just as uncomfortable as Leslie was. Obviously this rare family get-together hadn't been her idea. Leslie's guess was Eddie had set this up and convinced her mother to host it. Her brother was always trying to get them back on the same page. He believed their conflict stemmed from the fact that they were just too much alike. Too stubborn. Both unwilling to be the first person to apologize or try to make amends. Of course that's what everyone believed. Neither she nor her mother had ever told anyone about the pregnancy. There'd been no point. And she'd learned to be okay with her family never knowing her side of the story.

Her mother quickly turned toward Selena. "This must be your...friend?" She shook Selena's hand. "Welcome. I hope you're enjoying your first visit to Alaska."

Selena smiled politely. "It's been an adventure," she said.

"Well, Eddie's cooking, so you're in for a treat."

Selena looked impressed. "Cop and a chef? Wow, you know how to raise them right."

Leslie shifted uncomfortably.

"I can only take credit for the cop side of his personality. The cooking thing, he learned from his grandma," her mother said, gesturing her grandmother forward to meet Selena next.

They exchanged pleasantries as her mother gave Levi a quick hug and immediately launched into a conversation about the cabin.

"I assume it's unsalvageable," her mother said and Leslie felt the first kick to the gut. She didn't need to say it; she heard her mother's disappointment and disapproval in her tone.

Once again, Leslie was to blame for destroying more bonds with her family.

Levi glanced her way as he nodded. "We haven't gone out there since the day of the fire, but from what we observed, I don't think there's much left."

There was nothing left. This house and that cabin had been the only places where reminders of her dad had existed and now one was gone and the other didn't feel like home. The family home was actually suffocating and already the urge to escape was overwhelming.

Leslie took a breath. But a second later, both of her arms were behind her back and she was in handcuffs.

Her eyes narrowed as she swung around to face Eddie standing there on his crutches, which he alternated with his wheelchair. "Seriously?"

His stopwatch was already ticking the seconds. "Your time's running."

Damn it. She dropped to the floor. Lifting her legs through her arms, she brought her hands to the front of her body and raised them up to her head to retrieve a bobby pin from her messy bun.

The rest of the family watched as they joined them in the kitchen.

"What are they doing?" Selena asked Levi in amusement. She linked an arm through his and moved closer.

Leslie refused to let it distract her from the task at hand.

"Seeing how fast she can get out," Levi said, eyeing her intently. "It's a game they've played since they were kids."

Selena laughed. "Really? Whatever happened to throwing a football around?"

"Not this family," Eddie said. "You seem a little off your game today, sis," he told Leslie.

"Shut up and let me focus," she said, twisting the pin.

She was off her game, but in her defense, there was a ton of pressure what with both her client and a man she'd embarrassed herself with the night before watching…and getting cozy with one another. And she still had an injured right hand. She'd removed the bandages the night before as they only irritated the damaged skin even more, but now the metal from the cuffs was rubbing the red flesh.

Her grandmother cheered her on and her sister, Katherine, entered the kitchen and watched with interest.

"Who's the fastest?" Selena asked.

"Leslie holds the record with fifty-seven seconds," Eddie said, but he glanced at the stopwatch. "But it looks like she'll be losing that title to Katherine…and yep, a minute and six seconds," he said just as she freed her arms from the cuffs.

Damn it. She hated to lose.

She stood and handed Eddie back his cuffs.

"I think that sun and surf is making you soft," he said with a wink.

"Whatever. I can beat your ass," she mumbled.

"So…all of you are law enforcement or some type of public service hero?" Selena asked, glancing around at all the people in the kitchen.

Leslie nodded. "Except for grandma…and my dad." Why had she mentioned her father? He wasn't there. Bringing him up was just awkward and no one saying anything for a beat made it even more so.

Her gaze met Katherine's and once more, guilt washed over her. She sent a silent apologetic look for burning down her sister's yearly retreat and Katherine's single nod meant she was forgiven. Her sister wasn't big on words or emotions and she didn't hold grudges or ill will for long. Maybe Leslie had inherited all of the spite in the family gene pool.

Sometimes she wished she was more like her siblings.

The sound of the front door opening again made her tense even more. "Who else is joining us?" She felt her anxiety rise. What part of keeping Selena a secret didn't her family understand? Inviting the entire neighborhood to lunch was risky.

But Eddie touched her shoulder. "Don't worry, it's Montana and Kaia and I believe they've already met."

Selena's eyes lit up. "The kid from the bar?"

Eddie smiled as Montana and Kaia entered the kitchen. "That would be her."

Kaia was carrying a cake from the bakery on Main Street. "I brought dessert," she said. Then, seeing Selena, she dropped the cake onto the counter and reached into her coat pocket, pulling out a stack of paper. "Eddie said you were going to be here, so I brought the script for the school play...in case you wanted to help me rehearse?"

Selena nodded. "Absolutely. What play are you doing?"

"*Romeo and Juliet*."

"One of my favorites," she said.

"Awesome. Let's find a quiet place," Kaia said, taking Selena's hand and leading her out of the kitchen.

The star sent a parting glance to Levi, but he wasn't looking at her. His gaze was on Leslie. She cleared her throat. "Why don't you all go play a card game or something? I'll help Eddie cook," she said.

Her grandmother nodded, obviously sensing Leslie's need for space and fewer people, and ushered everyone else out of the kitchen.

"She's actually really nice," Eddie said, moving toward the stove and stirring the risotto sauce that was simmering. As he removed the lid, the delicious smell of garlic and white wine sauce had Leslie's stomach growling.

"You try spending every minute of every day with her then," Leslie mumbled, dipping her finger into the sauce to taste it.

Eddie swiped her hand away. "What irritates you so much about her?"

"She's just so...oblivious to the real world. How it works..." Selena wasn't a child, yet she seemed so sheltered from everything that she had no idea how serious her situation was. "She's just always so perky and optimistic."

Her brother nodded slowly, leaning his weight on his crutches. "And you think everyone should look at the world with the same bleak-colored glasses that you do?"

"No... I...I don't know. Maybe." She hated when her brother tried to make her feel unjustified for being practical and seeing the world as it was.

"Not everyone grew up hearing all the horrors of humanity, always prepared for the worst," he said.

"You make it sound like a bad thing that we were cautious and Mom made us realize we had to be careful...not trust everyone we met."

"I just think we were robbed of blissful ignorance sometimes."

Her brother had no idea what blissful ignorance she'd been robbed of. The wake-up she'd received at such a young age that had made her grow up a hell of a lot faster. Leslie grabbed a spoon from the drawer and tasted the risotto next. "This is delicious, but it tastes different from your usual recipe."

"It's cauliflower rice," Eddie said.

"You guys watching your carbs?"

He shrugged. "Wouldn't hurt for all of us to consume a few more vegetables, but I was actually trying to be considerate to Selena."

Leslie sighed. "She wouldn't starve to death, and it wouldn't kill her to eat a grain of rice."

"I'm trying to be a good host," he said, opening the oven door and checking on the roast turkey inside. "Besides, you just said it was delicious."

"It is. I'm just saying we don't all need to cater to her. I'm keeping her alive—that's enough."

Eddie laughed. "You know, all of this might be a little easier if you'd ease up a little and try to get to know her."

Leslie ignored the suggestion as she stared out into the living room where Selena and Kaia were rehearsing lines. She couldn't get to know Selena. Protecting strangers was so much easier than protecting friends. It was one of the first lessons taught at the academy. Don't get too close. Don't jeopardize the client's safety.

Twenty minutes later, they all gathered in the dining room to eat. The family members took their usual places around the table and Selena sat between Kaia and Levi.

"The food looks amazing, Eddie," her mother said. She picked up the bowl of seasoned cauliflower risotto and scooped some onto her plate, then passed the bowl to Leslie, but Leslie's attention was elsewhere.

Something was different about the dining room.

Her father's oil painting of the Chugach Mountains was no longer hanging above the old antique dish cabinet along the far wall. Now there was a thick mahogany wood–framed mirror instead.

"Hey, sis, wake up," Katherine said on the other side of her, nudging her elbow.

Leslie took the bowl from her mother and passed it along without taking any. Suddenly, she wasn't hungry. "Um... is that new?" she asked her mother, nodding toward the mirror.

Across from her, she caught her grandma's worried expression and Eddie's *Oh no, here we go* look. She ignored them.

"Well, not new," her mother's tone was chilly. "It's been hanging there for about a year and a half." She cut into her slice of turkey and didn't meet Leslie's gaze.

"Mirrors definitely make a room look bigger," Selena said.

Leslie continued to stare at her mother. "What happened

to Dad's oil painting?" The painting had hung on that wall since they'd framed it for him as a Father's Day present when she was eight. For twenty years, it had been there and all of a sudden, her mother decided to replace it with a mirror?

"I stored it in his garage," she said, daring Leslie to argue with the decision. Her steely gaze was like bait to Leslie. "Why?"

"Leslie, just eat," Katherine muttered next to her.

"The food really is delicious," Montana said, obviously hoping to turn the conversation around.

Enthusiastic nods and appreciative noises sounded around the table, but Leslie and her mother were locked in a battle of wills.

"I thought it was time for a change and I liked the mirror," her mother said.

"But the painting was special. It had meant something to Dad. It meant something to all of us...or I guess maybe not." She stopped. Everyone was quiet now and staring at their plates. She'd done it again. Made things uncomfortable for everyone.

Levi was the only one still looking at her and his sympathetic yet uncomfortable expression made her desperate for an escape. Why was he even here? She'd made her position on where they stood quite clear the night before... Why was she even there? She never should have let Selena bully her into this.

She stood and her chair scraped noisily against the hardwood floor as she pushed it in. "I'm going to get some air," she said, leaving the dining room.

She headed toward the front door, but her mother's voice in the hallway behind her made her stop.

"Where are you going? We are trying to have a nice family meal and we have guests. We'd like you to come back and join us," she said tightly.

Leslie turned around. "Who are you kidding, Mom? This is just awkward."

Her mother placed her hands on her hips. "Because you're making it awkward by storming off like a child over a silly redecorating choice."

"It's not just a… Never mind. It's your house. Do what you want."

Her mother walked toward her. "That's right. It is my house. One you've barely been inside in years, so forgive me if I didn't think it was necessary to consult you about the decision to hang the mirror."

"Don't you think maybe Katherine and Eddie might be upset about you taking down Dad's painting too?"

Her mother threw up her hands. "They don't live here either."

"Fine." She turned toward the door again. There would be no getting through to her mom. She wouldn't understand. Fighting was useless. Trying to get her mother to see her side in anything, ever, had always been futile.

"Leslie, please come back and eat."

"I don't think it's a good idea." All she'd be thinking about, stewing over, was the missing painting. How could her mother take it down? Didn't it mean anything to her? Couldn't she consider their feelings? Her feelings? She and her father had been close. There was so little of him left. Over the years, she was slowly forgetting the sound of his laugh or the way he looked. Her mother had to know how much this would upset her.

"Fine." Her mother gave up. "You never did want to be a part of this family, so I guess you running off again shouldn't upset me," she said behind her.

Leslie whipped around. "That's what you thought my leaving was? I was fifteen, mom. I was angry and sad and in the matter of weeks, I'd had to grow up very quickly." It was so long ago, but right now, all of the tough emotions and difficult choices felt like they'd happened only yesterday.

"Right," her mother said with a nod. "You were faced with some tough decisions and forced to deal with your mistakes."

Mistakes? That hurt. Maybe getting pregnant hadn't been planned and maybe it wasn't the best thing to happen to a fifteen-year-old, but her mother was still acting like it had been the worst thing that could have happened to Leslie.

"So what happened was…"

"If you say it was a good thing…," She was going to lose it if those words came out of her mother's mouth again. She'd heard it too many times.

"No. Of course it wasn't a good thing, but Leslie, look at things from my point of view. My baby was pregnant. I saw your future evaporating. I saw your life getting so much harder."

"Then why didn't you try to help instead of trying to tell me what to do, how to live? Convincing me that I should break up with Dawson and consider other options wasn't what I needed from you back then."

"I reacted the only way I knew. By trying to protect you. From Dawson. From having to grow up too quickly. From yourself."

"I didn't need protection. I needed support, guidance, a shoulder to cry on and a hand to help me get back up… especially afterward. Instead, you let me move out." Emotions strangled her and she forbade herself to break down right now.

Her mother gave a sad laugh as she said, "You were determined to leave and I didn't honestly expect you to stay away."

"Then why didn't you insist that I come back?"

"Because I was trying to give you space and I thought maybe your grandmother might have a way with you that I didn't. You were so headstrong." She shook her head as though feeling the defeat all over again. "Never listened to anything I said."

"Eddie and Katherine were stubborn too. You managed to deal with their rebellion and mistakes." That had been one of the hardest things about leaving home, not being with her siblings. Feeling left out—her own doing—but still painful. And knowing they were happier without her there.

"They weren't like you," her mother said.

Fantastic, so she was just the problem child. The uncontrollable one.

"If I could do things over..."

Her mother sounding unexpectedly remorseful was worse than her anger. But it was too late now. They couldn't go back and change the past and they couldn't move forward with this pain between them.

Desperate for an escape, Leslie stormed out of the house and across the yard to the garage. She slipped inside and closed the door behind her, then took a deep breath.

Her head hurt and her chest felt tight.

Why the hell had she let Eddie talk her into this? Her and her mother together was never a good idea. It always escalated into an argument and damn it if they hadn't reached the worst topic ever that day.

They hadn't talked about what had happened…since it had happened.

Avoidance had worked fine to keep things relatively peaceful for everyone else in the family all these years.

She forced several deep breaths as she walked around the garage. Her father's workshop, his hiding place, his own place to create. She touched his woodworking table, her finger leaving a trail through the sawdust still covering the top. No one ever came out there. It was as though they wanted to preserve it as it was, a way to honor their father.

But Leslie knew he wouldn't mind her being in there.

She'd spent a lot of time in there with him. Watching him build, watching him draw, watching him develop photos in his makeshift darkroom and watching him paint…

She stared at the last mural he'd created, weeks before he died. One full wall of the garage always acted like his canvas. He'd paint it white, then paint the most magnificent scenery images, based on photos they'd taken. He'd take a photo of it, then paint over it…and create something new.

It had always broken Leslie's heart to watch the designs disappear under layers of white paint, but he always reminded her he created for the love of it.

And then she'd smile seeing the next one.

He'd tried to teach her to paint and let her fool around on the white canvas wall sometimes, but her passion and talent had ended with photography. When he'd gotten sick, he'd stopped going out to take new photos, so he'd painted hers…

Like the one still on the wall now. The image of the Chugach Mountains in the middle of a rainstorm with thunder and lightning… Ironic that it was the last one he'd done before he'd died—and before her life had gone to shit.

She scanned the shelves and found the dining room

painting in the corner, a blanket draped over it. Would her mother be willing to let her have it? Send it to her in LA once she got back there? She hated to think of it here in the garage. And obviously Eddie and Katherine hadn't wanted it or they would have taken it already.

She wished she could explain how much this small thing meant to her and why she'd gotten upset, but she wasn't sure anyone would understand. So many important people had been stolen from her life far too quickly and she needed something to hold on to.

The garage door opened and Leslie quickly wiped her eye and voided her expression of any emotion as she turned around. Levi entered and shot her a concerned look. "Just checking on you. I saw you slip out."

Like she always used to. Like she did that day...

She swallowed hard. "I'm good. Eddie's cauliflower thing didn't look very appetizing." Jokes. Deflecting from real emotion. Her only way to cope.

And this time, Levi let her do it. "Definitely not his best creation," he agreed, scanning the garage. "This place looks exactly the same as it always did."

"Yeah... I was just looking for the painting," she said, slightly embarrassed for her reaction in the dining room. For once she'd like to say she was fine and holding things together and have her actions back her up.

"So you and your mom...everything okay?" he asked carefully.

She sighed and waved a hand. "Bickering as usual. Nothing new there." Making light of her relationship was the only way to survive it. For years she'd felt sad and guilty and angry. She'd longed for her mother's support during her teen years. She envied the relationship Katherine had with her and what hurt the most was the fact that her mother didn't seem to feel like she'd lost anything when Leslie had moved out. She'd never asked her to move back home. She hadn't made an effort to make things right at all. The more time that passed, the harder it had become to think that they could ever reconcile. She spotted her father's camera on the shelf next to his old photo albums and processing stuff. She picked it up carefully and blew the layer of dust away. She might not be able to take the painting with her right now, but she'd take the camera. No one was using it. No one else wanted it. It wouldn't be missed.

"You still taking photos?" Levi asked, looking slightly relieved. "I bet LA provides some stunning scenery."

She did and it did, but it was a hobby that she liked to keep to herself. She shook her head as she wiped the dust from the lens. "Not really. But I thought I might take a few while we were stuck here."

His attention caught the word *stuck* and his face fell slightly.

But she refused to feel guilty for distancing herself from him...from her past. It was a self-preservation thing and if he knew her at all, he'd know that and not take offense. She'd stupidly let her guard fall the night before and look how that had turned out.

Had he thought about the kiss? He must have, but she'd bet he wasn't replaying it in his mind the way she was. Levi had reacted exactly the way Leslie would have predicted. With distance, with a clear head, by pushing her away. Ignoring the conversation or any discussion about it was the best idea. Forget it ever happened.

"Do you know how much longer that will be?" he asked.

Unfortunately not and it was making her crazy. "No. Still no update on the stalker."

"I'm sure police in LA are working on it."

She wasn't but she nodded. "Is Selena ready to go? Are you ready to head back to the resort?" She'd had enough of the family get-together.

He nodded and looked about to say something, then closed his mouth and nodded again. "I'm good to go and I think Selena's ready anytime."

"Great. Um... I'll meet you both at the truck?" She needed a moment alone with her father's things, with his memory.

Levi nodded as he opened the door and left the garage.

She scanned the space, feeling the first sense of calm wash over her, the first feeling that things were going to be okay. Her father—even when he wasn't physically there—had a way of quieting her conflicted heart.

"Miss you, Dad," she said, turning off the light.

CHAPTER ELEVEN

LEVI NEEDED TO get back to the station.

As they drove in silence back to the resort—well, not Selena, whose chatter was incessant from the passenger seat—it couldn't be clearer that there was nothing left to stay in Wild River for. Despite the few moments of tension-free time together in her father's garage, Leslie was right back to ignoring him once they were inside his truck, her gaze lost somewhere out the window, clutching her father's old camera to her lap. When Leslie walked away from things, it was for good.

The visit to her family home had only put her more on edge and while he understood how hard this must be for her, she'd have an easier time if she'd just let them all in. Let them help. She'd said she'd moved on, but obviously not. The tension and conflict between her and her mother was still very much alive, eating them both up. He remembered the day he'd helped her move in with her grandmother vividly. He remembered her tears, he remembered her pain and he remembered her devastating confession. He'd never told anyone what had happened that day, but he'd never forgotten.

It was so long ago and he'd been a teenage boy dealing with his own adolescence and being in love with a girl who was both his best friend and his best friend's girl, so everything had seemed even more intense and there'd been a brief moment while he'd been her shoulder to cry on that he'd been tempted to tell her how he felt, to be honest with her. But the timing hadn't been right. He hadn't wanted to add to her conflicted heart. She'd needed a friend that day, not a confession of feelings, and then the moment was gone.

Leslie had been sad and withdrawn for a few months after moving in with her grandmother. He understood, having made that same difficult transition himself, and despite her troubles, it had connected them even more. She'd missed a few weeks of school, but with his help and support, eventually she'd gotten better and was back to her old self—at least, mostly.

If only she could find that same persevering strength now to somehow find happiness again and let herself be open, to feel...

He pulled into the parking lot of the resort and parked his truck in the fifteen-minute parking spot space. He'd pack his few things and hit the road.

Selena frowned. "I thought you were staying here?"

He shrugged casually as he cut the engine. "I think I'll head back to the station. I've got a bunch of pretraining stuff I should do...and I really should get back to Smokester... the station's German shepherd," he added for clarification.

That only made Selena more interested. "Ohhhh...a puppy." She sent a look full of daggers at Leslie. "*Someone* wouldn't stop at the puppy spa to pick up my adorable little girl on the way out of town. I haven't seen her or talked to her in days. Do you have pictures?"

"Um...no," Levi said, opening the door and climbing out.

Selena's mouth dropped open. "How is that possible? I take at least a hundred pictures of Unicorn every day. I named her Unicorn because she's unique and the groomer actually dyes her fur a fun rainbow of pink and purple."

Wow. "Well, Smokester's not really a pet. He's kind of a retired work dog that stays at the cabin," Levi said.

"Well, I have pictures," Selena said. Then she glared at Leslie. "No, wait, I don't because I don't have my phone."

"You'll get your phone back soon and maybe you can email them to Levi," Leslie said sharply as they entered the resort and headed for the elevators.

"That's a good point," Selena said. "I should get your email address to stay in touch, you know, in case you have questions about fundraising and charity event planning."

Right. "Um, yeah." He reached into his jacket pocket and retrieved a pen and an old grocery store receipt, then scribbled his email address on it. "Here you go."

Selena took it and tucked it into her pocket. "Great. Hey, before you go, want to have a drink?"

Wow, she really didn't give up easily. He was certain that he hadn't been giving off any kind of vibe that indicated that he would want to, but obviously the best approach with Selena was a direct one. "No, but thank you."

Did Leslie look relieved or was he imagining it? He'd caught her watching his interaction with Selena at her mother's house before the meal drama, but he couldn't tell if it was irritation or jealousy on her face, nor could he tell what the source of it was. She seemed annoyed with Selena all the time for everything. It might not have had anything to do with him. Yet, the kiss the night before made him think that maybe…

Selena seemed unfazed by his refusal for a drink. "Okay. Well, drive safe and I'll email you photos of Unicorn if I ever get my cell phone back."

"I'll look forward to it," he said, as they climbed into

the elevator. No doubt she'd forget all about him and the photos once she got back to her life in LA.

Inside the elevator, Leslie stood, arms folded, staring at the doors, and he had no idea what to say or if there even was anything left to say. The last two days had been a whirlwind—the fire, the kiss, the conflict between them, the tension, and the arguing...

He pressed his lips together and when the elevator doors opened on their floor and she hurried out without even a goodbye, Levi could only watch her go.

As SELENA BROWSED the spa menu in the resort hotel room twenty minutes later, Leslie dipped into the bathroom and shut the door.

Was it possible to have a heart attack at her age? Because it really felt like she was having a heart attack.

With each deep breath in, the air simply stuck in her chest, never making it to her lungs. Her exhales were shallow and she thought she might throw up.

How much longer could she physically keep this up? It might take months to find Selena's stalker... They'd have to return to LA at some point.

With a shaky hand, she dialed Eoghan's number.

He picked up halfway through the first ring as though staring at the phone, waiting for her call. It made her feel just a little bit better knowing he was there on the other side of the call, even if there wasn't much he could do.

She might not be in love with the guy, but it was refreshing to have someone she could count on who wasn't too close...who didn't know a whole lot about her past or demand that she be the person she used to be. Keeping things casual with Eoghan allowed her to rely on him in some capacity now without feeling like she had to completely open up or go all in.

He was safe. There was no fear that he might break her heart.

"How are you?" His concerned tone helped to ease the chest pangs, making her glad she called. Unfortunately, she had less than a minute.

"Not great. Hanging in there." Barely. "Any word yet?"

"Not yet, but the police think they might have a lead," he said.

A huge sigh of relief escaped her. Oh thank God. At least that was something. "Who?" She was convinced it was someone close to the star, someone who had intimate access. Someone with a vengeance, a vendetta against Selena. Not some stranger with a celebrity fetish.

"A guy was seen trying to jump the fence on her property last night," Eoghan said.

The house and gates were on lockdown so even her management team and family weren't permitted access right now—for their safety, they were told. "The agency is co-operating? Providing all the evidence I've collected to authorities?" She'd given everything to Eoghan, emailed him the files and photos to his personal email before leaving LA.

"Yes…" But there was a note of hesitancy in his voice.

"Maybe I should call Federico." She bit her lip. She hadn't reached out to the agency at all, still not completely trusting that she could, but the longer she withheld information on their whereabouts, the more shit she'd be in. Her boss would understand the delicate nature of all of this and why she'd done what she did. As long as she didn't continue to avoid him.

"No. I wouldn't. At first I thought maybe you'd acted drastically, but now I think you're right about not reaching out." He lowered his voice. "You're going to think this is crazy, but…"

Her heart raced, the pain returning instantly to her chest. "What?"

"I think someone inside the agency might be involved. Maybe working with someone on Selena's management team."

Her blood chilled in her veins and her stress level rose even higher. "Who?"

"I don't know yet…just a gut feeling."

Shit, time was up. "I'll check in again soon," she said, quickly disconnecting the call.

So, she was right about her instincts. She couldn't trust the agency. What about her boss? Why on earth would he somehow be involved in this? A former navy SEAL, thirty years of active service, then building up the company to be one of the best, most trusted in LA. It didn't make sense that he'd risk everything…for what? Why would he care about Selena Hudson or helping her stalker get to her?

Her mind raced; nothing added up. She pressed her fingers to her temples, hearing the television outside the bathroom door. Blaring.

She opened the door. "Can you turn it down a little? I'm going to take a bath." Might as well take advantage of the jetted tub she was paying for.

"I'm on TV," Selena said.

"That shouldn't thrill you anymore," Leslie said.

"No, I mean the case…the stalker." Selena leaned closer to the television and Leslie rushed to join her as her picture appeared on the screen with the caption *Hollywood royalty Selena Hudson in danger.*

Leslie stood frozen as the reporter recounted the situation. Sweat pooled on her lower back and she was now ninety-nine percent certain she was experiencing a heart attack.

How the hell did this make the news? Had the agency gone to the media? The police? Looking for public assistance? Or had Selena's management team needed to make a statement? "Do you think your team released a statement to explain your absence at the press conferences?" she asked tightly.

Selena shook her head. "Doubtful. They would rather hide this whole thing."

They had at first, but now with Selena being gone, maybe they were rethinking strategy. Or worse—if someone on her team was her stalker or involved somehow, maybe they wanted her found quickly and thought this was the way to go. But Leslie was careful not to reveal that thought process to the star. Selena was a big enough headache when she wasn't panicking or stressed about everything. "Isn't all publicity good, even if it's not positive?"

"Not in my case. I've been a poster child for wholesome, family content for so long and now all my movies are PG. I've been typecast as the good girl." And she didn't sound thrilled about it. "They wouldn't want this to ruin that image."

"You being in danger could ruin your image?"

"Having a stalker is typically associated with obsession and lust and in Hollywood, that could be misconstrued as my fault. Maybe my last few Instagram photos were too sexy or revealing," she said, sounding disgusted.

Leslie was disgusted for her. The double standards in the movie industry were rampant. She turned her attention back to the screen. So, if it wasn't the management team, maybe the media had been tipped off somehow... Would the stalker be that arrogant to go to them himself?

Did they crave the spotlight, any way they could get it? It was LA after all.

"The security company assigned to extra detail for Ms. Hudson had this to say about the situation," the reporter said.

"We firmly believe that Ms. Hudson's life is in danger and we are doing everything we can to prevent the situation from escalating." Her boss being interviewed on the screen made Leslie release a small sigh of relief. If Federico was part of this media release, then he knew how serious this was. They obviously believed Leslie.

"They believe Ms. Hudson is with their employee, Leslie Sanders…" the reporter continued.

A pic of Leslie appeared on the screen and she nearly hyperventilated. So much for staying undercover and flying under the radar. Her face all over the media was a very bad thing.

"Hey, you're on TV too," Selena said, glancing at her. "Not the greatest picture."

"Shhh…"

"At this time, it is uncertain whether or not Ms. Sanders is involved in an abduction of the star," the reporter said. "Or if she is in cahoots with whoever is responsible for the threats…"

Leslie's mouth fell and she felt for the bed behind her, lowering herself onto it. Her body was frozen but her mind was frantic as the words seemed to drift farther away. They thought she might have abducted Selena? That she was somehow a part of this? Why? Hadn't Eoghan explained everything to Federico?

Oh my God.

She fought for air.

Selena kneeled on the floor in front of her. "Hey, you okay?"

Eoghan was supposed to have briefed everyone at the office. Had he? Had they not believed him? Had the insider he believed was involved somehow gotten to Federico and convinced him that Leslie was the problem? Or was Federico really involved and trying to frame her?

The news concluded with a tip helpline for anyone to call in if they knew anything or saw the two of them and Leslie felt like vomiting. Not only was she in hot water with her employer, but now there was a wanted sign on her forehead and her boss was the one who put it there, for whatever reason—either way, it wasn't good.

And all for trying to do her job.

The room spun and a knock on the door made her heart nearly explode. "Don't answer," she said. Had hotel staff seen the news report? Had they already notified authorities? Of course she could explain all of this and Selena could vouch for her, but then they'd have to return to LA immediately and now more than ever, Leslie wasn't sure that was a great idea.

"Open up, it's Levi," came his voice on the other side.

She wasn't sure if it made her feel better or worse, but Selena went to the door and opened it.

Levi entered, a concerned, disbelieving look on his face. "I heard the news as soon as I turned on the radio in the parking lot…"

Leslie nodded, unable to find enough air to respond.

"Why don't you lie back? Take a breath? You look really pale," Selena was saying.

She tried to gently guide her back but Leslie stood. She couldn't take a breath or a moment to rest. Shit just went sideways—even more sideways—and she needed to react.

"We have to go." People in Wild River, the few who knew Selena was there, were fairly capable of understanding the urgency of keeping the sighting to themselves, but now that Leslie was deemed a potential criminal, who knew how far small-town loyalty went?

"Where?" Selena asked. "The most secluded place on earth burned down, remember?"

She shot her a look. Think. Think of something. Eoghan said the stalker was moving closer, so going back to LA wasn't an option. The cabin was gone. The resort ski town was no longer safe.

"I have a place," Levi said.

Leslie jumped. She'd forgotten he was even in the room. She turned to look at him. He was going to help? Obviously he didn't think she was an abductor. Having someone on her side made her feel a little better, but only slightly. "The station?" she asked, shaking off the fog of panic and forcing a clear head.

He nodded. "Pack your stuff quickly and meet me outside the lobby doors in ten minutes."

Leslie could do better than that. "We only need five."

LEVI WOULDN'T QUESTION his actions. This was the right thing to do. Leslie needed help and surprisingly, she finally realized it too.

Unfortunately, his co-worker had questions. "So, we are harboring fugitives now?" Chad said, popping his head around the corner of the office door thirty seconds after Levi had ushered the women into one of the bunk rooms across the hall.

He scoffed and waved a hand. Made light of the situation. Tried not to panic over the apparent truth of Chad's words. "I think we both know Leslie hasn't abducted anyone. It's a misunderstanding."

"A misunderstanding that's all over the news and one that the Levi I know wouldn't get tangled up in, so what's really going on?" Chad asked, entering and shutting the door.

"She's one of my closest friends." Understatement. The only woman he'd ever loved. "I need to help her. They had nowhere else to go," he said, removing his jacket and hanging it over the back of his chair. The four-hour drive from Wild River had been quiet and tense. Leslie had been lost in thought in the back seat of his truck and Selena had fallen asleep in the passenger seat, head propped against his shoulder. He'd need answers from Leslie—she needed to level with him about what was going on—but for now, he'd give her time and space.

Smokester woke from his nap on the couch in the office, one he knew he wasn't supposed to sleep on, saw that Levi was back and quickly jumped down. The German shepherd's sheepish look would normally garner a reprimand from Levi, but given the circumstances, could he really give the dog shit over breaking a rule? Instead he reached into his drawer for a treat and held it low for him.

The dog accepted it happily then curled up on his own bed in the corner of the office.

"Why doesn't she just go back to LA or go to the station? Selena obviously isn't going to press charges. Can't she clear up the whole misunderstanding?" Chad peeked through the office blinds toward the bunk room where they could hear Selena and Leslie talking.

"Selena is in danger. They aren't sure who they can trust. Leslie thinks there's a guy on the inside…"

"Or *woman*?" Chad gave him a pointed look, releasing the blinds.

Levi sighed. There was no way in hell Leslie was the bad guy in this situation. She'd been living by the law her entire life. Her family were all law enforcement in some way and she was the most honest person Levi knew. He could rest assured that he wasn't helping a criminal. "She's not guilty of anything but rash thinking and impulsiveness."

"How can you be so sure?"

"Because I've known her my entire life and I have no reason to believe she's lying to me. Besides, if she was helping Selena's stalker, wouldn't she have handed the woman over by now instead of hiding her in Alaska?"

Chad seemed to think on it. "Okay...but you know the risk you're taking having them here right? If anyone finds out, your job could be on the line."

He was aware of the consequences. He couldn't turn his back on Leslie when she needed his help and until they found the stalker, he had to help protect Selena too. The footage of the letters and the image of her vandalized room they'd shown on the news report didn't look like someone just out to scare her. Leslie had been right to flee LA. It may have been her only choice. "I'll take full responsibility for this if it goes sideways..."

"*When* this goes sideways."

Levi nodded. "If, when...it's all on me. Just please keep this to yourself, okay?" Chad was the only other full-time member at the station. No one else was scheduled to be there for another few weeks when preseason training would start. Levi hoped all of this would be over by then. At least, most of him hoped... A small, very stupid part of him hoped to have Leslie around for a little while.

Something was definitely wrong with him. He must be a sucker for punishment.

"Can I count on you?" he asked Chad. If the guy didn't agree, Levi wasn't sure what else he could do. His own apartment was being sublet and like Leslie, he wasn't sure who they could trust. Hell, even her family would be inclined to tell her to contact authorities and let the law figure it all out, but his gut told him that wouldn't be in Selena's best interest.

Someone wanted the star dead and there were too many people she couldn't trust.

Chad looked conflicted, but then he said, "You'll remember my discretion at review time?"

Levi sighed and pointed to the office door.

Chad grinned as he left.

Levi slumped in his chair and ran a hand through his hair. Through the one cracked blind in his office window, he saw Leslie and Selena setting up their bunks in the room across the hall. His gaze narrowed in on Leslie and his stomach twisted in knots. He better be right about his former best friend.

CHAPTER TWELVE

SHE HAD TO be doing the right thing. That was the only way she was getting out of this whole mess, saving Selena's life and having any hope of a future in law enforcement. And now she'd dragged Levi—and possibly Chad—into it as well. Levi had looked confident in his decision to help and had reassured her that it was no problem on the drive from Wild River and she almost believed him, but he had to be worried. He was putting his own neck on the line for her. Chad hadn't been as welcoming and she just hoped Levi could convince him to stay quiet about their whereabouts for a little while. A few days at most. That's all she was willing to put them at risk for.

She groaned as she splashed water on her face in the station cabin bathroom.

There had to be something she was missing, overlooking. Some clue. Shutting her eyes tight, she tried to push aside the stress clouding her usual clearheadedness and replayed everything over in her mind...

When the call came into the Executive Protection Agency three months ago, everyone thought Selena's management was just interested in upping her security with the upcoming release of her new movie. They hadn't been forthcoming about the amount or frequency of the threatening letters Selena had been receiving through her fan club, claiming it was just a random occurrence. They'd wanted to have extra protection just in case, but they hadn't considered the letters legit or anything to be truly concerned about.

Federico had called her into his office and explained the nature of the job. He'd told her what he claimed to know. Extra security for a couple of months. No imminent threat. It had sounded like a boring, mundane assignment. Federico had given no indication otherwise.

Think, Leslie, think! Had he displayed any cues that he'd known otherwise? Leslie had been working for him for two years, so she knew some of his tells, but no matter how hard she tried, she couldn't come up with a reason or anything to indicate that Federico had been lying or trying to set her up in any way.

Had he assigned her the security detail thinking she'd be easier to manipulate or overpower?

No, she wouldn't let any lack of confidence seep in while she was already vulnerable right now.

A week on the job, she'd found out about the stalker when she was scrolling through Selena's fan page and social media sites and noticed the same "fan" had commented over two hundred times a day. When she questioned the star's management team about it, they'd fessed up, admitting that they too had been a little worried about this particular admirer.

They blocked the fan from the sites and deleted the inappropriate comments, but a week later, more letters started arriving at the management office and Leslie discovered they hadn't been the first ones from the same person. Carefully constructed like ransom notes with cutout letters and no fingerprints on the paper or envelope, it was obvious the person knew what they were doing. All hope that it might be some kid messing around disappeared.

The letters were calm at first, claiming to be Selena's number one fan, apologizing for the frequent posts and the crude nature of them and asking why they'd been blocked from posting. When no one reinstated the fan's privileges, the wording became slightly more aggressive, demanding access to the star through her social media channels.

With each ignored letter, the language grew more threatening and abusive and Leslie informed the agency that the situation was more concerning than they'd originally understood. Federico had advised her to keep track of everything and keep him posted.

But almost immediately, the letters stopped.

The timing of that was suspicious, but she hadn't thought anything of it at the time and for three weeks, there was nothing. Everyone assumed the fan had given up, lost interest...

Until a letter showed up in Selena's own mailbox at home.

Up until that point, Selena's management team had kept the stalker situation to themselves, not wanting her to worry or be afraid when she was out promoting the new movie. Leslie had disagreed with the withholding and voiced her opinion to Federico, but he'd said that her management team knew best and they had to be careful not to damage her career in any way.

So, along with Selena's regular security team, Leslie worked at making sure event security was tighter than before and new security systems were installed at Selena's home. More cameras and alarms at the front gates, on all exits and windows, throughout the home.

Things were quiet for a few weeks. No sign of the fan. No more letters.

Everyone else started to relax, but Leslie knew that was

the time to be even more diligent. Selena refused to cancel any appearances and fought Leslie's suggestion of bringing in media for interviews instead of constantly meeting in public spaces, where the surroundings were unpredictable and difficult to monitor.

The star said everyone was paranoid until she arrived home one day to find blood splattered over the security fence. The words *Why did you abandon me?* were written in the thick dark red liquid.

Everything got more controlled, tighter. Leslie was grateful that the scare was enough for Selena to finally start letting her do her job more effectively. Fewer interviews, fewer media appearances... Her management team was pissed, but they handled it by saying Selena was sick. Things were quiet for a few days and everyone started to think that they'd done enough to deter the stalker.

Then the person got into her home. Into her bedroom. So close.

Selena had been in her downstairs gym with her trainer. Leslie was sitting on a bench in the hallway, bored stupid, scrolling through her phone's image directory, evaluating the photos she'd taken of the valley on her last hiking trip, when she'd heard a noise upstairs. Calling in backup to the security guard monitoring the gate, she'd made her way slowly, quietly throughout the house. Nothing in the kitchen or living room was out of place—then she'd entered Selena's bedroom.

The sight inside had made her blood run cold. The bedroom window was shattered, glass on the floor, yet the alarm hadn't gone off. Stuffed multicolored Chihuahua toys that looked like Selena's dog, Unicorn, were torn apart, their stuffing strewn all over the room. Blood was smeared on the walls and there was human feces on the floor. She'd nearly gagged at the gruesome display, but it was the words *I'm getting closer everyday* written in Selena's signature red lipstick across her vanity mirror that had Leslie reacting on impulse.

Fifteen minutes later, they were in her vehicle on their way out of the city.

And now she had no idea what to do next, except try to figure out who could have gained access to the house that day. The guard at the gate had claimed he saw no one drive up, so the person had to have been on foot. Security cameras hadn't caught him from her quick review of the footage, so it had to have been someone who knew about the new systems they'd installed.

Federico at the agency had known—she'd run everything by him. And of course everyone close to Selena, who also had more access to the house.

Leaving the bathroom, she went back into the bunk room.

"You okay? You were in there for a while."

Damn, Selena had seen her almost break down. She couldn't let that happen again. Her client needed to trust her…and Leslie needed to start trusting herself again. "I'm fine. It was just a bit of a shock seeing the news report, but I'm good." She reached for her cell phone and opened a notes app. "We need to go over the list of people in your life who could be *involved* in this," she said, choosing her words carefully. Selena respected and adored her team. Leslie needed her cooperation with full disclosure, not her on the defensive.

"I thought it was some rando," she said, sitting cross-legged on the bottom bunk bed.

"It could be…" Leslie hesitated. "But the messages seem really personal. They knew where you lived and despite the

upgrades in security, they knew how to access your home."
Plus, she needed to start somewhere and eighty percent of
the time, people were abused by loved ones. She was no
longer certain who was on her side. She couldn't just sit
there and not try to be proactive in solving this.

"Okay, well, I know it's not my family," Selena said,
confidently.

That they could agree on. Her mother and stepfather
were amazing, supportive parents. They had a bajillion
dollars of their own so they had no desire to defraud their
daughter or want her cash in the untimely incident of her
death. Leslie had met them both multiple times and they
were actually fairly down-to-earth, but then both hadn't
been born Hollywood royalty. They'd had to work hard to
pursue their goals and dreams to make it in the industry.
"What about your father?" Leslie asked carefully.

Selena shook her head. "He'd never hurt me."

Leslie would have to take the woman's word for it, having never met him. She wasn't entirely convinced they
should rule him out, but she'd circle back. "Okay, what
about friends?"

"I don't think so… I mean I used to have a lot of friends
when I was younger but now I'm too busy to keep in touch
with most of them."

Why did you abandon me? The words on the gate. "So,
maybe someone feels abandoned? Left behind? Jealous?"

Selena bit her lower lip. "I really don't think so. A lot of
the friendships I had were superficial. Based on the love of
acting and having to hang out together on set for hours on
end, but everyone from those days has gone on to do amazing stuff. I can't think of anyone that would be jealous…"

"What about nonactor friends? Wannabes that might
resent your success?" There had to be someone out there

who wasn't genuinely happy for Selena. Professional jealousy was rampant in Hollywood.

"There were a couple of extras from the set of my last movie, mean-girl types who would snicker and talk shit off camera... Nothing worth getting them kicked off set for, just petty insults about my acting or wardrobe, that kind of thing."

That was a start, even if not a great one. "Have you seen them since filming ended?"

Selena shook her head. "I know one of them moved to Atlanta to see if she'd have better luck in the industry there. Less competition and less expensive to survive while trying to break in."

Leslie made a note to confirm that. "Her name?"

"Alison Gray."

"What about the other one?"

"I heard her tell her agent that she'd decided to go into nursing." Selena shrugged. "I'm sorry, Leslie, but I don't know of any enemies."

Huh. So Hollywood wasn't as cutthroat as she'd assumed. At least not for Selena Hudson.

"Okay, let's move on to ex-boyfriends." Seemed more likely than a jealous female costar anyway. Women were more likely to slander one another on social media than exhibit the violence displayed by the stalker.

Selena rattled off the names of A-list stars that Leslie barely recognized, but she made a list of all of them. Twelve in total. Not great. But not a horrible place to start. "Okay, we need to do some stalking of our own. Come with me."

They left the room and a second later, knocked on Levi's office door. He opened it, holding a parachute in one hand and a sewing needle in the other. "Everything okay?" His dark eyes full of concern had Leslie's heart racing. He'd never know how grateful she was that he'd been at the resort and had stepped in to help them—probably because she wasn't going to tell him. She'd made the mistake of letting her guard slip momentarily the night before, that wouldn't be happening again.

She just needed to survive this nightmare, keeping things cool and casual between them and pushing the memory of his kiss out of her mind. Easier said than done as she stared at his lips right now, irrationally tempted by them.

He caught her stare and cleared his throat.

"Everything's fine," she said quickly.

"Are you sewing?" Selena asked.

Levi's cheeks flushed a little. "Yeah…well, not really. Repairing the parachutes… It's part of the job."

"That's actually really hot," Selena said.

Oh Jesus. "Can we use your computer?" Leslie asked briskly.

"Oh, sure…" He moved away from the door and Leslie headed straight to the laptop on the desk. "Password?"

His cheeks got even redder. He set the parachute down on the sofa and approached the laptop. "I'll do it."

Couldn't fault him for that. "We also need access to your social media accounts."

"For?"

"To cyber-stalk my exes," Selena said, sitting on the edge of the desk.

Levi turned to look at Leslie for clarification.

"What she said."

"Okay… Which site do you want? Facebook, LinkedIn, Twitter?"

Selena looked at him as though he were still in the dark ages. "Insta and TikTok."

"What the hell is TikTok?" he asked.

Leslie didn't know either, but she waited for Selena to tell Levi he was out of touch.

"We will create a profile for you," Selena said, obviously eager to get her hands on the computer and get online again. She forced Leslie out of the way and sat at the desk, then opened the page to create an account.

"Username… HotSmokejumper27…"

"Seriously?"

"What? He is hot," Selena said. She smiled up at Levi before adding, "I'll use my name as the password."

Leslie's back teeth clenched. So what if Selena was flirting with him? What did she care? Her impulsive actions the night before had nothing to do with actually being attracted to Levi. That would be insanely ridiculous. They'd been the result of stress and high emotions, and foolishly letting him get to her with memories of the past. She was not attracted to him. Not at all.

Then why couldn't she stop staring at the muscular forearms folded across his chest?

He glanced at her and she looked away quickly. She had to quit getting caught checking him out.

"All set," Selena said. "Now we can search…"

Leslie sat next to her and Levi hovered behind them. "Can we even see their profiles if we don't 'friend' them?"

"Yes. TikTok is more of a performance app. People doing karaoke routines and dance numbers, the flip the switch challenge…" Selena waited for either of them to clue in. When they didn't, she continued. "Anyway, believe me, these social media whore types never lock down their profiles. The more eyes on them, the better."

"That's so dangerous," Leslie muttered. Her own social media was limited to Facebook and she had every security measure in place and still rarely posted anything. She used it to see pics of Katherine and Eddie and friends from Wild River... Levi... There may have been more than one wine-induced night looking at old photos of him...

Selena searched the first name on the list of ex-boyfriends.

A video loaded of a guy standing on an outdoor patio with a breathtaking view behind him. "He's in Milan," Selena said.

"These could be old," Leslie said.

Selena laughed. "Ha!" She pointed to the date on the video. "This was ten minutes ago and there's four more from today alone."

She searched the next few names. Most of the men were filming on location and movie sets, eliminating them from the suspect list.

"I'll try Instagram," she said, sliding the laptop toward Levi to log in.

As he did, Leslie noticed his messenger icon pop up on the bottom right-hand corner of the computer screen.

One New Message from Angelica.

Who was Angelica?

Selena glanced at Levi. "Do you need to read that?"

His cheeks were flushed again. Obviously Angelica was someone important.

Oh my God, why did she care? Levi's dating life was none of her business.

"No... I can check it later," he said, turning the laptop back to Selena.

The next two guys she searched were on a yoga retreat. Together.

"Ahhhh...they finally came out. Good for them," Selena said, looking genuinely happy for her exes.

"You dated two gay guys?"

Selena turned to look at her. "Yeah."

Leslie checked her watch. "Moving on…"

The next guy's photos were from a hospital bed. "Oh my God. What happened to him?" Levi asked.

"Nose job," Selena said.

The next guy was in rehab. "It's just research for a movie," Selena said.

"Wow, that's commitment to a role," Levi said.

"I once spent four nights in jail to prepare for an indie project I was passionate about, but the funding wasn't there so it never got finished," Selena said, sounding disappointed. "It was a great story though, based on a true story of a woman wrongly convicted for killing her abuser."

That actually did sound fascinating. A movie Leslie would watch for sure. "I thought you only did rom-coms?" Leslie asked.

"That's all I do right now, but my agent is on the lookout for other projects all the time. Unfortunately, I'm currently pigeonholed as the rom-com queen, so it's difficult to be taken seriously by other filmmakers for their more offbeat projects."

She had no idea Selena was interested in doing anything other than the work she was doing. Not that she really knew much about her at all beyond the surface…or what she'd assumed based on her own preconceptions of the rich and famous.

And right now wasn't really the time to bond or get to know her client better. "Can we get back to this?" she asked as another message popped up on the screen.

Tracey would like to connect with you. Accept chat now?

Angelica. Tracey. Levi was a busy guy.

Selena glanced at him with an amused raised eyebrow. "Are we talking to Tracey?"

"Just hit Decline," Levi mumbled, obviously embarrassed.

Leslie couldn't define the source of her annoyance. It was completely illogical. What did she care if Levi had a healthy dating life? She wasn't jealous; that would be ridiculous... Or maybe she was a little. Jealous of the fact that she could no longer hang out with him the way these other women could. They'd never have the friendship they used to have. That's all it was. It had absolutely nothing to do with the fact that his kiss had rocked her and she'd been surprised by her body's reaction to it. She'd wanted him. That was true no matter what the reason.

"That's all of them," Selena said. "Ten out of the twelve accounted for as obviously not the guy since they aren't in LA."

"Well, at least we're down to two that I'll ask Eoghan to check out," she said.

Selena's face twisted into the look of disgust she always wore when Eoghan's name was mentioned.

But Levi's face held a different look. *She* may not be jealous, but he certainly looked it.

And she had no idea why, but that made her feel slightly better. Maybe he was missing their friendship too.

"He's our guy on the ground back there. And he's good at his job and would do anything to help me," she said, daring a glance at Levi. She wouldn't admit to Selena that her confidence and trust in him was fading a little. "We should go. Thanks for the use of your laptop."

Selena stood and touched Levi's arm. "Hey, do you want to show me around? Maybe go snowshoeing or something?"

Leslie pretended not to listen or care. If Levi wanted to entertain Selena, all the better. Get the woman out of her hair for a while so she could hear her own thoughts for a bit.

"Um… I can't tonight. I have plans. Maybe tomorrow?"

Plans with Angelica or Tracey? Or both?

Damn it, she *was* jealous.

And unfortunately, she wished it was just because these women got the pleasure of Levi's company, but she feared it went deeper than that.

Just another reason to get the hell out of there as soon as possible.

CHAPTER THIRTEEN

SUNLIGHT CRESTED THE mountains in the distance and a mild cool breeze held that sweet promise of warmer days to come as Levi stood in the clearing behind the cabin while Smokester procrastinated doing his business, instead preoccupied with a tree branch he'd buried in the snow the day before. Usually, Levi loved rare warmer Alaskan spring days like this, but that morning's brightness only helped to illuminate the shit show he found himself in the middle of.

The evening before, he'd been acting on instinct, following his gut and doing what he thought was the right thing.

That morning, all of the reasons that having Leslie and Selena at the cabin was a bad idea kept replaying over and over in his mind.

And the biggest one was that having Leslie so close was going to be the death of him.

Sleep had been impossible for Levi, lying in his bunk in the room next to where she was no doubt also not sleeping. All he could think about was the kiss and the slightly jealous looks he'd been catching when Selena flirted with him or when she'd seen the messages pop up on his computer screen... Was she actually attracted to him? He'd assumed their kiss had meant nothing to her, but what if it had?

She'd never given him any indication that she might have feelings for him before. But what if...

He groaned. What-ifs could drive a man insane and they

had far more pressing issues at the moment. Like keeping Selena alive and both not losing their careers over it.

He also had the added pressure of the charity fundraiser. The night before he'd filled out the documents that Mrs. Powell had sent to him and scanned and emailed them back to her and it had only made him more nervous. There was no backing out now, but having to come up with a tribute speech to deliver in his best friend's memory at the first event was unnerving. It wasn't that he couldn't sing Dawson's praises or explain what had made him so amazing at his job... It was just that in doing so, it reminded him just how much the guy had meant to him and that only compounded the guilt Levi fought for having feelings for Leslie.

A kiss could never happen again. Nothing could ever happen between them. It didn't matter if she was suddenly seeing him in a different light or not, he couldn't act on his repressed feelings. Not and still be loyal to his buddy's memory. He'd feel like a fraud.

He checked his watch and whistled. "Okay Smokester, time to head back in."

The old dog glanced up at him, then reburied the stick in its hiding place and sauntered on over. He nudged against Levi's leg and he bent to pet the dog. "I'm in trouble, aren't I?" he asked, scratching behind the dog's ears.

Smokester's single bark confirmed it as they stood and headed back inside.

"Ahhhh the puppy," Selena said excitedly, seeing them enter. The night before, Smokester had hidden out in his office, not exactly a fan of strangers, but when Selena stood and patted her legs, encouraging him to go to her, he did. "Oh! You're so pretty! Look at the pretty girl."

Smokester was a male dog, but it seemed irrelevant. The dog didn't take issue with it, rolling onto the living room floor and allowing himself to be adored. "I miss my dog so much... We'll be great friends," Selena told the dog.

With Smokester taken care of, Levi glanced into the women's bunk room on his way to the office, but he didn't see Leslie. The sound of running water coming from the bathroom had him envisioning her in another towel and he quickly dove into the office and shut the door.

Almost immediately there was a knock, then Chad entered. "That woman's making a wuss of our dog," he whispered.

Chad's only issue was that Selena wasn't rubbing *his* belly. The movie star hadn't shown the same flirtatiousness toward his co-worker the night before, and for a guy who thought of himself as a bit of a Casanova, that must have been a hit to Chad's ego. "The dog's not complaining," Levi said, and he was happy that Selena's affection had been turned elsewhere. "What's up?"

"We still need to get out to the Sanders property with a cleanup crew."

Levi nodded. He'd meant to arrange a team that day, but then he'd been preoccupied. And now, the cleanup might have to wait awhile. He couldn't risk bringing in more crew members right now with the women at the cabin. He trusted his team with his life when they were on a mission, but this was different and he'd already put Chad in a compromising position. That was enough. "Yeah, I'll set something up..."

Chad shot him a look, but he didn't say anything as his cell phone chimed with a new text message and he left the office.

"What was that about the cabin?" Leslie asked, entering the office next.

Obviously, she'd heard Chad. The station cabin wasn't

big enough for any kind of privacy. He nodded. "We will have to get a team out there soon to take care of the debris."

She lingered at the door. "Do you know the extent of the damage?"

Unfortunately. He hesitated. She had enough to deal with right now, but there was no point sugarcoating it or keeping the truth from her. "Aerial views show that there's not much left…" he said sympathetically. "Sorry, Leslie."

If she was upset, she hid it well. Something she'd perfected over the years. When he'd first met her as a kid, she'd been so different. Before she'd started dating Dawson and her home life had gotten complicated, she'd been so open, so happy… He'd kill for a glimpse of that girl again.

"I suspected that, anyway…thanks," she said, turning to leave.

He hesitated. "Hey, did you want to go out there?" He wasn't sure if seeing the remnants would make her feel better or worse, but he wanted to give her the option.

She shook her head quickly, her blond ponytail whipping her in the face. "No, that's fine. There's really no point."

"Okay…"

She turned to leave, then stopped. "How would we even get out there?"

So she did care. "We could take one of the Ski-Doos. There are several trails leading that far inland." They weren't well traveled and the snow wouldn't be packed down yet, so it would take the better part of the day. He swallowed hard and forced out any feelings of excitement at the idea of spending the day with her.

He'd just resolved to bury his attraction and not let anything happen between them again. Still, the idea of being alone with her made his heart soar.

She looked less enthusiastic as she bit her lip, then slowly nodded. "Maybe we should. See if there's anything left to salvage."

He knew she was thinking of her father's paintings and photographs that had decorated the walls and he was nervous about what they'd discover. "Sure…give me a couple of minutes, and we can head out."

She nodded then sighed as though having forgotten about their other guest. "What about Selena?"

There was no way he was bringing both of them. They'd have to take separate Ski-Doos and he knew which woman he'd end up riding with. He couldn't deny that he wanted to go with Leslie. Alone. Damn, his pulse was already racing. "Chad's here. He'll keep an eye on her."

"I don't need a babysitter—where the hell would I go?" Selena yelled from the other room, obviously eavesdropping on the conversation.

Levi shrugged. "She's got a point."

"Chad won't mind being left here…?" she asked quietly.

"I mind!" the guy called from the kitchen.

Seriously zero privacy.

Levi shook his head. "He's kidding."

"I'll meet you outside," Leslie said, obviously feeling a desperate need to escape the claustrophobic quarters.

Ten minutes later, Levi had given himself a serious pep talk about boundaries and keeping things light, and the two of them met near the back shed where the Ski-Doos were parked. He climbed on and started the engine, the machine revving to life before he reached behind him for two helmets and handed one to Leslie.

He'd loaned her a ski suit from the cabin's supply room and despite it being two sizes too big for her, she looked insanely hot wearing it. The ends of her blond hair sticking out from under the hat blew softly in the wind and the overwhelming urge to grab her and kiss her and see if he'd imagined the spark between them was strong.

So much for the pep talk. Luckily, he didn't expect her to make the same impulsive mistake again. He was relying on that.

She put the helmet on and then tossed one leg over the seat, climbing on behind him. Levi braced himself and waited for her arms to wrap around his waist, but a quick glance over his shoulder revealed that she was holding on to the handles in the back instead.

Probably for the best.

He didn't need the extra distraction. The proximity to her and her thighs against his hips even with layers of fabric between them was enough.

"Ready?" he asked.

"Let's go," she said.

He started toward the trail leading south toward the lake. Visibility was clear and the thick wet snow on the trail made for a smoother ride. Thank God, because the ride was rough enough. Keeping his eyes straight ahead and his hands on the bars was a challenge.

"Why are you driving like my grandmother?" Leslie called over the roar of the machine.

The trash talk caught him by surprise. It was the first thing she'd said to him that wasn't full of tension or awkwardness. The slightly teasing tone gave him far more hope than it should have. He shot a quick glance at her over his shoulder and hit the gas harder. A little too abruptly. She flew backward slightly and reached out for him before she could fall off the back of the Ski-Doo. "What was that about my driving?" he called back as her arms encircled his waist. Another quick look at her revealed she was smiling and it nearly took his breath away. This was the first time he'd seen that smile since she'd arrived. And it was directed at him…or this activity anyway.

He didn't care if he had to fly over the snowy trails; he was determined to keep that smile on her face as long as possible.

LESLIE'S ARMS TIGHTENED around Levi as he drove even faster down the tree-lined trail, snow blowing up all around them. The adrenaline pumping through her from the speed and exhilarating ride gave her an almost euphoric feeling, one she desperately wanted to last as long as possible. The wind whipping against her cheeks, the motor vibrating between her legs and the small bumps and hills along the way that added an extra element of excitement to the ride had her heart feeling a little lighter than it had in a week.

The smile on her face was definitely new. She hadn't even been able to force a convincing one in days, but right now she couldn't help but enjoy the moment, the sense of freedom and letting go—while she held on tight to Levi.

Her chest pressed up against his back and her thighs clutching his hips added a sensuality to the moment that she wished she could explain…or at least understand.

She'd been on the back of Ski-Doos and Sea-Doos and dirt bikes with Levi a million times over the years, but it had never felt this intimate.

Her mind told her she needed to get a grip, focus on what was important and not let anyone from her past get too close while she was stuck there. Her heart told her she might not have any say.

Levi was breaking her down bit by bit. She'd crumbled completely two nights before in his hotel room and unfortunately the wall she'd rebuilt around herself seemed to be made of straw. And more and more of it was being blown away in the wind the kinder Levi was, the more considerate, the more helpful and understanding.

As much as she didn't want to need him, she did and that was leading to a whole lot of other confusing emotions within her.

She moved even closer, breathing in the scent of his familiar cologne on his jacket. The smell combined with the feel of his muscular body beneath the coat had her body reacting in ways it really shouldn't be. She clenched her thighs around him—the vibration from the Ski-Doo was definitely not helping the situation.

Selena was right. Levi was hot.

But Levi was also her former best friend. Her former *fiancé's* best friend too. This attraction to him was not right. Oh God, what would have happened if he hadn't pushed her away the other night? She'd be feeling guilty and embarrassed and awkward on top of everything else right now. Even more so. Thankfully, he'd had enough wits about him to see the impulsiveness of the situation for what it was… Still, his rejection stung. He didn't want her? Not even in the context of a one-night fling that would mean nothing?

She took a deep breath and loosened her hold on him a little.

Levi was just a friend from her past helping her out in a shitty situation. Nothing more. He couldn't possibly be more than that. She needed to remember that and not fall into the trap of vulnerability that would swallow her up before she had an opportunity to escape Wild River once again.

STOPPING IN FRONT of the cabin a few hours later, Levi turned off the Ski-Doo and removed his helmet.

About halfway there, he'd felt the atmosphere around them completely change. Leslie had stopped laughing, stopped smiling. She'd retreated once again. For a brief time, she'd had her body wrapped around him and he could feel the chemistry sizzling between them on the adrenaline rush through the woodsy trail. Then suddenly, it disappeared. Her body had tensed, she pulled away, creating as much of a gap as possible between them, and her mood had sobered. He had no idea what she was going through and the emotional roller-coaster ride she seemed to be on. She seemed hell-bent on keeping her guard up and he wondered what would have happened had he let something happen between them two nights before. Would she have continued to open up to him? Or would she have retreated even further?

Leslie avoided his gaze now as she removed her helmet and scanned what was left of her family's cabin. Charred logs and wood beams, broken glass and roof tiles littered the plot of land where it had stood. Pieces of unsalvageable furniture, kitchen appliances nearly unrecognizable in the places where they'd once been inside the cabin. Everything else—photos, clothing, fabrics had been reduced to ash, covered by freshly fallen snow. It was tough to see and Levi swallowed the large lump forming in the back of his throat.

Leslie walked toward it, careful not to fall between cracks in the rubble, and stood among the remains of some of their best childhood memories.

Should he go to her? Would she appreciate that? Or did he give her space? Give her this time to process?

He wanted to go to her, provide any support or comfort she needed, but he suspected she wanted a moment alone and he couldn't trust himself not to cross another line, so he moved farther away, examining the extent of the wildlife damage caused by the fire. They'd reached it early enough that the burn through the surrounding forest was minimal. They'd contained the damage to the wildlife, but unfortunately they hadn't been able to save the cabin. Cleanup wouldn't require much... He and Chad could handle it.

He still couldn't believe it was gone. It had been a big part of his past—amazing memories had been made there, summer days and nights he'd never forget. Now it was gone and it was just another part of their shared past that he and Leslie no longer had.

Slowly, everything tying them together was disappearing and soon the only thing that would remain would be the completely useless feelings he had for her. And those had never been enough.

Everything was gone.

Standing among the remnants of the cabin, Leslie was staggered by the force of the sentiments hitting her. It was just a cabin—four log walls and old furniture. In reality, the furniture fabrics had all faded to become unrecognizable, a lingering musty smell from the fires and wet clothing sitting on them, the beds had been uncomfortable paper-thin mattresses with springs sticking out and old wooden frames, the kitchen appliances were green and dated, having been owned by her grandmother. All items that no one had any reason to feel bad about losing; they were well past their expiration date. She hadn't been there in years. If she hadn't come back with Selena now, it could have been many more years before she'd be there again. Feeling this distraught was silly. It was just stuff. Stuff from her past. Stuff she'd already walked away from.

Yet the deep ache in her chest made it difficult to breathe in the frigid air.

It was as though the cabin burning had taken with it the memories she'd tried to repress, ignore, forget. Now they were rushing back, reminding her that she hadn't held on to them, cherished them…just like the cabin itself and now they were slipping away for real—unappreciated.

"I'm sorry." Levi's voice beside her made her jump. He'd been so quiet, she'd almost forgotten she wasn't alone. How long had she just been standing there? Obviously she looked wrecked, because the sympathy on his face said he was worried about her.

That was the last thing she needed or wanted. She cleared her throat quietly. "It's nothing. We barely used the place anymore and most of it was old junk anyway. Stuff Mom didn't want in the house anymore. Nothing of value."

"Maybe not monetary value, but this place definitely meant something to you and your family. To me too."

There were too many emotions, too much meaning in his words and in his tone. She shifted uncomfortably under the intensity in his gaze as she shrugged. "Sometimes it's better to have no other choice than to let go of something. Mom should have sold this land back to the city years ago. It's in the middle of nowhere and too hard to even get to, especially in winter." She heard herself making excuses, giving reasons to not feel so bad and just hoped they sounded like she actually believed them.

Levi studied her, his expression telling her he wasn't buying her act. But he remained silent instead of calling her out, which somehow annoyed her even more. As though he didn't want to hurt her or start a fight. As though she might be fragile.

She placed her hands on her hips. "What?"

He shook his head. "Nothing."

"You obviously have something to say, so go ahead."

He blew out a long deep breath, the cold creating a white fog around his head as he said, "You really don't care?"

"Why would I care, Levi? I haven't been here in forever." And the last time she had, the place had started to lose its charm. The summer of her lost innocence with the miscarriage had almost been like lifting a veil off her childhood and she no longer saw the cabin as a safe, fun place. It was here that she'd missed her period and had started to suspect. It was here that she'd cried herself to sleep with worry that long summer weekend. It was where she'd had a blowout fight with her mother when she'd accused her of moping around and ruining the weekend for everyone else. She just needed to keep remembering those times at the cabin and the pain of the loss would ease a little. "This was just a part of my past."

"A big part," he said, pushing on. "I remember. You used to love this place...more than anyone else in your family. You couldn't wait for school to let out to get here. Swimming and fishing in the lake with your dad in summer, ice fishing in winter, hiking and taking all of those amazing photographs..."

"Stop!" Damn it, too loud, too forceful, but he'd struck a nerve. Exactly the way he'd been trying to. Memories of her dad were sacred to her and she didn't appreciate him using them to get to her.

He clamped his lips together, obviously realizing he'd gone too far.

"Don't try to make me feel like a bad person just because I've moved on, learned to let go of things," she said. What choice did she have? Things were ripped away; things were lost whether people wanted to let go of them or not. Life had taught her that cruel lesson time and time again.

This cabin was the most recent symbol of how nothing in life lasted forever.

Levi shook his head and lowered his gaze to the ground. "That wasn't my intention. I'm sorry."

Intention or not, he'd gotten to her. He was right; this place had meant something in good times and in bad and it was devastating to know there would be no going back. No opportunity to recreate old memories or make new ones.

Levi stepped toward her and placed his hands on her shoulders. His eyes beneath snow-covered eyelashes burned deep into hers and he gently touched her cool cheek. The warm, gentle caress was intimate and full of affection. "I'm sorry," he said again and the apology seemed to linger heavy in the air, full of unspoken intention.

Her heart picked up its pace and her sadness was overshadowed by a different feeling entirely. An unsettling connection simmered around them as his hand lingered on her face. She stared at Levi, questioning his action, questioning his motive... Was he once again just trying to get her to open up as a friend? Or was there something more going on between them? Her body's reaction to him in recent days was definitely something she couldn't pretend wasn't happening. And if things were just friendly between them, why was the urge to kiss him so strong?

Was he simply trying to be there for her or was he feeling this attraction too?

Neither was what she needed right now.

She shook her head and stepped quickly away from his touch, stumbling over a charred log. "You need to stop with these mixed signals," she said and winced. Damn, why had she said that? Why open up this conversation at all?

"Me?" He looked genuinely confused. "Mixed signals?"

"Yes. You rejected me the other night in the hotel room and then you keep sending these…vibes… I don't know." *Jesus, Leslie, just stop talking. Let the subject drop.*

"I didn't reject you. I put the brakes on before you did something you'd regret." His tone was defensive and frustrated as though he were tired of protecting her.

Well, she hadn't asked him to. "I'm a grown-ass woman, Levi. You don't need to protect me from myself," she said, her annoyance rising. He'd always taken on that role of protector, always looking out for her and Dawson, whether they needed him to or not. He'd assumed a big brother position in the group, keeping them all on the straight and narrow. And while she might be at the mercy of accepting his help with Selena, she didn't need him acting like a martyr regarding her feelings.

He ran a hand through his hair and looked almost defeated as he said, "Maybe it wasn't you I was protecting. Maybe I was looking out for myself."

Her pulse raced through her veins as she stared at him. "What are you talking about?" He'd been completely in the driver's seat. Manipulating her feelings until she broke, then pushing her away when she'd given in to the desire of wanting him.

"Damn it, Leslie." His voice rose slightly and he stared at her like she was completely obtuse. "Maybe I didn't want to have sex with the woman I've been in love with my entire life while her mind and heart are still with my best friend." The raw frustration in his voice was something she'd never heard directed at her before. Things between them had always been light, friendly, caring. He'd never sounded so completely destroyed before—and yet, he'd said *love*.

Shock made her completely numb to the cold wind and

their devastating surroundings as she struggled to process what he'd just said. "Love?" Had he really said he was *in love* with her, not simply that he loved her, which would have been a reason for not having sex with her that she could have understood. But, in love? That made no sense at all. Since when? Why? What the hell was happening?

"Yeah," he said with a sigh. "Love. I love you. I always have."

So the attraction between them was real, but it went deeper than just a physical lust. At least on his end. She knew her feelings about him were different in the last few days, but she couldn't pin them down. Stress and exhaustion were taking their toll and there was a lot at stake. She was fighting nostalgia and heartache and her defenses were down... But there was no way she was in love with Levi. He was her friend. Dawson's friend.

They couldn't be in love.

"Look, I know the timing on this confession isn't great, and I already regret telling you..."

Why did that sting? She wished she didn't know, that he hadn't told her. It just confused and complicated the hell out of things even more. Yet, his regret was worse.

"That came out wrong," he said, reading her expression correctly. "I just meant, I know you have a lot to deal with right now and adding more to it wasn't my..."

"Intent," she finished, her tone distant, cold. All his good intentions could go to hell. She didn't need him to help her feel something again. She was desperately trying not to feel anything at all because if she opened herself up to one emotion, they'd all spiral right out of her control and she couldn't lose that right now.

"Leslie, I'm sorry I told you. I was... I don't know. Tired of holding it in maybe. Wanting to help you understand why I didn't..." His voice, full of emotion, trailed as he reached out to her.

She moved away. She refused to let him touch her. She couldn't do this with him. He wouldn't get inside her head or her heart. She was tired of losing the things she cared about and she'd already left Levi in the past along with every other heartache.

He was in love with her.

To say it was the last thing she'd ever expected would be an understatement.

She scanned her surroundings, overwhelmed and unsure what to say or do. She headed back toward the Ski-Doo and listened for his footsteps behind her. She just wanted to get away from this place. Needed to get as far away as she could.

Seeing it, being there with him had only made her question just how much she really had left the past in the past and moved on, the way she claimed.

CHAPTER FOURTEEN

THE AXE CAME down hard, splitting the log in two, the sound echoing across the forest, but not loud enough to drown out the thoughts in Levi's head.

He had to be the dumbest man on earth. Confessing his twenty-year-old feelings for Leslie now? In the middle of this huge mess she was in? Quite literally standing among a mess that used to be her family's cabin?

What the hell was wrong with him?

This situation was already so far out of control and could implode at any second and he went and made it worse.

Smokester lay on the ground a few feet away, playing with his stick. His brown tail flopped back and forth and his pointy ears were piqued. The dog sensed Levi was in a mood and shot him a look occasionally that suggested he needed to sort his shit out fast because he'd like to go back inside but wouldn't leave him alone out there.

"You can go in," he told the dog. Levi couldn't. Not yet.

The dog just sighed and collapsed onto his paws and closed his eyes.

Levi replaced the log and swung again, split pieces of wood falling in opposite directions. Chopping wood usually gave him a sense of accomplishment and the physical exertion was the only way to get his frustration out. Plus, he needed to stay out of the cabin. Away from Leslie. The space had gone from feeling small to feeling impossibly claustrophobic.

Mixed signals.

She'd accused *him* of that?

She was the one who'd kissed him, who'd tried to have sex with him... He'd been trying to protect her from making a mistake. Because he sure as hell knew she hadn't been acting on feelings as deep as his were for her.

That had been confirmed by the look on her face after his confession.

He swung hard over and over again, cutting more wood than they'd need all year. Sweat pooled on his lower back and dripped down his forehead, but he kept cutting.

He didn't know what else to do. She obviously wanted nothing to do with him and now he'd pissed her off and pushed her away even more. Talking to her about it, trying to explain wouldn't help. He'd kept his feelings a secret for so long, he wasn't even sure what he could say. And putting all of this on her now had been a horrible lapse in judgment.

He should never have tried to get her to open up. He'd been selfish in wanting his friend back...in any capacity. He missed her. He still loved her. But he needed to accept the fact that he still was nowhere close to getting her back in his life.

And maybe he never would.

SHE WOULD NOT go out there. It was just asking for trouble.

Leslie stood in the living room window of the station watching Levi chop firewood near the back shed. He'd removed his jacket and the sight of the sweat at his lower back on the tight gray T-shirt he wore made Leslie a little flushed as well. Where had this attraction to him come from? And why couldn't she shake it off? There had been undeniable chemistry sizzling between them on the Ski-Doo, but she'd blamed it on the adrenaline rush. Then when he'd touched her cheek, there had been a definite spark, but combined with the emotional sight of her destroyed cabin, she couldn't be sure that electricity between them meant anything.

But she was running out of excuses for the way her body was suddenly reacting to Levi.

And he loved her. He'd always loved her.

That had her mind and heart in an even more conflicting battle.

Common sense said stay as far away as possible, fight the physical attraction she had for him even more. Leading him on and hurting him when she couldn't return the feelings would be wrong. But she had no idea what to do with his revelation. Why had he never told her? Why tell her now? They couldn't be together now any more than they could have been before.

But two things were obvious—her heart wanted her friend back and her body wanted her friend.

He swung the axe and his biceps and forearm muscles tensed and contracted and her mouth watered. The block of wood broke apart, falling away from the log, and Levi reached for a new one. His ass was sexy as hell and his big, thick hamstrings were strong and sturdy as he bent to retrieve the broken pieces.

No one she'd met since Dawson had attracted her like this. Not Eoghan, not any man she'd met in LA. So why was the one man she really shouldn't want leaving her overcome with a desire to have him?

He lifted his gaze and it met hers through the frosty windowpane. The burning intensity could have defrosted the entire forest around them. He stood staring at her for a long moment, his chest rising and falling with his exertion, and Leslie held her own breath, lost in a moment of indecision.

Levi turned away and she released the air she'd been holding as she watched him pick up an armful of wood and head into the shed.

As he closed the door behind him, he cast a final…inviting look in her direction.

Damn it… They needed to talk, clear the air, get things straight. Otherwise, being in this cabin together would be impossible. She couldn't ignore how they were both feeling and hope it would go away. Maybe if they talked about it, they could diffuse the situation before things got even more out of hand.

She reached for her jacket and checked quickly on Selena napping in their bunk room before slipping out the back door and heading across the path to the shed. The snow crunching beneath her boots did nothing to drown out the pounding of her heart in her ears and the cold wind couldn't cool the heat coursing through her body.

She hesitated at the shed door, then opened it and went inside before she could talk herself out of it. "Hey… I think we need to talk."

Levi didn't turn around, just continued stacking the wood in a pile near the wall. "Leslie, either do what you came in here to do or get out. I've got work to do."

Her mouth dropped, but her body was on autopilot and in less than a second, she was turning him around to face her. Standing on tiptoes, she gripped his cheeks between her hands and kissed him. Hard. Desperate. With purpose. It wasn't an act of unplanned impulsivity. It was done with a clear head, if not a clear heart.

Frustration and confusion were all there in the kiss. On both ends. But he didn't pull away and neither did she.

He lifted her up and she wrapped her legs around his waist as she deepened the kiss, searching for…what? The reason she was doing this, maybe? Testing him to see if he'd put on the brakes again?

He pulled back abruptly as though reading her very thoughts. "If you were expecting me to show restraint again, I'm sorry, but that won't be happening this time," he said, his voice deep and gruff with an unconcealed desire.

For her.

She swallowed hard, her mind reeling as she met his gaze full on.

What should she do?

Listen to her body that was screaming for him or continue to follow her common sense as it rattled off the million reasons why this was such a bad idea?

"I know what I want and I'm exhausted from fighting it, so this time it's all on you," he said.

Shit. She was going for it.

Her entire life was in chaos right now anyway, how much worse could it get?

She crushed his mouth with hers again and reached for the edge of his sweaty T-shirt. She raised it up over his abs and chest and he allowed her to remove one arm at a time, still holding her beneath her ass and only briefly breaking contact with her mouth to yank the shirt over his head for her. His strength was sexy. Being so strong herself, it took a man like Levi—rock hard, solid and sturdy—to make her feel like she'd met her match.

Her hands roamed over the sculpted muscles in his shoulders and back, then along the front of his pecs and down his incredible washboard abs.

Damn, he rivaled every hot guy in LA. Every hot guy anywhere.

She wouldn't try to make sense of what was happening. Seeing Levi in a different light. Wanting him in a different way. Her body was taking over and Leslie wasn't willing to fight her attraction any longer.

She wanted Levi, right now, in this moment, and she was going to let herself have him. She'd worry about the consequences later...much later.

He backed them up to the wooden work table and swiped the tools from the top. He lowered her down onto it and buried his head into the crook of her neck. Soft, wet kisses along her neck, her ear, her collarbone. "You smell amazing," he murmured against her skin, his breath making her shiver. He removed her jacket and then her sweater, looking at her briefly for confirmation.

She nodded and he continued his trail of kisses across her chest.

Leslie arched her back, enjoying the feel of his lips against her skin, the rough graze of his short beard along her soft flesh. It had been so long since she'd had a sexy hunk of a man like Levi desiring her, enjoying her.

When his head dipped even lower to her cleavage, she tangled her hands into his hair, holding his head there. His tongue licked along the swell of her breast as he reached behind to unclasp the bra. "If you're going to stop me, please do it now."

She didn't.

He lowered the straps slowly down her arms and Leslie's body trembled with the chill in the shed and the anticipation of his touch. He paused to look at her, the unconcealed lust in his expression surprising her... Had he always been this attracted to her? How had he kept it to himself for so long? She'd never felt uncomfortable around him. She'd never imagined his feelings ran deeper than friendship. He'd never made her feel uncomfortable at all.

He'd hid his real feelings for her sake...for her happiness. Content to be there for her in whatever way he could.

"Why didn't you ever...?" She wasn't sure why she needed to know, but she did.

"Tell you?"

She nodded.

"Because I loved you more than I desired you," he said hoarsely and her breath caught.

He must have loved her a lot then, because his desire for her was evident. He was straining against the front of his jeans and she tentatively reached forward, cupping him through the fabric. He was so hard already and the size of him did not disappoint.

Her pulse raced. It had been a long time since just the touch of a penis had her body reacting, aching... What would it feel like to have him inside of her?

He took one nipple into his mouth and she closed her eyes, savoring the feel of his warm mouth on her, the tantalizing flick of his tongue over the bud. With his hands, he massaged both. Then he took the other nipple and worked it into a hard bud.

She could feel her underwear getting wet and she reached for the button on his jeans. She undid them and pushed the fabric down over his hips. His cock stood out straight in his underwear and she swallowed hard.

She didn't want to stop. For the first time in so long she felt something other than pain. She was no longer numb. Her heart beating wildly in her chest and the desire coursing through her veins made her feel very much alive.

Levi was making her feel alive.

Was it just the situation—the familiarity and comfortable way Levi made her feel—or was it something more? Could her former best friend actually be the only one who could help bring her back to life? And was it fair of her to allow him to?

Too many questions and no answers.

He lifted her down from the table and reached for the waistband on her leggings. He slowly slid them down over her hips, over her ass, down her thighs, then he lifted her back onto the table and wedged himself between her legs. His cock pressed against her through their underwear and she could feel his wetness join hers.

She wanted him inside of her so badly, but their impulsive move meant no protection, so this would have to satisfy them for now. She wouldn't try to pretend that this would be the only time.

Levi gripped her ass and pulled her forward until she was grinding on him, up and down...over and over again. She clung to his shoulders, her nails digging in as the arousal mounted and her breath became labored.

Levi's grip tightened on her ass and he quickened her movements, his head buried into her neck. He continued to kiss and suck and lick, his actions becoming more frantic, more desperate as she rode him harder.

Her mouth was dry but sweat covered her entire body as her breasts rubbed against his rock-solid chest and her thighs brushed against his.

"Damn, I want to be inside you," he said.

"I want you inside me," she whispered. She wanted to be as close to him as possible. Feel him fill her. All of him. All of her. This was hardly enough.

He pushed hard against her as she ground even faster, feeling her orgasm rise to nearly a breaking point. "Levi..." she said, holding on to him tighter like a life preserver when she thought she might float away…be lost…once again. He was the grounding rock she needed. The one he always was for her, and right now, she wouldn't let go.

He groaned his own release the same time she felt the first ripples of orgasm erupt inside of her. Her body trembled and Levi's grip on her ass tightened even more as he held her still, as his head fell forward onto her shoulder and he moaned his final release.

She fought for a breath as she enjoyed the last sensations of pleasure flowing through her. Her grip on him relaxed, but she didn't move away or release him completely. A tornado of emotions raged through her and she waited for the reality of what they'd just done to set in, for the high to dissipate…but all she felt was a euphoria that erased all other sensations.

"Gotta say, I didn't think you'd call my bluff like that," Levi said, gently, pulling back slightly to look at her. He brushed her hair away from her face and studied her for any sign of regret or guilt.

He wouldn't find any…at least not yet.

LEVI WAS COMING down from the high and didn't know what to do with himself. He'd just had sex with his best friend. No matter how many times he repeated it to himself, it felt surreal, like he'd imagined it, like it had only happened in one of his fantasies. He struggled to believe it had actually happened.

They hadn't said much afterward, both not really knowing what to say. And now back inside the cabin, the tight quarters with Leslie had him inventing make-work projects to stay in his office and away from her.

He had no regrets, but the guilt was hitting him a lot harder than he'd told himself it would. No amount of reasoning or excuses was easing the heaviness in his chest during a time when he wanted to be celebrating. He'd been with the woman he'd always loved. She'd opened herself up to him. Her body at least. Just a little... He should be the happiest man on earth.

But if he was feeling this conflicted, she had to be as well.

Which was a double kick to the groin.

Maybe he shouldn't have goaded her the way he had. Maybe he should never have told her the truth about how he felt. Maybe he shouldn't have allowed things to go this far...

He ran a hand through his hair in frustration.

Disappointment in himself and his actions mixed with annoyance. Why the hell did he always have to sacrifice what he wanted? Why did he always have to be the good guy? The honorable guy who was so fucking heartbroken and miserable?

Life had determined this situation they found themselves in. Fate had intervened in a cruel way to allow him this opportunity to be with her. But the fact of the matter was that it sucked. Getting the girl of his dreams by default and at such a high cost was not the way he wanted to finally have love, be accepted, get his own chance at happiness.

He sighed as he glanced through the open blinds of his office to the living room, where Leslie was using his laptop. Damn, she was so beautiful, so amazing...and despite the guilt, his body reacted to her again already. Remembering her kiss, her urgency, the way her hands had caressed his body...his entire body.

What was she thinking? What was she feeling?

Did she want to continue exploring what they'd opened themselves up to in the shed just moments before? Or had one impulsive time with him been enough? Would her common sense kick in? Or was she ready to consider a new future—with him in it. Not as her friend, but as something more.

And when all of this was over, where would they go from here?

The unknown and the uncertainty were terrifying. He'd taken a leap of faith into stormy waves and he just hoped he could breathe with his head underwater.

Right now, he'd give them both a little space and time—as much as physically possible given the circumstances. If she wanted to talk or needed him, she knew where to find him. He'd move at her pace, on her agenda.

Approaching the office door, he shut it a little too hard and loud and closed the window blinds to block the sight of her.

Then he collapsed onto his sofa next to a sleeping Smokester and allowed all the years of unexpressed heartache to come crashing in all around him.

OH SHIT, OH SHIT, oh shit...

Levi was obviously spiraling. The loud bang of his office door had Leslie frozen. Was he pissed? Was he annoyed? Had she done something wrong?

Well, obviously it hadn't been the right thing. Having sex with him was arguably the dumbest thing she could have done. She felt guilty as shit, but she wasn't really regretting her actions. Or at least, she hadn't been...

What did she do? Go to him and talk about what happened?

And say what?

She had no idea where they went from here or what it had meant.

"What's his problem?" Selena asked, coming up behind

her with a meaty-looking sandwich that was definitely not vegan or gluten-free.

"I have no idea." That much was true. It could be that he regretted what happened or it could be that he was annoyed at her for the impulsive act, then her not being able to reciprocate feelings beyond a physical connection.

But what did he expect?

She'd only recently learned he had feelings for her. She'd kept her own heart guarded for so long, it had been a huge step just allowing herself a brief moment of connection in any way with a man—with her best friend.

She loved Levi...but could she ever have the same feelings for him that he had for her? Could she ever be *in love* with him? She didn't know. She'd never allowed herself to think of him in that way before.

And now she knew she was attracted to him...but real love? Like what she'd had before...

"I thought actresses didn't eat carbs," she said grumpily.

"I eat carbs. Don't project your prejudices against skinny, rich, famous people on me," Selena said, sitting next to her. "Besides, this is gluten-free. Levi got Chad to pick some up at the grocery store when he was made aware of my dietary requirements."

Oh, for the love of... Why was everyone catering to the star? First her brother with his cauliflower substitute risotto and now Chad? In LA everyone did what Selena wanted— sure they were paid to, but here in Wild River people were expected to fend for themselves. No one had ever doted on Leslie this way. Not that she wanted them to.

"Can we look up TMZ?" Selena asked, moving even closer to see the laptop.

Leslie inched away. "No."

"Entertainment Weekly?"

Leslie sighed. "No." The last thing she needed at that moment was to see her face with a wanted sticker all over the internet. For a brief respite out in the shed, she'd forgotten all about the mess she was in, the stalker trying to kill her client and the fact that they were thousands of miles away from where they needed to be and that sooner or later they'd have to go back.

"How was the cabin?" Selena asked, with a mouthful of sandwich.

"Completely destroyed," Leslie said, feeling yet another tug at her chest and not entirely because of the cabin.

Levi loved her—she still couldn't quite believe it.

"Is that what's got you upset?" the star asked carefully, any trace of her annoying self disappearing.

It would be easier to allow her to think that was all it was, but Selena looked remorseful when she glanced at her. "No…that's not it. I'm just trying to figure out a way to get us out of this mess as quickly as possible."

And put some distance between her and Levi before she could do something stupid like fall in love.

SELENA ENTERED HIS office and closed the door behind her.

Oh no… If the star tried flirting with him again right now, Levi might actually have a nervous meltdown. "Hey, I'm just in the middle of…"

"What did you do to make Leslie even more annoyed?" she interrupted.

Oh, he was to blame for that? The way he remembered it, it had been her who came out to the shed, her who had initiated the kiss—and other things. He'd warned her, given her time to change her mind. She hadn't.

He folded his arms across his chest as he leaned back in his chair. "What makes you think I did something?"

"Because both of you are acting even more awkward and tense around one another since the ride out to the cabin."

The woman was perceptive. But it was since the mind-blowing sex in the shed that things had been more awkward. Like neither of them knew what to do or say to one another. What did you say to your off-limits best friend after crossing a line like that?

"Did you two have an argument?" Selena asked when he wasn't forthcoming with information.

The opposite actually. They'd connected in a different way, a much deeper, raw, emotional way. And they were both shaken up about it. And now neither of them knew how to handle it or what to do next. "Sort of... I guess," he said. He wasn't going to tell Selena the truth. That would be up to Leslie and so far, he got the impression that she really wasn't trying to form any sort of friendship with her client. He understood that. Keeping someone safe relied heavily on being aware and cognizant and not blinded by emotion in times of extreme decision making. Life-or-death decisions couldn't be made effectively if Selena was too close...

"Well, if we all have to be cooped up inside here together, you need to apologize and make it up to her because she's even more unbearable than before."

"Apologize and make it up to her?" For giving her the orgasm that she asked for? This was bullshit. He wouldn't do it. She was the one who was playing with his heart and real emotions. She knew how he felt about her now. It hadn't just been sex for him. In fact, it was because he cared so much about her that he'd rejected her advances the first time. He wasn't sure what had gotten into him when she'd come out to the shed.

Part of him had thought she would never do it. Another

part was hoping there was a deeper meaning in it for her as well.

Which would be another kind of problem.

He'd always had to deal with unrequited love, hiding his feelings and feeling guilty over them... What would he do if there was a real chance for them? If they actually decided to give a relationship beyond friendship a go? Could he do that? Or would his loyalty to Dawson prevent him from allowing his own happiness?

Either way, this new source of conflict was Leslie's fault.

Nope, he wouldn't apologize and he wouldn't suck up to her...

"Look, you're the man," Selena said, "and whether you're right or wrong, it needs to be you who caves first, because Leslie won't and this elephant in the room will just spiral and grow bigger until we are all grumpy and ready to kill one another."

Unfortunately, she was right. The tension in the cabin was nearing an unbearable level already. "Fine. I'll apologize to her," he said through clenched teeth. And tell her straight out that their actions were a mistake; she didn't have to tell him that. And that he could control himself in the future and give her the space she'd been asking for all along. It wouldn't be happening again. Despite how badly he wanted it to.

"That's not enough. You need to do something nice for her," Selena said. Her own attraction to him obviously fading, was she now moving on to matchmaker? He wasn't sure which Selena he preferred. Both were slightly irritating.

Levi sighed. "Leslie's not the type to want a big elaborate gesture..." She hated flowers and surprises and didn't like jewelry. She'd be only more annoyed at him if he groveled.

Selena rolled her eyes. "Just because a woman doesn't come across as needy and demanding and soft doesn't mean she doesn't want to feel appreciated. Feel like she matters."

Leslie was so appreciated and she definitely mattered. Given the chance, he'd show her that she was the only thing that ever had to him. "Well, what do you suggest I do?" he said tightly.

Selena seemed motivated by having something to plan. "You should make her a nice dinner. She hasn't eaten much in days...stressed out and all."

"Dinner here?" The cabin wasn't exactly a five-star restaurant and definitely didn't give off a romantic vibe. Besides, Selena and Chad were there as well and if they needed to talk, Levi knew neither of them would want an audience.

"Yes. But not in here. Out in the yard, surrounded by a view of the mountains. It's a clear sky out there, so a picnic would be perfect." Selena was obviously as romantic as the characters she played in movies. Her eyes had taken on a dreamlike quality as she talked.

But reality check. "A picnic in minus-four-degree weather?" He wasn't a genius when it came to women, but he could confidently say that he doubted most wanted to freeze to death while trying to eat.

"Not completely outside. In an igloo. I saw one in the supply closet when I was helping Chad put new gear away earlier today."

Levi frowned, then realization dawned. The inflatable igloo that Chad had bought to sleep in on nights when the aurora borealis was at its clearest in this part of Alaska. It was completely transparent and would shelter them from the elements while still providing an amazing view of the scenery and night sky. Still, he hesitated. "I'm not sure..."

"I'm telling you, it's perfect. These dinner-under-the-stars dates are all the rage in LA. They pop up all over the city and within hours, it's impossible to secure reservations. And the scenery is hardly as breathtaking as it is out here." Selena refused to be deterred.

Levi wasn't sold. Would Leslie like that? She had been avoiding him as much as he'd been avoiding her since they'd come back inside. Would she agree to have dinner with him? A real dinner, just the two of them, alone, under the stars? "She might be too pissed to agree to it."

"Then we keep it a surprise until everything is set up. She'll come around. Trust me," Selena said with a confident smile.

He saw no point in arguing. He was fairly certain the star was used to getting her way in the end and he was just relieved she was no longer suggesting the dinner for the two of them. "Okay," he said, reluctantly.

"Great! I'll go distract Leslie and you get the igloo ready." She opened the door to leave, then turned back. "Remember—don't say anything until it's ready."

Levi nodded but unfortunately, he knew his best friend better than Selena did and he wasn't sure this surprise dinner was what she wanted. Then again, he had no idea what she wanted and he refused to even give himself the glimmer of hope that someday it could be him.

CHAPTER FIFTEEN

SELENA HAD LOCKED her out of the cabin. She'd literally pushed her outside and shut the door when Leslie had refused to go outside to see the full moon.

She banged on the door now. "Selena, open the door. I've seen the moon a thousand times."

"Look again because I don't think you're really seeing it," the star called out, shooting her a pointed look through the tiny glass windowpane.

What the hell did that mean?

She was in no mood to figure out what Selena was talking about. She looked up at the night sky, which was clear and full of stars, but the moon was far from full. "You need to check your astronomy chart again—that's not a full moon." And even if it was, staring at it wouldn't provide any clarity to her conflicted state. All afternoon, she'd barely seen Levi. They were clearly avoiding one another and the longer the silence went on, the harder it was to find a way to talk. She'd tried to focus on the case, but her mind kept wandering to their rendezvous in the shed and even calling Eoghan hadn't helped as he hadn't answered her call. She was desperate not to read too much into that, but she sensed she was losing her eyes and ears in LA. "Selena, let me in!"

Instead, Selena just waved.

Levi cleared his throat behind her and she jumped. "Oh thank God," she said, turning to face him. "Can you unlock…?" She stopped, really seeing him then. Showered, hair gelled back away from his face, his beard trimmed so it was neat and tidy… He was dressed in jeans and his winter coat, a black crew neck sweater visible underneath and he looked gorgeously nervous.

Like he was up to something.

She glanced back at Selena and saw her wink at Levi.

Great. They were both up to something.

"What's going on?" she asked cautiously. Had Levi told Selena about their time together in the shed? Had he convinced the star to help him try to…what? Seduce her? Too late for that. She hadn't exactly needed much seducing to attack him earlier that day.

"Um… I was hoping you'd join me for dinner," he said, looking unsure.

Ah, so this had been Selena's idea. Had her client felt the energy shift around her and Levi that day? "Dinner?"

"Yeah, out here…well, actually," he gently guided her around the side of the cabin, "in there." He pointed to an inflatable igloo structure set up in the yard behind the cabin. Inside, she could see several blankets set up and cushions from the couch. Tea lights illuminated the space in a romantic glow and a picnic dinner sat in the middle of it all.

Her heart raced.

A picnic under the stars. With Levi.

"You did all that?" For her? Holy shit, her emotions were going wild. It was the nicest thing a man had ever done for her. Ever. Dawson hadn't exactly been the romantic wine and dine type.

Neither was she. She'd never been the type to want wooing and a man to put in effort to impress her, but her reaction to this was betraying. Obviously some part of her did want someone to make an effort.

He nodded. "Selena suggested it, but I put it together, yeah." He cleared his throat. "If it's a bad idea—if you'd rather not…"

"No!" She forced a calming breath. "It looks…really nice."

He smiled and it simultaneously eased some of the tension that had been simmering between them all day and increased it tenfold.

He looked so good and she was a mess. Not having expected this.

Thanks for the heads-up, Selena.

Though no doubt the secrecy was so that she couldn't preemptively refuse. They both knew her well and she was grateful they hadn't told her.

Levi led the way to the igloo and unzipped the door. He held the flap open for her to crawl in and she did, ignoring the way her pulse was racing. This was just a dinner. Their actions earlier that day had been far more intimate. Though not really. That day had been impulsive and physical, this had been planned and held a lot more meaning.

She took a seat, cross-legged on one of the cushions, and was surprised that it was actually quite comfortable. The temperature inside the igloo was just right. She'd expected it to still be either cold or humid, but it was big enough inside that it was neither.

Levi zipped the door and joined her, sitting on the cushion across from her.

"I've seen a few restaurants in LA do something like this," Leslie said, desperate to keep the mood and conversation light.

Only in the city, it was nothing like this. In LA, the neon lights shone so brightly, you couldn't see the real stars and the city was so alive and vibrant that the slow serenity that this kind of experience was supposed to provide just didn't happen.

Here, the starry sky above, the snow-covered mountains and wilderness all around them, the glistening of the ice on the lake in the distance, the igloo illuminated by just candlelight was almost magical. Definitely the most romantic setting she'd ever experienced.

And she wanted to blame Selena and all her rom-com talk for the way she was feeling in that moment, but she knew it was all because of Levi.

What she didn't know was what to do with that just yet.

She glanced across at him quickly, taking in their surroundings, and her chest tightened and she wiped the palms of her hands on her lap. "This is really nice," she said again.

He looked relieved as he reached for a bottle of champagne. "I wasn't sure you'd be into it…"

Into it? Or into him? Was he trying to gauge her feelings? Or was she reading too much into his words. "I think it's one of those things that I didn't realize I'd like until it happened." Damn, now was she doing it too? Intentionally or was the subtext just coming out unconsciously?

He seemed to catch it too, but a second later, the cork popped on the champagne bottle and they both jumped. "Champagne?" he asked, pouring a glass.

"Thank you," she said, accepting it.

He'd removed his jacket and the sight of him in the jeans that fit tight across his thighs and the black crew neck sweater that accentuated the muscular body made her hungry for something other than whatever they were about to eat.

He'd always been attractive, so how had she never felt this attraction before?

Was it just their shared history and the magic of the moment messing with her head and her heart?

No. That should only be making her feel guilty or sad or anxious.

In that moment, she felt none of that. She just felt a desire to be with him, to let go of the what-ifs and what-comes-next and what-it-all-means questions that continued to surface. She needed a break from conflict and drama and he was giving her that. And for right now, she'd take it. This dinner didn't have to mean anything more than two friends eating together. She knew he wouldn't push for anything she wasn't willing to give.

She took a deep breath and released it slowly, catching his attention.

A look of concern flashed in his dark eyes. "Is this too much?"

She shook her head. "It's really amazing…thank you." He was making an effort—for her. He was opening himself up when she knew it must be just as hard for him as it was for her to push aside all the reasons they shouldn't be doing this.

He finished pouring his own glass of champagne, then raised his glass in the air. "To…reconnecting," he said.

Such an understated way to put what was happening between them, but she would be hard-pressed to define it any better, so she clinked her glass to his and took a sip. The liquid tasted sweet on her tongue and warmed her as she swallowed. A few more sips and maybe her pulse would start to settle down a little.

Levi sipped his own drink, his eyes locked on hers over the rim of his glass.

Okay, nope. Pulse was just increasing.

"You look really beautiful…can I say that?" He looked

like he was afraid of spooking her and she understood. She'd been so on edge since arriving and it hadn't taken much to switch her moods from hot to cold.

She nodded. Compliments were okay, right? Friends complimented one another. "You look nice too." More than nice.

"Are you hungry?" he asked.

"I'm not in a rush to eat." This rare moment of letting go and forgetting about the mess she was in wouldn't last long enough, so she didn't want to hurry it.

Levi smiled and leaned back against his cushions. "So, life in LA—how is it?"

Of all the questions he could have asked, this was probably the most complicated and difficult to answer. "It's different." Growing up in Wild River wasn't exactly as secluded as other parts of Alaska, but it still wasn't busy, fast-paced California. "It took a little while to get used to. The traffic and crowds and the noise. The city always seems to be in motion—day and night. There's an overall feeling of hustling." That part she did enjoy; being busy kept her from being alone with her thoughts and feelings too often, but she kept that part to herself.

"The heat must be nice though," Levi said.

"The heat is definitely a perk. I live close to the beach, so I run every morning along the pier and swim in the ocean almost all year round. The workout scene in LA is no joke. Rollerbladers, cyclists, people working out on the equipment on the public beaches. It's definitely a community vibe in itself."

"Well, the city is definitely full of beautiful people," he said.

"Yeah…it's almost a little too much. Like here, you see an attractive person and you can appreciate the beauty, but in LA, everyone is beautiful, and in a way, it dims the appeal of outside appearances." And unfortunately, it took too much time and commitment to invest in someone long enough to see who they truly were…and if she was being honest, she wasn't ready to.

Was she ready to see Levi?

He nodded. "And your job…you enjoy protecting the rich and famous?"

Another tough one. "I do." She'd leave it at that.

Unfortunately, in true Levi nature, he pressed for more. "But you could have specialized in other aspects, right? Property? Events? Why pick personal security detail for Hollywood?"

She sighed. "I think I was attracted to the idea of film, being on set," she admitted. "I actually enjoy that part most—watching the camera crew and sneaking peeks at the takes and sometimes getting to watch the post-production editing of the footage." Selena had zero interest in the behind-the-scenes work of her movies, but it was a perk of the job for Leslie.

"That makes sense. You always loved being behind the camera." He sounded nostalgic and she too couldn't help but remember those days when she'd make her own movies starring him and Dawson and her siblings. She'd never fully commit to her hobby as a career—doing what she loved to survive would dim the passion she had for it—but she did miss her time behind the lens.

He sipped his champagne and studied her. "Do you keep in touch with your family…friends back here?"

Was he asking because he'd felt her avoidance over the years and wanted to know if it was just him? She shook her head. "Not often. Mostly through Facebook…and in cases of emergency like Eddie getting shot or Grandma getting married again." The last few months there had been more contact with them than usual. Would there be after this was all over? And would it take another extreme circumstance to get her back to Wild River? Staring at Levi, she really wished she knew the answer.

"I'm sorry things are still what they are with your mom," he said softly.

Her too, but she'd come to accept that things would always be that way. People didn't make amends until both parties were willing and accepting and she wasn't sure if she or her mother needed to reach that place but they weren't there yet.

But they'd been talking about her for far too long and she wanted to avoid where the subject might lead.

She cleared her throat. "So, how's your life? You were promoted to full-time, clearly. That's really great." Smoke jumping was for the elite and highly skilled. Only the best firefighters made the cut and Levi making it as far as he had in this career spoke volumes about his abilities and dedication.

It didn't surprise Leslie that he was excelling in his chosen career. He'd never half-assed anything in his life. She thought maybe it was his military upbringing that had made him so diligent and hardworking.

"The year-long position is definitely what I'd been working toward," he said. "Hoping for. So yeah, it's good. Things are slower this time of year, but we stay busy inspecting gear and going out on training missions, that kind of thing." He grinned. "Rescuing women in towels."

Her cheeks flushed. "We are never to discuss that again," she said.

"Hey, I said I wouldn't tell anyone. Doesn't mean I can't think about it," he said, winking at her.

The simple, casual gesture had her nearly spilling her champagne. He'd winked at her a million times. Why was this any different? Why had this set her heart pounding again?

He was sexy as hell. How was he still single? He'd never really dated much in the years that she'd known him...

He was in love with her. Had that been the reason he hadn't gotten involved with anyone else? Were his feelings for her that strong?

But obviously, he dated. Angelica...Tracey...just two women who sprang to mind.

"Is there anyone special?" She coughed. "I mean any women in your life?" Why had she asked? That was none of her business. Although after that day's events, maybe it was?

He grinned. "I tend to strike out a lot in that department."

The women he dated must have something wrong with their eyesight. "Have you tried online dating?" She was curious, but mostly she just wanted to see if he'd been actively trying to find someone.

He shuddered. "Chad set up a profile on Tinder and Match.com and I've perused them, I won't lie, but I don't think you can catch a spark that way. Call me old-fashioned, but I like real connections." He stared into her eyes and her mouth went dry. "I guess I'm just not interested in dating unless it's going somewhere."

"But how do you know if it's going somewhere unless you go on a date?" Why was this so important to her? Why was she nudging him in that direction? To make sure he knew that what had happened between them didn't mean...what? What did it mean? And unfortunately, she knew pushing him away was just her own way of self-preservation.

"Fair enough," he said, looking slightly disappointed as he asked, "So, you're dating a lot then?"

She shook her head quickly. Too quickly.

"What about that co-worker guy Selena mentioned?" Definite jealousy in his tone and oddly enough it made her feel good. "She said you two were boning."

She was going to strangle Selena.

"We're um, he's...um..." What was Eoghan? A friend... with benefits? Neither of them really defined what they were beyond their casual hookups and after-work drinks. They definitely weren't serious. He was a nice guy, fun, easy to be around. He understood her lifestyle; they had common interests and goals. Could she see a real future with him? Did he leave her breathless and weak in the knees? Could she see him as the father of her future children? No to all of that. "There's not a real spark," she said finally.

Levi smiled, looking almost...relieved?

Her heart raced. "Hey, I'm sorry to have just disappeared...before."

He nodded slowly.

"You understand why I did, right?"

"Sometimes I think I do. Other times, I'm not sure."

"I didn't really know what else to do. I was hurting and desperate to get away from that feeling, you know?"

"Did it work? Did you get away from it?" he asked, his blue eyes like waves crashing over her.

"No," she said honestly. It wasn't until that moment, with him, that she wasn't constantly aware of the lingering pain and hurt.

"I wish you'd stayed. I was hurting too. And it would

have been nice to have someone..." He shook his head. "To have *you* here."

She swallowed hard and a long silence fell over them. Maybe she should have stayed, but she couldn't change the past.

He sat forward and reached across the blanket, his hand slid toward hers and covered it gently. "Is this okay?"

Was it? She had no idea. She felt like they needed permission from someone who used to be important to both of them to be acting this way, giving in to feelings and attraction this way...but they'd never get it. Was it really okay to move on like this?

"I don't know," she said honestly.

Levi nodded and pulled back but she grabbed his hand and held tight. "But we won't know unless we try, right?"

He tightened his grip on her hand and his gaze burned into hers.

And there was most definitely a spark.

The night was ending too quickly, but Leslie's yawn across from him told him she needed to get some sleep. The last few days had been emotionally draining on her and he knew he hadn't made anything easier. He'd been relieved to see her relaxed for the first time that evening. He'd have to thank Selena for her idea. She may have saved his ass. He'd had no idea how to act around Leslie after their encounter in the shed, but this dinner had definitely helped to ease them back from going too far, too quickly.

Squeezing Leslie's hand, he glanced at his watch. "I guess we should call it a night, huh?"

She looked disappointed to end their picnic, but nodded, suppressing another yawn. "Unfortunately, I think so. I can barely keep my eyes open," she said, starting to pack up the leftover food from the picnic.

"No, don't worry about all of this. I'll clean up," he said.

"You sure?"

"Positive." He brought her hand to his lips and placed a soft kiss on her palm. There was so much more he wanted to do, to say…but they'd already crossed a line earlier that day, several actually, and he didn't want to push her away by repeating the impulsivity.

And when his gaze lifted to hers and he saw the conflict in her expression, he reined in any emotion that might frighten her away or make her retreat. He'd already told her he loved her, he'd already put his heart on the line… He'd let her decide what happened next.

Releasing her hand, he unzipped the igloo and crawled out into the cold. The wind had picked up and the late night chill made him shiver as he held back the flap for her to exit.

"Brr…" she said, rubbing her arms for heat as she stood next to him. "Well, thank you for a nice evening."

He nodded, hesitating before touching her cheek. She was so beautiful and he longed to tell her just how much. He wanted to hold her and kiss her and be with her in every way. But he wasn't crazy enough to think that this connection between them would be enough for her to leave everything in the past and move forward.

His own guilt was overwhelming—not only had he been intimate with Leslie on a physical level, but their date had meant so much to him as well and he had no right to be with her like this. She'd always been his best friend's girl, not his. His only reprieve was knowing Leslie didn't love him in return, therefore the choice of whether or not to be together wouldn't be up to him.

She stepped closer and he wrapped his arms around her and held her close. He closed his eyes, wanting to savor this time together, but he could feel her uncertainty, her conflicted heart. She wanted to take comfort in him, but thought she shouldn't. "Hey, I'm here for you. Anything you need..." This last part would be torture, but he needed to reassure her that her feelings and actions weren't wrong. That they could live in the moment without consequences or expectations. "And none of this has to mean anything more than it does right now."

She pulled back slowly, and her gaze flitted from his eyes to his lips, her expression clearly debating whether what he said was true. Could they act on their impulses without having it become another complication or source of regret?

Levi knew what he wanted and he knew it was wrong to want it, but damn if he could put on the brakes without hurting her and torturing himself.

But like before, he waited for her to act first.

Standing on tiptoes, she bridged the gap between them and only a brief hesitation flashed in her eyes before her lips met his.

He wasn't going to think. He was going to shut off all thoughts that could destroy this moment. He wouldn't think about the past or their complicated history. He wouldn't think about what happened next, the day after or when she would eventually leave again.

Living in the moment was something he wasn't particularly good at, but he'd just assured her that's all this was and when Leslie's soft, delicious lips pressed against his, it was easier. He grabbed her hips and pulled her body tight into his as his lips parted and he gave her tongue access to his mouth.

His hands caressed her ass through the fabric of the skin-tight leggings. So firm. So sexy. Her entire body was strong, sculpted. She wasn't skinny; she was solid muscle, with a tantalizing amount of curves. Her hips, ass and breasts would make any man weak at the knees.

Her arms went around his neck and he lifted her, wrapping her legs around his waist as he deepened the kiss. This was his best friend, someone he never thought he could have, yet here she was in his arms for the second time that day and he didn't want to let go, didn't want to lose her again. He wanted this. Wanted her. He groaned against her mouth as he felt himself thicken instantly. Her kiss was everything he'd fantasized about over the years, but so much more than he'd ever expected. He wanted to believe he wasn't imagining the intensity of her passion or the emotions he felt being reciprocated. "Leslie..." he said through a strangled sound.

"Take me inside," she whispered.

Damn, how he wanted to. "Selena and Chad are in there." Both occupying separate bunk rooms. The cabin wasn't exactly the best place for any kind of privacy.

"The igloo?" she whispered against his lips, kissing him eagerly again.

The igloo it was. Quickly, he set her back on the ground and unzipped the door flap.

Within seconds they were inside and he'd cleared space on the blankets. He lay back against the mountain of cushions and she straddled him, leaning down to capture his mouth with her own once more.

Levi gripped her thighs as he returned the kiss with everything he had. He didn't know how many chances he'd get to kiss her, so he wasn't wasting any opportunity to show her how he felt. His tongue explored her mouth, savoring the taste of the champagne still on her lips. She moaned and her hands roamed all over his chest and shoulders and arms.

Knowing that she wanted him was driving him insane.

She slipped her hands under his sweater and her fingers gently grazed his flesh. She broke contact with his mouth and lowered her face to his neck, kissing gently along his ear and down the side.

His breath caught, then quickened and his grip tightened on her waist. "Leslie, you're killing me." She had to know the power she had over him. He was helpless against her advances, his guilt not strong enough to give him the energy to resist. But he wouldn't tell her his heart was also on the line or that she held it in her hands. He'd meant what he'd told her—this meant only what she wanted it to.

She sat up and lifted her sweatshirt over her head, tossing it aside.

He swallowed hard at the sight of her beautiful breasts swelling over the top of the white sports bra she wore. He wanted to touch them, kiss them…

The shape of her body illuminated only by the flickering tea lights and the moon above them was breathtaking. He stared at her, unable to tear his eyes away. He wanted to commit this image to memory. Something to keep once all of this was over.

He sat up slowly and removed the bra. His gaze locked on hers and he searched for any sign of hesitation, uncertainty… "You sure?"

She nodded.

He tossed her bra aside and his hands stroked along her chest, downward to cup both breasts. He massaged gently, then more aggressively when her eyes closed and her head fell back in pleasure. He wanted to make her feel incredible. She deserved to feel amazing. She deserved to know just how incredible she was.

He lowered his head to her neck and left a trail of kisses from her shoulder to her collarbone, up toward her earlobe and back down across her chest. She smelled so good, like the wild outdoors and a hint of cinnamon from the body soap in the shower stall. He ran his tongue along her skin, enjoying the sweet taste of her.

"Levi, I want you," she said, gripping his shoulders.

The bulge in the front of his jeans should tell her just how badly he wanted her too. "You can have me." All of him. But right now, it was clear she was asking for only his body.

Within seconds they were naked and as he lay back against the cushions and she placed one leg on either side of his body, his heart felt as though it would explode any moment.

Earlier that day had been amazing but now here they were, completely naked, exposed, vulnerable…and this time he could have her more fully. The thought of being inside of her was enough to make him come, so he steadied his breathing and forced a deep breath, desperate to make this experience a memorable one for her.

He wanted to be memorable to her when she left this time.

She ran her hands along his chest, over his abs and lower. Her eyes never left his as she wrapped a hand around him. "Guess we can't actually…" she said, desire in her voice revealing how badly she wanted to.

He cleared his throat. "Actually, we can," he said, reaching for his discarded jeans. He reached into the back pocket for his wallet and retrieved a condom.

She studied him. "Are you always prepared or were you hoping this might happen?"

"Which is the right answer?" he asked. Truth was, he'd slipped it into his wallet last minute with no expectations, just a lot of hope and wanting to be prepared.

She grinned. "Maybe it's best to not answer at all," she said, opening it.

He watched as she slowly rolled it on over his exposed, straining cock and fought the intense sensations rippling through him at her touch. This moment was never supposed to be...the two of them hadn't been destined for one another. He'd learned to live with that but now here they were and he had no idea how he should be feeling or acting. All he knew was that he needed to be with her. He couldn't let his guilt or his desire to protect her or himself make her feel like he didn't want her. Nothing was further from the truth.

They'd live in the moment.

She lowered her body down over him and rode him slowly at first. Closing her eyes, she moved her hips forward and up and down over the length of him.

He held her thighs, his fingers digging in hard as he stared at her beautiful body above him. Her blond hair fell over one shoulder and the strands glistened in the light from the moon. The tea lights, flickering their last remaining light, cast a breathtaking shadow across her face, but he knew every inch of it by heart. The deep blue eyes, the tiny adorable nose, the high cheekbones and the full, delicious lips.

Her breasts bounced slightly as she quickened her pace, her breathing labored, and Levi was mesmerized by the rise and fall of her chest and abdomen.

His hands slid upward on her thighs and wrapped around

her back, cupping her ass. He lifted her higher until her body reached the top of his penis, then plunged her back down over his hardness.

"That feels so good, Levi," she said and he nearly came undone hearing her say his name. He might not be what she needed or wanted long term, but he was what she needed and wanted right now. And right now, he'd convince himself that that was enough.

She rode him harder and faster until they were both panting and desperate for release. "Leslie, I'm not lasting much longer," he said, staring up at her.

"Come for me, Levi," she said, her hands pressed against his chest and her gaze locked with his, full of lust and desire and so incredibly sexy, he couldn't hold back any longer. His body erupted in rippling waves of pleasure and his grip on her tightened as he throbbed inside of her. Behind her, he could see the moon and the stars and the shadow of the mountains and forest in the distance, and it was as though he was seeing it all for the first time. He released a satisfied moan as his body shuddered his release and his hands went to her face. He pulled her closer and kissed her hard.

Leslie pressed her pelvis forward, leaving no gap between them as she ground her hips back and forth the full length of him.

It wasn't a challenge to stay hard for her. He was wanting her all over again already.

Her breathing hastened and her grip on his shoulders tightened as she got closer to the edge. "Levi," she said, sounding almost afraid of the sensation, of the passion, of the connection between them.

"I've got you," he whispered. "It's okay to let go." He'd catch her. He'd never let her fall. Never ever hurt her...

She took his face between her hands and kissed him

hard as her orgasm erupted. He groaned against her mouth, holding her close to his body as she rode out the waves of their passion.

A second later, she tightened around him and he could feel her pulsate and tremble. A moan escaped her lips and she pulled back, fighting for air as she rested her forehead against his.

"That was..."

He held his breath. If she said it was a mistake, he would never forgive himself for giving in, letting go...allowing himself what he wanted.

"Everything in this moment," she said softly, her gaze locked on his.

Relief flowed through him but his heart still ached. It was everything in this moment, but was it enough?

CHAPTER SIXTEEN

LEVI DECIDED TO postpone finding out which Leslie would be waking up that morning—the guarded, regretful, walls-up Leslie or the open, trusting Leslie she'd been the night before. He wasn't sure how to handle either. Things were bound to be awkward and tense no matter what, albeit in different ways.

So, before the women woke, he'd headed out to the site of the cabin fire with Chad to start the cleanup. Normally, they would have called in a few other members of the team for assistance, but given their hidden fugitives situation, Levi had downplayed the amount of work involved and told the others that he and Chad could take care of it.

As they pulled up now into the clearing, as close to the cabin as the trails would allow with the cleanup dumpster truck, Chad was still mumbling about the early wake-up. "Thought there was no rush to get this done," he mumbled, his eyes barely open behind his sunglasses.

"There wasn't…but snow is in the forecast for the next week, and lots of it, so I thought we should get on it," Levi said.

Chad glanced at him. "Sure it has nothing to do with a certain blonde who has a warrant out for her arrest?"

What did he know about it? The guy had obviously seen them having dinner in the igloo the night before. Had he seen other things? "Only considering this is her cabin,"

Levi said. He wasn't ready to talk about Leslie with any-one yet. He still had no idea what was happening and he couldn't quite get his emotions sorted. He loved her. Now he'd been with her. Essentially, his heart was doomed with no chance in hell of recovery. And he was desperately push-ing aside the fact that he felt like he was somehow betray-ing his best friend. In the light of day, it was harder to face himself in the mirror. Not that he regretted being there for Leslie, he'd never regret that…but he wished he could do it with a clear conscience. His loyalties were divided but he knew whom he'd choose given the choice. Unfortunately, that didn't make him feel any better.

"Last night looked interesting," the guy said as they climbed out, grabbed their supplies and headed down the trail toward the debris.

Levi looked at him. "Which part?"

Chad laughed. "Don't worry, man. I wasn't snooping. I just meant the picnic setup you had going. Not exactly your thing."

"It was Selena's idea and I thought taking Leslie's mind off things would be a nice thing to do," he said, taking big strides through the deep snow.

"Well, did you?"

Levi glared at him. "Did I what?"

"Take her mind off things," Chad said with a grin.

"Look, it was just two friends reconnecting after far too long, that's all." He walked faster, putting distance between the two of them, and Chad took the hint that he wasn't into discussing it.

Not that he wasn't replaying every detail in his own mind as he trudged through the snow. Leslie's kiss, her touch, her desire for him had him feeling ways he never had before. He was happy with his life and he'd mastered the art of being alone. As a child, he'd never had any real, lasting connections with people except his two best friends and so not having them now seemed par for the course. He'd learned to be okay on his own, depending on himself, offering support to others, but never really needing it. He didn't need to be with someone out of fear of being alone or just wanting a warm body next to him at night. He wasn't interested in settling and until someone else came along who made him feel the way Leslie did, who commanded his heart the way she always had, he wasn't interested in getting involved. And now that he knew how amazing being with her was, even in this partial way, he was doomed.

As they reached the site, he put on his work gloves and immediately got to work picking up the larger pieces of charred logs.

Chad joined him a few minutes later and scanned the area. "Really nothing left, huh?"

"Nope."

"Sorry, man. This can't be easy on you either," Chad said, his rare display of concern throwing Levi slightly off guard.

"It's harder on Leslie." Even if she was putting on a brave face.

"So, you two were best friends and she was Dawson's girl?" Chad had far too many questions that morning. When had the guy gotten so chatty?

"Yeah…she was engaged to Dawson before he died." He couldn't get into the details. It would be that much harder.

"And then she left Wild River?"

"Yes." Two weeks after the funeral.

"And she's leaving again once all this blows over?"

"Yes." Levi huffed. "What are you getting at?"

Chad stacked more logs onto one arm. "Just making sure I have all the facts straight, that's all."

More like making sure *Levi* had all the facts straight. Chad was looking out for him and he appreciated it, but it was no use to warn Levi not to get too invested in Leslie—that warning was far too late. "Well, less talk, more work," he said grumpily.

"Yes boss," Chad said, carrying the logs back out the trail.

Unfortunately, now that Chad had brought it up, he couldn't quit thinking about the truth of the man's words. Leslie was leaving again. Soon. Would she keep in touch this time or disappear from his life again? He knew how he felt, but he had no idea where Leslie's heart was. He didn't expect her to feel the same way about him and he meant what he'd said the night before about no expectations. He didn't regret telling her he loved her—she deserved to know, even if now they were both at a standstill as to what to do with that knowledge.

Could they be together? For real? Would she ever consider him more than a friend that she'd had stress-induced sex with? Would she ever move back to Alaska? Would he give up everything here to move to LA for her?

So many unanswered questions and he was getting way too far ahead of himself.

Sorting through the debris of the fireplace, he noticed a broken photo frame. Bending to pick it up, he shook away the shattered glass and carefully took out the remaining piece of the picture from the charred frame. The edges were burned, but the central image was still relatively intact. He blew the soot and ash gently away from it and stared at the photo of Leslie, Katherine and Eddie that their father had taken the year before he died. The lake in the background and the bright sunny day reflecting the happiness in the siblings' faces was a true reflection of simpler times—better times.

This picture had hung in the cabin for years and it had meant a lot to the Sanders family. To Leslie.

It was a miracle that most of it had survived the blaze.

Was there a way to restore it? Fix it for her?

Maybe he couldn't help her with everything she was going through, but maybe he could give her back this small piece of her past.

Remind her that not everything needed to be forgotten.

Levi had disappeared early that morning and so far, it had taken a hundred push-ups and fifty sit-ups not to read too much into it. Leslie had heard the truck starting just after 7:00 a.m. and had seen it drive away through the bunk room window. She'd been slightly relieved to have some time that morning to gather her thoughts about what had happened between them before she was forced to face him.

But him needing that time as well had her on edge.

What was he thinking? Feeling?

She suspected he was battling the same conflicting emotions as she was. They'd been friends for years, they'd recently lost contact (her fault) and now when her world was in chaos and her job, and quite possibly her life, was on the line, they'd connected on an even deeper level than ever before. On his end, he'd apparently always loved her—a huge surprise to her—and now she'd no doubt opened a can of emotional worms that she wasn't sure she was ever going to be able to contain.

And neither of them had actually even mentioned the elephant not in the room, the third member of their triangle, who was still very much a reason for her and Levi to stop whatever was happening between them immediately.

She couldn't confidently say that she was over Dawson. She'd spent the last few years burying her pain, never fully acknowledging the impact his death had had on her, changing her life so completely, and here Levi was, about to launch a charity honoring him.

Things were a mess.

One emotion she hadn't expected to come from their night together was inspiration, but she'd woken up that morning feeling the desire to take some photos for the first time in weeks.

Getting up off the floor, she dressed quietly, careful not to wake Selena, who was cuddled in her bottom bunk with a snoring Smokester. Then, grabbing her father's old camera, she slid into her boots and jacket and headed outside.

It was so quiet out there in the middle of nowhere. The trees were still. The ground was frozen solid, so there weren't the usual spring thaw sounds like the crackling ice or snow falling from tree branches. There was no one around for miles. Everything was soundless and still.

And the overcast sky with just a few cloud breaks illuminating the forest in a beautiful early morning glow was the perfect lighting for photos.

She hung the camera strap around her neck and then snapped a few shots of the snow-covered evergreens surrounding the cabin and checked the images on the display. They were crisp and clear. The old camera was still one of the best ones on the market. Spotting a bird perched on a fallen tree trunk about ten yards away, Leslie zoomed in and captured the shot as the bird flew off. She took a deep breath, appreciating how much easier it was to breathe out here in nature. No smog, no traffic noise, no people... Nature definitely had a way of soothing a soul.

She hiked through the deep snow toward the trail they'd taken on the Ski-Doo and then followed it farther into the forest. Turning back around, she captured several images of the station cabin through the trees.

They weren't amazing shots or anything worth framing, but just being out there alone with the camera, capturing nature, gave her a sense of peace, which was something her conflicted spirit needed that morning.

She didn't regret being with Levi. She'd wanted him and her attraction to him had shocked the hell out of her, but giving in to it had felt right in the moment and one thing she knew for sure was that you couldn't change the past, so regrets were a waste of time.

However, she did feel bad for having taken advantage of him. Knowing how he felt about her, it had been unfair to lead him on when she had no idea how she felt... She was happy to have him back in her life, but she wasn't sure what that meant. Obviously a physical relationship wasn't possible when she returned to LA, so did they go back to being friends? Was that even possible after being so intimate with someone? And was friendship enough?

The loud crack of a tree branch made her jump and she turned in a slow circle. There was nothing out there for miles. Levi and Chad wouldn't be back so soon and Levi had assured her that no one else would be stopping by the station.

She scanned through the trees all around her, but didn't see anything or anyone.

Must have been wildlife. Hopefully not a bear...or a moose. She wasn't exactly equipped to fend off an animal attack.

"Those pictures would be nicer with someone in them."

Selena snuck up behind her and Leslie sighed. So much for her peaceful, contemplative alone time. "I told you I don't take pictures of people." Anymore. Scenery shots couldn't break her heart. The ones with people in them remained after the people were gone and she had enough of those for one lifetime.

"You could try. Believe me, if some of the photographers I've worked with in LA can get work…"

"I didn't say I couldn't do it." Suddenly, she didn't want to seem incompetent. She did have skills. Other than keeping people safe, photography had been her only other passion, the only other thing she was proud to say she was good at.

"So, let's do it," Selena said. "Come on, Leslie. I'm bored stupid in that cabin."

"I thought you were watching those rom-coms Chad downloaded for you." Before Selena had locked her out of the cabin the evening before, she'd caught Chad watching them as well.

"I've seen them all a million times. They're no different than the stuff I'm always receiving from my agent." She scanned the surroundings. "It's because of how I've been perceived up until now…the jobs I've accepted. But maybe with new headshots, I could convince producers that I don't always have to play the sidekick to the leading man. Dramatic photos showing a different side to my personality might be a start…"

Leslie hesitated. "But you're not…camera ready."

Selena placed a hand on her hip. "You're saying I need makeup and hair products to look good?"

"No. I'm saying I thought you'd want those things."

Selena shook her head. "No, I told you. I don't want

posed, fabricated photos with a thousand filters. I want real, fresh-faced and authentic."

That she could do. "Okay. Why don't you head down the trail a little ways to where those bigger trees are…?" She pointed and Selena actually followed her direction. "Great, right there," she said.

"You sure this lighting is good? It's kinda overcast," Selena said, glancing at the clouds in the sky.

"Trust me. It's perfect." Leslie set up the camera, adjusting the lens, one eye to the sky. She knew these thick clouds, the way they passed over these mountains and illuminated the trail through the breaks in the trees. Timed perfectly, she'd get the shot she was aiming for.

Selena posed and Leslie snapped a few photos, scanned them, and adjusted the lens filter.

The clouds acted just as she'd predicted they would and she was ready when the break happened and a beam of sunlight streamed through, surrounded by the shadows. She took the photo and then smiled as she reviewed it. Perfect.

Selena jogged toward her. "Let me see."

Leslie turned the camera toward her.

"Oh my God, this shot is amazing. You totally lied to me. Hobby, my ass. You could be a professional photographer."

The praise made her feel better than she thought it would. "Thanks. Let's move farther along the trail and set up a few more." This wasn't so bad and she'd never admit it, but Selena was right—the pictures did look better with people in them.

"So, where did you learn how to take pictures like that?" Selena asked. "From your dad, right?" She looked pleased with herself to have been paying attention.

"Yeah, I mean, I took a few courses when I was younger

too, but my dad was really into it. He was the one to introduce me to all kinds of art."

Selena eyed her. "So, you share a passion with your father, the way I do."

"Yeah, I guess so."

"I wanted to be an actor before I could even read a script and I know that intense passion had to come from watching my dad in movies."

She hadn't thought she and Selena could possibly have anything in common, but maybe there was something they could connect on. *If* she wanted to connect with the star… which she didn't. She needed to keep her alive, that was all.

Leslie cleared her throat. "We should get back. I should check in with Eoghan." Not hearing from him in over twenty-four hours was starting to concern her. What the hell was going on back there? There hadn't been any new updates on the news channels she was monitoring.

And just like that, the tension and stress erased by her photography session were back. She wasn't on holiday and the brief respite she'd taken from her assignment was long enough.

Selena's smile faded, but Leslie refused to feel bad. She was her bodyguard, not her friend.

"Yeah…sure. Hey, that Eoghan guy, are you two…?"

She wanted to say it was none of Selena's business, but if she was relying on Eoghan to help them, Selena had a right to know Leslie's level of confidence in him. "No… I mean not really. Nothing serious." Especially not now. Whatever casual relationship she'd had with her co-worker had ended after the day before. She might not be sure of her feelings for Levi, but she knew the reason she was conflicted over him was because she cared. She couldn't claim to have that with Eoghan. She'd known before that the relationship wasn't going any further, and the previous few days had only confirmed that fact.

"I'll be honest— the few times I've met him, I got a weird vibe…" Selena said.

Probably because he was one of the only men in the office who didn't fall at Selena's feet or ogle her. No doubt the star found that odd. "He's just quiet, serious, more reserved."

"If you say so," she said as they reached the cabin. "But while we're on the subject of your love life…"

"We're *not* on the subject of my love life," Leslie said. Selena had meddled in that area quite enough with the igloo dinner idea; Leslie didn't need any more help nudging her and Levi closer together. As it was, they'd gotten far too close already.

Selena grinned as she shrugged. "Okay. All I'm saying is that that igloo looked pretty steamed up last night."

She disappeared inside and Leslie took a final calming breath of cool mountain air.

How on earth had she gotten herself into this complicated disaster?

CHAPTER SEVENTEEN

LEVI KNEW EXACTLY where to bring the damaged photo.

Pulling his truck up in front of Flippin' Pages bookstore on Main Street hours later, he took the plastic bag containing the picture and headed inside.

The door chimed as he entered and he scanned the interior. He'd expected the store to be quiet on a Thursday afternoon. In truth, like most independent bookstores, his grandmother's didn't get a whole lot of traffic anymore. But the store hosted many reader events, bringing in the local book club of thirty women every month, and it looked like Levi had walked into the middle of one of these events. Only there were a lot more than thirty women inside the store.

He scanned over the heads to see a table set up in the back of the room with a woman signing books. His grandmother sat next to her and prepared the next book for her to sign, opening to the signature page and asking the next person in line their name.

Even in her seventies, Meredith Grayson liked to run these events herself. An avid reader, she'd taught Levi to appreciate literature from a young age. When his friends were reading comic books, he was reading the classics and enjoying them—for the most part.

"Hey, Levi," Callum McKendrick said, coming up to him, carrying another box of the author's books. The twentysomething store clerk was a doppelganger for Clark Kent, with dark gelled hair, a strong jawline, muscular build and dark-rimmed glasses that only made him more attractive to the patrons of the store. His look screamed hot nerd.

"Hey, man," Levi said. "Wow, I can't remember the store ever having so many people in it at once."

Callum nodded. "It's our best reader event yet. Huge turnout. The author is originally from Wild River and she draws a great crowd whenever she visits."

Apparently.

"What brings you in?" he asked, leading the way through the crowd toward the signing desk.

"Just here to see my grandma… But she looks really busy."

She hadn't noticed him yet, engaged in a discussion with one of the readers waiting in line. Her enthusiasm for books was really what had kept the store open so long. Engage her in a conversation about one of her favorites or a hyped upcoming release and she could talk for hours.

Callum set the box down under the signing table and checked his watch. "We're about to break anyway. The author needs a cigarette—it was one of the conditions of her signing," he said with a laugh. "Can you stick around for a bit? I'll tell Meredith you're here."

He should get back to the cabin and he definitely was *not* avoiding it, but this was important. "Great. Thanks. I'll just wait in her office," he said. He weaved his way through the crowd and into the back hall, leading to her office.

Ellie Mitchell collided with him as he opened the door. "Whoa… Sorry, Ellie," he said, catching her before she could come up short on his chest. At five-foot-nothing, with her girl next door looks, it was impossible to tell she was almost thirty.

"Levi—hi!" she said, her smile bright as she hugged him quickly. "Nice to see you."

"You too," he said. Ellie had been the manager of his grandmother's store for the last ten years, after her mother retired from the job. A total bookworm with a passion for old books that rivaled his grandmother's, Ellie was the perfect person to run the store day-to-day. The weekly book club and frequent author events had been her idea and it had definitely saved the store from having to close years earlier.

"You here for the signing?" she asked, blowing her wispy light brown bangs off her forehead. She showed him the cover of a fantasy novel featuring a dragon and a woman in metal armor wielding a sword. "It's already a *New York Times* bestseller."

"Actually I'm just here to see Grandma. Callum said she was due for a break in a few minutes," he said, taking a copy of the book anyway. He liked to support the store and its authors whenever possible…and he was there to ask his grandmother for a favor, so the least he could do was buy a copy.

"Yeah, feel free to wait in here. I'll tell her you're back here as soon as she's available."

"Thanks, Ellie," he said as she closed the door behind her.

Levi breathed in the familiar scent of the office. So many afternoons had been spent there, doing his homework and reading while his grandmother worked in the store. As a teen, he'd stocked the shelves and cleaned the store… It had been a second home.

He scanned the cluttered bookshelf of his grandmother's own collection, running a finger along the spines. All the classics she'd made him read and literature featuring Alaska or its authors held those coveted places on her personal shelf.

His gaze fell to a picture of him and his father hanging on the wall above the bookshelf. His father was in his military uniform. It was the day before he'd officially left Levi in his grandmother's care. Of course, Levi hadn't known. He'd thought the situation was temporary...but he'd long forgiven his dad. There was no point holding grudges and he was happy that they hadn't had any conflict or bad blood between them before his father died six years ago from a heart attack.

He stared at his own young, smiling face. To anyone else, it was just a nice father/son photo but Levi recognized the internal conflict in the boy he was then. Moving around a lot had a way of making him feel unsettled all the time. No real roots had ever been set down until he'd come to live in Wild River.

And even then, he wasn't sure if the town would have felt like home without Leslie and Dawson. And now neither of them were there.

He didn't need to dig too deep to know that moving again would be something he'd consider for the right reason...or right person.

The office door opened and his grandmother entered. Wearing her usual smock that read "I put the 'lit' in literature," one pair of reading glasses hanging around her neck, another pair of bifocals holding back her long gray hair, she was the picture of a bookseller. "Hi, darling..." She gave him a quick hug and immediately went to her Keurig machine to slip an Earl Grey pod in to brew. "You picked a crazy day to visit. I only have a few moments," she said.

He didn't take it personally. His grandmother's life revolved around the store and while they loved one another, they weren't close in the traditional sense. He'd been basically old enough to look after himself by the time he moved in with her and she'd essentially let him do it. She offered advice only when asked and stayed out of his business out of respect, not a lack of caring. She was always there for him when it mattered, but Christmas and birthdays were the only time they made an effort to get together since he'd moved out on his own at nineteen.

"The store is packed. That's great."

"Harriet Jennings always draws a crowd when she visits. I wish she could release a new book every month," she said, then noticing the copy in his hand, added, "You a fan of the series?"

"Um… I don't know yet, but thought I'd give it a shot. So, I won't stay long." He placed the picture in the plastic bag on her desk. "I was just wondering if you knew of a way…or someone else who might be able to restore this."

She lifted her glasses up to her eyes from the chain hanging around her neck and peered at the picture. Levi shifted as he waited. Would she recognize the photo?

"Fire damage?"

"Yeah, the Sanders cabin," he said.

She tsked. "I heard about that. What a shame. You used to spend a lot of time there."

He nodded. "There's nothing left. We did the cleanup this morning. I was lucky to find this."

Her furrowed expression wasn't optimistic as she studied it. "It's old and the damage is extensive."

"But you've restored worse." He remembered watching her replace old and worn covers on first editions of books. How meticulous and careful she'd been. How her expertise hadn't faltered even as she'd aged and a slight quiver had entered her hands, but never dared to while she was working,

"I have," she said. "But books are a little different. And I've never dealt with fire damage before."

Damn. "So, no saving this one?"

She glanced at him, a knowing look on her face. "Leave it with me. I'll see what I can do," she said.

That's all he could ask for. "Thanks, Grandma. I'd appreciate that."

She smiled at him as her tea finished brewing, signaling her break was over. "So, how's she doing anyway?"

He blinked. "Who?"

"Leslie," she said, adding honey to her favorite mug.

"What makes you think I know?" His heart raced under his grandmother's perceptiveness.

"I just meant about the cabin burning down," she said with a knowing grin above the rim of her mug.

Oh, right. "I'm sure she's disappointed, but I think she's got bigger issues right now."

Meredith nodded as she blew on the hot liquid. "Yes. Wanted for possible abduction of a Hollywood movie star?" She raised an eyebrow and the amused flicker in her light blue eyes suggested she'd be fascinated if it were true.

Levi scoffed. "Don't believe everything you see on the news. Leslie's not involved, she's just trying to keep the woman safe... I bet," he added quickly.

"I'm sure. Anyway, I hope wherever she is, she's safe," she said with a wink, opening the office door and leading the way out into the hallway.

He followed and she hugged him quickly. "Give her a hug for me," she whispered.

Entering the station later that day, Levi held his breath. He wasn't sure what to expect from Leslie but inside everything was quiet. "Hello?" he called out as he entered the kitchen.

Silence, except for the running dishwasher.

Checking the living room, he saw it too was empty. Even Smokester was gone. He headed toward his office and saw a Post-it note stuck to the door.

Gone for a hike.

It was Chad's handwriting, but he knew the guy must mean all four of them, otherwise he wouldn't have left Levi a status update about his own whereabouts. A hike was probably a great idea. Being cooped up inside the cabin with no real contact with the outside world must be driving the women insane. Levi loved the quiet solitude staying at the cabin provided. Big cities with their crowded streets and noise pollution weren't his thing.

Could they *be* his thing if Leslie asked?

What the hell was he thinking? One incredible day together didn't mean anything. It hadn't escaped his notice that she hadn't brought up his confession of love at all…as though wanting to forget about it maybe?

As if he could.

He sat in his office chair and opened his laptop. Several new messages waited in his email inbox from Angelica with questions regarding his preference of menu for the event and a list of wine choices…and an invite to dinner Saturday evening. If only he could go to dinner with her and not be thinking about Leslie. If only he'd ever had the pleasure of a woman's company without feeling like something was missing. Unfortunately, he suspected no other dinner date would measure up to the igloo picnic, which was depressing as hell.

Seeing a new message arrive, his stomach twisted.

Mrs. Powell's subject line made his heart race.

Charity Event Speech.

He'd been putting it off. The biggest responsibility he had regarding the event. The last few days he hadn't been in the right mindset...

He heard the front door open and voices in the entryway and he shut his laptop, thankful for the excuse to avoid the emails a little longer.

Footsteps echoed down the hall toward the office before Leslie appeared in the doorway. "Hi," he said. "How was the hike?"

"Good. It was good to get some fresh air and exercise," she said.

"Yeah, that's always helpful to clear the mind," he said.

She nodded. "Yeah, so... Chad said the cleanup went okay." She entered the office and closed the door behind her.

Did she want privacy? Or was she there to say something she didn't want the others to hear? "Yeah. We'll finish the report and send it to your mom in the next few days. She'll need it if she decides to file an insurance claim—if she had any on the cabin...or maybe tax purposes or something. And the tow truck will be there later today to tow your car into a shop in Wild River, where I thought you'd eventually be able to pick it up," he said. He was talking too much, but he wasn't sure he could handle silence or the conversation taking a different direction.

He couldn't quite read Leslie. She didn't seem upset or annoyed, but she wasn't giving any kind of vibe at all really.

"Sounds good," she said. She stared at her hands, folded in front of her, and he stared at the top of her head. He wanted to go to her and wrap his arms around her, breathe in the fresh mountain air on her skin, kiss her cold cheeks, but he remained in his chair.

So far this had all been at her pace and it still was. Whatever she wanted. Or didn't want.

But damn, could this awkwardness get any worse? He needed to say something. "Listen, I…"

"Levi…"

They both spoke at the same time.

"Go ahead," he said.

"Well, I just wanted to say that I'm not sure how long we can keep this up."

His heart plummeted but he prayed his poker face was still in place. "Us?" he asked.

"That too, yes. But more specifically, I mean us hiding out here. I can't keep running with Selena, hiding her. We need to go to the police or head back to LA."

He couldn't argue that it made sense. They couldn't stay there forever. Selena would clear up the misunderstanding about Leslie being involved with the stalker. Leslie might lose her job still, but at least she wouldn't face jail time. They needed to go back and figure things out. Running may have been an ill-thought-out plan, but then again, maybe not. "Is it safe for her there?" he asked.

She sighed. "I'm not sure. But Eoghan, my co-worker, said that the police have a suspect in custody."

Levi knew his expression was definitely on the jealousy spectrum as he cleared his throat. "You spoke to him today?"

"Yeah."

She'd told him they weren't serious, but was she still planning on continuing her casual relationship with Eoghan when she returned to LA? Did it matter? Would things be continuing between him and Leslie when she went back? Probably not.

"I'm not going to be…um, dating him anymore," she said awkwardly.

There was no hiding his relief. "Because of us?"

"Not *not* because of us."

So there was an us? This whole thing was super confusing. But he was afraid to ask what she meant. He suspected she had no idea what she really wanted…except for the physical. And he'd promised not to push for anything more than she was willing to give. Despite the torture and torment it might cause him.

She moved farther into the office and her eyes were worried as she said, "About last night…"

He held his breath.

"I just want you to know that it was incredible. The whole thing—the picnic, the champagne…" Her cheeks flushed and he stood quickly, not wanting her to feel out there, exposed in her feelings alone.

He moved toward her and wrapped his arms around her waist. "I'll admit, I was worried you'd be having regrets."

"Well, I'm not *not* having regrets," she said, but her gaze was on his mouth and when she licked her lips absentmindedly, he knew she'd be okay with adding to those regrets should they exist.

"So, does that mean I shouldn't kiss you?" he asked.

"Probably. Do you want to kiss me?"

"I always want to kiss you," he said, lowering his head closer to hers. He could feel her heart pound in her chest, the steady rhythm matching his own.

He held back slightly. Waiting for her okay. She gave a small nod as she stared into his eyes.

His mouth connected with hers and her arms immediately wrapped around his neck. He'd been thinking about things all day and was no closer to an answer about what they were doing or where this was leading…but when he was kissing her, all other thoughts vanished and he was grateful for the opportunity to turn off his brain.

He ran his tongue along her bottom lip and she captured his lip between her teeth.

She pressed her body even closer and he bent at the knees and lifted her. She wrapped her legs around his waist and he carried her to his desk. He set her down on the edge and wedged his thighs between her legs. His hands tangled in her hair as he deepened the kiss. The same passion ignited between them as before and it both invigorated and terrified him.

He pulled away and studied her. He didn't need to say anything. She could read his thoughts on his face.

She reached for his jacket and removed it down over his shoulders, letting it fall to the floor. She removed his sweater and undershirt in one quick move and sighed, taking in the sight of his sculpted chest and stomach.

He reached for the buttons on her plaid button-up shirt, unbuttoning quickly.

Holy shit. His intake was a low whistling sound seeing that she wore nothing underneath.

"I'm washing clothes in the sink. Hope you don't mind," she said with a teasing flirtation in her voice that he'd never heard directed at him before.

His mouth was dry and his voice sounded hoarse as he said, "Not at all…"

She wrapped her hand around the back of his neck and pulled his head down to hers again. Damn, she was so sexy and he'd never get enough of her.

His hands cupped her bare breasts and he massaged gently, his thumb running over her hardened nipples.

Her hands traced the muscles along his abs, dipping

lower into the waistband of his jeans. His erection was on full display. She reached for the button on his jeans and opened them, sliding her hand inside of his underwear. He moaned as she wrapped her hand around his erection and she pressed her lips to his, muffling the sound.

Chad and Selena were in the other room and for once, things were quiet. No blaring television or music to drown out the noises in the office. "Can we really do this? In here?" she asked, slightly out of breath.

"I'm not sure I have a choice. I want you so bad, Leslie," he said. The other two already knew there was something going on between them. This wouldn't come as a surprise to either one of their friends. Bottom line was, in that moment, when his desire for her was so strong, he really didn't care what they heard or what they thought.

He reached for her jeans, unbuttoning them and easing her backward onto the desk. His hands slipped inside and he felt how wet she was between her legs. At least the desire was mutual.

And damn, what was it about it that turned him on so much he could lose sight of all the reasons they shouldn't be doing this? Nothing else mattered when he was kissing her, holding her, touching her... *No one* else mattered.

The office door opened and Levi's worst nightmare seemed to move in slow motion in front of his eyes despite the fact that he and Leslie moved fast as lightning away from one another. She pulled her shirt closed and hopped down off the desk. He reached for his shirt off the floor and not a single explanation—lie—about why they'd both been half-naked and all over one another, alone in his office, came to mind as they were caught.

By Mrs. Powell. Her former future mother-in-law and the woman who'd practically raised him as her own son.

Fuck.

Leslie kept her eyes downcast as he walked toward Mrs. Powell. His pulse raced even faster than it had seconds before and his hands shook as he clumsily struggled with the button on his jeans. This was not good. Not good at all.

"Mrs. Powell, I didn't know you were stopping by," Levi said, pure awkwardness in his voice.

"Obviously." The chill in her tone could have frozen the entire backwoods. Her steely gaze was locked on Leslie. "Leslie? I wasn't aware that you were back. But then, I guess taking *this* situation into account, I wasn't aware of a lot of things."

Leslie met her gaze. "Hello, Mrs. Powell. Nice to see you," she mumbled as she moved past them quickly. "I'll let you two talk."

Levi cleared his throat and sent her a desperate look as she escaped the office. But Leslie shouldn't have to stay and explain herself to Mrs. Powell. Obviously she felt guilty getting caught by her former mother-in-law-to-be, but Mrs. Powell had made it very clear that Leslie wasn't part of their family anymore. She'd never wanted Leslie in their family, yet she adored Levi.

So, this was all on him to explain.

LESLIE'S DEVASTATION HAD reached an all-time high. This was by far the worst thing that could have happened. Her ex-fiancé's mother catching her and Levi in a compromising situation was a thing of nightmares. Levi had looked guilty as shit and she knew they both should be. Things had gotten out of control. She'd allowed them to get out of control. This was on her.

But she'd sensed her presence in the office would only make things worse. Mrs. Powell had never liked her, so it would be Levi who would reap the woman's disappointment. Damn, why had she put him in all of these tough situations?

She hovered near the door frame of her bunk room to listen, out of sight.

"What are you doing?" Selena asked, getting up from her bunk to join her.

"Shhh…"

"That was unexpected," she heard Mrs. Powell say carefully.

"Yeah…for me too, honestly," Levi said.

Unexpected for him too? Which part? Getting caught or getting physical with her? Most likely both hadn't been planned. They certainly hadn't on her end.

"What is she even doing here?"

Was Alaska off limits to her now? Leslie's irritation grew. She'd never given Dawson's mother any reason to dislike her. If anything, she'd helped keep Dawson's head on straight at times, forcing him to study and take his academics seriously when all he wanted to do was play sports and cut class. She'd helped him graduate. When he'd fallen in with a rougher crowd in high school, with Levi's help, she'd pulled him back and made him realize he couldn't throw his life away for a few stupid choices. Of course, the Powells hadn't known anything about all of that. To them, their only son could do no wrong.

"There was a security risk to her client in LA," Levi said.

Leslie winced, but it was too late now. Mrs. Powell had seen her. He needed to tell the woman something.

"Yes, I heard about the cabin and I saw her on the news."

Her disdain was evident. She'd condemned Leslie already without having any idea what was going on. As usual.

"Leslie needed my help and it's a confidential situation I couldn't talk about. With anyone. She's not guilty of anything they are accusing her of in the media," he said.

"You believe that strongly enough to put your own career on the line?" Mrs. Powell asked, her tone a fraction more threatening than concerned, which made Leslie's blood boil. She could be rude and dismissive to Leslie, but Levi didn't deserve that.

"Who is this woman?" Selena whispered, looking ready to barge into the office and set her straight herself.

Oddly enough it made Leslie feel a little better. "Our mutual…friend, Dawson's mother," she whispered, stumbling over the word *friend*. She didn't need Selena knowing more about the situation than that.

"I believe in Leslie," Levi said and Leslie felt her conflicted heart grow even more confused. He was such an amazing guy and her unexpected attraction to him had only magnified in the last few days, but could it be more than that?

He'd always been the one she could count on. He'd always made her laugh. He was smart and handsome and hardworking… Oh God…

Mrs. Powell's appearance had given her a very real reason why they shouldn't even be thinking about it, yet here she was realizing that maybe she did have feelings for Levi. Ones that might go a lot deeper than she ever could have thought possible. Years ago, she'd dismissed any feelings she thought she had once he'd made it clear that they were just friends, but obviously things had always been far more complicated than she'd realized.

"That was sweet of him to say that," Selena whispered.

"So you two are together now?" Mrs. Powell asked.

Leslie held her breath as she waited for his answer.

Selena seemed to be holding hers as well. What would Levi tell her? What did he think was going on?

Levi's sigh was loud but his voice was respectful and gentle as he said, "Again, I'm not sure that's something I want to discuss with you."

Was she disappointed or relieved? He didn't owe Mrs. Powell any explanation. Still, she'd have appreciated some clarity as well. From his viewpoint.

"Well, I'm not sure I can move past it and forget what I just saw," Mrs. Powell said, sounding disappointed and on edge.

"Understandable."

"I mean how are you supposed to be the face of this foundation when you're…having relations with my dead son's ex-girlfriend?"

Fiancée, actually. Damn, Mrs. Powell's unacceptance of her still stung and she hated that she was still letting the woman get to her. She didn't need or want her approval anymore.

But Levi still might.

"This is all very new," he said. "Things are very complicated right now. I'm not entirely sure what's going on between Leslie and me."

"Well, from what I witnessed, it's unacceptable."

Levi was quiet and Leslie held her breath. For what she wasn't sure. She didn't know what she expected him to do. Mrs. Powell and this foundation meant a lot to him. She knew his loyalty to Dawson ran deep. She could see his conflicted heart when he looked at her with affection in his eyes. Besides, Dawson had never stood up for her—for them—she couldn't expect Levi to.

He cleared his throat. "I'm sorry this came out the way

it did and that you feel the way you do, but Leslie is important to me."

Her heart raced.

"And she was important to Dawson," he continued. "I'm not sure I'll ever understand why you refuse to acknowledge that…but I'm sorry to say that your opinion of her is wrong—it always has been and it won't affect how I feel about her."

"So, you'd walk away from the foundation, all the work we've put in together, all the great work this foundation would do to raise awareness and help others? You'd give all that up…for her?"

No…please don't do anything rash, Levi. Her heart was ready to explode in her chest from the way he'd stood up for her. Dawson had always just ignored his mother's disdain, had told Leslie not to worry about what his mother thought. She'd never known where she actually stood with the woman or if Dawson's unwillingness to stand up for her was because he really didn't care what his mother thought or if he'd never held Leslie in high enough regard to fight for her, to walk away from his family if they didn't accept her.

The way Levi was prepared to.

"I don't want to," she heard him say. "And I don't think I need to…but that's up to you, Mrs. Powell."

A long silence followed and Leslie swallowed the lump forming in her throat. This had to be so hard on Levi. Feeling as though he'd let Mrs. Powell down and having to choose between something he was passionate about or defending Leslie.

The sound of Mrs. Powell's shoes in the hallway had Leslie moving farther into the room, out of sight as she passed the bunk room door. A second later the front door closed and she released a breath.

"Wow. I can't believe Levi just did that," Selena said, admiration in her voice.

Neither could Leslie. What the hell had Levi just done? Choosing her over the Powells and the foundation. She'd expected to feel happy that someone had put her first, but her stomach only churned. Her anxiety peaked and she couldn't define the source of the uneasiness washing over her.

What if Levi had just stood up for something that could never really happen?

CHAPTER EIGHTEEN

WHAT A COMPLETE shit show.

Despite knowing he'd done the right thing, Levi was destroyed by the sight of Mrs. Powell's disappointed expression as she'd walked away. This foundation meant so much to her. It meant a lot to him too, but he couldn't just ignore the fact that he was more in love with Leslie now than he'd ever been and he wasn't prepared to lose her.

Or let anyone devalue her ever again. Not even someone as important to him as Mrs. Powell.

Leaving his office, he searched the cabin for her. She must have overheard the conversation and he needed her to know that this decision regarding the foundation wasn't her fault in any way.

He scanned the living room and kitchen, but didn't see her.

"She went outside with her phone," Selena said, appearing in the hallway behind him.

"Is she okay?" A heads-up about what to expect would be appreciated.

"Mostly confused I think, but what you said in there meant a lot to her. I could tell," she said.

He nodded before heading outside. He heard her voice at the back of the cabin and slowed his pace, listening to the one side of her telephone call.

"Yeah…that's good to hear. Thank you. I, uh, couldn't have survived this without you," she was saying.

His chest tightened. Eoghan? Her co-worker. She'd said there was nothing serious between them, but her tone now as she thanked the guy suggested otherwise. Levi had always taken a back seat to his best friend, but he'd be damned if he lost Leslie to some guy in LA he knew she didn't have real feelings for.

She had feelings for *him*. Fear was preventing her from admitting it. He could sense her attraction and affection growing the more they were together. It had become more than physical for her too. They'd been friends for so long, they knew one another, trusted one another, mutually respected one another. All of that, combined with the intense sexual chemistry they had, made for the basis of something real.

"We will head back tomorrow," he heard her say and he felt the kick to his gut. She was leaving. He'd always known she would and she'd given him the heads-up that it would be soon, but he couldn't help but think that Mrs. Powell's appearance was the cause for her decision right now. No doubt any guilt or second-guessing that she'd been repressing the last few days being with him was all coming back.

She disconnected the call and he cleared his throat and took several steps toward her, not wanting to startle her or let her know he'd been listening.

She turned and he searched her face for any indication that there was still a hope for them, that she hadn't started rebuilding the walls he'd fought to tear down, but there was none. "Hi," she said. "Um, I'm sorry about all of that."

"Hey, none of that was your fault. You okay?" he asked, reaching out to touch her arms.

She folded them and he slowly let his hands fall away. Body language spoke volumes and hers said they wouldn't be tearing the clothes off one another again anytime soon.

Ever?

"Yeah. Fine." She coughed. "I just spoke to Eoghan. They have the guy being charged on several accounts— harassment, breaking and entering... Selena should be safe to go back."

He nodded slowly. "So, you're leaving."

"Tomorrow morning, we will head back. There's no point in staying any longer."

Ouch.

"I mean, it's a long drive and it's time to face the music," she said in an attempt to soften the blow a little too late.

It was a long drive and she did need to get back there, but he knew the real reason she was suddenly so eager to go. "Look, I'm sorry about Mrs. Powell," he said quickly.

She held up a hand to stop him. "It's fine. Actually it's not fine that I created this problem between you two."

That's what she thought? Of course she'd internalize it and use it as a reason to back away from him. "You didn't. I needed her to know how important you are to me, and it may not have been the way I would have liked her to find out but I'm glad that it's out there now." Keeping his love for her a secret all these years had gotten him nowhere. She knew the truth now and he was no longer hiding it.

"I appreciate you standing up for me, but it really wasn't necessary," she said. "This foundation is important and I really hope that you two can work this out...after I'm gone."

He swallowed hard. So that was it. She'd gotten a re-minder of the biggest reason of all that they shouldn't be to-gether and she was using it because she was afraid of what they had. She was running away again. Denying how she felt and pushing down the feelings was her way of dealing with issues when things got too hard.

He reached for her hand, but she stood firm. "Leslie, I

know that everything has been one big mess…but somehow within all of that, we've reconnected. More than that, we've connected in a different way. I know you feel this too and I know it goes deeper than just the physical." He'd felt it in her kiss, in her touch, in the way she looked at him. She couldn't fake passion like that.

She shook her head. "I should never have crossed that line with you."

"Because you don't care about me or because you think that us being together is wrong?"

She sighed. "Does it matter?"

"Absolutely, it matters. I know how I feel about you and it's enough to walk away from…" This was going to really terrify her, but he refused to hold back the truth. "Well, just about everything."

"Levi…"

He ignored the warning note in her voice and pushed on. This might be the only chance he'd have to say everything he needed to. And if she still walked away from him, he'd have to live with that, but at least he'd know he gave it everything. "Leslie, I've loved you for so long, never ever thinking there could ever be a chance for us. And as much as I miss my friend and would give anything to have him back, the reality is he's not coming back. But I'm here and you're here and I know we have something special."

She looked torn as she listened. He was putting it all on the line and he desperately hoped she wouldn't turn away from him. From his love.

"All I'm asking is that you don't shut me out again. You don't leave and never look back." Because that would break him more than anything else. "I've waited a long time for my friend to find her way back to me and I'm not sure I can lose you again."

She took such a deep breath it felt as though she were sucking in all the air around them. "Levi, I'm not sure how I feel. I know that I misled you and I'm sorry about that. I'm sorry I dragged you into all of this."

Was she not hearing anything he said? He didn't care that he'd put his career at risk. He didn't care that she'd complicated the hell out of his life. "Leslie, you can't say you don't have feelings for me."

She stared at him for a long, excruciating moment and with each second his confidence in her, in *them*, slipped away.

She lowered her head, her gaze on the ground. "I'm sorry, Levi. I never meant to hurt you," she said as she moved past him quickly and disappeared inside the cabin.

Levi shut his eyes, feeling all his energy drain from his body, all the fight leaving his soul. He was open, raw and vulnerable and unlike before when he'd held it together by holding it all inside, he had no idea how to mend this new version of his broken heart.

IF SHE COULD leave that night, she would. The faster she could get out of there, put some distance between herself and Levi and the million emotions clouding her judgment, the better.

What had she been thinking being with him? Giving in to her attraction? Pushing aside all consequences and living in the moment often led to regrets and mistakes. He was neither but unfortunately, without reassurance from her, he was bound to feel like both.

Damn.

It had been unfair to him to let things get out of hand and his words ringing through her mind had her feeling worse and worse. He was right. She did have feelings for him, but she had no idea how deep they ran or if they were something she could continue to act on.

He'd said he was ready to give up everything for her.

That terrified her. Because what if she wasn't ready to do that for him? What if she wasn't ready to let herself be fully committed to someone ever again? Keeping her guard up had helped her ignore the ache in her chest, helped her forget what it was like to be in love with someone. To be vulnerable to heartache again wasn't something she was ready for.

Going into the living room, she heard Levi's truck engine revving outside and fought every urge to go after him. This was for the best. They both could use some space right now.

"Where's Levi going?" Selena asked, eyeing her carefully.

"I don't know," she said. She swallowed hard before saying, "But good news, they've arrested and charged a man they believe is your stalker, so we can head back to LA."

Selena looked both relieved at the news and disappointed. "There's no need to leave right away. My touring schedule is already messed up. I could call my team and let them know where we are and that we will head back in a few days."

Leslie knew how desperate Selena was to get back to her life and yet the star was putting Leslie's feelings and her relationship with Levi first and an unexpected lump rose in her throat. She forced her expression to remain neutral as she said, "No need. We'll head back in the morning."

"You sure?"

No, but unfortunately it was the only decision she knew how to make right now. She had no idea what to do about Levi, but she could do what she knew best—finish the job of protecting her client and hope she could get her life back on track.

Unfortunately, she wasn't sure it was possible to go back to the life she'd been living now that she'd gotten a glimpse of what could be a better one.

THE CALL FOR assistance from the Florida Department of Fire Safety couldn't have come at a worse time...or maybe a better time. After their argument, it was difficult to be in the close quarters of the cabin with Leslie and resist the urge to talk to her...touch her, beg her to stay open, stay vulnerable...but he sensed she needed space. Any attempt at trying to make things better would likely backfire.

He'd laid his cards on the table. He was wearing his heart on his sleeve and every other cliché metaphor for putting himself out there to get his ass kicked by love. There was nothing else he could do now but wait and see if she could move past the past, if she did love him too.

Or thought she could eventually...

This space was a little more than he'd like to give though, given the circumstances. Being around her was challenging, but she was leaving in the morning and he hated the thought that he was now leaving first. The Florida fire department needed his team right away to help with forest fires blazing due to the dry, hot weather and lightning storms the East Coast had been experiencing that week.

He'd called in the other members of his team and now that Leslie and Selena were leaving, there wasn't really any danger in the other men finding out that they'd been hiding there that week.

He didn't like the idea of leaving the two women there alone overnight, but they had everything they needed— food, Ski-Doos, his truck in case of an emergency, firewood… They should be fine. They were both capable of looking after themselves.

"Hey, you ready to go?" Chad asked, popping his head around the office door frame.

Levi hesitated. "Yeah… I'm ready." He grabbed his jacket and his gear and shut down his laptop.

From the corner of his eye, he saw Leslie packing her things into a backpack in her bunk room across the hall. She wasn't looking at him, but she was aware of him. They'd been tiptoeing around one another all evening, avoiding even superficial contact.

But she'd heard the emergency call and she knew he was leaving. For a dangerous mission, at that.

Would she at least say goodbye?

He took his time turning off the office lights and locking the office door. He bent to retie his boots in the hallway.

She was sitting on her bed, reading one of Selena's magazines. Only he knew she wasn't actually reading. She hated those magazines.

He coughed. Loudly.

She didn't even glance up.

Guess that was it then.

"Levi, plane's leaving, man," Chad called out from the front door.

"Coming," he called, hoping to catch her attention.

Last chance…

Nothing.

Okay then. That's where they were once again.

JUST STAY IN the room.

Nothing good could come of talking to Levi right as he was leaving. Leslie wasn't sure how she felt and she didn't want to confuse things further, by wrapping her arms around him and kissing him goodbye, which was what she desperately wanted to do. Without words of reassurance, acting on her impulses again would just be a dick move. So she stayed put as he got ready to leave and headed toward the front door, ignoring his attempts at capturing her attention.

But he was going to fight wildfires. He was putting his life at risk.

What if…

Nope. She wasn't going there. Levi would be fine and the time apart would be good. Give her time to clear her head without him in her space—in her peripheral vision at all times, smelling his cologne that she swore he'd only started wearing since they'd had sex. It was a scent she knew she'd soon be missing.

She heard the front door close and fell backward onto the bed. Grabbing a pillow, she put it over her face and muffled a scream into it. She kicked her legs against the bed and cursed herself for being so damn stubborn all the time.

"You were really going to let me go without saying goodbye? That's a dick move." Levi's slightly teasing tone had an element of hurt when he reappeared in the bedroom doorway.

Embarrassed, but happy to have a do-over, Leslie jumped up from the bed and hurried into his arms. She hugged him tight and he kissed the top of her head.

She wanted to stay there. Right there. Forever. Or until she got her heart and head sorted out. But she couldn't rely on him anymore and she couldn't keep messing with his heart. "Stay safe," she whispered.

"You too," he whispered back, squeezing her one more time before releasing her and heading out of the station cabin…for real this time.

CHAPTER NINETEEN

EIGHT HOURS AND four rom-coms later, Leslie was tapping out. As the credits rolled on the last movie, she reached for the television remote and turned it off. Next to her, Selena was wiping a tear off her cheek, her knees pulled into her chest, looking completely wrecked by the onscreen love.

Unreal. The woman had seen this movie eighteen times and she starred in these things, yet she was still sobbing over a happy ending?

Leslie felt nothing. In the last eight hours, she'd effectively closed herself off again. Years of practice had immediately come to her rescue before the pain and disappointment could fully envelop her. Maybe there was something wrong with her, something broken inside that she wasn't sure how to fix. Or was it that she didn't want to fix it because that would mean being open and vulnerable?

"Ready to change your opinion on these movies now?" Selena asked, a smug look on her face.

Was she serious? Selena thought this marathon she'd forced Leslie to endure would actually result in some type of enlightenment. "Absolutely not," she said.

"What? Why?"

"Because they are completely anti-feminist, that's why. In every one of these movies, it's been the woman giving up something for love. Career, family, her home, her country… How about the dude giving something up for a change?"

"He opens his heart to the heroine."

"Pfft…so what? Why is that enough for the guy, but not the woman? Why isn't he expected to make major life changes?"

Selena looked ready to argue, but she paused. "Huh… I guess I didn't really notice that before. But you do have a point."

Now Leslie looked smug. "Ready to change *your* opinion of them now?"

"Not completely. I see your point, *but* what you're not acknowledging is that the woman who claimed to be happy with her life, her career, whatever, wasn't truly happy. And meeting the hero and falling for him is what taught her that. In the end, she ultimately got it all."

"No one gets it all. It's unrealistic." Leslie looked into the popcorn bowl between them, but only unpopped kernels sat at the bottom. She licked her finger and dipped it into the salt.

"That's not true. My parents are a perfect example of having it all. They have careers they love, they are still in love with each other, they are happy."

Well, money tended to help happiness along. The Hudsons were rich and beautiful; to not be happy would mean there was no way they could ever be satisfied. But Leslie kept her comments to herself. They were nice people. "Well, I'm sure you'll get it all too," she said. She wasn't being sarcastic but Selena thought she was.

She reached across the couch and punched Leslie in the shoulder. "Don't be so jaded all the time."

Leslie sighed. Maybe she was jaded, but she had good reason. She'd thought she was getting, well, maybe not a perfect life with Dawson, but close enough, and that was ripped away, but she wasn't going to get into that. "I meant it," she said. "You have a career you love, a wonderful, supportive family and there's no shortage of men who would love to cater to your every whim for the rest of your life."

Selena frowned. "You think men cater to me?"

"Don't you?" Everyone catered to Selena. It was the job of most people in her life to do so.

"People, including men, do help me and make my life easier, sure. But I choose to believe that in a relationship, the couple—both parties—should look out for each other."

"No one's ever taken care of me," Leslie said, before she could stop herself. Unfortunately, she'd just realized how true that was. Dawson had never treated her like other girls—he didn't open doors or pull out chairs for her the way he did for his mother or other female friends. He'd never really checked on her to make sure she was okay after a stressful workday, knowing she could handle the emotional toll of the job. When she was sick, she made her own damn soup.

And she hadn't minded being independent. Right?

Selena was looking at her like she'd grown another face. "What?"

"No one takes care of you because you don't need anyone to take care of you. You take care of everyone else. It's your thing. You'd probably punch someone if they even tried to imply you needed help or protection."

"You're probably right about that, but it would still be nice if someone at least wanted to risk the punch in the face." Why had she admitted that? She wasn't insecure or soft. She wasn't actively looking for someone to share her life with... Was she? Was she ready to move on?

Selena raised an eyebrow. "I think Levi would be up for it."

Leslie shook her head quickly. "That's, um...nothing's

happening between Levi and me." She'd pushed him away earlier that day for his sake. She was a mess. Her life was a mess. Things had gone too far and now the best thing for them both was for her to shut down again.

Selena turned on the couch to face her. "Look, if you want to push everyone else away, that's okay. But I think you should reconsider on that one."

Too close. She was letting the star get too close, too involved in her personal life, but it seemed far too late now. Selena had played a part in her and Levi's igloo dinner date and she'd witnessed what had been going on the last few days. "Things are complicated."

"Hello. When is love not complicated?" She gestured toward the stack of DVD cases on the coffee table.

"That's not real."

"Okay, well, let's hear your version of this complicated *real* love."

God, she really didn't want to get into this. Selena didn't need to know about her past. But she was staring at her expectantly. "Fine. The woman who was in here—Mrs. Powell? She's Dawson's mother."

Selena nodded. "Right…"

"And Dawson was my fiancé," she said, quickly.

Selena's eyes widened. "Holy shit. I thought there might be more to that story, but I never expected you to actually tell me." She paused. "And his mother—she didn't like you?"

"Not particularly."

"But you're so delightful," Selena's tone was teasing and Leslie gave a small laugh.

"She didn't think I was good enough for him. They are super wealthy and my family is just average, middle class…" Dawson's parents had struggled to have a child.

Dawson had been the result of years of in vitro and fertility treatments. Mrs. Powell always referred to him as her miracle baby and basically worshipped him.

"That shouldn't have mattered."

"But it did."

"Did it matter to Dawson?" Selena asked softly.

Leslie shook her head. "Not at all. Dawson had lived a privileged life, traveling all over the world. He'd had the best of everything, but he shared it with his friends." She smiled, one particular memory returning. "He once told his parents that he was joining the junior hockey team just so they'd buy him all the gear, then he gave it to the poorest, but most talented kid on the team. When his parents found out, they donated thousands to the league to make sure all the kids who wanted to play got the chance."

"Wow—that was sweet. So, charity runs in the family," Selena said, her own voice clouding with emotion.

"No one in his family loved the idea of him going into the police force. Not when he could have gone to any university, followed any path, but I joined the force and he decided it was what he wanted as well."

At the academy, they'd pushed one another to be better, work harder... They'd grown even closer in that year and by the time they'd graduated, she knew he was the man she wanted to spend her life with.

"So they blamed you for his dangerous career choice?"

"I guess so," Leslie said. It hadn't helped the relationship she'd had with the family.

"But surely, things would have changed after you two got married, right? The families would just have been forced to accept it and grow up. I mean, it was Dawson's choice to make—both his career and who he wanted to be with—you."

"Guess we will never know." She paused. "He died on

our wedding day," she said. Might as well paint the whole picture so that Selena could understand why being with Levi wasn't an option.

Selena's eyes glistened with tears. "Oh my God...you don't like watching rom-coms because you starred in your own...but one without a happy ending. More like a tragedy, like a Nicholas Sp—"

Leslie held up a hand. "Please don't."

"Sorry." She was quiet for a minute. "If it was your wedding day, how was he on the job?"

"Officers are always on duty. Especially Dawson. He lived for the job. Anyway, he heard a call come in—a breaking and entering suspect had shot a gas station attendant over forty dollars in gas. He fled. Dawson chased. The guy was on a suicide mission." She shrugged. There was no more to the story than that. The message on her phone that she'd missed because she was putting on her makeup was the last she'd heard from him. *Don't start forever without me.*

But now he was gone. Was it okay to start forever now?

For the next few days, he'd be living in his boots.

After a quick initial assessment of the area and the streamer wind test, Chad determined the landing location and Levi and his team prepared to jump. This being the first official jump of the season for his crew, Levi's name was at the top of the jump list, so this fire belonged to him.

As always, the knowledge of that responsibility weighed heavy on him as he jumped out of the plane. Dropping into any wildfire held its own unique challenges, but the Florida heat and humidity had Levi soaked through his gear already.

As his feet hit the ground, the aircraft circled above,

dropping their seventy-two hours' worth of provisions. Seeing their cargo drop by parachute, landing in a nearby tree, Levi shimmied up quickly to retrieve it, then reached for his chainsaw. He started at the heel of the fire and began cutting away.

Heavy dark smoke impaired his visibility and his shallow breaths were hindered as he worked alongside his crew, digging and hacking to cut the fire off from the fuel and preventing the spread. Next to him, Miller overturned sections of the hot ground, mixing it with the cool soil below.

Levi blinked exhaustion from his eyes and commanded his attention to focus on the hazardous and arduous task at hand. He'd slept a few hours on the plane, but Leslie hadn't been far from his thoughts and he needed to get his head on straight and worry about the potential dangers he and the team were facing out there, but his mind kept wandering back to the station.

He also couldn't help the nagging feeling in his gut that he shouldn't have left them.

Hours later, they loaded up their gear and hiked the eight miles out to base camp, where they'd spend the night before heading to another region. Levi's eyes were heavy and his limbs were aching. He wiped the soot-filled sweat from his forehead as he trudged along after the others to where a meal of Spam and coffee awaited.

At the campsite, the team debriefed and then as Chad joined the others to eat their freeze-dried dinners, Levi set up his sleeping area on the ground. It was far from the luxury king-sized bed in the Wild River Resort, but right now, after the long, exhausting day, it would feel almost as good.

Sweat pooled on his lower back on top of the sleeping bag as he stared up at the hazy sky, the thick smoke from the fires blocking any view of the stars. Even in his T-shirt, the Florida heat was killer. Living in a hot climate year round didn't appeal to him at all. But would he consider it if Leslie asked?

His gut twisted. He hadn't had time to check in with them since arriving in Florida and now it was after midnight in Alaska—she was probably sleeping.

He took several deep breaths of the thick air as Chad set up camp next to him. "You okay, man?" he asked, gearing down.

"Yeah," he said. Leslie and Selena were safe. A man believed to be Selena's stalker had been arrested in LA. They were heading back in the morning.

Still…

And it didn't help that Eddie had called a few times.

Like now.

Should he answer? Eddie calling after midnight meant it might be something important. Leslie had asked him not to talk to her family about the situation, but that was when everything was still uncertain. Letting Eddie know what was going on now was fine though, right? He wondered if Leslie would go see her family, say goodbye before she headed out of town.

The cell phone continued to ring and Chad shot him an annoyed look as he lay on the ground. "Dude, either answer it or silence it. We've got three hours till we hike out. I'm planning to get as much sleep as possible."

Levi cleared his throat and answered the call on the last ring. "Hey, Eddie."

"I've been trying to reach you," Eddie sounded on edge.

"Yeah, sorry, man. I'm at a base camp in Florida. We got a call to assist—"

Eddie interrupted. "Do you know where Leslie is?"

The sense of urgency and concern in the other man's

voice made him sit up. "Yes, and I'm sorry I didn't tell you before but..."

"Levi, where is she?"

"At the station cabin. They've been there for a few days. She didn't know what else to do when that news report dropped, but apparently they have a guy arrested in LA so she's planning on heading back in the morning."

"He was released," Eddie said. "Wrong guy—they dropped the charges."

Shit. Levi took a deep breath. It was fine. Leslie was still in Alaska and she was monitoring the situation in LA. She wouldn't head back if it was unsafe. "Well, she's still there, so we have time to warn her."

"I think the guy might be headed here."

He frowned. "What? How would he know where they are?"

"Leslie's car was towed into the shop on Main Street. I noticed it sitting outside earlier today."

That, Levi knew—he'd called for the tow. "Yeah, she was planning on picking it up this morning before heading back."

"I don't think that's a good idea," Eddie said.

"Why not?"

"I found a tracking device on it."

Shit.

"ARE YOU PLANNING on saying goodbye to your family before leaving?" Selena asked as they drove through town the next morning to the shop where Levi said her car would be ready and waiting for the trip back to LA.

Leslie had gone back and forth about it over and over again, but she'd ultimately decided against it. They'd be pissed that she'd been avoiding them, not filling them in on her whereabouts and everything that was going on, so the only way to avoid a whole shit ton of arguments was to keep avoiding them for now. And she'd already started putting her walls back up...no need to compromise them again. "We should hit the road." Fifty-seven hours of driving awaited them and she needed to call the agency to update them. Selena also needed to call all of her people to let them know she was okay and headed back.

As soon as Leslie's phone charged.

She'd forgotten to charge it the night before and it was dead. She'd plug it in at the shop while Selena ate breakfast at the diner next door, then they'd be good to go.

She ignored the tug at her chest that said otherwise.

The familiar scenery of her hometown wouldn't get to her. Her guilt about not saying goodbye to her family wouldn't derail her plans. This trip hadn't been a vacation. She had a job to finish and she needed to focus on getting Selena back to LA safely and quickly.

Her phone being dead, she hadn't had a chance to find out if Levi had tried to call or text her from Florida. She hoped he was safe. She missed him already. Which made leaving that day already difficult. Maybe the way they'd said goodbye was for the best—hurried, short and bittersweet. A long, drawn-out farewell would have been harder and she'd have had time to question her choices and what came next.

Pulling into the shop parking lot, she parked Levi's truck next to her car and gathered her things. "Okay, we have an hour. Go eat, I'll charge my cell phone inside, pay for the services and then we are good to go." She'd also make a very quick stop at the tech shop to grab a new mobile charger.

"Do you want anything?" Selena asked.

"No, I'm good." She didn't have an appetite that morning. Heading back to face the music was only half as hard as leaving all her unfinished business here and her stomach was a mess about all of it.

Leslie headed into the noisy shop that smelled like gas and other car fluids and scanned the wall for an outlet. Locating one near the old woodstove in the corner, she bent to plug her phone in and the sound of a familiar voice behind her made her jump.

"Could you have picked a farther place to hide out?"

Eoghan's teasing tone, thick with his Australian accent, seemed to hide an eerie urgency. "Eoghan? You're here… In Wild River." How? Why? What the hell? And why was her first reaction guilt about what was going on with Levi when there were a million other issues with Eoghan being there, like how he'd found them.

"Hey, Leslie. You here to pick up your car?" Doug, the shop owner, asked from behind the counter.

She blinked and nodded to him. "Yeah, Doug…just, uh, give me a sec?"

"Sure thing. Ring the bell when you're ready," he said, setting a dirty, oil-covered bell on the counter and heading into the back.

Leslie turned back to Eoghan. He was dressed in jeans, hiking boots and a winter coat that was obviously new. The North Mountain Sports Company logo suggested he'd been in town long enough to go shopping. Just how long had he been here? "What's going on?"

He didn't answer as he hugged her, his strong cologne making her hold her breath. "It's good to see you. I'm glad you're okay."

Why wouldn't she be? She pulled back abruptly and frowned. "What's going on? When did you get here?"

"This morning. I took a red-eye flight last night when I couldn't reach you."

"How did you even know where to find us?" She looked around. She shouldn't have left Selena alone.

"From these." Eoghan handed her his phone, his expression now serious.

Instagram pictures with Selena tagged appeared. Pictures dated three days before. Leslie scanned the photos of the star that looked like they were taken on Main Street. But she could be anywhere. All small towns looked similar. But still, these photos were not good. Not good at all... How the hell had they gotten posted? Had Selena hijacked her phone at some point? Damn, the star really hadn't listened to her about the danger she was in at all.

But Leslie frowned. "I still don't know how..."

Eoghan stood behind her and zoomed in on the image. "Behind her. That street sign in the distance."

Leslie squinted. Even zoomed all the way in, the street sign was unreadable. Too small and not at all in focus. She took a breath. "This is unreadable."

Eoghan took the phone and opened an app. "Not if you upload the photos to this app." He showed her the new image—crisper, clearer...readable. Wild River Resort. Oh no... But...

"But someone would have to use the app...or one like it."

"Someone motivated enough—like me—could have," he said. His mood turned deadly serious as he touched her shoulders. "The man they had in custody was released. His alibi checked out. He wasn't the guy."

Her entire body froze. Selena was still in danger. "They let him go?"

"No other choice, but don't worry, the company is surveilling him."

The company, right. Her boss. People who actually had believed that she was in on it, that she may have abducted the star herself. She shook her head. "I'm still confused though. Why did you come here?"

He looked slightly sheepish and his tone was affectionately embarrassed as he said, "I came here when I couldn't reach you on your cell phone last night—you frightened me. I thought maybe the real stalker had found you and Selena."

An awkwardness fell between them but telling him that whatever was happening between them was officially over had to wait as her guilt subsided quickly to panic. The real stalker was still loose and might know where they were. Selena should have known better than to take those selfies. And then post them to social media? What the hell had she been thinking?

Leslie started to pace. "Okay, but...we're assuming the stalker is tech savvy...or still very motivated. Even if he did know where she was, he wouldn't actually come all the way to Alaska, right?" In most cases, stalkers lost interest when the target was removed from sight or availability. They moved on, became obsessed with a new one.

"I wouldn't be so sure. There's more," Eoghan said. "You should sit."

She didn't want to sit. She wanted to grab Selena and get the hell out of there. But she also needed to know all the details and think with a clear head this time, so she lowered herself down into the plush chair near the woodstove. "What's going on?"

"There have been more letters, messages... Actual death threats now. Her management team are freaking out," Eoghan said, taking one of her hands in his.

She tensed at the touch. Now wasn't the time to call off their casual relationship, but she added it to the list of messes she needed to deal with once Selena was safe. Death threats. Things had escalated even more. Whoever the stalker was wasn't messing around anymore. And they might know where they were.

She had to get to Selena. She stood quickly. "We should leave. Right away." Hiding out was one thing, but if the guy actually found them, it was better on home turf, with more security detail. Being on the road was safer.

Eoghan nodded. "Yeah, I agree. Let's get your car and head back to LA. We can drive back together. That way, we're on the road for the next few days and whether the guy is in LA or Alaska, he won't be able to get to her. And if he does travel here, we may have a better case to prove it's the right guy."

Leslie was nodding. That all made sense. "Yes, okay."

Eoghan touched her hand again. "Don't worry. It's okay. I'm here. We'll get Selena back where she belongs…safely."

She did feel slightly better with backup. Unfortunately, Eoghan's affectionate touch and concerned, caring expression made her uneasy. Would he have come all this way to help if it had been another agent? Or were his feelings for her motivating this? Damn. She really couldn't deal with this right now. "Okay. Thank you," she said.

"Where is she anyway?" He glanced around the shop.

"Eating at the diner. I had to charge my phone," she said, turning to unplug it.

Eoghan stepped closer. "Let it keep charging for a few extra minutes. I'll take care of getting your car. Go get Selena and I'll meet you both outside in five minutes."

Leslie checked the battery life—still only at thirty percent. She nodded. "Okay. Meet you outside."

Entering the old fifties-style diner seconds later, Leslie ignored some familiar faces and a few waves in her direction. She didn't have time for reunions right now. She ignored the rumble of her stomach at the smell of frying bacon and fresh apple pie as she looked for Selena and spotted her in the corner, at a table near the window, sipping an espresso. Leslie hurried over to her. "Hey... We need to go," she said.

Selena frowned. "My breakfast hasn't even arrived yet."

"We will have to grab something on the road," she said.

The actress must have heard the note of urgency in her voice because for the first time she moved fast, without argument. She stood and drained the contents of the cup. "I have to pay," she said, heading toward the counter with the cash Leslie had given her.

"Hurry," Leslie said, scanning the restaurant, in full paranoia mode. She could strangle Selena for posting pics online. Hadn't she been clear that this was serious? She'd put her career and her own safety on the line and the star couldn't follow one simple rule.

"Do you want to tell me what's going on?" Selena asked, rejoining her a moment later.

Leslie sighed. "The man they arrested was released. He's not the stalker."

"Okay...so shouldn't we stay in Wild River?" She stopped walking.

"That would be a great idea except the stalker might know where you are. Wild River isn't a safe option for us anymore," Leslie said, her annoyance causing her voice to rise.

Diners at nearby tables turned to look their way and she led Selena out of the restaurant. "There were pictures of you on Instagram."

Selena's eyes widened. "How?"

Leslie resisted the urge to scream. "Because somehow—and not entirely surprisingly—you posted them."

"No, I didn't."

Was she seriously going to lie about this right now? "I saw them."

"Leslie, I have no idea what you're talking about."

Damn, if she didn't sound sincere, but Leslie had seen the photos herself. "Look, the damage is done. We just need to leave."

"Is he here? The stalker?" Selena looked genuinely worried as she scanned the quiet street. It was just after ten and stores were opening for the day, but there were few people around.

"I don't know. But Eoghan is here and if he could figure out where we are based on the Instagram photos, so could the stalker. So, we have to leave."

"Wait. Eoghan's here?" Selena paused near the front door.

"Yes. Come on, we're meeting him at the car." Leslie zipped her jacket higher as the cold air blew through her hair. "Come on." She gestured for the woman to follow her toward the shop.

Selena shook her head.

Great, the annoying Selena was back. The attitude had returned. It was going to be a really long car ride back to LA.

Her teeth clenched as she walked toward her. "What's the problem?"

"Why is Eoghan here?"

"To help. To let me know what was going on."

"He couldn't have done it by phone?"

Leslie sighed. "Look, I know you're not a fan, but he's here to help and right now, I'll be honest with you, I'm doubting my own ability to keep you safe, so I could use his assistance on this."

"Bullshit. You don't need him."

The vote of confidence was coming a little too late. Leslie had made mistakes...both personally and professionally and she really just wanted to get out of there and put all of this behind her, even if that meant heading back to LA to face the music. "Well, he's here." She guided Selena down the street. "And this is kinda your fault," she mumbled.

Selena looked enraged. "I told you. I didn't post any pictures online, Leslie!"

Reaching the shop, she saw Eoghan waiting near her car and Leslie extended a hand toward him. "Can I have your phone to show Selena the pictures she claims don't exist?"

Eoghan hesitated, but then clicked on his Instagram app and handed Leslie his phone. She turned it to face Selena. "Don't remember somehow stealing my phone and posting these?"

Selena squinted to look at them. "That's not Wild River..." She looked harder. "Except the Photoshopped parts."

Leslie frowned. "What are you talking about?" Her head hurt and right now she actually didn't care about the photos, she just wanted this whole ordeal to be over. It was tempting to let Eoghan take over and walk away from this mess.

Selena pointed to the picture of her on Main Street. "This picture is on set at Universal. The background has been doctored to look like Wild River...but look closely."

Leslie peered at the photo. It did look off. Where was North Mountain Sports Co.? It should have been in the corner of the picture...but it wasn't. That space on Main Street looked under construction.

"And look at my clothes. I wasn't wearing that anytime we were here," Selena said, pleased that she was in the right.

It was true. These photos weren't real. She was really slipping not to have noticed those things herself… Why had she let her personal life throw her off her game so hard? Eoghan's unexpected arrival hadn't helped. She rubbed her aching temple. "You're right. But they say they were posted from your Instagram three days ago."

"Someone must have hacked my account. Happens to celebrities all the time," she said with a shrug.

"But how would they have known to change the photo to a shot of Wild River?" Leslie asked. This made no sense. She owed the star an apology, but first she wanted to figure out how this happened.

"I don't know," Selena said, but her mistrusting gaze was focused on Eoghan.

Leslie turned toward him to ask, but a right hook caught her cheek and she stumbled backward. Eoghan had punched her? Her brain felt rattled as she steadied herself and prepared to fight back.

"Leslie!" she heard Selena's voice, but another quick jab had her blinking furiously to maintain focus. She staggered, struggling to comprehend and recover, but a final hard blow had her lights out.

CHAPTER TWENTY

OKAY, SO SELENA'S gut feelings about Eoghan were right.

Her eyes opening slowly, her head throbbing, Leslie forced her brain through the fogginess swirling around her. The events replaying in a haze. Eoghan in Wild River. Eoghan knocking her out, Photoshopped photos…by him? Why? And how the hell had he known where to find them?

What the actual fuck was going on? Had Eoghan been somehow involved with Selena's stalker this entire time or *was* he Selena's stalker? Leslie blinked away a wave of dizziness and swallowed the saliva gathering in her mouth, as she quickly assessed her current situation.

Her hands were tied tightly with a thick rope and fastened to the door handle in the back seat of her own car. Her cheek and left eye felt swollen and she could barely see over the puffiness. Her stomach was queasy—low blood sugar queasy—which meant they must have been on the road a little while.

Outside it was dusk and she couldn't pinpoint their location. It was just stretches of highway and trees as far as she could see.

Selena sat next to her, her hands in handcuffs behind her back, her mouth covered—she talked too much and had probably tried screaming for help. Eoghan knew that once awake, Leslie wouldn't jeopardize their safety like that. It would be futile anyway in this secluded section of the Alaska Highway. They could drive for miles and not see another vehicle.

Selena's eyes were wide and bloodshot when they met hers. She was obviously scared, but looked slightly relieved to see Leslie had regained consciousness. Leslie forced her own expression to be calm as she whispered, "It's going to be okay." It had to be okay. She needed to get them out of this.

Leslie took a moment to stare at Eoghan behind the wheel, trying to assess his mental state—and his motive. Why would he be interested in the Hollywood star? The Eoghan she thought she knew wouldn't be, but the man sitting in the driver's seat right now was barely recognizable. His shoulder-length wavy hair looked dirty and messy in a low ponytail, not his usual carefully styled man bun. His hands clutched the wheel and he was mumbling to himself. Incoherent babbling that she couldn't decipher.

How the hell had she been so stupid not to see who he really was?

She cleared her throat and his gaze shot to the rearview mirror as though she'd scared him with the noise. His wild-eyed expression made him look unhinged. Wonderful. She was indeed dealing with a dangerous person. "Don't make any noise or do anything stupid or I'll shoot you and throw you out of the car," he said.

Her own gun and handcuffs were in her bag, sitting on the front seat, and she didn't have her cell phone.

Her heart thundered in her chest. Just what was Eoghan capable of? What had he done already? The break-in at Selena's house, the messages in blood—was that all him? How had she missed the signs? The connections?

She took a deep breath. Gauging his mental state and finding out his intentions was the first step in getting them out of danger. "Eoghan, let's talk about this. How do you plan on executing this kidnapping?"

He stared at her through the mirror. "You made it very easy. No one knows where you both are. Only I knew where to find you."

About that . . If it hadn't been Selena's fault, if the photos weren't real, then what had given away their location? "How *did* you know? I mean if you doctored the photos to convince me it was Selena's fault...then how did you know?"

"I put a tracking device on your vehicle months ago," he said, returning his gaze to the road. "On all of Selena's vehicles too."

Jesus. He'd had access to the star because of Leslie.

All the clues—the letters, the photos, the intimate details about Selena, the knowledge about her daily schedule, when she'd be on set, when she'd be at home...everything had been because of her relationship with Eoghan, their closeness, her trust in her co-worker. Letting her guard slip had put them in this position.

The first person she'd tried to open up to in years and this happened. Maybe she was right to stay closed off, guarded.

Or maybe she needed to trust the right person...

Thinking of Levi only made her stomach twist in the worst way. What if their last goodbye really was the last one? What if she never saw him again? Panic at the thought made it hard to breathe; and her regret was so strong it had her chest tightening, so she pushed all thoughts of him aside. Survival was the priority right now.

"So why didn't you abduct her before?"

"You know the answer to that," he said.

Right. The toying, the intimidating, the pleasure of watching a victim become more paranoid, then scared...

"But all things have to end," he said casually. "I knew once you heard about the suspect being released, you wouldn't head back to LA and I was tired of waiting. And besides, you really did create the perfect situation for my next steps."

Next steps. Truly abducting the star. Where would he take her? They certainly weren't heading back to LA right now. He could take them anywhere. No one would know.

He'd never tell her where they were heading, so instead she asked, "Why Selena?" Hollywood royalty had never really seemed to interest him. He claimed to hate LA and said the job was a stepping stone to a career with the NYPD. That mutual sense of not really belonging in California and not identifying with most people living there had been one of the things that had bonded them. Either he'd really presented himself as someone he wasn't or he had a reason for targeting Selena.

He glanced in the rearview, but this time his gaze was locked on Selena as he spoke. "I was fifteen when she starred in *Surviving Junior High*."

The after-school special that taught morals in a fun, often lighthearted and touching way. Leslie vaguely remembered watching it as a teen. Selena had said she'd been ten acting like a tween in the popular show. She'd seen her sign posters for her fans with catchphrases from her character.

"In the show her parents were going through a divorce— so were mine," Eoghan said. "I felt like she understood what I was going through. Her struggles were my struggles, even though she was only twelve in the show."

Leslie nodded. "I can understand that." He was a teen and going through a hard time. Easier to sympathize with that than the stalker he was turning out to be, but plenty of children lived through divorces and deaths and tragedies; it didn't turn them into dangerous people.

"For three years I watched her on that show. Our connection grew stronger and stronger..."

Connection? He really was twisted up in this tortured, warped kind of way. Confusing fiction with reality...as a means to escape?

She glanced at Selena, but the woman just looked even more terrified as Eoghan continued to explain the origins of his obsession.

"Then out of nowhere, the show was canceled." The irritation in his voice warned Leslie to tread carefully. He was driving really fast on snow-covered, slippery, winding roads.

"She abandoned me," he said, his glare icy as he stared at Selena.

An oncoming transport truck wailed on the horn as the vehicle started to swerve into the other lane.

"She abandoned me," he repeated, hitting the steering wheel and pressing down on the gas a little harder.

Jesus, they may not even survive wherever they were going.

Could she talk him down? Help him realize that his anger was misdirected? "It wasn't her choice," she said softly. "Shows get canceled all the time..."

"She wasn't there anymore," Eoghan said and the car sped up. He struggled to keep it from sliding off the road and Leslie saw Selena shut her eyes tight.

"I'd turn on the television and she was gone," Eoghan said, to no one in particular now, as though talking to himself. "She left me all alone. I had no one. My father left and my mother was useless. Kids were assholes." He hit the wheel with his fist over and over and then drove even faster, coming up close to the bumper of the truck in front of them. "I had no one and she didn't give a damn. I wrote letter after letter and she never responded." He looked in the rearview at Selena. "You never responded! Why didn't you respond, April?" Calling her by her character's name, he wasn't seeing Selena Hudson. He was seeing the young girl he'd watched on his television, the one he'd felt understood him, was there for him. "You left me all alone," he said.

Tears slid down Selena's cheeks and Leslie knew the star could sense the immediate danger they were in. Engaging Eoghan in this conversation had been a mistake. He was losing his temper and with it, his ability to navigate the treacherous roads.

She had to do something. She tugged on her hands, desperate to loosen the ropes enough to break free. She scanned the back of her vehicle for something—anything— to use as a tool or a weapon, but Eoghan had wiped the back seat clean.

Selena glanced at her and her expression changed. Gone was the terror and the tears had stopped. Now there was only a look of sheer determination.

Shit. What was she going to do?

"Selena…" she whispered, a note of caution in her voice. One wrong move and this guy could snap—or worse, they could go off the road. Plunging to their death off the side of the highway wasn't the way Leslie wanted to die.

Selena motioned toward Leslie's head and Leslie inched slowly and quietly as close to her as possible. She saw her raise her hands and quickly slide a bobby pin from Leslie's messy bun.

Eoghan glanced at them over his shoulder and neither of them moved.

Her heart pounded in her chest as she watched Selena maneuver the bobby pin into the lock… She struggled with her shaking hand but Leslie nodded her encouragement to keep trying. There was no way she could get free of the ropes.

Selena wiggled the pin desperately in the lock as the car continued to pick up speed on the highway and finally the cuffs broke open.

She did it!

Leslie clamped her lips together and tried to signal Selena to make a dive out of the vehicle. She might get injured but at least she'd be out of this car. She'd have a fighting chance.

Instead, the star gripped the handcuffs in both hands and, leaning over the seat, she wrapped them around Eoghan's neck.

Surprise registered on his face as he reached up to try to free himself, but Selena leaned back, using all her strength and body weight to choke him out.

"Selena, the car…" Leslie said. With Eoghan out at the wheel, they'd surely crash. But the car was slowing…his foot releasing pressure on the gas as he struggled with Selena. His eyes bulged and Selena tugged harder.

She had to help. Yanking with all her might, she felt the ropes cut into her hands as they broke free from the door handle. Her hands still tied, Leslie crawled over the seat and took control of the wheel as Eoghan's head fell forward, passed out.

She pressed her foot to the gas and slowly brought the car to the side of the highway, putting it in Park and exhaling a deep breath.

Oh my God…

Selena collapsed back against the seat and ripped the tape away from her mouth. "Motherfucker!" she said, rubbing her lips. She kicked the back of the seat and glared at

Eoghan, slumped to one side, his head against the driver's side window. "Can you believe this asshole?"

"No...but you called it." And she hadn't listened. "Can you untie me?" She extended her hands toward Selena but the movie star folded her arms.

"So, I was right about him."

Leslie sighed. "You were right about him."

"And you were wrong?"

"Seriously?"

"Say it."

"Okay, I was wrong. Now untie me before he wakes up and murders you."

Selena moved closer and untied the rope quickly.

Leslie grabbed her bag and retrieved her gun and handcuffs, then she dug around in the console for her cell phone. Battery was at twenty percent...but no cell service.

Fucking fantastic.

But at least they were no longer at the mercy of a stalker.

ARRIVING IN WILD RIVER twelve hours after receiving the call from Eddie, exhausted and fueled only by coffee and adrenaline, Levi headed straight to the police station. Leaving his crew to fight the fires in Florida on their own had been one of the toughest, quickest decisions he'd ever had to make in his life, but he couldn't ignore his gut feeling that something was wrong. Leslie's vehicle had a tracking device on it. That meant Selena's stalker could know where they were. At least they'd been safe at the cabin, but the shop had reported that Leslie had picked up her vehicle hours ago.

"Any word from her?" Levi asked as he hurried into Eddie's office. He'd had no luck reaching her on her cell phone and by now, he must be looking like a stalker himself with the number of missed calls she'd find on her phone.

He hadn't showered or changed and he was dirty and he stank, but none of that mattered right now.

"No," Eddie said. "But I've been tracking her car with the tracker and they've been driving south." He looked worried, but not entirely convinced that something was legitimately wrong. "I tried calling you, but it went straight to voicemail," Eddie said, taking in his gear.

"I was on a domestic flight back here," Levi said.

"I hate to say it, man, but I might have put out the emergency call a little early," Eddie said. "This could just be Leslie being Leslie."

No way. His gut told him something was definitely off. "Normally, I'd agree but we've both been trying to reach her and by now she'd have at least sent a 'Fuck off' text," he said.

Eddie nodded. "You're right about that." He paused. "So what should we do? They are about ten hours away already and other than asking a highway trooper to pull her car over, I'm not sure how to reach her."

"Could we do that?"

Eddie grinned, reaching for his cell phone. "Probably not, but I can threaten it," he said, texting her.

Levi sat in the chair across from Eddie's desk, exhaustion catching up to him. He'd left base camp and hiked to the Florida station ten miles away, where he'd gotten a ride to the airport. He'd been prepared to pay anything for a last-minute flight back to Anchorage and the entire eight-hour flight, he'd been on edge. Desperate to get back, hating to be out of range, out of contact.

Now maybe Eddie was right. It could have been an insane overreaction.

"So, she was at the cabin these last few days?" Eddie asked, leaning back in his chair.

"Yeah. Listen, I'm sorry, man. She didn't want me to tell anyone. She thought maybe your family might have a difference of opinion on how she was handling things." He ran a hand over his scruffy beard.

"She's not wrong," Eddie said, then he frowned. "So, were you done in Florida?"

Levi shifted in the chair. "Not exactly." And if Leslie was fine and just ignoring them the way Eddie thought, his rushing back there, following a gut instinct, was enough for him to maybe hand over his position to Chad. He'd made a judgment call that he never would have made for any other reason, for any other person.

"But you came back early?"

"Yep." This would be an amazing time for that Forrester guy to be around. Levi's actions would have highlighted his point exactly. The woman he loved might have needed him and that had taken priority.

"Because you thought Leslie might be in trouble?"

"Yep."

The knowing look on Eddie's face told Levi it was time to go before this conversation took a different turn. He stood.

"Are we going to talk about that or…?"

"I'd rather not," Levi said, heading toward the office door. "Keep trying her and I'll let you know if I hear anything." Right now he needed a shower and a nap and time to reevaluate his priorities. The last week he'd taken far too many chances with his career and while he'd give up anything and everything to be with Leslie, he had to start facing reality—a future with her might not be in the cards and he had to salvage what he did have left.

"Sounds good, man. Take care," Eddie said.

"Hey, Eddie…call for you on line two," said Jan, the department receptionist, paging his office.

"Do you know who it is?" Eddie asked as he nodded his goodbye to Levi and reached for the landline on his desk.

"I think it's your sister," Jan said.

Eddie sat forward and Levi paused in the doorway. "Katherine?"

"Leslie," Jan said.

IT WAS ALMOST forty hours since he'd last slept, but the adrenaline pumping through Levi's body as he paced the station had him wide awake.

"They're here," Eddie said, tapping him on the shoulder as the station doors opened and the highway troopers led Selena's stalker in through the doors, his hands in cuffs behind his back. Eoghan. Leslie's co-worker. Another agent. She'd been right about it being an inside job and not trusting anyone. Unfortunately, she'd trusted the wrong guy.

Six-foot-two and at least two hundred pounds, the guy's long hair blocked the view of his face as he kept his head down, shuffling his feet as he passed Levi in the hallway.

Son of a bitch. Levi's hands clenched at his sides. Resisting the temptation to knock the guy out took everything he had. And several officers watching him.

If this man touched one hair on Leslie's head…one hair on Selena's head…

But when the door opened again and Leslie entered, all anger disappeared, replaced only by relief. She was okay. They were okay.

Only her face wasn't okay. Deep bruising around her right eye and cheekbone, swelling that made one side of her face balloon had Levi's heart racing and he turned to head back toward Eoghan.

Eddie intercepted. "Hey, it's okay. He'll get what he deserves. Channel your energy where it matters most," he said quietly, nodding toward Leslie and Selena walking their way.

Levi took a breath. "Yeah. You're right."

"Hey, sis…looking good," Eddie said, as the two women reached them, but even Levi could detect the note of concern in his teasing as he pulled Leslie in for a hug. "You good?" he heard the other guy whisper.

"Yeah," Leslie said. "Fine."

Her voice was steady and strong. No sign of fear or anguish. Forever the professional badass, she would never let on if this experience had shaken her.

When she pulled back and her gaze met Levi's, she looked happy to see him but also slightly confused. "Weren't you…?"

"I came back," he said awkwardly, staring at his feet.

Two arms were wrapped around his waist, but unfortunately, they were the wrong ones. "So happy to see you," Selena said, smiling up at him.

He forced one of his own, squeezing her quickly with one arm then releasing her. "Happy to see you in one piece as well," he said. She looked tired and she was dirty and wet from the hike along the highway to get cell reception, but other than that, she was injury-free.

"I knew not to trust that guy," she said and he saw Leslie's irritation mount.

Eddie saw it too and quickly addressed Selena. "Hey, why don't I start taking your statement? Get you some coffee and something to eat."

The movie star nodded, but then glanced at Leslie as though for reassurance.

"It's fine. Go with Eddie. I'll be there in a minute," she said.

Selena followed Eddie to his office. Leaving the two of them alone.

Levi cleared his throat. "I want to kill him for doing that to you," he said.

"It's not as bad as it looks," Leslie said, forever tough, forever strong. "Um, aren't you supposed to be in Florida?"

Obviously she didn't want to discuss what had happened. Unfortunately, that meant he had some explaining to do. "I am, yes, but Eddie called."

She shook her head. "You were supposed to be ignoring Eddie's calls, remember?"

"I knew something was wrong. When you weren't answering… I just had a feeling that something was wrong, that's all."

She stared at him as though conflicted by his actions. That made two of them, but he couldn't regret his decision. He wanted to give himself shit over putting his career on the line, but ultimately it was a decision he'd make over and over again. What if something had happened to her? The thought of potentially losing her for good was too much. He was glad he was there. This was the only place he should be right now.

Although standing there, not touching her was torture.

She looked like she'd been through hell that week and he was a mess, but he didn't care, he'd wrap his arms around her, if she'd give any indication that she'd welcome that.

She didn't. Instead, she folded her arms across her chest. "What about the assist call?"

"I can't say I'm even thinking about that right now." He stepped forward and touched her arms anyway. "All I care about is you being okay."

"I'm fine. And you could have risked your job…"

"It's a risk I was willing to make. For that matter, it's a risk I'd make over and over again."

She shook her head, irritated by his concern. "That doesn't even make any sense, Levi. This is what we do. We all know there's an element of danger in our careers. The job comes first."

"Not for me. Not when it comes to you," he said gently. Of course she'd feel that way. She'd grown up with a family of law enforcers who put their careers above all else. She'd been prepared to marry someone who would do the same... Who had done the same.

He wasn't like the rest of them. He'd never had a real, solid family, anyone he could rely on, depend on...and Leslie was the person he trusted and loved the most in the world. That was worth putting above all else, even if she didn't feel that way.

Her expression changed, softened slightly, then she looked away quickly. "I should get cleaned up and get ready to give my statement."

He nodded slowly and let his hands drop. What had he expected? This love had always been one-sided. Thinking that things might have changed that week between them had been foolish. "Yeah. I should go too." He was covered in sweat and soot and he smelled like a wildfire. He wasn't exactly making it hard for her to resist him.

"Levi, I..." She stopped as though she had no idea how to finish the sentence. No matter what she said, it wouldn't be what he longed to hear.

"Yeah, I know. Take care, Leslie." Walking quickly, he headed down the hall and out of the station, hoping he didn't look as pathetic as he felt.

CHAPTER TWENTY-ONE

THE NEXT TWENTY-FOUR hours were a blur and it was only when she was in her seat on a plane from Anchorage to LA that Leslie let herself relax. The Alaska state trooper department was holding Eoghan in custody until he could be transferred back to California. Leslie and Selena had provided their statements and she'd received medical treatment for a fractured cheekbone. Her call to Federico at the agency had been short and sweet—he'd advised her to get Selena back to LA as soon as possible and he was glad they were both okay. Flying back was faster. She'd figure out how to get her car back later.

The movie star looked like she wasn't suffering any aftereffects from the trauma. Sitting in the first-class window seat next to her, Selena thumbed through a fitness magazine and sipped a glass of wine.

"Hey… How on earth did you do that anyway? With the handcuffs." She hadn't had a chance to ask Selena about her quick-thinking skills with everything else going on.

"I pay attention sometimes," Selena said with a grin. "At your family's house. I watched and learned."

Leslie laughed, but it was more strangled relief. "I think you might have saved our lives."

"Might have?"

"Okay, definitely did." She hesitated. "I'm sorry about all of this. I should have listened to you when you said you didn't trust Eoghan and when you said you hadn't posted those pictures." She shook her head. Disappointment in herself—her judgment, her perception of things, her inability to listen to Selena—was starting to set in now that the immediate danger was over.

Selena shrugged. "Don't beat yourself up over it. We've all been gaslit by a man before."

"Yeah, but I shouldn't have been. Not by Eoghan. I'm trained to see the signs, the dangers, the warning patterns of behavior, but I...just didn't." Maybe she wasn't as cut out for this career as she'd thought. How could she not question her abilities when she'd failed the first time she'd really been put to the test?

Selena closed the magazine and touched her shoulder. "Why are you being so hard on yourself? Of course you didn't see it with Eoghan, because he didn't show any of that. He was trained the same way you were, so he knew how *not* to act. He knew you'd pick up on anything suspicious, so he made sure not to fall into any of those recognizable patterns."

She had a point, but... "But I still let him get close. To both of us. That never should have happened."

"Why? Are you immune to the need to have connections with people? Leslie, you're only human and as much as you push people away, even you needed someone in your life— even if it was just casual. Eoghan was a safe choice for you because you knew there was no chance of getting hurt because your feelings for him weren't that deep," she said.

Wow, when had *Selena* gotten so deep? Having misjudged the woman and not actually getting to know her before making assumptions compounded Leslie's guilt. "Still, I'm sorry."

"Apology accepted and I'm sorry if I was...difficult at times."

Leslie laughed. "Understatement."

"We're safe now. I can return to my life. And for what it's worth, I think you did everything right," Selena said.

Leslie swallowed the lump in her throat. "Thank you." Unfortunately, her superiors wouldn't see it that way

THAT PAST WEEK took the award for craziest week of Levi's life.

He'd struggled with every emotion possible—heartache, love, fear, disappointment, and now that it was all over, he wasn't sure what to feel. It was as if his body had shut down, gone numb in a form of protective mode.

Leslie and Selena were back in LA. The stalker was in custody and everyone was safe.

Her goodbye this time had left him with the impression that he was nowhere on her mind right now and he understood—she had a lot to deal with still back in LA. She'd just escaped an abduction and there were far more pressing things for her to focus on. He wasn't sure he'd ever make her priority list.

But damn if he didn't miss her already. Maybe if they'd had more time and the circumstances hadn't been so intense.

He'd give anything to see her right now.

"Hey, turn on *Channel 5 News*," Chad said, entering his office without knocking. He and the rest of the team had just gotten back from Florida a few hours ago. Levi still had a tough decision to make regarding his own career. He needed to meet with his team and find out whether they all still felt confident with him at the lead.

Levi grabbed the remote and turned on the news. On the screen, Selena was being interviewed by the media at a press conference. Dressed in a pale pink sundress, her hair and makeup done, Levi almost didn't recognize her. No wonder Leslie had believed she could keep the star safe from her usual fans. Gone was the girl next door look she'd sported here in Alaska, replaced with a glamorous Hollywood persona. Next to her stood what he assumed was her management team while several LA officers kept the crowd back and under control.

"It's been a scary few weeks," she was saying, "but I'm just happy to be back in LA, knowing that the bad guy is behind bars."

The bad guy. Eoghan. The guy Leslie had been casually dating. He knew she'd be beating herself up over that right now, blaming herself for allowing Eoghan to get to Selena through her. Once again she'd feel validated in keeping people at a distance.

Keeping *him* at a distance. She hadn't called or texted to let him know they were settled, and resisting the urge to reach out to her was nearly impossible. He didn't need answers about them... He just wanted to hear her voice. Selena was safe, her nightmare was over, but he was still worried about Leslie. She'd push through this the way she always did by shutting down, putting walls up and pushing everyone away.

"We know it's been tough on her fans, but we needed to do what was in her best interest, to keep her safe," her PR rep said, speaking next.

Bullshit. Leslie had made that call all on her own and now she'd be the one owning up to that decision, her future on the line. She deserved praise for her actions, but unfortunately, Levi knew the agency was going to want to make a clean break, distance themselves from this mess, and that would include letting Leslie go.

Next, to his surprise, Leslie appeared on the camera, her right eye still swollen and bruised. Levi's fists curled and anger raged through his body. That son of a bitch. If he could have five minutes alone with the guy...

He stood and moved closer to the television as though it could somehow bring him closer to Leslie and studied her expression as the interviewer questioned her.

"So, the Executive Protection Agency had no idea that one of their employees was the suspect?" the female reporter asked, turning the microphone toward Leslie.

"No. Eoghan Hartright's background checks came back clear of any indication that he could be a threat to any of the company's clients." Her voice was confident, clear and sure, and her demeanor was professional and calm, but he knew she had to be fighting turmoil within. The agency hadn't taken her concerns seriously enough. They hadn't listened to her and now she'd be the scapegoat. "The company's emphasis on safety is the number one priority." No doubt she'd been coached to make sure the agency's reputation was protected and while he admired the hell out of her for her show of respect, this was bullshit.

"Were you authorized or advised to take Ms. Hudson away from LA?" the reporter asked.

Leslie hesitated. "No, that was my decision. It was impulsive and could have ended badly. I take full responsibility for my actions."

They were the right actions. From what he'd learned about the case from Selena and Leslie, she'd had no other choice. Her decision to leave LA had ultimately saved Selena's life. And then Selena's quick thinking had saved hers.

What if something had happened to her? His blood chilled in his veins at the very thought. For so long, he'd kept his feelings to himself. Then that week everything had changed. He didn't know what would happen next, but he knew he wasn't ready to just let her go again. If this experience had taught him anything, it was that life was too short to have regrets or let doubt—or guilt—prevent him from living his life the way he most wanted to.

With her in it.

But how could he help her reach the same realization?

Turning off the television, he left the station and climbed into his truck.

Walking into Flippin' Pages a few hours later, Levi's heart was even heavier. His grandmother's call saying she'd been able to restore the photo should have been good news, but the events of the last few days only made it harder.

He'd been looking forward to surprising Leslie with the photo, but now she had so much else going on, so much to deal with... Would she even care?

"Hey, Levi, how are you?" Ellie asked, touching his arm gently.

Everyone in town knew by now about the situation and how he'd helped the women by letting them hide out at the station.

"I'm okay... Just here to see Grandma," he said.

"She's in her office," Ellie said.

He ran a hand over his face as he headed toward the back office.

"You look horrible," his grandmother said as he entered.

"Thanks. It's been a rough few days," he said, accepting the cup of hot coffee she extended to him.

"I heard about the kidnapping..." She shook her head. "So glad Leslie and that young starlet are okay," she said.

"Me too," he said, emotion thick in his voice. He sipped his coffee—the fourth one that day—but the liquid held no taste and the caffeine seemed to have little effect.

His grandmother eyed him. "You still didn't tell that girl, did you?"

His forehead wrinkled. "Tell her what?"

"That you love her."

"You know that?" No sense denying it. His shocked expression must say it all anyway.

"Always have. I may not have been one of those...helicopter parents, but I paid attention."

He nodded. He wished she had been more hands-on, but she'd been there when it mattered and he couldn't fault her for focusing on her own life. She'd raised her kids and he'd been dumped on her.

She sat across from him. "Look, Levi, you were a good kid and you were mature for your age. I never worried about you. You had a good head on your shoulders. And the Powells had kinda taken you under their wing..." She shrugged. "But I did pay attention to the important things and my heart has always hurt just a little, knowing you were keeping your love to yourself for her sake...for her happiness."

The heart-to-heart might be coming a little late, but he held no grudges. He sighed as he stared into the dark liquid, watching the swirls of steam escape the cup. "I did tell her. Probably wasn't the best timing or situation. And I was starting to think she might have feelings for me too."

"That's good. Progress," his grandmother said, looking truly engaged.

"Yeah, but now she's gone again and things have always been complicated. Even more so now."

"Complicated, sure. But not impossible," she said, handing him the restored photo. "Just like this picture."

HAD THE LA sun always been this blinding?

Despite her dark sunglasses, Leslie's eyes hurt as she entered the Executive Protection Agency later that week. Exhausted from lack of sleep and worry, her body still aching from the attempted abduction, she longed to put off what was sure to be her firing, but she had to face the music today. Get this over with, then decide what was next for her.

Entering her boss's office, she slid her sunglasses to the top of her head.

He winced, a note of sympathy in his expression seeing the black eye and bruised cheek she still sported. "That looks like it hurt."

"I've been through worse." The emotional toil of the last few weeks had her hurting more than the physical damage she'd suffered on assignment.

Levi's confession of love replayed in her thoughts and in her dreams and her own conflicted heart was killing her. A month ago, she was successfully keeping her past in the past, along with her feelings. Now, everything had been dug up from where she'd kept it buried and she didn't know where to begin to start healing. She never really had.

"Have a seat," Federico said, standing and closing his office door. Several other agents were standing in the hall, no doubt eager to listen. It didn't matter, she didn't care what they all thought. She'd be walking out for the last time in a few moments anyway.

Federico returned to his chair and sat. He cleared his throat and got straight to it. "Leslie, you've been a great agent, and we were fortunate to have you on this assignment." He folded his large wrinkled hands in front of him on his desk. "Your quick thinking and skills helped to save Ms. Hudson's life."

But...

"But your impulsiveness and unauthorized decision

making is questionably what put her in more danger in the first place."

She wished she could argue that, but she couldn't. She'd reacted on instinct that day instead of policy.

"Fleeing the state and not advising anyone of your plans was rash and unfortunately, we aren't able to overlook the... liability you are to this company." Federico shook his graying head.

She nodded. Liability. That stung more than she thought it would.

"I'm afraid we have to let you go," Federico said, looking genuinely saddened by the decision he felt forced to make. "Effective immediately."

"I understand, sir." She stood. "I apologize for putting the agency under scrutiny and for not recognizing the danger that Eoghan proposed to my client sooner."

He nodded quickly at the mention of Eoghan, almost as though he'd hoped not to have to discuss the agency's own lack of judgment in hiring the man. "Yes, well..."

The office door flew open and Selena burst in.

Federico stood. "Ms. Hudson, what are you doing here? I mean, nice to see you... Is everything okay with the new security detail?"

The agency had convinced Selena's management team to allow them to stay on and had replaced Leslie with another agent.

"No, everything's not okay," Selena said, sliding her Tiffany sunglasses up over her dark hair. "I got up this morning expecting my peppermint herbal tea with my two scoops of Swerve and honey made the way I like it to be waiting for me after my workout and it wasn't there."

Leslie hid a smile at the overdramatic outburst. This

wasn't the Selena she'd gotten to know but she was enjoying the theatrics.

Federico looked confused. "Um…"

"Do you know why it wasn't there?" she asked, hands on her tiny hips.

"No, Ms. Hud—"

"Because Ms. Sanders wasn't there. Instead, I have this eight-foot-tall beast scaring the shit out of my Chihuahua and handing me a plastic one-use water bottle." She said the words in a whisper hiss as though the environment police were in earshot.

Federico stammered, unsure how to respond.

Despite the deep ache in her chest, Leslie felt a smile tug at the corner of her mouth. She hadn't realized she'd missed this five-foot-six, hundred-pound terror until that morning when she wasn't swearing over making the herbal tea. She hadn't seen Selena since the press conference. She hadn't returned the ten thousand text messages from her either, thinking it best to cut all contact.

"I apologize, Ms. Hudson, but given the circumstances…" Federico stammered.

"Circumstances? You mean, the fact that this woman saved my life?" Selena gestured to Leslie.

Technically, in the end they'd saved each other and to her surprise, Leslie had felt a small void not being in contact with her the last few days. Must be the shared life-and-death experience. That was all. A common bond of having gone through something traumatic.

"Yes, she did, but—" Federico said.

Selena waved a finger, silencing him. "I'm still breathing and bullet hole–free, so there is no 'but.'"

Federico's cheeks flushed and he shifted from one foot to the other. It wasn't every day someone almost two feet shorter than him could intimidate him but Leslie could al-most see his balls shrinking up into his body as he said, "Well, she also broke protocol…"

"If she hadn't, I'd be dead—or worse," Selena said, cranking up the drama.

Only in Hollywood…

Federico looked at a loss for further excuses or rationale, and glanced at Leslie.

Leslie remained calm and professional as she turned to her former client. "Selena, I appreciate you coming to my defense like this, but Federico is right. My actions put you in danger."

"Bullshit," Selena said, looking at her like she was disap-pointed that Leslie hadn't already filed a lawsuit for wrong-ful dismissal. "Do not let these assholes gaslight you like that. You followed your instincts and you were right to do it. Unlike this agency hiring someone without completing a full credential verification. Your agency," she said walking toward Federico, "put my life at risk by hiring a dangerous person and then allowing him access to private informa-tion. Not Ms. Sanders."

Selena did have a point. She'd been selective about the information she'd disclosed to Eoghan, yet he knew things he shouldn't have been privy to. Information she'd told only Federico, like when the new security system had been in-stalled and when Selena was making public appearances. The agency really hadn't done everything in their power to keep Selena safe. If she hadn't taken Selena away, Eoghan would have gotten to her.

"Ms. Hudson does raise a valid point," she said, feel-ing her fighting energy return. She wouldn't ask for him to reconsider his decision about firing her because she no longer wanted to work for an agency that didn't have her back or one she couldn't completely trust. And she had no intentions of going to the media to blame the agency to protect or reclaim her own credentials. But at least now she was seeing this parting of ways in a different light, one where she wasn't completely at fault. And her confidence returned slightly.

Federico looked back and forth between them. "So, you want Ms. Sanders to continue as your security detail?" he asked Selena.

"Yes," she said. "But not through this agency. I'm terminating my contract, effective immediately." She ripped the papers she had in her hands, which looked like a take-out menu from the sushi place down the street and not her actual agency contract, then she turned to Leslie. "I want to hire you privately."

"Oh…um…" Did Leslie even want to continue in this line of work? She hadn't made any real decisions regarding her future career yet.

"You can name your price," Selena said.

Caught off guard, Leslie hesitated. Was Selena serious? For months, she'd complained about not having a big burly man protect her and now she had that and she wanted Leslie back? Or maybe this was all a show for Federico's sake. Her way of helping Leslie regain face in front of her employer.

Selena waved a hand. "You're right. We shouldn't discuss business in front of your former employer. Let's go. My driver will take us somewhere for lunch where we can discuss this privately," she said with as much Hollywood flair as Leslie had ever seen and she hid her grin as she stood, put on her sunglasses, and followed the star out of the office.

Dramatic exits weren't normally her thing, but when in Rome…

CHAPTER TWENTY-TWO

Two weeks later...

THE CHIHUAHUA WAS wearing a suit.

Leslie refused to admit that Unicorn looked adorable in the black-and-white dog outfit with the fake bowtie that Selena had bought him to wear to her movie premiere that evening. She was just relieved that the dog was okay. He'd enjoyed his extended stay at Posh Puppy Spa and the reunion with his owner had been about as dramatic as possible.

Now, he ran around the posh Beverly Hills hotel room with a plastic bone in his mouth. He brought it to Leslie and dropped it at her feet. "No. I'm not touching that," she told the dog.

Unicorn's tail wagged so fast it blurred and he nudged the bone closer.

Leslie sighed, picked up the disgustingly wet bone and threw it across the room. Then a knock on the room door had her jumping to her feet. "Who is it?" she asked, looking through the peephole. A tall, lanky guy with a handlebar mustache who she didn't recognize stood there with a garment bag draped over his arm.

"Antonio from Versace. I have a dress for Ms. Hudson," he called through the door.

"She already has a dress," Leslie said, glancing toward

the bathroom, where Selena was already outfitted for the movie premiere in a dark green floor-length backless gown. Her makeup artist was finishing up and her hair stylist sat ready to do her job next.

"I was told to bring it," the guy said.

Leslie sighed. Selena had tried on sixteen dresses the day before at the fitting and had spent hours agonizing over the right choice. If she was changing her mind again, they *might* make it to the theater for the movie premiere before the final credits rolled. "Hey, Selena...this guy, Anthony, says he has another dress."

Selena nodded, smacking her lips together in the bathroom mirror. "Yes—and it's *Antonio*. Let him in."

Instead, Leslie opened the door and stepped out into the hallway. She patted the guy down and unzipped the garment bag to look inside. No concealed weapon. She went back inside the hotel room and let him in.

Selena met him with a warm smile. "Antonio! Thank you so much for bringing this last-minute."

"No problem, darlin', but it's the wrong size. They said at the shop that they confirmed with you that this was the one you wanted, but it's going to hang off you all wrong." The guy looked sincerely distraught at the thought that the dress wouldn't show on the red carpet properly.

And Leslie was relieved. They wouldn't have to waste more time on another dress. She couldn't wait to get Selena to the premiere, so she could relax in the back of a dark theater for a little while. She'd agreed to return as Selena's security temporarily until she decided what she wanted to do moving forward...and if she was being honest, now that Eoghan had turned out to be a stalker, Selena was the only real...friend?...she had in LA. Her family were still reaching out to check on her—primarily Eddie—but she was keeping up the facade of being okay.

But the truth was, emotionally, she wasn't sure she'd ever not feel so exhausted. Her conflicted heart had her yo-yoing between reaching out to Levi or leaving the week they'd had together in the past. She hadn't made any promises to him when they'd said goodbye and he wasn't expecting anything from her...

Which made things a million times worse because it was really all on her. She knew where he stood and despite him not reaching out to her, she didn't doubt for a second that he wanted to, but she had no idea what *she* wanted.

"This dress is not for me." Selena turned to grin at her and Leslie's head was shaking.

"Absolutely not. I'm your security detail. Not your date."

"Look, I'm still freaked out by the whole experience and I'd like you to stay close."

Lies. The star had bounced back after the incident faster than a wrongly addressed email. "I can do that better not in a dress." The last dress she'd worn had been to her grandmother's wedding months ago and that had been under extreme duress and she loved her grandmother and just barely, recently started tolerating Selena.

"They only let stars on the red carpet," Selena said, reaching toward her belt. "And their plus one."

Leslie sighed, slapping her hands away. "I can take my own clothes off," she mumbled. "And he has to leave."

Selena smiled warmly at Antonio. "Thank you again," she said, tipping him and seeing him out. He kissed both of her cheeks and wished her luck at her premiere. Then she turned back to Leslie. "Okay, well, hurry. We're going to be late."

This was insane. She had to be crazy for agreeing to

this. But before she knew it, she was out of her pants and shirt and sliding into the long, simple black gown. Which cost more than she made in a year.

"It's on loan. So be careful," Selena said, helping her zip it up.

Her pulse raced. Wonderful, so not only was she going to be uncomfortable all evening, but she needed to make sure she didn't spill anything on it or rip it?

"Wow. You look amazing. Who knew this curvy body was hidden under all those unflattering clothes you wear?" Selena said, turning her toward the full-length mirror.

The dress fit her perfectly. Actually suited her as well. Nothing too flashy or over-the-top. No sequins or bows or revealing cut-outs. She ran a hand along the soft fabric as she stared at her reflection.

What would Levi think if he saw her in it? Would it be silly to snap a selfie and send it to him with the message Help, I've been abducted?

Yes, it would and also, it would open up the lines of communication again and she wasn't sure she was ready for that. Unfortunately, the more time that passed, the less ready she was.

"Some makeup and a few curls and you might actually steal some attention away from me," Selena said.

"Yeah. Right." It would take more than a dress for that to happen. Leslie picked up her gun and scanned the available places on her body. Where the hell could she put it?

Selena handed her a leg holster. She'd actually thought this through, meaning this hadn't been the last-minute thing she tried to make it appear. "Strap it in here, like Angelina Jolie in…"

"*Mr. and Mrs. Smith*." Leslie couldn't help but laugh.

"Yes, I know." Taking the holster, she wrapped it around

her right leg through the slit in the dress and secured the gun out of sight.

"Nothing wrong with being sexy and lethal," Selena said with a wink.

Damn, if it wasn't actually the most empowering feeling ever.

WHAT'S SAFER THAN bringing your bodyguard as a date?

Selena's caption on the photo had Levi smiling, while his chest tightened. Leslie looked drop-dead gorgeous in an elegant, simple tight-fitting black evening gown, despite looking completely terrified and uncomfortable standing next to the star on the red carpet. Her blond hair was hanging loose in waves around her sexy bare shoulders and she was wearing slightly more makeup than he'd ever seen her wear. She looked like she could be on the movie screen herself.

Damn she was beautiful.

And obviously staying in LA to continue working as Selena's security.

What had he expected? That his confession of love and their time together would have been enough to make her want to come back here? Be with him?

They'd had a connection. She couldn't deny it, but for Leslie, that would be all the more reason to stay away. Running away from the guilt and conflict that opening her heart to him would definitely cause was her self-preservation method.

He'd go to her if he thought she wanted him to. If there wasn't a certainty that she'd push him away. He'd move halfway across the world for her—no question. His career meant a lot to him, but she meant more.

He stared at the photo of her awkward, forced-looking smile and the right thing to do hit him like déjà vu.

He'd let her go once before for her happiness; he could do it again.

Smokester sauntered over and sat at Levi's feet. The sad expression, floppy ears and low whine from the dog echoed his sentiments. "I miss them too, buddy," he said petting the dog's head. It had been weeks but it seemed the dog was having as hard a time of it as he was.

His gaze landed on the photo he'd had refinished for Leslie. He should probably just send it to her in LA. That would be the easiest. Or maybe her mother might like to have it…

A knock sounded on the door before Mrs. Powell entered. "Oh…hi. I didn't hear the front door." He hadn't heard from her or spoken to her directly since she'd walked in on him and Leslie together. He wasn't sure of his responsibility to the foundation now, if she still wanted him involved.

"It was open. I hope you don't mind me stopping by." She was wringing her hands and struggling to make eye contact as she said, "Levi, I owe you an apology and I'm not very good at them, so um…"

He smiled and stood. "Then let's just say that was it." He opened his arms and she stepped into them with a sigh of relief. He hugged her tight. "And I'm sorry if I upset you."

She pulled away and sighed. The fine lines around her eyes looked deeper that day and this conversation seemed to be taking a lot out of her. "Darling, it's your life. You can love who you love and be involved with anyone your heart desires…" She glanced at her shoes. "And I should have been more supportive."

He sensed she was talking about support she should have given in the past as well. To her son and maybe even Leslie. He knew from experience how regret could manifest in different ways and could be spurred from new realizations after it was too late to make amends. His had certainly re-surfaced, allowing himself to open up to Leslie, but he was understanding now that guilt was just one emotion and it didn't need to fuel his actions.

"I know you two have never really gotten along, but Leslie is a wonderful person," he said gently, not wanting to make her feel worse.

"I know that. I do. As a mother, you want what's best for your children and I may have been a little blinded by my own prejudices when it came to Leslie. I worshipped my son and no one is good enough for your kids." She paused. "But she was always lucky to have you in her life. You're quite wonderful yourself, young man." She looked past him and, seeing the photo on his desk, she picked it up. "Her father took this?"

"Yeah. Unfortunately, it was the only thing I could save after the fire." His grandmother had done an amazing job restoring it and he hoped it would give Leslie a little clo-sure to have it.

Mrs. Powell studied the photo, then studied him. "You've always loved her, haven't you?"

No sense denying it and he never wanted Mrs. Powell to mistake his actions in his office that day as simply lust or a physical attraction. He nodded. "With all my heart."

She put the photo down and took his hands in hers. "My son was so lucky to have you. They both were—are," she said. "Keeping your own feelings to yourself all these years had to be hard and even though you don't need my permis-sion to finally go after what you want, I'm giving it. I want to see you happy, Levi."

He took a deep breath, feeling the weight on his chest get that much lighter. She was right, he didn't need her bless-ing, but it made him feel better to have it. She'd been like a mother to him for so long and he felt as though getting her approval was the next best thing to getting Dawson's. "Thank you. That means more than you know," he said.

She nodded. "I really wish I could do things differently... but I can't change the past."

"No one can. We just have to do the best we can going forward."

She wiped a tear from the corner of her eye. "You'll still be there at the event? You still want to be involved in the foundation?"

"Of course."

He'd never let his best friend down before. He wouldn't start now.

LESLIE TOOK SELENA'S laptop and plugged in the cable to the camera the next afternoon, after they'd both slept half the day away. They hadn't gotten back to the hotel after the premiere and after-parties until almost 3:00 a.m. Her job was feeling more like hanging out with the star now—dare she even say, hanging out with a friend. Which meant it was time to move on. They could still stay in touch, but Leslie felt the lines between personal and professional blurring and ultimately that put Selena at risk. She hadn't gotten the nerve to tell Selena yet, but she would. Soon.

"I'm not sure how great these turned out," she said, clicking on the link to the photos she'd taken in the Alaskan wilderness three weeks before.

Three weeks. Felt like forever.

"From what I remember, they're really great," Selena said, bringing her chair super close and curling her legs under her as she sat.

Normally the close proximity and Selena's disregard for personal space would annoy her, but knowing she was planning on handing in her resignation made Selena that much more tolerable. Damn it, she was going to miss the pain-in-the-ass movie star.

"Okay, here they are," she said as the images loaded.

Selena leaned closer, examining each photo of her in the snowy woods with the mountains in the distance. "You were so right about the lighting being perfect. I barely have any makeup on and I don't even need a filter on these."

"You never need a filter," Leslie said.

"Aw…thanks. I like those three best," she said, pointing to the same ones Leslie would have chosen.

"Yeah, they are really nice, but are you sure your team is going to want these more candid shots going on your site and audition material?"

Selena scoffed. "After neglecting to inform me of how much danger I was in before, I think I'll be taking over more of the decisions regarding my career moving forward."

Well, good for her. Still, Leslie was self-conscious about the images. It wouldn't just be Selena putting herself out there with this new look. Leslie's photography had always been private. Now millions of people would see it. "Okay, but maybe we should take new ones, here in LA. On the beach maybe?"

Selena shook her head, her long brown braid swishing back and forth. "These are perfect."

A message icon popped up on the screen and Leslie's heart all but stopped.

A new message from Levi.

"Is that Levi, my Levi?" she asked, staring at the name on the screen.

Selena shot her a look with one perfectly arched eyebrow raised. "Oh, so he's *your* Levi, now?"

She flushed. "You know what I mean." She hesitated. Selena and Levi corresponding was none of her business. She knew the star had "friended" most of the people she'd met in Wild River as well. Hell, she'd Skyped with Kaia two days ago. She was an extrovert and liked connecting with people. And staying in touch with the man who'd helped them out was completely natural, expected even. So why was Leslie jealous again? "You're still in contact with him?" she asked.

"Of course. I told him to reach out if he needed advice or had any questions regarding foundation stuff," Selena said, casually.

So he was still working on that. Good. That was good. She was glad she hadn't gotten between him and Mrs. Powell. "Oh, right. That's good." She paused. "How... How is he?" Did that sound casual?

"Good. I've set up a GoFundMe page for the foundation on the new website. It will help them collect donations throughout the year, not just during events."

"Wow. Does he ever mention—I mean, does he ask about me?" Damn, why had she asked that? What did it matter? And if he wanted to check in with her, he could text or call anytime.

She'd answer the phone, wouldn't she?

She'd definitely answer a text.

"Don't answer that," she said quickly.

Selena did anyway. "He does. Every single time we chat."

Her heart had lodged itself in her throat and she nodded casually. "So, these three photos, then?"

"You're in love with him."

She swung toward her with a scoff designed to make people keep their distance. "No... I'm..."

Selena eyed her. "I'm the expert on love, remember?"

"You're the expert on *fake* love," Leslie argued, but her words were only half-hearted.

"I spent a week and a half glued to your side and the only time you were even remotely relaxed or happy was when things started getting friendly with Levi. And the tension between you both was full of sexual chemistry even in the beginning. You were different with him."

"Okay, fine… I love him." It was the first time she'd even admitted it to herself and she knew it was true. "But you know why it's complicated."

Selena shot her a look. "You want complicated? Try dating your on-set intimacy coordinator."

Leslie almost laughed. Leave it to Selena to find the most awkward situation to put herself in. "Well, so you get it." She hadn't been able to erase thoughts of Levi from her mind in weeks; she really didn't want to talk about him. It hurt too much.

But the star was adamant. "No, I *don't* get it. He loves you. You love him. As much as you adore me, I'm not enough to keep you in LA. Neither is this job. You want to make a real difference in the world, maybe start by making a difference in Levi's."

Leslie studied her. "I don't remember that line from any of your movies."

Selena slapped her arm. "That's because it's not. It's from the heart. Look, I know I can be a pain in the ass and out of touch with reality, but what I saw between you and Levi? That shit's real. The pain you both went through connects you."

"Right. We're connected by my fiancé's death." How could they both move forward together with Dawson's ghost overshadowing their future? And if Levi was continuing with the foundation, then obviously he and Mrs. Powell were okay again and Leslie didn't want to come between them or cause unnecessary conflict.

"No. You both knew Dawson. You both loved Dawson. But you both lost Dawson. And as hard as that was and no matter how much you both still miss him and want to respect his memory, no one would fault either of you for moving on. And I truly believe that Dawson would be happier knowing you'd found one another in a true connection, than for both of you to blame him for not taking the chance on what you both want most. More than that—what you both deserve."

"I don't know. It's been a long time." Really only a few weeks, but the longer the silence grew between them, the harder it seemed to get back to any kind of progress they may have made during their time together.

"You have to stop running when faced with conflict," Selena said.

"What are you talking about? I face conflict all the time. It's my life. My career."

"Right. When you're protecting other people. But when it comes to your own personal conflicts—*your* fears—you run. You ran when you and your mom couldn't see eye to eye, you ran after Dawson died...now you're running from this. Running from Levi."

It was so true. But how did she stop running when it was her way of self-preservation all these years?

It would be so easy to listen to Selena. To use her friend's words as permission to go for it with Levi. But she still wasn't sure she could do it. "I don't know. I need more time to think about everything that happened... With some distance comes perspective, right?"

Selena nodded. "I thought you'd say that, so..." Reaching into her purse, she took out an envelope and handed it to Leslie.

A plane ticket for Anchorage. Leslie's eyes widened as she saw the date and time on the ticket. "This leaves in two hours."

Selena nodded. "In my experience, impulsive decisions are always the right ones."

Leslie raised an eyebrow. "Yeah, I don't think so."

"When it comes to matters of the heart—absolutely. Stop overthinking this. Remember how you felt when you were with him."

She did. It was all she could think about.

"Hold on to that feeling and go get him, before you throw yourself back into work and once again try to hide who you are and what you really want. You don't want to keep living this shell of an existence, Leslie."

She hesitated.

"That line was from a movie," Selena said, getting up and easing Leslie up from her chair. "My driver's waiting for you."

Her heart raced. Oh God. Could she actually do this? "What about you? I can't just leave you. I'm your security detail."

"I called an agency already. They are sending a guy over right away."

"So, you fight to get me my job back, and now you're firing me?"

Selena hugged her. "I just wanted more time to turn you into a friend. Some people say, I'm an acquired taste."

Leslie laughed, then sobered, staring at the plane ticket in her hand. "What do I say to him?"

"Tell him you love him and that's enough. After all," Selena said with a wink, "this isn't some cheesy rom-com."

CHAPTER TWENTY-THREE

STARING AT HER family home the next day, Leslie couldn't help but wonder if maybe not all families could resolve their issues, overcome their differences. So many years had passed and a lot of life had happened. They'd never been able to bring up the past without arguing. Maybe they were too late?

The only way she'd know was if she went inside.

"You don't have to go in," Eddie said, putting his van in Park and turning to face her.

Didn't she? Since this whole mess had happened, the weight of her past mistakes and unresolved issues weighed heavier on her now that she was acknowledging them. She'd never find peace if she kept running. Selena had been right to call her out on her usual way of handling uncomfortable situations.

"She's probably seen the van by now," Leslie said.

"I can run in and make up some excuse for stopping by," Eddie said. "She doesn't know you're back in town yet."

She'd crashed at his place the night before but could she be back permanently in Wild River and not have this heart-to-heart? Family gatherings had always been stressful. Everyone always suffered because of the tension between them. It had to stop. If there was some way to come to a truce, it would benefit everyone she cared about.

"Thanks, but I think I need to do this." Even if they

could never see eye to eye or have a close mother-daughter relationship, Leslie needed to offer the olive branch. Her mother had hurt her, but she'd hurt her as well and forgiveness couldn't start, healing couldn't start, until someone said they were sorry.

And if she was moving back to Wild River, she didn't want the strained relationship or the what-ifs plaguing her new future…whatever that may look like.

She unbuckled her seat belt and gave Eddie a quick hug. "Thanks for the ride."

"No problem…want me to wait?"

A getaway driver would only make it easier for her to escape if things went sideways. No more running. She was facing conflict head-on. One step at a time. "No. I'll be okay." If things didn't go well, she could jog back into town to let off steam.

"Okay. Don't forget Kaia's school play is tonight at seven at the junior high school."

"I'll be there," she said, climbing out of the van. She shut the door and took several deep, calming breaths as she walked up the stairs to the front door.

Knock? Or just go in?

She still had her old house key on her key ring. So many times she'd thought she should get rid of it, but could never bring herself to.

She knocked.

Her mother's look of surprise quickly evaporated, replaced by one of tremendous relief as she stepped out onto the porch and wrapped Leslie in a hug.

The lump in her throat was so thick she could barely breathe. This had to be the first real hug she'd gotten from her mother…in years. She couldn't even remember the last one. Even at Christmas, they'd do an awkward one-arm, shoulder squeeze thing. Never a full hug. Realizing her arms still hung at her sides, she lifted them slowly and hugged her mom back.

From the corner of her eye, she saw Eddie watching from the van and waved him on. Their rare display of affection for one another wasn't a spectator sport. She heard the van drive away as she pulled back slowly.

Her mother wiped an eye quickly and then scanned Leslie's face. Her black eye had faded to a yellowish hue, but the look of concern on her mother's face was still there. "I'm so grateful you're okay," she said, sounding slightly choked.

She wasn't the only one. "I'm fine. Just a few bruises, that's all." And a fractured cheekbone and third degree burns still healing on her hand, but she wasn't there to talk about the craziness of the last month. Injuries were part of their chosen careers. "I'm moving back home," she said. Then realizing her word choice, she said, "I mean to Wild River…not home…home."

Her mother nodded slowly. "I mean you could. I mean if you wanted to… Just temporarily obviously, we're not going to be permanent roommates or anything. That would be weird. But until you find a place of your own."

To say the offer came as a shock would be an understatement and she couldn't find the right words.

"I'm just putting it out there that you could stay here— if you want," her mother added awkwardly.

Could she though? She hadn't lived with her mother in over twelve years. Would they be able to put their differences aside that easily? Had it really only taken this experience for them to realize life was far too short to shut out the people who loved them? She'd done a lot of thinking in the last few days and she understood now everything her mother had been trying to do. She didn't agree with all of it, but she suspected her mother regretted some of it as well. And she was finally able to acknowledge her own part in everything. "I'm not sure that's the best idea… It's not a terrible idea," she said quickly when her mother looked disappointed, "but I think maybe we start slow? Baby steps."

Her mother nodded eagerly. "Like brunch?"

Leslie laughed. "Like brunch."

An awkward silence hung over them. "Um…should we hug again or…?"

"I think one was enough," she said.

Her mother looked relieved. Baby steps. "Did you want to come in? Were you here to visit?"

"Yeah, if you're not busy."

"Not at all. Actually, I received a bit of a surprise the other day." She moved back into the house and Leslie followed her inside. The usual gripping feeling in her chest she normally experienced upon being in her former family home, around her mother, didn't appear and she took it as a good sign.

In the kitchen, her mother handed her an envelope.

"What's this?" Leslie took it and read the return address. LA. Selena's address. She frowned. "Selena sent you a letter?" That was old school. Leslie had assumed Selena wouldn't have known what to do with a stamp.

Then again, she'd underestimated her quite a bit. If she was being completely honest, she missed the woman already. Which was unexpected—the star had driven her insane.

"Yes," her mother said. "And um…she's right about everything she says."

Oh no. "What did she say?" she asked slowly.

"Just that family was too important to throw away because of differences. That a bond between mother and daughter should be stronger than anger and hurt."

Leslie took a breath. "I'm sure she stole that line from a recent script," she said with a teasing grin.

"She also sent this," her mother said, taking a check out of the envelope. "To cover the cost of the cabin."

Leslie's eyes widened at the number of zeros. Holy shit! This was quite the apology.

The sticky note attached read "Hoping this will help with the rebuild. Still lots of memories to be made."

"Wow." This amount of money could build two cabins. "This was generous of her."

"Yep." Her mother leaned against the counter and stared at her for a long moment. "I mean, I was thinking of just sending it back... We can't really accept it, can we?"

"If I know Selena, she'd just hire someone to come build the cabin for us. She's a little headstrong when she cares about something."

"Oh...okay. So, we should keep this gift from her?"

Leslie nodded. "She'd be offended otherwise."

"But do we even want to rebuild the cabin?"

Suddenly, Leslie wanted to rebuild so much more. So many aspects of her life had been put on hold the last few years while she buried her feelings and held on to a past that no longer let her choose her own happiness.

"I definitely think we should rebuild," she said. "Selena's right—there are still more memories to be made."

THE JUNIOR HIGH school gym was standing room only by the time the play was about to start that evening. Leslie scanned the auditorium from the second-row seat they'd been able to snag because Eddie had insisted on getting there two hours early. Her brother's affection for his girlfriend's daughter was obvious and it didn't surprise Leslie how wonderful he was at this future stepdad role. Eddie really knew how to step up to responsibilities and seeing the three of them together, Leslie knew the admiration they all held for one another was mutual.

"I think there's more people here than at Selena's movie premiere," she said.

"I heard that," Selena said, as her face appeared on Leslie's phone via FaceTime. She was filming on set, but had insisted on being there remotely to see Kaia's performance. Leslie wouldn't admit how much that meant to her. Since leaving LA the day before, Selena had texted six times. And Leslie had texted back.

"Seriously, check it out," she said, holding the phone up and scanning the auditorium for Selena to see the crowd.

"Holy shit, that's awesome. Is Kaia nervous?" she asked.

Leslie had seen the little girl only momentarily when she'd arrived with Tank and Cassie, to wish her good luck with her performance, but she'd been almost vibrating. "I think she's excited." Leslie scanned all the parents around her. They were the ones who looked nervous. It had to be every parent's worst fear that their kid would embarrass themself or feel disappointed in their performance, especially after working so hard...but Kaia was so lucky to have her brother and Montana and Tank and Cassie so invested in her. She was a lucky kid.

The school's drama teacher appeared on stage at the microphone and a silence fell over the crowd as she welcomed everyone to the performance. A round of applause later and the red velvet curtain lifted.

The set was really well done and the familiar balcony from *Romeo and Juliet* had Leslie's emotions acting up even before the iconic, romantic tragedy began.

What was wrong with her? These were preteens acting out Shakespeare and yet her heart was in her throat throughout the entire play. Lovers that weren't destined to be together. Lives lost, wasted because of young love…

Beside her on the right, Tank and Cassie held hands, leaning into one another. On her left, Eddie and Montana were shoulder to shoulder, knee to knee.

Being the fifth wheel kinda sucked. She had thought of reaching out to Levi…but a junior high play with her brother and friends wasn't really the right time, the right way she wanted to talk to him. She'd missed him these past few weeks and he'd been constantly on her mind. That meant something. Since admitting her feelings to Selena, they'd only gotten stronger. As if saying it, acknowledging them had given them permission to grow and overwhelm her with their intensity.

The final scene left not a dry eye in the room and a standing ovation rippled through the crowd as the final curtain lowered. Leslie wiped her eye quickly as the auditorium lights came back on and turned her cell phone to face her.

"She was so amazing!" Selena said. "I have flowers being delivered backstage right now—a lot of flowers. You guys might want to go help her with them," she said.

"We're on it," Eddie said. "Meet you at the van," he told Leslie before the four parents headed backstage to collect Kaia.

Leslie left the row and moved through the crowd to the back of the auditorium.

"So?" Selena said.

"So what?"

"I want to hear all about it. Every last detail. Leave nothing out."

Leslie hesitated. "Hear about what?"

"You're stalling…" Selena peered at her through the phone screen. "Oh my God, you haven't seen him yet, have you?"

"I just got back to town."

"Two days ago!" Selena's shrill voice caught the attention of several parents and Leslie lowered the volume on the call as she headed outside.

It was actually a day and a half.

"Look, I'm just wanting to do it organically, you know. Let him find out I'm back through the grapevine and then…"

"Come to you?" Selena raised an eyebrow.

Yes. "No. Not like that. Just reconnect naturally…a casual encounter. Nothing forced or planned." Truth was she was terrified. She had no idea how Levi was going to respond to her being back, to seeing her again…especially since the two of them hadn't spoken in weeks. What if she'd hurt him too many times and he wasn't interested in getting involved anymore? She loved him but was that enough? He was still working on the foundation, so maybe he'd decided that he wanted to put his commitment to Dawson's memory above all else.

"He's going to misread that as you friend zoning him again," Selena said in a huff. "He'll think you're not madly in love with him. That you're back because you lost your job over questionable judgment and have nowhere else to go."

"That's not true." She'd decided to come back. And he'd been the most important factor in that decision. The only factor really.

"*He* doesn't know that," Selena said. "And no guy wants to feel like the fallback guy. Eoghan turned out to be a criminal, so you decide to choose Levi."

"Again, it's not like that." But no one could argue her right to be careful. She'd lost one fiancé to his job and the first time she let her guard down again around a man—however casual—the guy turned out to be a stalker. Taking things slow with Levi was the only thing that made sense.

Though they hadn't exactly taken things slow a few weeks before.

Selena moved closer to the screen. "Look, you need to go to him."

"I'm not sure I can."

"I'm telling you, you can. He's in Wild River tomorrow night at the resort for the charity event. You need to go and you need to tell him you love him."

Leslie winced. At an event honoring her former fiancé? One she wasn't a part of or even invited to? "You really think that's the best time?"

"Yes. Because it will bring you both closure and assure him that he's getting all of you. All of your heart. Convince him you're ready to move on."

She hated when Selena was right. "What if I'm not entirely ready?" She loved Levi. He was her best friend, always had been. He was the only man she wanted in her future, but she wasn't good at this. She'd started opening herself up only a few weeks ago...

Selena gave her an encouraging smile. "Then Levi will help you get there. With patience and understanding and love. Damn, girl, if you don't go after him soon, I'm making another play for him."

Leslie laughed as she nodded. "Okay... I can go to him. I can do this." In fact she wasn't sure she could do this, not even a little bit, but Levi was worth shooting her shot.

CHAPTER TWENTY-FOUR

THAT SEASON'S TRAINING was scheduled to start in two weeks and sitting across from Levi was the latest recruit. Tyler Forrester's smile might be wide now, but it wouldn't be for long when he was enduring eighteen-hour days preparing for the upcoming wildfire season. "Welcome to the team," Levi said, extending a hand to the guy.

Tyler stood and shook it. "Thank you. You won't regret this."

"Make sure I don't," Levi said.

Tyler hesitated as he headed toward the office door. "Can I ask—why the change of heart?"

It was a fair question. No doubt his call to the guy the day before had come as a surprise. "I, uh, just realized that maybe I'd been unfair before. We'd be lucky to have someone as qualified as you." He wouldn't admit to the guy that his own actions had only amplified how hypocritical he'd been in his applicant assessment. How could he turn the guy away for having someone in his life that he'd choose over the job in a hypothetical situation when Levi had actually done it?

"Well, thanks again."

"See you at training," he said, sitting back in his chair as Chad entered the office.

"So, you reconsidered?" he asked with a knowing grin.

"Seemed like the best decision," Levi said. He cleared

his throat. "Speaking of decisions…" Time to have the hard talk. "I realize mine wasn't what was best for the team. I chose to leave Florida on an instinct and I'll be happy to step down if the team thinks that's the best thing."

Chad looked at him as though he'd lost his mind. "What are you talking about?"

"I abandoned the team."

Chad shook his head as he entered. "No. You prioritized. And you made the right decision. Besides, you'd completed the jump. Lead member or not, your name would have been moved to the bottom of the jump list…the next one was Miller's fire."

"But I would still have assisted…"

"Levi, give yourself a break, man. You've chosen a life of serving and protecting, no matter what that looks like— jumping out of a plane into a fire or being there for a loved one." Chad patted his shoulder. "Now stop stressing and get ready to have your ass handed to you by that new recruit at training camp," he said as he left the office.

Levi nodded and sighed as he fell back in his chair.

Now that that was over, he had something even heavier weighing on him.

He stared at his computer screen, the blinking cursor at the top of the page, where it had sat all morning, taunting him. He had twenty hours before he'd be standing in front of a crowded room and delivering a speech to honor his best friend, and a blank page was all he had so far.

Thinking of things to say about Dawson wasn't the hard part. It was putting all of his respect and admiration for his friend into coherent sentences that would ring true and give everyone in the room a sense that they knew him.

He started to type…

Dawson Powell was a hero.

He backspaced over the stale introduction and ran a hand over his face. "Come on, Levi...get it together," he mumbled.

Take care of my girl until I see her again.

His buddy's last words had replayed in his mind every time he'd sat down to write this. Maybe that was it. Maybe that was what he needed to convey.

Sitting forward, he started again...

Dawson Powell cared about everyone the same and that made him the kind of hero not everyone can be. He didn't make decisions based on his own heart, but on prioritizing the needs of those around him, a trait that those of us who loved him often didn't understand...

Levi's fingers flew over the keyboard, the words spilling out of him now that he was allowing himself to be honest. His best friend may not have been able to be everything to him or to Leslie because he was trying to be everything to everyone...especially the ones who needed him most.

It had taken Levi a long time to understand but he did now.

He finished the speech and hit Print, then rested his head on his hands, his elbows on the desk. "I hope to make you proud, buddy."

WALKING INTO THE Wild River Resort the next evening, Leslie could barely feel her legs beneath her. Her heart was about to burst out of her chest and her sweaty palms refused to stay dry, no matter how many times she wiped them on the legs of her dress pants.

Dress pants and blouse. No fancy, sparkly dress. Selena would not approve, but Leslie had to draw the line somewhere when it came to accepting the star's advice. This was Wild River. Not Hollywood. And she was just an un-employed police officer. Not an actress.

And she knew that wouldn't matter to Levi.

She took a breath as she stopped in front of the ball-room doors.

This was what she needed to do. No backing out. If she let more time pass between them, she was afraid her heart might close off again, the walls would start to build back up and the possibility of what could be with Levi would disappear.

She didn't want that.

She wanted Levi.

She opened the door and the sight of the decorated ball-room made her smile. Round tables of eight, adorned with white silk tablecloths, beautiful pale pink flower center-pieces, and candles were placed all around the room. White string lights draped from the ceiling, creating a beautiful, intimate ambience in the large space.

At the front of the room was a podium with a large dis-play screen containing information about the foundation and how to donate and next to it was a large framed photo of Dawson in his state trooper uniform. It wasn't the posed, serious shot that was featured at his funeral, but a candid shot of him laughing, and it warmed Leslie's heart.

That was Dawson captured perfectly. Always smiling, always happy... No one could say that Dawson hadn't en-joyed life. Every aspect of it.

Selena was right. He'd want her and Levi to enjoy their lives too, even if that was together...maybe especially if that was together.

The event wasn't scheduled to start for another hour and she scanned the otherwise empty room and spotted Levi with a man hooking up the media equipment. She swallowed hard. He looked amazing in jeans and a white T-shirt, his hair messy and uncombed. A scruffy beard that she suspected would be trimmed and combed to perfection by the time the event started, which was soon. She didn't have much time.

When he turned, she froze, waiting for his expression to settle on one emotion…beyond surprised. Would he be happy to see her? Relieved? Stressed?

His gaze softened and her shoulders sagged in relief as he gave a small wave.

She raised a hand and fought to control the urge to run toward him and jump into his arms.

Damn, those movies Selena had forced her to watch were messing with her brain.

He spoke to the technician, then headed toward her. "Hey…"

"Hey…" Okay, now what? Wait for him to speak first or say something? Confess her love immediately or keep it casual? "This place looks beautiful…" She scanned the room because looking at him and not being in his arms was damn near impossible.

"Yeah, the decorators Mrs. Powell hired did a great job," he said.

She nodded toward the picture. "Great choice."

He glanced at it. "I thought so. Really represents his spirit, you know?"

She did know. And right now, seeing all the effort and commitment Levi was putting into this foundation represented his spirit. He'd always preferred being behind the scenes, letting Dawson shine, and he was still doing just that.

"So, how are you settling in?" he asked.

She blushed. So he did know she was back in town and

was only now reaching out to him. "I would have called or texted, but…"

He lowered his head. "I get it."

What did he get? Her heart raced as he smiled up at her. The look in his eyes suggesting that she didn't need to vocalize it. He knew she was there to let him down easy.

She took a deep breath. "No, I don't think you do." She stepped forward and reached for his hands.

The look of surprise on his face gave her courage.

"I didn't call or text because I wanted to say this in person."

He searched her face for a clue of what was coming next. Hesitant, but hopeful.

Just say it. Quickly. Before her natural instincts kicked in and she ran out of the room. "I'm in love with you. That's why I came back. It wasn't because I was out of a job and had nowhere else to go. Or because I missed my family. Or because I was tired of LA. And you're not a fallback guy…" she said. What else had Selena mentioned that she needed to clarify?

He gave a strangled-sounding laugh. "I would never have assumed that."

Right. Of course not. Her friend was getting an earful.

"But um…can we just back up a little? You're in love with me?"

She nodded. "Madly."

He laughed, drawing her closer. "Madly, huh?"

"I've been watching a lot of sappy movies and there's always the big gesture. When someone is in the wrong and they need to make things right. I know this isn't exactly big, but this is it. My…big…gesture."

"I like the influence Selena has on you," he said, releasing her hands and wrapping his arms around her waist. He pulled her into his body and she cuddled into him. A sigh of relief escaping her. This felt right. Real. Exactly where she wanted to be. This moment and always.

"I'm sorry about everything before," she whispered.

He kissed the top of her head. "There's nothing to apologize for. These last few years have been rough on us both. I'm just happy you're back."

She knew he meant more than just physically. More than just being home in Wild River. Back to the person she'd been before, the person she'd lost for a little while, the person she'd forgotten she was.

She looked at him and their eyes met and held. "In case you were wondering, I'm still madly in love with you too," Levi said, lowering his head to hers. "I always have been and I always will be."

His lips were just an inch away and Leslie stood on tiptoes to meet them. They were soft, warm, and welcoming and he deepened the kiss as his grip on her tightened.

When Levi kissed her, it was like everything familiar and nothing familiar all at once. He was so much of her past that she felt secure, safe in his arms, but experiencing him in this new way was different, exciting...terrifying.

She knew him. Every little detail. Yet he was showing her a new side that she never imagined was there—passionate but controlled, strong but vulnerable, open yet guarded. He was both the Levi she knew and a man she wanted to get to know better. And it wasn't a shared tragic past that had her feeling this way. It was him. The man he always was, the man he'd always been for her and the man he always would be.

His lips savoring hers and his arms holding her tight told her he'd never hurt her or let her down and she wanted to be that same safe place for him. And maybe that was enough to give this a chance, see where years of friendship could lead, what they could turn into. They didn't owe anyone anything—not an explanation, not an apology. They weren't doing anything wrong by being together. Dawson was gone and she missed him every day, missed the life they were supposed to have had—should have had—together, but she couldn't bring him back. Her pain and guilt could never bring him back and she was tired of living as though she too had died that day on the highway. She wanted to live again, laugh again, feel love again and be loved.

And right now Levi was making all of that a reality for her. His touch, his kiss, his caress all brought her back from the brink and she couldn't get enough of the life he was breathing into her with every look of desire and love.

She closed her eyes, enjoying the moment. She wanted it to last forever. She wanted this second chance at a forever love…with him. She'd been blessed to find love in the past and she refused to take this new shot for granted. Loving Dawson had taught her so much, but loving Levi was her future.

He held her close as he made her feel every ounce of love he'd always had for her. The respect and admiration and longing all revealed itself in his desperate, loving kiss.

And when she pulled away and caught the photo of Dawson out of the corner of her eye, she knew somewhere, somehow, he was giving them his blessing.

And finally she opened herself up completely to the new chapter waiting for her in Levi's arms.

EPILOGUE

Three months later...

THE LATE SUMMER SUN was high in the sky and the light breeze blowing through the Alaskan wilderness was mild and smelled of sweet honeysuckle.

A flatbed truck backed slowly down the recently widened road toward the cleared lot where Leslie's family cabin used to be. On the back, there was several thousand dollars' worth of lumber and building materials. Courtesy of Selena Hudson.

A tornado of emotions swirled through Leslie's heart.

They were rebuilding the family cabin. After so many years, they'd all decided that it was time to have a new place to help them hold on to the memories of the past, but also make new ones. They were all moving on, moving forward... The mistakes of the past forgiven and opening up to new life adventures...wherever they may lead.

Her mother, grandmother, Eddie, Montana, Katherine and Levi were all there, ready to get to work. They were doing this together.

Leslie glanced at Levi, who was guiding the truck to a stop in front of the lot. She'd once thought her heart could never be mended, that the love she'd once had was as strong as love could get and there was no such thing as second chances... She'd been wrong.

Levi was not Dawson, but she loved him just as fiercely. In a different way...a more mature, steady kind of way. A love that she felt in her entire being, one that was solid. One that would last.

The last three months together, their connection had only grown stronger and she wanted to spend the rest of her life growing even closer, opening herself up to everything a life with him had to offer. She'd let her walls come crumbling down faster than she'd ever thought possible and being with him, she felt safer and more secure than she ever had in her life.

Returning to work as a state trooper, she felt like she was back where she belonged and she and her mother were working through things at a weekly brunch. Somehow, Montana had talked her into becoming a freelance photographer for SnowTrek Tours and truly, it hadn't taken much convincing. Spending time behind the camera again helped to balance the stress of her job. For the first time, she was optimistic about what the future would hold for all of them.

Levi turned to look at her now and his wink had her heart racing. Dressed in old ripped jeans, a tight white T-shirt and work boots, his muscles on full display, Leslie knew she was going to struggle with focusing on the job ahead of her. They'd barely been able to keep their hands and lips...and all other body parts off one another for months.

"Do you have the original plans?" Katherine asked, coming up behind her in full contractor gear. Hard hat, tool belt and work boots—her older sister was taking this very seriously.

Leslie almost laughed. Between the eight of them, there was zero knowledge of how to build a cabin, but they were going to make a mess of it together. "Yes." She handed the original cabin building plans to her sister, and Katherine headed toward the others to start implementing a game plan as Levi approached.

He wrapped his arms around her waist and kissed her gently. She'd never felt so content, safe and at ease in her entire life. "Okay. We have the wood. Now what?" he asked.

"I have no idea," she said, glancing at her family members, who looked equally lost about where to start, but they were eager.

"Well, I do have something that might help us get started," he said with a mischievous grin.

"You do?" What was he up to? "What?"

"Give me a sec."

She watched him go to his truck and open the back door. Her family joined them as he returned carrying a large, framed picture. When he turned it toward her, her eyes watered and a lump rose in her throat. The photo of her and Katherine and Eddie—the one that had hung in the cabin all those years, the one she thought had been lost in the fire, gone forever.

Here it was. He'd somehow saved it and was giving it back to them.

Beside her, her grandmother smiled and took the photo, staring at it. "Wow. Thank you, Levi…this is the most perfect gift you could give us, besides making our girl here smile, of course," she said, squeezing Leslie's shoulder.

Her brother and sister laughed and made fun of each other's goofy expressions in the picture and she caught her mother wipe the corner of her eye.

Leslie's heart was so full of happiness in that special moment that it was impossible to care that they were going to make a huge mess of the build. The walls might not be perfectly straight, the roof might leak, the doors might not be secure on the hinges, but none of that mattered.

Because the best things in life often came without a blueprint.

* * * * *

ACKNOWLEDGMENTS

Thank you so much to my readers who have continued to support this series! I love spending my time in this small Alaskan ski resort town and you all make that possible. Thank you as always to my agent, Jill Marsal, who continues to keep me sane and to my editor, Dana Grimaldi, for always making each book that much stronger and more enjoyable to work on. And a big thank you to my husband and son who can always play another round of Fortnite (if they have to ;)) to give me more time to write. Love you guys the most!

A Wild River
Match

CHAPTER ONE

THIS HAD TO be a joke.

When Mike Toledo had asked for a chance to prove he could lead his own Alaskan wilderness tours, the Valentine's Day Blind Date Ice Fishing excursion was not what he'd had in mind.

Normally, spending the weekend ice fishing was his idea of a great time. Fish and get paid to do it? Sign him up.

But Valentine's Day was really not his thing. He didn't get the whole chocolate, flowers and jewelry thing. Candlelight dinners and rose petals weren't in his wheelhouse. Not that he even had a wheelhouse...

Maybe that was why he was still single at thirty-two.

He stared at the adventure brochure, pretending to review all the details, but his mind reeled. What legit-sounding excuse could he use to get out of this one?

The whole idea was ridiculous, but crazy enough, it was one of SnowTrek Tours' most popular events. Outdoor enthusiasts signed up to be matched with other like-minded singles to fish and flirt out on a frozen lake for two days, in an attempt to find that elusive love connection. Cassie's rationale made sense. Similar interests *were* a basis for a strong relationship, but Mike wasn't exactly feeling the love that year, finding himself once again alone.

His last semi-girlfriend, Jade Frazier, had been hot as hell but the least compatible match for him and his lifestyle.

It was almost hard to believe they'd made it six weeks. His initial attraction to her had been solely based on her blond hair, gorgeous green eyes, amazing body... She'd definitely turned his head the night they'd met at The Drunk Tank, the local watering hole in Wild River.

But when she'd tried to make him wear a suit jacket and tie for a dinner party with some of her friends, it was obvious that they weren't the right fit. He wasn't looking for someone to change him. He was who he was. A six-foot-three burly guy raised mountain tough by another big burly dude along with his three big burly brothers.

Plaid was their family crest.

To say he lacked finesse would be an understatement. His mother had left when he and his older brothers were young, and growing up in a house full of men who enjoyed hunting, fishing, camping and roughhousing hadn't taught him how to have a softer side. But when had it become necessary for men to be both strong and vulnerable?

Clearly he'd missed the memo.

"So, what do you think?" Cassie asked him from across her desk. His boss was an amazing, fiery ball of energy in a five-foot-nothing frame. She'd built her company from the ground up and had successfully survived a big adventure chain store opening on Main Street because of her smart business sense and grit. He had respect for what she'd accomplished and the reputation she'd built in Alaska as one of the best adventure tour companies in the North. If he wanted to prove to Cassie that he was a team player and could handle any tour she gave him, he needed to accept this challenge.

He'd been working at SnowTrek Tours for two years, he had all the proper certification and even wilderness survival skills based on his volunteer position with the Wild

River Search and Rescue, so he was more than qualified to handle group tours on his own.

He could keep this group alive out in the Alaskan wild. Helping them fall in love...*that* would be the hard part.

"Yes," he said, nodding with more enthusiasm than he felt. "This is...great. I won't let you down." He stood and left the office determined to survive the toughest challenge his boss could have thrown at him.

MADDIE FRAZIER OPENED her duffel bag on her bed and scanned her packing list for a weekend of ice fishing and finding her perfect match out on the lake.

"You're insane," her sister said as she entered the bedroom. Jade picked up a thin, silky-looking nightie from Maddie's drawer and tossed it into the bag.

Maddie shot her a look and stuffed it back into the drawer, opting for her fleece pajamas instead. Sexy could wait until summer. February in Alaska meant practical clothing unless she was out to catch more than just fish and feelings that Valentine's Day weekend.

"Seriously, you're actually hoping to find love out on a frozen lake in a tiny stinky fishing cabin?" Jade wrinkled her nose as though she could already smell the bait.

"Why not? I love fishing, so if the guy isn't 'the one,' I'll have a few rainbow trout as a consolation prize." She shrugged, hoping to make light of how optimistic she was about this matchmaking process. But SnowTrek Tours had an amazing success rate with this annual event. Three couples who'd met on previous years' excursions had already gotten married. One couple had a baby on the way.

At twenty-nine, Maddie wasn't quite ready for that, but she was overdue for a relationship that lasted more than a few weeks. Her last long-term relationship had been in high school and it had ended horribly with her boyfriend dumping her for her best friend. Former best friend. That had been the toughest part—losing the guy she loved and her closest friend at the same time. But her heart was finally over that and she was ready to trust again.

Optimistic with zero hang-ups—that was the goal.

"How are we related?" Jade asked, shaking her head.

Maddie had asked herself that same question a lot over the years. They were only two years apart, but more different than any sisters could be.

Jade was studying to be a fashion designer through an online degree program. She had impeccable taste and never left the house without her hair and makeup done. Which was one of the reasons she hated camping and hiking and anything outside, really. Too messy, too dirty... Rain and wind were not a friend to Jade's two-hour beauty routine.

Maddie was definitely more like their father. Maybe it was because he had two girls and not the son he'd wanted that he'd taken her fishing and camping and hiking... Either way, she loved the outdoors. As an educator at the Alaska Wildlife Conservation Center, she spent most of her time in the wild, protecting nature from humans and vice versa. Hiking, mountain climbing, biking, off-roading were all ways she loved to spend her days off and growing up in a ski resort town gave her ample opportunity.

Unfortunately acting like "one of the guys" meant that the guys she'd grown up with had trouble seeing her in any other way.

"Are you going to be okay here alone all weekend?" Maddie asked. They'd been roommates since their parents died and she hated the idea of leaving her sister alone on Valentine's Day after her recent breakup. She'd been dating Mike Toledo for almost two months but had complained about the guy almost as long. Maddie hadn't said anything but she hadn't really seen the connection between the big quiet guy and her outgoing, extroverted sister the few times she'd seen them together. It had surprised her that her sister was dating an adventure tour guide who was over six feet tall and beefy. Jade preferred shorter, fitter, more…polished men. Still, Jade had seemed really distraught when things hadn't worked out, claiming Mike was an insensitive brute that she'd wasted her time on.

And while February 14 was just another day to Maddie, Valentine's Day was one of Jade's favorite holidays. Usually she had a boyfriend more than willing to make it special for her, so her first year single in forever would be a tough one.

Maddie had signed up for the weekend away before Thanksgiving…before Jade's breakup.

Still, if her sister wanted her to stay…

But Jade shook her head quickly. "Yes, I'm totally fine. Go. Have…fun."

Maddie wasn't convinced and her protective instincts over her baby sister outweighed her desire for a romantic weekend. "You know what, I'll stay home and we can have a Galentine's Day instead." Decision made, she started unpacking.

Jade stopped her. "No way—you're going. I'm one hundred percent over the breakup. Believe me, he was not worth the tears. I just wish I'd found someone else in the last few months, but I can buy my own chocolate and flowers this year."

"You're sure?"

"Absolutely," Jade said reassuringly, then she paused. "But if you see Mike, feel free to slap him with a fish for me."

CHAPTER TWO

OF ALL THE TOUR GUIDES at SnowTrek Tours, Mike Toledo was assigned to her excursion. Fantastic. That wouldn't make things awkward at all.

Maddie took a deep breath and squared her shoulders. She wouldn't let this bother her. She wasn't there to spend time with Mike. She would just ignore him. Once they were paired up, she'd be too preoccupied getting to know her match to even notice him. She scanned the group as everyone arrived and loaded their gear into the back of two vans that would be taking them out to the lake.

They hadn't been assigned their matches yet, but there were a few great-looking guys so far...

"Hi, everyone!" the owner of SnowTrek Tours, Cassie Reynolds, addressed them. "Thank you all for signing up for our fifth annual Blind Date Ice Fishing event. My expert tour guide Mike Toledo will be hosting you all this weekend. He's very qualified and capable of ensuring everyone's safety and comfort..."

Yeah, except when it comes to matters of the heart.

So far, Maddie wasn't entirely impressed with SnowTrek's choice to allow this guy to be in charge of whether they found love that weekend.

But she refused to worry about him. *Her* Mr. Right could be standing right next to her right at that moment.

"Most of you are here already, but a few are running

late, so Mike will load one van and then I'll drive the others up to the lake once they arrive," Cassie said. "Have fun!"

Everyone was all smiles and chatter as they loaded into the van and headed out to the lake. But sitting behind the driver's seat moments later, Maddie couldn't help her gaze from shifting to Mike's reflection in the rearview mirror as he drove.

Please don't let this inconvenient coincidence ruin my weekend.

MADDIE FRAZIER.

Wonderful. He was stuck hosting Jade's sister for the weekend. He assumed Jade had told her all about him. Or her version of him anyway.

Didn't matter. He wasn't the one needing to impress her. That job fell on her match. And what an impossible feat that poor guy had if Maddie was anything like her sister.

"Okay, everyone, gather around." Mike called the group in to the edge of the frozen, glistening lake.

His gaze fell on Maddie, and her piercing look revealed she wasn't thrilled by this turn of events either. Well, hopefully they could both be adult enough to get through the weekend.

"So, this is how the event will work," he said. "You've all been expertly matched by our selection process and questionnaire. But, you will also get a chance to meet everyone at tonight's firepit dinner, where we'll have a speed dating opportunity. If you're not feeling your connection or want to explore something else, the option will be there."

The group nodded and he saw a few of the guests sizing each other up.

The heat sizzling off these people already could potentially melt the ice and they hadn't even gotten started yet.

Mike scanned the matchmaker sheet Cassie had given him and then forced all the enthusiasm he could muster as he glanced up at the hopefuls waiting to be shot by Cupid's arrow.

Unfortunately, there was an uneven number. Shit, someone was missing. He scanned the name tags on everyone's jacket and then reviewed the list.

Darrel Lovejoy wasn't there. Maddie's match.

"Um… I just have to make a quick call," he said. Cassie had dropped off the last of the group a few moments ago but she hadn't said anything about the missing guy. He walked farther away and dialed her cell.

"Hey, Mike, everything okay?" she asked.

"Darrel Lovejoy isn't here… Maddie Frazier's match."

"Shit. I knew I forgot to tell you something. He canceled last minute…"

"So, do you want to come back for Maddie?" He hated that he had to call Cassie with a problem only two hours in, but he could hardly be blamed for this.

"Not really," she said. "I have another tour scheduled… Unless, of course, she wants to leave."

"I don't know. I haven't told her yet," he said, dreading the conversation. No doubt she'd cause a scene and demand her money back.

"Well, there's still a possibility that she'll connect with someone at the speed dating thing, so maybe try to convince her to stay and in the meantime, just make sure she has fun?"

Damn it. He clenched his teeth. "Yeah. Of course."

Disconnecting the call, he returned to the group. "Okay…as I pair you all up, meet your partner at your sled, load your gear inside the wooden box and you can head over to your shared hut. Get settled, get to know one another and I'll be around to make sure everyone's comfortable and has everything they need."

The group nodded, eager to get started.

Mike called all the names and everyone looked pleased as they headed off toward their huts. Except for Maddie, who was left standing there alone. He approached with caution. "Unfortunately, it looks like your match couldn't make it."

Disappointment clouded her face momentarily before she hid it. "Oh, well, should I leave?"

He shook his head. "There's still the speed dating round tonight. Cassie suggested you stay and see if you find a connection there… But it's up to you."

She nodded and shrugged. "I guess a solo cabin retreat doesn't sound all that terrible."

It would in a minute.

He cleared his throat. "Actually, our release form requires two people in a hut for participants' safety…so I guess you're stuck with me." He'd been looking forward to a hut all of his own for two days with forecasted perfect winter fishing conditions but that had been shot to hell.

"Like a fill-in match?"

Her horrified expression at the prospect would be reason enough to say no, *if* that was the situation. "No. I'll just be filling the vacancy from a safety perspective."

"Oh really? I'm safer with you?" she huffed.

Just let it go…

"What's that supposed to mean?"

Maddie shrugged but it was anything but a casual gesture. She obviously had a lot to say. "Just that you're not exactly the most…attentive."

"According to your sister?" Jade's idea of attention bordered more on doting. He couldn't even check his cell phone while out with her or she thought he was being rude or ignoring her. Constant talking was the only way to convince her he'd been engaged in their conversations and her frequent texting and calls when they weren't together had been borderline stalking... It had been exhausting.

"Are you telling me she's wrong?" Maddie asked.

Mike sighed and fought the urge to set her straight. "It doesn't matter." He picked up the handle of the wood sled box containing their gear and headed toward their fishing hut.

What mattered was making sure everyone survived, most had a good time and he proved to Cassie that he could handle anything the great outdoors threw at him.

Even Maddie Frazier.

THIS WAS JUST GREAT.

Not only did she miss out on an opportunity to connect with a like-minded outdoor enthusiast, but now she was trapped in a six-by-ten hut with her sister's ex for forty-eight hours.

Only her own stubbornness prevented her from leaving.

That and the fact that she really wanted to ice fish. Who knew when she'd get another opportunity to use her favorite fishing pole in such comfortable surroundings.

She could ignore Mike—and those startlingly blue eyes—for two days. She'd never noticed how light they were. The shade of blue was almost crystal clear, yet they held a deep intensity.

Following him toward their hut, she cast a glance toward the other "couples" making their way across the ice. They all looked to be getting along already. SnowTrek had really done their research to pair everyone with their ideal mate.

Mike stood at the door, holding it open for her as she approached.

Entering, she momentarily forgot her frustration as she took in her accommodations.

The space was already toasty warm, heated by a small woodstove, and the dim lighting from the 12-volt interior spotlights in the ceiling created a warm glow. Two comfy club folding chairs sat side by side in the center of the intimate space, two lock-down hole covers in the floor in front of them. Behind were two cots made up with plaid bedding and a down comforter, and along the wall was additional bench seating with storage boxes underneath.

The hut door closed and Mike cleared his throat. "Take whichever cot you prefer—I'm cool with either."

She scanned the options. One was visibly bigger than the other and probably the better choice for him considering his height and build. "I'll take that one," she said, pointing to it, leaving him with the smaller one.

The only sign of annoyance was the way he pursed his lips. "No problem." He handed over her duffel bag from the wood sled box and she carried it to her cot. She could do this. She wouldn't argue with him. She'd ignore him and fish.

"You brought your own pole?" he asked behind her.

She turned to see him examining her Fenwick Elite Tech Ice Spinning Rod. "I don't go anywhere without my own pole," she said.

She couldn't tell if he was impressed or in disbelief as he slowly handed it to her.

"Well, it's a good one. We supply everything you need, but this pole will definitely be the best one out here this weekend, if the pole has anything to do with the catch."

She raised her chin. "It all comes down to skill."

"And you've got skills?"

"I guess you'll see," she said.

His smirk actually softened his features just a little. "Well, what are we waiting for? Let's get you started." He unlocked her portal on the floor, revealing the hole already drilled in the thick ice, and handed her the tackle box. "There's plastic ice fishing lures in there as well if you'd rather not touch the live bait."

Was that a note of challenge in his voice?

He obviously thought she and Jade were the same person. Her sister would definitely opt for the nonliving bait, but she wasn't going to catch anything big that way. "I'll take the live minnows, please."

Again, the slight look of surprise. But he simply cleared his throat as he handed her the bait. "Good choice."

Painfully aware of his gaze on her, she baited the large hook at the end of her line. Watching to see if she was bluffing?

Maybe other women pretended to like these kinds of things to impress a guy, but that wasn't her game. She *had* no game. She was who she was—take it or leave it. All the men she'd dated so far had chosen to leave it.

Her dating profile consisted of about a dozen guys over the last ten years. All of whom had claimed to want a down-to-earth, outdoorsy type of partner, but ultimately they hadn't expected her to keep up with them or outdo them when it came to the great outdoors. Fragile egos weren't something she found attractive.

"So, what made you sign up for this? What was appealing about meeting someone this way?" Mike asked.

"I'm a vegetarian," she said.

He frowned.

"You know...bars are meat markets..." She waited.

Nope, right over his head. "You know what, never mind." This was another reason she was still single. No one got her jokes.

But Mike's delayed chuckle made her chest twist. It sounded genuine and sincere. And it was the first indication that he wasn't completely hating this entire experience so far. As much as he tried to appear upbeat, it was obvious he wasn't thrilled about being the one to lead this tour. His enthusiasm had seemed forced since they'd boarded the SnowTrek Tours van and she suspected he'd rather fight off a bear than coordinate a speed dating event.

"Do you mind?" he asked, gesturing toward the other fishing hole.

She shrugged. "I guess not." The guy may have pissed off her sister but she wasn't cruel enough to deny anyone this experience.

Removing his coat, he sat in the chair next to hers and opened his own portal. Then he rolled up the sleeves of his flannel plaid shirt and set up his own line.

Her gaze fell to a long scar extending from the base of his thumb to his wrist. Ouch, that would have been a nasty injury...and relatively new judging by the pale pinkness of the flesh. Her eyes traveled upward and grew even wider at the tattoo sleeve disappearing under the fabric of the shirt. She frowned. Her sister hated tattoos.

Whatever had attracted Jade to him at all?

"Something wrong?" he asked, catching her stare.

No doubt he was reading her reaction wrong. She loved tattoos—was the proud owner of several herself—but not Jade. She nodded toward the scar. She couldn't help herself. Scars fascinated her. "How'd you get the scar?"

"It was actually during an emergency response mission.

I volunteer on the Wild River Search and Rescue," he said as he baited his own line.

Her mouth gaped, and she was relieved he wasn't looking at her. Her sister had never mentioned that detail. Maddie had considered becoming a volunteer member over the years, but after a bear had been put down because of an attack on hikers who'd wandered into an off-limits area several years before, Maddie had realized she was too anti dumb people not to deliver lectures instead of rescuing the lost. "What happened?" she asked.

"It was late November, and four hikers had gotten lost on Snowcrest Peak. One of them got a call through to 911 and dispatch was able to get a location on them. They'd stumbled into an avalanche high danger area so the situation was upgraded to an emergency."

Maddie's eyes were wide as she waited for him to continue. Having grown up on the mountains, she understood the importance of staying clear of those areas and the severity of what the team must have faced that day. Snowcrest Peak in winter wasn't for the beginner hiker, and the weather conditions on that mountain could change from a sunny, cloudless day to a blinding snowstorm of sleet and ice in minutes.

"We located the missing hikers with the cell in less than twenty minutes, but then the worst-case scenario happened and the mountain gave way. Three team members and their rescues were able to get clear of the danger, but...well, my rescue was a little older and heavier...and we were trapped."

Maddie held her breath as he paused.

"As the snow enveloped us, I wrapped a leather strap around our wrists, not wanting to be separated from him as we were tossed down the side of the mountain. It worked, but the leather tore into my flesh...leaving the scar."

"And the rescue?"

"It was a success by most measures. The other team members found us within an hour. We got lucky...just suffered some minor frostbite." He shrugged as his gaze met hers.

She tried and failed to conceal her awe. Her sister's ex was turning out to be nothing like she'd expected. In fact, he was the most fascinating, attractive and *off-limits* man she'd met in a long time.

IT HAD BEEN a while since a woman had looked at him the way Maddie was right now. Often when he told the rescue story there was the look of admiration that followed. Heck, he'd admit it had even gotten him laid a time or two, but not once had he seen the complete and utter respect and intrigue he saw in her emerald eyes. Resisting the urge to brush her blond hair away from her face and place a trail of kisses on her pink flushed cheeks and hypnotizing eyes took every ounce of his strength. "So, what do you do?" he asked, forcing his gaze away.

"I'm an educator at the Alaska Wildlife Conservation Center."

His expression was one of surprise as he turned to look at her.

"What?"

He shook his head quickly. "Nothing… I guess I just hadn't expected that." Jade was so anti outdoors, anti animals, anti everything Mike considered fun and interesting, it was hard to believe her sister could be the complete opposite. But he was quickly realizing the two were nothing alike.

"Just because Jade isn't exactly outdoorsy?"

He shrugged. "I shouldn't have assumed."

"It's okay. Jade and I are so different it's sometimes hard for me to believe we're related."

It wasn't so hard from an outside perspective—they both shared the same blond hair and green eyes, but Maddie's were darker, more seductive. Her overall features were softer. She was curvier and less put together than Jade. No makeup or fake eyelashes. Sitting next to him in jeans, hiking boots and a thick plaid jacket, she looked comfortable in the hut.

He couldn't picture Jade sitting there.

"So, I take it you enjoy your job?"

"Love it," she said. "Educating people about the wildlife out here is exciting, especially the kids. They really light up seeing the animals up close. Every day is different and I just love being outside. I couldn't imagine being cooped up in an office all day every day."

He couldn't have said it better himself. He'd tried and failed to be happy in a corporate job. He had a degree in accounting and he was great with numbers. But suits and desks would drive him to an early grave. Giving it up to become an adventure tour guide might have been a step down financially, but there was more to life than money.

"It might not be the most lucrative career, but happiness has to be a factor in life choices, right?" she said.

Once again, caught off guard by their similar philosophies, he simply nodded.

Was it possible that he had more in common with his ex's sister than he could ever have thought? It was quickly becoming obvious that he might have dated the wrong sister.

CHAPTER THREE

"Guess the fish just aren't biting today," Mike said as the sun started to set outside the hut windows.

"I wonder if the others had more luck." Maddie pulled her line up and frowned at the slightly frozen bait at the end. Her disappointment over not catching anything wasn't as strong as it would normally be. Surprisingly, she'd had a good day...fun, even.

The hut was cozy with the stove giving off heat and the smell of burning wood and fresh mountain air all around them. It was peaceful and serene.

Mike was easy to be around. He didn't feel the need to fill every moment with chatter and yet, sitting in silence while they fished together had felt like they were actually getting to know one another. He seemed to get better looking as the day went on, with each sneaky glance in his direction. The muscular, burly build and long legs, the full, thick beard that was trimmed neat along his square jawline, and those light blue eyes that were kind and slightly intoxicating in their depth had her attraction growing.

And she sensed he was shooting glances her way, as well.

The few times their gazes had met, there had definitely been some type of unspoken connection...a spark.

"I think I hear everyone outside. If you want to head out and join them, I'll go let the cook know we're ready to eat," he said, locking their fishing holes and grabbing his coat

Maddie put on all her gear and still shivered as she stepped out onto the frozen lake. It was even prettier at night. The ice stretching far in both directions and the stars above in the clear night sky were breathtaking. Taking out her cell phone, she snapped several photos before joining the others near the fire grill. Thick hollowed-out logs were set up for each couple.

Everyone looked caught up in their partner, so Maddie quietly sat on her empty log, taking in the group. Smiles and laughter, light touching… One man had his arm draped around his match as they snuggled together.

Looked like so far so good…for the rest of them anyway. Cassie had obviously done a thorough job pairing everyone.

What would her match have been like?

The questionnaire had asked everything from preferred physical characteristics to personality traits. She'd been honest. Maddie was looking for a strong, smart, capable man with a quirky sense of humor—or at least some sense of humor—who enjoyed the outdoors and being in nature. No pressure for expensive, fancy dates. No pretenses. She'd prefer to skip the highlight reel and get to the core of the person. She'd wanted someone with similar goals, similar life philosophies…

She'd basically described Mike.

She watched him approach with the cook from the ice fishing company, chatting amicably and looking so at ease out there in the frigid weather. Any doubts she'd had about his abilities to lead a tour had vanished. He was capable, strong and competent. Of course, he didn't come across as a heart-on-his-sleeve type of guy, so why he was assigned to this trip was still a bit of a mystery.

As the cook collected the fish from those who'd caught some and prepared the grill, Mike sat next to her on the log. "So, I hope you brought a protein bar or something," he said with a wink.

She felt her cheeks warm at the simple blink of an eye. "Maybe we can convince the others to share?"

Mike glanced at them. "They look too preoccupied to eat anyway."

Maddie scanned the others, then turned back to Mike. "How did you get stuck leading this excursion anyway?"

"What makes you think I got stuck with it?"

"You just don't come across as a big relationship guy." The words came out wrong. She'd meant he wasn't the romantic, Valentine's Day, flowers and chocolate kinda guy, but it was too late to clarify.

"Jade tell you that?" he asked, his voice slightly cooler and she regretted the question. It only reminded her that this guy had dated and dumped her sister three months ago.

"You're not exactly her normal type, if I'm being honest," she said carefully.

He turned to face her. "No? Well, whose type am I?"

Mine.

But somehow the word stuck in her throat, so she looked away.

In theory, on paper, he was exactly her type, everything she was looking for in a man but unfortunately, being her sister's ex unchecked all the boxes he'd ticked.

ONCE THE FOOD had been cleared away, Mike drained the contents of his thermos and stood to address the group. Back to the dating element of the weekend.

Forcing as much enthusiasm as he could fake, he said, "Okay, so we're going to begin our speed dating round."

Only one couple who had clearly friend zoned one another looked eager to mingle. The others seemed content to retreat back inside the individual huts, and Mike was tempted to let them do it, but this was part of the experience and Cassie was right—Maddie deserved to see if there was someone there she might hit it off with.

And he wasn't at all jealous about that.

"Remember, there's no obligation to switch partners, it's just so you all have a chance to get to know one another," he said.

Maddie glanced at him, a slight questioning expression on her face.

"You'll participate too." Mike had noticed the friend-zoned man's attention on Maddie while they'd eaten. The two had chatted and joked...they'd seemed to be getting along.

And that's what she was there for. To make a real connection.

He was not there for that reason.

He checked his notes from Cassie...this dating part of the excursion was the bit he was least comfortable executing, but he needed to pull it off. Good evaluations from this group would go a long way in ensuring Cassie trusted him with future excursions. "Ladies will stay put and the men will rotate from log to log. A five-minute alarm will chime when it's time to rotate again."

The men stood, ready, and Mike hit his stopwatch. "And start."

He poured more coffee into his thermos and sat on a log away from the group, desperate not to watch but feeling his gaze shift back to Maddie as the men did their rotation.

Most of the original couples seemed happy together. He wasn't an expert on love but he could read body language and it appeared everyone was keeping their speed dates casual, friendly.

If Cassie ever wanted a career change she could definitely become a professional matchmaker. Maybe next year he should sign himself up as a participant. Finding a potential mate who liked ice fishing and the great outdoors, someone not worried about how they looked or having to pee in an outhouse...

Someone with a nice sense of humor who was interesting to talk to but who also didn't mind the stillness and silence.

Someone like Maddie.

He sighed as his gaze landed on her again. His ill-timed attraction for her had him foolishly hoping she'd say no to his next question as the speed dating wrapped up. "So, anyone want to switch?"

Three women shook their heads, to the relief of their partners, but Friend-Zoned Guy's hand went up slowly. He glanced at his current match and she nodded her approval. "I'd like to hang out with Maddie...if she's up for it."

His match smiled at Mike, but Mike's palms went clammy as he turned to Maddie. Would she switch? It made sense seeing as how this other guy was available and there for the same reason. "It's totally your choice."

She hesitated, smiling politely at the guy. "Um, actually I think I'll stick to my original hut."

Her original hut, meaning her original "stand-in" partner—him.

"Okay, well, everyone can head back inside. Have a good night," he said quickly before Maddie could have a change of heart.

CHAPTER FOUR

THE VIBE INSIDE the hut was definitely different now. Maddie's choice to stay with Mike had him all kinds of conflicted, and she seemed uneasy, as well. As if they both knew her decision meant something but weren't sure what to do about it.

At her cot, she opened her duffel bag and took out her pajamas.

"Turn around, please," she said when he continued to stand there awkwardly.

"Oh right." Mike turned and when he caught a glimpse of her removing her sweater in the reflection of the window, he shut his eyes tight. Unfortunately, not fast enough. The image of her bare, shapely back and shoulders would now be engrained behind his eyelids, along with those piercing green eyes and wide, easy smile. The inventory of images he was collecting was sure to stick with him long after the weekend was over.

"Okay, I'm good," she said a minute later.

He turned around in time to see her pull the heavy comforter back and climb into her cot. Her white fleece pajamas with grizzly bears all over them made him smile. "Cute pj's."

Her laugh sounded slightly embarrassed. "Yeah right. I'm sure the pajama choices in the other huts are a little less...cozy."

He opened his own duffel bag and retrieved a pair of pajama pants that could be the male version of the ones she was wearing. He held them up. "Yeah, but are they matching?"

Her laugh broke any lingering tension between them and made his body tingle with that same fight-or-flight response he always got on rescue missions. Unfortunately, he wasn't sure what the right actions were this time. He didn't want to run away or fight the crazy attraction he was feeling for Maddie, but the fact that she was his ex's sister meant he needed to do one or the other, and running away wasn't exactly an option at the moment.

"That is an odd coincidence," she said, fluffing her pillow behind her.

"Yep." Though it didn't exactly shock him. He and Maddie seemed to have a lot in common—not just their preferred choice of sleepwear.

He turned around and removed the plaid button shirt and then lifted his undershirt off over his head. He caught Maddie's stare in the window reflection and she looked away quickly.

Not before he caught the glimmer of unconcealed attraction in her eyes though.

He quickly removed his jeans and pulled on the pajama pants and then climbed into his cot across from her.

An awkward silence fell over the hut and he cleared his throat. "Comfortable?"

"Yeah…this is actually surprisingly comfortable."

At least she was. He wasn't sure he'd be able to roll over without falling onto the floor. His legs hung over the end of his cot. "Good. That's good."

"Hey, did you want to switch?" she asked. "I chose this one to annoy you, but I'd be happy to swap with you."

"Nah, I'm okay. You're the client, after all," he said, immediately regretting the word choice. She was so much more than just a client, but he had no right to see her in any other way.

"Okay," she said quietly.

He stared at the ceiling, still kicking himself for the comment. He couldn't claim to be great with words. One of the reasons he preferred not to talk too much. "Lights off?"

"Sure, yeah. Probably be easier to sleep."

He sat up and hit the switch on the wall and immediately the hut was dark, except for a small beam of light streaming through the blinds.

"Well, hopefully tomorrow we have more luck catching something," he said.

Something other than these unexpected feelings.

MADDIE LAY AWAKE on her cot, listening to Mike toss and turn on his. It was late and she'd been up early. Normally, she'd have no trouble falling asleep, but she was hyperaware of him just a few feet away.

She also couldn't shake the nagging question that had plagued her most of the day. "Hey, Mike, you awake?"

"Yep." His bedsprings creaked as he rolled onto his side to face her. She could faintly make out the outline of his naked upper body. "What's up?" he asked.

She hesitated. The question was embarrassing, but she had to ask. "When you spoke to Cassie, did she say what happened to Darrel?"

"No...just that he'd had to cancel last minute."

She bit her lip, straining to see her hands in the dark as she played with her nails. She swallowed hard. "You don't think he drove past SnowTrek Tours...saw me and then bailed, do you?"

Mike scoffed, then made an odd coughing noise to cover it up. "No... I don't think that's what happened."

She nodded, even though he couldn't see her.

"I mean, the guy would have to be crazy if that were the case," he said softly but also slightly gruffly, as though sentimental comments took a lot out of him.

Which had the butterflies in the pit of her stomach fluttering on full speed. She was grateful for the dark so he couldn't see her flushed cheeks. "Okay. Thanks, Mike."

"But I'm sorry he didn't show up," Mike said, an odd note in his voice.

"I'm not," she said. "'Night, Mike."

CHAPTER FIVE

MADDIE YAWNED AND stretched before her eyes opened the next morning and she quickly scanned her surroundings before remembering where she was. She hadn't expected to sleep so well in an unfamiliar bed, but the silence out on the lake had been like nothing else, and once she'd finally dozed off, she'd been out cold.

She glanced toward Mike's cot but it was already made and he wasn't in the hut.

Maddie got up quickly and peered outside. Two couples sat on the logs, drinking from thermoses. Smoke spiraled into the air from the outside grill and the smell of breakfast cooking made her stomach growl. She dressed quickly and was about to reach for her coat when the hut door opened.

Mike entered carrying her thermos and balancing two plates of food. "Hey, morning," he said, seeing her up. "I thought you might sleep past breakfast, so…"

He was bringing it to her.

It was probably a sad reflection on her past dating life, but this was the nicest, most thoughtful thing any guy had done for her. Twenty-four hours ago she'd have thought it out of character for Mike, but she was realizing there were far more layers to the guy than her sister had bothered to peel back.

She accepted the food and coffee from him with a smile. "Thanks."

"No problem." He set his own plate down and shoved his hands into his pockets. "Did you sleep okay?"

"Once I finally fell asleep, yeah." She picked up a piece of toast and took a bite, savoring the buttered homemade bread. "This is so good. What is it about eating food outside that makes it taste better?"

He stared at her.

"What?" she said.

He shook his head and looked away. "Nothing. I was just saying the same thing... Should I get the fishing holes ready?"

She nodded, taking another bite of the toast. "Absolutely. I'm not leaving here without catching something."

Other than feelings for her sister's ex.

HOT COFFEE IN HAND, line cast through the hole in the floor, Mike settled into his chair next to Maddie. He hadn't slept so great on the tiny cot, but he wasn't tired. He hadn't needed his cell phone alarm to wake him.

Something about the outdoors invigorated him. Waking up to silence, stillness, the smell of food grilling and fresh coffee brewing in the chilled air was the closest to heaven he'd ever get.

And being there with a woman who enjoyed all those things as much as he did made it even better. He'd dated a lot of women and no one seemed as compatible for him as Maddie. He'd always thought compatible would mean settling on chemistry or physical attraction.

You got one or the other, right? Relationships were either comfortable or passionate.

It didn't feel that way now.

He was both comfortable with Maddie and insanely tempted to grab her and kiss her. He took a gulp of coffee and cleared his throat. "So, it's just you and Jade? In your family, I mean."

Maddie nodded. "Yeah, our dad died of cancer a few years ago and our mom had an aneurysm..."

"Sorry," he mumbled. One tragedy was hard enough, two in the matter of several years had to be really difficult.

"That's why Jade and I are so close. It's just us now," she said quietly.

He nodded. He understood. He could also clearly hear the note in her voice that said she'd never do anything to hurt Jade or jeopardize that strong sisterly bond. Mike didn't want to come between sisters, but damned if he could deny that he wanted to see where things could lead with Maddie.

She was everything he'd look for in an ideal partner, and those green eyes were dark emerald pools that just sucked him in.

"This fishing pole was my dad's," she said. "He'd wanted it for years but refused to splurge on it. Jade and I saved up and bought it for him for Father's Day the year before he died. He only had a chance to use it a few times, but he loved it."

"I'm sure it meant a lot to him that it came from you both," Mike said. He didn't have many memories of his mother—she'd left him and his brothers with their dad after the divorce—but he had a picture of her in his wallet that had been there as long as he could remember. Everyone had a different way of holding on to the past.

Maddie nodded and a silence fell over them.

"Hey, I feel something," she said suddenly, sitting straighter and holding the pole tighter in both hands.

Mike put his thermos aside and moved closer. Her line

tugged and his eyes widened. "Looks like it could be a big one."

She started reeling it in and he stood back, impressed by the skill.

Most fishers were too eager. They yanked the reel and went too fast, causing the fish to retreat from the bait and take off if they weren't already hooked. Maddie was patient, calm, reeling in a little at a time…keeping the fish interested, letting it chase the bait. More desperate, more confident in its conquest…until it was too late. It was hooked and met its fate.

She pulled the fish up through the ice and the wiggling, struggling rainbow trout had to be a ten-pounder. And when she carefully removed the fish from the hook herself—delicately, thoughtfully, respectful of the catch—he was a goner.

She picked it up in both hands and displayed it proudly. "Think it's the catch of the weekend?"

She was the catch of the weekend.

He couldn't stop himself. He strode toward her and cupped her face between his hands. Her eyes registered surprise first, then mirrored his own attraction. The fish in her arms was the only thing between them as he leaned toward her, brushing her blond waves away from her face. He paused—unsure and more than a little hesitant.

Her gaze flitted from his eyes to his lips and back again. "Well?"

"Well what?" he asked, his voice slightly hoarse.

"Are you going to kiss me or not?"

IT FELT LIKE an eternity as she waited for his answer.

His eyes burned into hers, his attraction evident, his desire intense. He was just inches from her, holding back... contemplating.

She should be moving away, putting the brakes on...contemplating, herself. But in that moment, she just wanted him to kiss her. She'd worry about the consequences later.

She stood on her tiptoes, raising her face even closer. "I mean, I should get something for catching this fish, shouldn't I?" she whispered.

He seemed satisfied with the justification as he pulled her toward him and his lips pressed against hers. She closed her eyes and savored the feel of his mouth, the taste of coffee on his lips. His beard tickled her flesh and a shiver danced down her spine.

His fingers tangled into her hair as he deepened the kiss, intoxicating her with his passion. She'd wanted this. Her attraction to him had been growing with each minute they'd spent together, every new thing she learned about him...

He pulled her in closer, kissing her harder, stealing her breath away, and she gave in to the moment fully, completely, wishing it could last. His touch, his kiss, the way he'd looked at her all had her body reacting in ways it never had for anyone else.

When he reluctantly pulled away, disappointment washed over her. Would she ever get a chance to kiss him again? Could they enjoy the day together without promises, without consequences, without guilt and then go their separate ways?

They couldn't actually date one another...

"Mike, you know this can't happen, right?" Every part of her wished there was a way and if he had any ideas on how they could be together and not hurt Jade, she was all ears. But she'd been on the receiving end of a betrayal like this and she could never do that to Jade. She knew the hurt and pain that went along with having to put on a brave face and act like everything was okay, when deep down her heart was aching. Jade would never admit that she was upset, but Maddie would know.

"Are you sure? I mean, Jade and I weren't serious. We dated six weeks."

Six weeks too long. If it had been one bad date, maybe... but they'd given it an actual shot and Jade had been disappointed things hadn't worked, which meant she'd obviously had feelings for Mike. "I can't risk hurting her." She shook her head. "I think this weekend is all we have and then..." Her voice trailed off and she was unable to verbalize the rest.

He sighed as though his thoughts had just completed the same spiral to the same disappointing conclusion.

He took the fish from her and placed it into the ice bucket then, taking her hands, he moved backward toward his own chair. Sitting, he pulled her down onto his lap and she snuggled into him as he reached for his own fishing pole and they continued to fish.

CHAPTER SIX

THE DAY PASSED far too quickly and night fell over the frozen lake, bringing the weekend closer to its end. The couples had opted for dinner inside their individual huts and Maddie was grateful for the extra alone time with Mike.

As she finished the last bite of the rainbow trout she'd caught that day, she sat back in her chair and said, "Well, this was one of the most unexpectedly fun weekends I've had in a long time." Fun but also disappointing that their time together couldn't last.

He nodded. "Me too. And you were right when you said this excursion wasn't really my thing. The fishing part of course, but the whole romantic thing is definitely not my strong suit."

"I don't know. I mean, I think there's different kinds of romance. You might not be the big gesture guy, but small gestures are the way to some women's hearts." Like hers. His bringing her breakfast that morning, or the way he'd refilled her coffee every time it was low or too cold, or the way he'd given up the bigger cot... His silent, unassuming way made him far more appealing than any lavish, over-the-top show of affection ever could.

"Well, it takes a very special kind of woman to appreciate that," he said with that same soft gruffness that appeared in his voice whenever the conversation moved to emotional territory. Oddly enough, his struggle with vulnerability only made him more endearing. The effort counted for more and there was a level of sincerity that she hadn't seen in other men she'd dated.

"You said you were raised by your dad?" she asked.

"Yeah. Growing up it was a house full of testosterone. I have three brothers," he said, sitting back in his chair and crossing one ankle over his other knee. His thick, broad thighs captured her attention and the memory of sitting on his lap that afternoon had her cheeks warming.

"What are they like?"

"Exactly like me. Only hairier," he said with a grin.

She laughed. That explained why he'd assumed she and Jade were alike.

"And now that I know your type, I'm never introducing you to them," he said teasingly, but she suspected there was truth in the words.

She smiled but the ache in her chest grew. She'd never met anyone like him. She didn't want to meet anyone else like him. She liked *him*. Far more than was safe for her heart.

He sat forward and reached across, taking her hands in his. He lowered his head and stared at their joined hands, gently stroking hers. "Maddie, I haven't had a connection like this in… I don't think ever."

She swallowed hard.

"The hardest part is knowing we have to leave here tomorrow morning and you don't want to explore this further."

"It's not that I don't want to." She paused. "I wish things were different."

Choosing her sister over a man she barely knew was the right thing, so why was it so hard?

Mike's gaze held hers for a long moment. He looked

ready to argue but respected her enough not to. He slowly released her hands and stood. "We should probably call it a night?"

She didn't want to, but it was after ten and all the other huts were dark and...not exactly quiet, but definitely out for the night. They were packing up and leaving for the drive back to Wild River first thing the next morning. "Yeah, we probably should." She stood and collected their plates, but he took them from her.

"I'll take care of all this if you want to get ready for bed."

She nodded and she desperately wanted to tell him how she was feeling, but the words refused to surface. Why make this harder by confessing that she was falling for him? What good could come from that?

He put on his coat and left the hut with the dishes and Maddie changed into her pajamas...but instead of the big fleecy shirt, she pulled on a light-colored tank top with her pajama bottoms.

Then immediately second-guessed the decision when Mike returned and his gaze took in her body. He didn't say a word, but the look of desire in his eyes had her heart pounding out of her chest.

"You sure you don't want the bigger cot?" she asked as casually as possible.

"Only if you're in it too."

Her pulse raced as her mind came up with all the reasons that was a bad idea.

Their attraction for one another was obvious. There'd been more kissing than fishing that day. No talking about what it all meant. They'd agreed that it was a one-time, one-day thing.

One-night thing, as well?

What happens in the fishing hut, stays in the fishing hut?

But it was already going to be hard to walk away from him the next morning. If they shared a night together, it would be a million times harder.

"I just want to hold you a little longer," he said.

Unfortunately, that was almost worse. Sex was one thing. An emotional connection was a whole other thing.

But it was too late anyway and if they were on borrowed time, Maddie was desperate to prolong the inevitable.

She climbed into the bigger cot and pulled the sheets back, inviting him in.

Mike quickly removed his clothes, grabbed his pillow from the other cot and climbed in next to her, wearing only his underwear. "This okay?" he asked.

"Sleeping next to an insanely hot guy in only underwear—probably not." It was certainly going to test her self-control, but she was going to do it anyway.

She pulled the blankets up over them and cuddled into his large, muscular chest. He was so warm and his arms wrapped around her felt secure, safe. Where she was meant to be.

He kissed her forehead as he held her tight. "Today was probably the best day I've had in a long time," he said quietly.

"Me too."

"I really wish I'd met you first," Mike said, and she released a deep, heavy sigh.

"Me too," she whispered again as she closed her eyes and he held her even tighter.

CHAPTER SEVEN

MIKE GLANCED INTO the rearview mirror of the SnowTrek Tours van as he pulled onto Main Street the next day. His gaze met Maddie's and his heart raced. Those eyes. He was going to miss the hell out of those eyes. And every other part of her.

Things had happened so quickly between them, yet he knew it was the real deal. He'd never connected with anyone the way he had with her. And he had no other choice than ignore it. Hope it faded?

They'd agreed that they couldn't actually see one another, given the circumstances. But it was bullshit. How was he supposed to forget one of the best weekends of his life? How was he supposed to shut off the feelings he'd developed for her?

Could she really turn them off like that? Walk away from him?

Was her loyalty to her sister just that strong? If so, that made her even more incredible. He'd do anything for his brothers, but he'd be hard-pressed to walk away from her if the situation was reversed.

He sighed as he stopped the van in front of the shop, and ran a hand over his beard. "Okay, everyone, here we are—safe and sound." Everyone was accounted for, and other than one couple who'd kept each other in the friend zone, everyone in the van had fished, flirted and possibly found their match.

Mission accomplished. Cassie had to approve.

Unfortunately, he'd lost focus on what the weekend was supposed to achieve. He'd been caught up and caught off guard by Maddie.

The guests climbed out and Mike took their things from the back of the van. Then they all headed inside to fill out the SnowTrek Tours event evaluation form, but Maddie lingered after she'd shouldered her bag.

She jammed her hands into her pockets and rocked back on the heels of her hiking boots, looking as reluctant to say goodbye as he was. "Well, thank you for a memorable weekend."

He nodded. "You're welcome." He stared at her, waiting, hoping…

She pointed toward the shop. "Guess I should go in and fill out my evaluation."

"Yeah…"

She turned to walk away and he reached for her hand. "Maddie?"

Her eager expression when she turned back gave him a glimmer of hope. "You sure? About us…not seeing one another again?"

She hesitated and he held his breath. "I would like to see you again."

Oh thank God. He smiled. "You would?"

"Yeah, I mean, there's no reason we can't be…friends? Hang out sometime."

Friends. He shook his head. "You really think we could be just friends after this weekend?" That hurt. He'd thought they'd gone way beyond friendship. And while he'd love to have her in his life, that way would never be enough.

"It's better than nothing, isn't it?" She looked as pained as he felt.

"I'm not sure I can do that, Maddie. Being around you and not being able to hold your hand or kiss you..." He'd never felt this magnetic pull to anyone before. Spending time with her, knowing it couldn't lead to a deeper connection, a real relationship would be hell. And what if she started seeing someone else? The thought alone made his stomach drop—he'd never survive witnessing it.

"So you'd rather not have me in your life at all?" Her disappointment shattered him even more.

He hated hurting her, but if she could honestly say that she could be just friends, then she wasn't feeling this connection the same way he was. Maybe he'd read this wrong. It was best to leave the weekend in the past and move on before either of them got hurt. "I know my limits and any attempt to be your friend—" he shook his head "—I think I'd just let you down."

Her chest rose and fell on a deep sigh. One full of heartbreaking resolution. He released her hand and shoved his into his pockets. "Well, I'm glad you enjoyed the experience."

She looked ready to say something more, but instead she simply nodded, gathered her things and headed down the street, away from SnowTrek Tours and away from him. All he could do was watch her leave.

As she climbed the stairs to her apartment a half hour later, Maddie's emotions were a mess.

The first time she'd ever met a guy who had her feeling all the feels in all the right ways and he was off-limits. The weekend had been amazing. Even the awkward tension at the beginning had signaled something, had foreshadowed an attraction. One she'd struggled to fight.

Not hard enough.

She could still taste Mike on her lips, still feel his beard tickling her skin… Still drown in the guilt of having made out with her sister's ex. Slept in his arms last night. Years before she'd felt so betrayed by her best friend and boyfriend. She hadn't understood that maybe the two of them had had a stronger connection, that maybe they'd been a better fit and that sometimes things just happened when you least expected them.

Now she was seeing things a little differently, occupying a different angle of the triangle. But unlike her former best friend, she'd chosen her connection with her sister above all else.

But damn, why had she let it go that far? Getting over him now would be torture. How was it possible that after only two days, he'd completely captured her heart?

No more. She had put an end to it before it could get out of hand…though neither of them was thrilled about it. The look on his face when she'd said they could be friends had broken her. She didn't want to be just friends any more than he did, but the fact that he was turning down an opportunity to at least have that…hurt. A lot.

The sadness and disappointment in his tone as they'd said goodbye had made her stomach twist as though she wasn't doing the right thing. But what else could she do? She couldn't betray her sister.

Not for a man she'd known for only two days.

A man she'd fallen hard for in two days.

She unlocked the front door and dragged her duffel bag inside. Sighing, she leaned against it and fought the tears burning in the backs of her eyes.

As Mike unloaded the gear into the back room of SnowTrek Tours, he could hear the laughter and happy voices of the tour guests as they mingled at the End of Weekend event and filled out their evaluation forms.

Maddie hadn't stayed to fill hers out.

And Mike hadn't been able to stay out front with everyone. Their flirtatious gazes and praise of Cassie's matchmaking skills were too much and he'd needed some space away from it all. He was glad everyone had a good time and the connections had worked, but his own bruised heart couldn't handle being among the festivities.

"Hey, there you are," Cassie said, popping her head around the corner.

"Yeah, just putting everything away."

She entered the room and tapped him on the shoulder. "Well, good news—everyone rated you highly and the excursion was a success, so you can officially lead your own tours."

At the start of the weekend, that had been the goal. He should be thrilled, and he was…or would be. Right now he could barely summon a smile. "Great. Thanks, Cass."

She lingered. "So, were the fish biting?"

He nodded, not really in the mood to chat but unable to ignore his boss. "I think everyone caught at least one." He hadn't. With Maddie sitting on his lap, his attention hadn't exactly been on the fishing pole. Her body so close to his, the sound of her gentle laugh, the moments of silence that had been filled with so much left unspoken…

"Too bad about Maddie," Cassie said. "She didn't stay to fill out an evaluation form so I hope she wasn't too upset about her match having to cancel. Did she still have fun?"

"I don't know. That one's hard to read," he said a little too briskly.

"You okay?" Cassie asked.

He sighed and ran a hand over his beard. "Sorry. I'm sure she did. I'm just tired."

She studied him. "That's not tired. That's emotionally torn. I'd recognize that expression anywhere."

He avoided her perceptive gaze as he continued putting the fishing gear on the racks.

"Um, Mike...you two hit it off, didn't you?" She sounded intrigued that she might have created an even more successful event than she'd thought.

There was no point denying it. "Unfortunately."

Cassie frowned. "What do you mean? Isn't that a good thing?"

"It would be...if I hadn't already dated her sister."

Cassie's expression was full of sympathetic understanding as she touched his shoulder. "Sorry, Mike."

"Not as sorry as I am," he said with a heavy sigh and even heavier heart.

CHAPTER EIGHT

JADE WAS ON HER the moment she returned from the library. Trying to conceal any sign of guilt was taking more strength than Maddie had as she ate ice cream straight from the carton.

"So? How was it?" her sister asked, a glint of excitement in her eyes. She set her backpack down and sat beside Maddie on the sofa, waiting to hear all the juicy gossip.

Maddie avoided looking at her. "It was fine…"

"Just fine?"

"Yeah…fine."

Jade looked unimpressed. "After all those matchmaking questionnaires and all the promises from SnowTrek that you'd find your perfect match and it was just fine?"

"SnowTrek didn't promise anything." Maddie sighed, dropping the spoon into the carton. Even her favorite treat wasn't cheering her up. She suspected it would take more than chocolate chip cookie dough to heal her conflicted heart. "I'm going to take a shower," she said, unfolding her legs from their cross-legged position and getting up. She needed some time to process the whirlwind of emotions raging through her and be alone with her memories of Mike before she was forced to move on. And being around Jade—the unblamable source of the situation she was in—was too much right now.

"Hold up," Jade said as she walked away.

Maddie paused and turned. "I'm really not in the mood, Jade, we can talk in a bit."

Unfortunately, her sister was relentless. "Just let me get this straight—you didn't make a connection this weekend?"

"My match canceled at the last minute." That part was true. She'd focus on the truth and avoid the rest of the details.

"But you stayed anyway?"

"I'd paid to fish." She shrugged, hoping her sister would drop it.

She didn't. "Well, who did you fish with?"

Oh God... "Mike."

Her sister's face didn't take on the look of annoyance Maddie had been expecting at the mention of her ex. Instead, she looked impatient as she said, "And?"

"And what?"

"Was there a connection?" Jade asked.

Uh-oh... Why was her sister cornering her into either lying or coming clean and potentially driving a wedge between them? She hesitated. "He's a nice guy," she said carefully.

Jade grinned. "So, you *did* like him?"

More than she'd ever liked anyone in her life. Including her sister right now. "Can I be honest or are we still supposed to hate Mike?" she asked, losing her cool a little. Truth was, her sister had had a great guy and she hadn't recognized it. Jade couldn't see how perfect Mike was, but Maddie could. Unfortunately, sister code prevented her from having him. It seemed really unfair.

"You can be honest," Jade said, getting up from the couch.

"I like him a lot and we did...connect," she said, still unsure how much to reveal. The sleeping together part she'd definitely keep to herself. "In fact, I've never connected so well with any guy before." She expected her sister to be annoyed or tell her she was crazy for liking Mike.

But Jade's smile was wide as a Cheshire cat's as she said, "I knew it would work."

Maddie narrowed her eyes. "Knew *what* would work?"

"Okay, don't get mad but there may not have ever been a Darrel Lovejoy," Jade said quickly.

"No Darrel Lovejoy?" What the hell was her sister talking about? "Wait, how did you know my match's name?"

"I may have invented him," she said sheepishly.

"I'm sorry, what?" Either she was more tired than she'd thought or her sister wasn't making any sense right now. Invented him? Why?

"Look, I knew you and Mike would really hit it off, but I also knew he probably would ignore me if I said I had someone he should meet. And you get annoyed whenever I try to introduce you to men…so…"

"So, you set this up?"

Jade nodded and her grin said she was proud of herself. "Yep. And it worked."

Maddie swallowed hard. She forced herself not to reach out and strangle her sister. "Yeah, only it *didn't* because I told Mike I couldn't see him…because of you."

"What?" Jade looked confused. "Why would you do that?"

Right now, Maddie had no idea.

A FEW DAYS LATER, Mike loaded the SnowTrek Tours van for a winter camping expedition. His first one leading a group of six campers on a two-night trip in the Alaskan backwoods. Getting out of town again would give him a reason not to reach out to Maddie and hopefully help take his mind off her. The past few days had been torture not hearing from her.

He kept hoping that maybe she'd change her mind...

"All set to go?" Cassie asked, coming outside.

"Just about," he said. The campers were seated inside the van and the gear was loaded. He closed the back doors and turned to his boss.

"Hey," Cassie said, "I was wondering—have you read those evaluation forms from the ice fishing excursion yet?"

"I read some of them," he said. "Everyone seemed to have enjoyed it." Was she still worried about his ability to lead the tour? Had someone had a concern?

"Did you read this one?" Cassie asked, extending one toward him.

He took it and his heart pounded in his chest, seeing Maddie's name at the top of the page. He read her evaluation of the excursion, skimming her praise for the accommodations and the food and the overall tour rating.

Then his breath caught in his chest as he saw the guide evaluation section.

At first I was disappointed to learn that our guide was Mike, seeing as how I believed him to be a gruff, egocentric guy who'd broken my sister's heart. Turns out I couldn't have been more wrong about him. He's kind and considerate and strong and capable and all the things I'd look for in a...guide. When my "match" didn't show up, I thought being trapped in a fishing hut with Mike for two days would be difficult. The only thing difficult was the weekend coming to an end much too quickly. Mike is the perfect...guide. And I hope to experience more excursions with him in the future.

He released a deep breath as he raised his gaze to Cassie's. "So, I guess she enjoyed the experience." Her evaluation was great, but he already knew she felt those things. Trouble was, they still couldn't be together.

Cassie grinned. "So much so that she booked another one." She cocked her head to the side and nodded down the street.

Mike turned to see Maddie headed their way, bundled warm in a thick ski suit, knitted hat, scarf and gloves, rugged thermal winter boots on her feet, and an overnight backpack and winter sleeping bag on her back. His mouth dropped. "She's coming?"

Cassie patted him on the shoulder. "Just keep your wits about you and bring everyone back safe, okay," she said with a wink as she went back inside.

Maddie stopped in front of him on the sidewalk. "Hi," she said.

"Hey."

She was here. She was coming on the trip. They were going to spend two full days and nights together out in the Alaskan wilderness. And she looked so breathtakingly beautiful...those emerald eyes lighting up his day.

But she'd said they could only be friends, so his stomach turned at the thought that she might still be sticking to that.

"So, it turns out my sister really doesn't have an issue with us seeing one another," she said quickly, sounding slightly nervous. "In fact, she thought we'd be perfect together. So, if you were still wanting to ask me out or something, that would actually be okay."

Oh, he wanted to ask her out. Over and over again.

But right now, he wanted to kiss her.

He stepped closer and pulled her into him. "Maddie,

would you like to go on a real date sometime?" he murmured against her lips.

"Only if it includes the outdoors and the night sky and hours of just being together," she said, moving even closer, wrapping her arms around his neck.

"Where have you been all my life?" he asked with a smile, touching her flushed, cool cheek.

"Waiting right here while you dated the wrong girl," she said with a grin before kissing him, hard, her passion making his heart soar as he held her tight and deepened the kiss.

He wouldn't be letting this amazing catch go anytime soon.

* * * * *

Sergeant Hayden Mitchell's mission: give every canine veteran the perfect forever home. But when it comes to Sierra, a sweet Labrador, Hayden isn't sure Lizzie Vega fits the bill. When a storm leaves her stranded at his ranch, the hardened ex-military man wonders if Lizzie is the perfect match for Sierra...and him...

Read on for a sneak peek at
The Rancher's Forever Family,
the first book in the Texas Cowboys & K-9s miniseries
by USA TODAY *bestselling author Sasha Summers.*

His fingertips traced the curve of her jaw.

"This is the strangest day of my life," she whispered, entirely focused on him. His touch. His gaze. His proximity.

"Agreed." His voice was low, gruff and toe curling.

"I'm not complaining." She wasn't breathing. Was she? Did it matter?

"Agreed." He stepped closer, his hand resting against her cheek. "But that's not going to stop me from asking if I can—"

"Kiss me," she finished, sliding her hands up his chest, his impossibly warm, wall-like chest, and around his neck. "Yes, please."

It was the softest sweep of his lips against hers, but potent enough to induce a full-body shudder from her and a ragged— bone-melting—hitch in his breath.

He lifted his head, just as caught off guard as she was…

But then her hands gripped his shoulders, his arm slid around her waist and she was pressed against him. Being wrapped up in Hayden Mitchell's arms was just as intense as he was. His lips met hers and every single fiber of her being was alive with want. Every sensation seemed magnified. The firmness of his mouth against hers. The cling of his lips, seeking   And when she opened for him, the sweep of his tongue against hers.

No breathing. No thinking. Just this. Just him.

Don't miss
The Rancher's Forever Family *by Sasha Summers,*
available soon wherever
Harlequin Special Edition books and ebooks are sold.

Harlequin.com

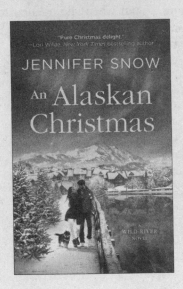
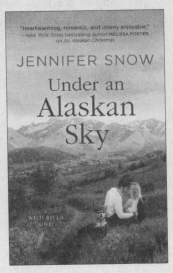

Get 4 FREE REWARDS!

We'll send you 2 FREE Books plus 2 FREE Mystery Gifts.

FREE Value Over **$20**

Both the **Romance** and **Suspense** collections feature compelling novels written by many of today's bestselling authors.